SO *not* MEANT TO BE

MEGHAN QUINN

Bloom *books*

Published by Bloom Books, an imprint of Sourcebooks
P.O. Box 4410, Naperville, Illinois 60567-4410
(630) 961-3900
sourcebooks.com

Originally published in 2022 by Hot-lanta Publishing, LLC.

Cataloging-in-Publication data is on file with the Library of Congress.

Printed and bound in the United States of America.
VP 11 10 9 8 7 6 5 4 3 2

PROLOGUE
KELSEY

"KELSEY, IT'S A KNOWN FACT men and women can't have a working relationship and be friends at the same time."

JP Cane leans against the edge of the conference room table, tattooed arms crossed at his annoyingly brawny chest, sleeves of his dress shirt folded up to his elbows, and sporting a smirk that is more infuriating than charming.

"What on earth are you talking about?" I ask as I sit hunched over a mountain of design papers.

Still leaning against the table, he lowers his hands casually and grips the edge as he says, "The other night, when we were having dinner with Huxley and Lottie, you said we could be friends."

Lottie is my older sister—by twelve months—and my best friend. She's engaged to the incomparable Huxley Cane, our boss and the brother of the bane of my existence standing before me.

How we all came to know each other is still an extremely fascinating story of luck. The quick and dirty explanation? Lottie was looking for a rich husband to save face with an archenemy; Huxley was looking for a fake fiancée in order to secure a business arrangement. They bumped into each other on the sidewalk. They formed a deal to help each other, signed a contract, and she moved into his mansion. It's all *Pretty Woman*-esque, without the hooker aspect. Although…Lottie had a hard time staying away from Huxley's alpha advances.

But while she was playing the role of the doting, madly-in-love fiancée, she was helping me with my business, Sustainably Organized. That's how we were hired by Cane Enterprises and how I found myself working closely with JP, because he was the one assigned to my projects.

Like I said, a whirlwind. I still can't believe it happened this way.

"Do you have a rebuttal?" JP asks, pulling me from my thoughts.

Seeing that this meeting is going nowhere, I toss my pen to the table and stand tall. "First of all, we weren't having dinner *together* with Huxley and Lottie. It wasn't a double date—"

"Jesus, I know," he says, exasperated. "You made that very clear three and a half times." He uses his fingers to tick off the instances. "When we rang the doorbell, because we happened to arrive at the same time. When we were in the kitchen, both reaching for the same champagne. Outside by the pool when we happened to get left at the table alone. And in the living room, you were midway through telling me we weren't on a double date when Lottie interrupted you to show you a new 'toy' she got." He grins, flashing those annoyingly straight teeth of his. "Still waiting on the details of the new toy."

"And *secondly*…" I continue. No way am I telling him about that… device, Huxley got Lottie. Nope. I'm blushing just thinking about it. "Why on earth can't we be friends?"

"Isn't it obvious?"

I glance around the room, trying to see if I've missed any clues, but I spot absolutely nothing. I look back at him and say, "No. No, it's not obvious."

He shakes his head and moves around the conference table to sit on it, right next to me. "Because, Kelsey, there's a palpable attraction between us."

I snort so hard I spray snot on the design plans in front of me. Casually, I wipe away the droplets with my hand. An attraction?

I mean…sure, JP is a very handsome man. An obvious handsome, if you're into the steep cut of his jawline that's peppered by a thick dark beard. His sexy, tousled hair curls ever so slightly on top but is faded short on the sides, and the hidden tattoos that only appear when he's comfortable with his present company. Yes, he's handsome, sexy, I might have said a time or two.

But there's more to a human being than just finding them physically attractive, at least for me. For me to actually find someone attractive, they need to have a good heart, a desirable personality, and be able to make me laugh.

Not sure JP has a heart, and his personality reads like that of an attention-seeking middle child with an aptitude for not taking anything seriously. He might have a good one-liner here and there, but his overall ability to provoke, annoy, and irritate me wins out.

He must have one of the messiest offices I've ever seen, *whispers* which is a complete turn off for a detail-oriented person like I am. Who could look at someone sexually when his desk is stacked in papers and covered by coffee cups and pens with mismatched lids?

So, am I attracted to JP? That would be a definite no.

"You really think there's an attraction between us?" I ask.

"Babe, I can smell the sexual chemistry, and because it's so palpable, so thick, so…musky—"

"Eww, it's not musky."

What am I saying? It's not anything. There's no chemistry. Nothing is palpable, and there's absolutely no thickness…none.

Nor is anything musky. *Who even describes attraction as musky?*

But he ignores me and continues his far-fetched diatribe. "We can't possibly be work friends because the attraction between us will always and forever put the thought of sex on the table."

This time I hold back my snort and let silence fill the air for a few breaths before I close the space between us until our faces are only a few inches apart. Despite him being almost a foot taller than I am, I can still look him in the eyes as I ask, "Are you feverish? Is that what's happening? You've come down with something and this is how you act?"

"I'm a specimen of health. You should know that. You check me out enough."

"I do not."

I don't.

Just need to make that clear. I really don't.

He guffaws, a sound so annoying that my molars grind together. "Why do you think my sleeves are rolled up right now?"

I glance down at his inked forearms—okay, sure, those are sexy, probably the best thing about the man. That's it, though, the forearms. Can't blame a girl for delighting in some arm porn, right, ladies?

He leans in close. "Because I know how much they turn you on."

I press my hand against his face, stopping whatever he's attempting to do. "Do you understand how massively inappropriate this is? I'm your employee."

"Technically, you're Huxley's employee; I'm just the overseer of things."

"Is that the professional term?"

He flashes that irritating grin of his. "It is." He wets his lips but I keep my eyes trained on his eyes. There's no way I'll give him the satisfaction of glancing at his mouth. "Not sure why you're getting all flustered and red in the face."

"I'm not flustered." I straighten my arms at my sides.

"I'm trying to be an honest do-gooder right now, attempting to educate you on why we can't be friends. I should be praised, not disparaged with your sneer." Before I can respond, he keeps moving forward with his so-called do-gooder's education. "A man and a woman who find each other attractive and who work together will never be able to be friends. There will always be a giant elephant in the room, and that elephant's name is Sex. It's basic human math, Kelsey. We all need to climax, and when we find someone who's attractive, we want that person to help us climax."

Is anyone else hearing this?

God, he could not cheapen the act of making love any more. Is it an ego boost JP thinks I'm attractive? Yep. But where's the romance these days?

Where's the wooing?

Where's the spontaneity?

Even Lottie and Huxley will admit there was nothing romantic about how their relationship started. It all seems so clinical these days.

As a true romantic who loves everything about love, I can't help wondering if there's a man out there who checks all the boxes of the perfect rom-com hero.

Noooo, now we have to deal with catfishing, followed by an unsolicited dick pic, and then finalized by a solid ghosting.

I'm so sick of it.

Hands on my hips, I turn toward him and ask, "What the hell happened to make you like this? I asked you what you thought about bamboo filing cabinets and it turned into this argument about why we can't be friends. I don't see how this conversation is relevant to my question."

"It's relevant," he says, sliding in closer, his shoe now pressing against my heel, "because when your hungry eyes are devouring me from across the conference table but your attitude is attempting to put me in the friend zone, I'm going to call you out on it. You said you want to be friends, but that's not going to happen."

A delusion, that's what he's experiencing. And someone needs to put him in his place.

I press my finger to his chest and say, "Trust me, JP, if I found you the least bit attractive, you'd know it. What you're believing are hungry eyes for you, is a ravenous woman who had one waffle slathered in peanut butter at six this morning. Hunger hallucination has set in, and your meager body—"

"Meager? *Pfft.*"

"—has morphed into a giant meatball sub in my mind, nothing more. Convince yourself all you want about what you assume is my attraction toward you, but from my mouth to your headstrong ears, I couldn't find you any more revolting."

His brows shoot up in surprise. Honestly, I'm slightly surprised myself. *Revolting* isn't the right word, but I'm on a roll.

"And if I had any romantic inkling toward you, I wouldn't be wearing this simple, almost homely blouse that does nothing to show off my perfect bouncy breasts."

He wets his lips as he glances down briefly at my chest and then back up.

"And I wouldn't be wearing underwear, either, on the off chance that you pulled me on top of this conference table and spread my legs for a small taste."

His Adam's apple bobs.

"And I sure as hell wouldn't be mentally pleading for this conversation to end so I can pack up and retreat to my studio apartment to eat dinner peacefully alone without an imperious imbecile like yourself chirping in my ear about work relationships. Because, JP, if I wanted you, I would want to steal, consume, and savor every second I had with you."

He reaches out to me just as I twist away to gather my papers. "But that's not the case here." I smile at him. "I can't get away from you fast enough." *I am woman! Hear me roar!*

His nostrils flare.

His jaw ticks.

And he stuffs his hands in his dress pant pockets where they belong.

"Now that we've cleared that up, I'll leave since we're getting nothing done here and a meatball sub is calling my name. I'm going to assume you approve of the bamboo filing cabinets." I collect the papers together and then tap them on the table, evening them into one solid stack.

"We still can't be friends," he says, his voice strangled.

God, is he still on that? Let's add mental ability of a gnat to his list of incompatible qualities.

"Good. When I said that the other night, I was just attempting to be kind, you know, since your company hired mine, but now that our feelings are out in the open, we can live our lives without this fake, bullshit friendship." I gently place my papers in my folder and then in my bag along with my pens, keeping them color-coded, of course. "Now, if you don't mind, I have an appointment to stuff my mouth full of meat."

I move past him, my shoulder bumping against his, but he places his hand on my hip, pausing my retreat. His touch is barely a blip on my bodice, but I shiver reluctantly. Our shoulders meet, side by side, and when I look forward, avoiding eye contact with him, he leans in and whispers into my ear, his lips inches away.

"The only bullshit thing between us is that spiel you just laid out. Deny it all you want, but I know you want me. The quicker you accept that, the better you will feel."

Despite the heavy beat of my heart, I know it's my time to turn my head, and when I do, our noses nearly touch. With all the bravado I can muster, I say, "The sooner you realize I'm out of your league...the better *you* will feel."

It wasn't always like this between us. When I first met him, all I could think about was how truly, stunningly handsome he was, with his mossy-green stare and a cocky air about him that demanded my attention. He was everything a girl fantasizes about. For the briefest of moments, I thought that maybe, just maybe, there could be something between us. That if he asked me out on a date, I would've said yes. But when my business was toeing the line of becoming successful under his leadership, I knew I wouldn't mix business with pleasure, not when I worked so hard to get to where I was.

So I pushed my initial thoughts to the side and, sadly, I've come to see him differently now.

He regularly waltzes into meetings smelling like last night's perfume. He's often distracted by his phone, and when I've looked over, there's always been a different woman's name on the screen. He's flirty and clearly not someone interested in long-term anything. He teases about love, he jokes about forever, and he's never serious. And that's not what I want despite my initial attraction.

With my head held high, I move past him, out the door of the conference room, and to the elevators. I have no idea why JP is droning on about this *attraction* between us. It's not as though I've led him on. I'm a firm believer in love. Therefore, I'm looking for love. Not a fling, not a sexy one-night stand. I'm looking for my soulmate, just like the soulmates on my semipopular podcast. *I want forever.*

JP Cane can believe what he wants, but if there's one thing I know for sure in this romance desert that is my life, he and I are so not meant to be.

JP

Let me guess…Kelsey told you we're so not meant to be, right?

Rolls eyes

Of course she did. Not that I'm looking for forever, because I'm not. I'm just looking for a good time.

I've had too much loss in my life to commit to anyone. Yeah, I'm *that* guy. Psychoanalyze me all you want, but it's not going to change the fact that my fear of commitment is a real thing.

But I'll say this—if anyone was going to change my mind about that, it would be Kelsey.

She's…hell, she's all kinds of special.

From the first moment I saw her during her pitch meeting with us, I was wowed. But working closely together, I was enamored. Her smile, her positive outlook on life, her fucking gorgeous eyes, she stole my breath, and it was the first time in my goddamn life that I actually thought to myself... *She could be my forever.*

Talk about scaring the shit out of myself. It was like a Nordic breeze shot right up my ass. Absolutely chilling.

I couldn't be thinking that way.

I couldn't be thinking about *gulp* forever.

So, being a mature adult, I've chosen to deflect. To annoy. To keep her as far away as possible. And boy, was it working. I got under her skin. Whenever she looks at me, she wants to murder me. Whenever I look at her, I think... *Well, she's hot, but she wants to murder me, therefore, stay away.*

And like I said, it worked. It worked so fucking well... until it didn't anymore.

You can ONLY imagine what happens next...

CHAPTER 1
KELSEY

MEANT TO BE PODCAST

ALEC AND LUNA

Kelsey: Welcome, listener, to the *Meant to Be Podcast*, where we talk to madly-in-love couples about the way they met. Alec and Luna, thank you so much for joining me today.

Alec: Our pleasure. Luna could not stop raving about you.

Luna: Guilty. I'm obsessed with this podcast.

Kelsey: Thank you so much. So then, you must know how we run things over here. The intro is you two giving us a quick rundown on your meet-cute. Think you can do it?

Luna: We can.

Alec: She made me practice.

Kelsey: Ha-ha. Well then, take it away. How did you two become meant to be?

Luna: My brother got engaged to his boyfriend and they couldn't afford a big fancy wedding, so I signed him up for a DIY wedding show called *The Wedding Game*.

Alec: My brother, Thad, was a groomzilla and wanted to win the grand prize at the end of the show, an apartment overlooking Central Park, and laid a guilt trip to force me to help.

Luna: First day of shooting, Alec assumed I was a PA and demanded I get him coffee.

Alec: Asked, not demanded. Let's keep things straight, but, yes, I did. And you can imagine how the little spitfire next to me reacted.

Luna: I had it out for him. He was the competition and he was going down.

Alec: I didn't care about the competition at all and was counting down the days until it was done. Then I realized what a bad brother I was being and how sad Thad was, so...I put in the effort.

Luna: *Effort* meant following me around a baking store so he could learn how to bake a cake.

Alec: I knocked over some nuts, and she helped me pick them up and found me out. She took pity on me and showed me how to bake a cake to help Thad.

Luna: That day in my apartment changed everything. I didn't see him as competition. I saw him as a brother trying to make a difference.

Alec: She's a sucker for family, and so shortly after that, I asked her out.

Luna: We got married last spring.

"Can you two stop making out? Honestly, I came here to have dinner with you, not see you lick each other's faces."

Lottie pauses and looks over her shoulder. "But he smells so good. Have you smelled him?"

"I haven't, because he's not my boyfriend."

Huxley twists Lottie off him onto the outdoor couch they're sharing and lifts her chin to his lips. "I'm going to go check on the pizza." He presses the lightest of kisses to her lips and then stands. "Kelse, can I get you a refill on your drink?"

I hold up my wineglass to him and say, "Please, thank you."

Huxley has the best wines. He doesn't drink much of it, so I always make a point to put a dent in his labels when I'm over for dinner, which is at least once a week. And eating outside is always my choice. Huxley and Lottie have a gorgeous coastal-style house with white walls and black accents just outside Beverly Hills in The Flats. The backyard has a breathtaking infinity pool that stretches the length of the property and expensive yet massively comfortable patio furniture. Tall palm trees add privacy. Their backyard is my favorite place.

When he disappears into the house, Lottie leans toward me and asks, "Kelsey, you know that vibrator I showed you the other night?"

"Yes?"

She looks over her shoulder, checking on Huxley, and then says, "I blacked out. He legit had to shake me back to consciousness. He won't use it on me anymore even though I'm begging desperately for it."

Keeping my expression neutral, I say, "Isn't that lovely? Congratulations on the intense orgasm."

Lottie's brows tilt down. "Hey, am I sensing some sarcasm?"

"What clued you in?" I cross one leg over the other, wishing I didn't ask for a refill on wine.

"Uh, the attitude. What the hell is going on?"

Sighing, I look my sister in the eye and say, "I'm very happy for you and Huxley and your love, but I'm the perpetually single one, and it's hard to watch."

"Are you jealous?" she asks.

"Yes," I answer, not even trying to avoid the truth. Lottie is my best friend and I tell her everything, even if it makes me look bad. "I'm very jealous that you have this consuming relationship with a man who worships you, and I don't even have one prospect."

"That's not true," Lottie says as Huxley rejoins us, handing us both glasses of wine. "What about JP?"

"Oh, please," I groan and then send my apologies to Huxley. "No offense to you since he's your brother, but JP is a moron."

"No offense taken. I agree with you," Huxley says as he drapes his arm behind Lottie and pulls her against his side while bringing his beer bottle to his lips.

"How is he a moron?" Lottie asks.

"Where to start?" Huxley asks, looking so composed and regal. If Huxley, JP, and Breaker—their other brother—didn't all look so much alike, I would question their relationship to each other.

I've always liked Huxley, even when Lottie hated him. It was easy to get along with him because he's very business-minded, smart, and can remain impartial. He's savvy with work decisions, enjoys helping, and loves deeply. He's the total package. I'm very grateful Lottie found him, but God, if only JP had an ounce of Huxley in him, it would make being around him bearable.

"JP is fun, the kind of fun you need," Lottie says. "I love you, Kelse, but you're a bit uptight."

"I am *not* uptight," I defend. "I just know what I like and what I don't like, and trust me when I say I don't like JP. He's annoying and thinks too highly of himself and, frankly, he's far too messy for me."

"All facts," Huxley says. "Kelsey deserves better."

"That's your brother," Lottie says.

"I'm aware, babe. But I agree with Kelsey. They aren't a good match."

"Thank you." I sip my wine. "And since we're on the topic, I'll let you know I'm thinking about joining that local dating app. You know, the one with the blind date restaurant?"

"Wait, the one that Noely Clark from *Good Morning, Malibu* has boasted about? The one where she found love? What's it called?"

"Going In Blind," I say.

"Yes." She snaps her finger at me. "Oh my God, didn't you interview her and Jack on your podcast?"

I nod. "Yes, that's where I got the idea. She was telling me all about it while we weren't recording, and it seems really interesting. Like, maybe I could actually find someone like-minded."

"How does it work?" Huxley asks.

"It's all anonymous through an app, but everyone is put through a background check and screened to make sure there's no catfishing. Then, the app matches you with people. You don't know who the person is by name or what they look like, and you meet up at the restaurant, Going In Blind, where you share a meal together and see if you're a match. Like a blind date."

"That's pretty neat," Huxley says.

"I love it," Lottie adds. "God, I should've thought of that when I was trolling for a rich husband."

Huxley's arm tightens around Lottie as he says, "I think you did pretty good for yourself."

Lottie cups his cheek and pulls him in for a kiss. "I did decent, though you can be quite grumpy."

I watch Huxley's hand curl around my sister possessively as he whispers something into her ear. *Ugh, great, you're in love. WE ALL CAN SEE THAT!*

I lean back in my chair and drain my wineglass, while they do some sort of secret whispering thing to each other, which, frankly, I have no desire to be a part of. Not that they want me to be a part of it either.

What I would like is to be a part of a relationship like theirs where you're so infatuated with each other that you completely forget the world around you and get lost in each other's eyes.

I want to be worshipped.

I want to be important in someone's life.

I want to be the person someone calls when they need advice or have big news...or just want to hear my voice.

I want to be surprised with flowers at my apartment door. Whisked away to somewhere I've never been. Thought of nearly every second of every day because I consume someone's thoughts.

I want the real.

The ugly.

The pettiness that comes with relationships.

The teasing.

The arguments.

The laughs.

The love.

The romance.

I want it all. And sitting here, watching my sister experience exactly that, yes, it makes me jealous, but it also makes me realize that if I want all those things, I'm going to have to make them happen myself. I can't sit back and wait.

If I want love, I need to go find it.

"Oh God, I feel like throwing up," I say as I shake my hands at my side. "Why did I think this was a good idea?"

"Because you want to be in a relationship," Lottie says calmly from where she sits cross-legged on my bed.

"I do." I nod as I stare at myself in my full-length mirror, examining the purple strapless dress I chose for my date tonight. "I really want to be in a relationship."

"And you yourself said this guy sounds nice. Likes dogs, has his own business—something you have in common—and has a secret desire to be in a boy band, which is charming."

"It is." I nod again, still staring at myself. "The boy band thing really got me."

"And what was his favorite quote again?"

"'Buzz, your girlfriend! Woof!'" I say, chuckling as I turn to the side, checking out my back.

Lottie chuckles too. "See, he seems like a good time as well."

Now I turn toward Lottie and ask, "What if he's the one?"

"Okay, you can't go into this thinking like that. You need to be calm, composed, and just have fun. You can't go all crazy romantic on him and ask him to have your babies fifteen minutes into the date."

I give her a glaring look. "I would never do that."

"Just checking, because earlier you asked me if purple accented your elbow pit veins too much. Who asks that?"

I flash my arms at Lottie and say, "Mom gave me these veins, and they are far too prominent. I don't need the purple of this dress making them even more prominent."

"With the way that dress makes your boobs look, I'm pretty sure the last thing he's going to be looking at is your inner elbow veins."

I clutch my chest. "Oh my God, do I look like I'm trying too hard?"

"Noooo," Lottie moans. "You look perfect. Now, if you don't leave soon, you're going to be late and I know what you hate most in life is being late."

"That's true. Being late just means you're either a 'time bender'— that's a real thing—or you don't care about other people's time. And time is the one thing in life you can't get back."

"Yes, I know." Lottie stands from the bed and ushers me toward the door, but before she can push me out, I turn toward her and grip her arms.

"What if this is it, if he's the one? I'm going to start sweating when I see him. I won't be able to act cool. What if this is my one and only chance at love?"

"This is not your one and only chance. This is a blind date with a guy that some computer algorithm thought would be a good fit for you."

"A proven algorithm. The success rate is as high as ninety percent. Do you know what kind of pressure that puts on me?"

"You're overthinking this. It's supposed to be fun."

"Nothing about dating is fun. You lucked out with Huxley. Maybe I should walk a rich neighborhood, looking for a husband."

"Or you could just go out with JP…"

That calms my nerves right away and I put distance between myself and my sister. "By now you should know I have zero interest in him. I'd have better luck dating a houseplant than JP Cane. Now"—I straighten out my dress—"if you will excuse me, I have a blind date to go on."

"One mention of JP and you're all fixed and ready to go?"

"Yes." I pick up my purse and sling it over my shoulder. "Because if there's one thing I know for sure, it's that any date is better than a date with him."

CHAPTER 2
JP

"I TRULY, TRULY HATE YOU," I say into the phone as I stand outside the restaurant.

"Do you hate me or do you hate yourself?" Breaker asks. "Because you're the one who lost the bet."

"My shoe was untied, I called a time-out, you didn't listen, you scored the winning basket, and basically...you cheated."

"Jesus," Breaker huffs. "What a load of crap and you know it. You didn't call a time-out until I juked you, you lunged, and I blew past you. I beat you fair and square."

Hand in one pocket, I toe the sidewalk and say, "Well, we needed a replay."

"Why don't you act like a man, own up to your loss, and take the consequences without complaining?"

"Because I don't want to do this."

"Then you never should've placed the bet."

"Yeah, well...I didn't think I was going to lose."

He laughs into the phone. "Not my problem."

"Fuck...fine." I push my hand through my hair. "But this is fucking stupid."

"Let me ask you this—are you mad because you lost, or are you mad because you're going on a date that isn't with the apple of your eye?"

"There's no apple of my eye."

Breaker snorts. "Dude, you're not fooling anyone. You're infatuated with Kelsey and it bothers you that she wants nothing to do with you."

"Kelsey?" I guffaw so loudly that I draw the attention of a man walking into the restaurant. I give him a nod and then turn around for some privacy. "Kelsey is a pill. She's uptight, annoying, and doesn't know a good thing when it's standing right in front of her."

"Meaning you," Breaker says, his voice full of humor.

"Uh, yeah, clearly. Why would I want to go on a date with someone who thinks more highly of a piece of gum stuck on her shoe than me?"

"Hmm, maybe I should ask Kelsey out. We seem to have a lot in common."

"Fuck…off," I groan as I turn toward the restaurant. He better not ask Kelsey out. If she doesn't want me—*and I'm extremely likable*—then she wouldn't want Breaker. Kelsey is blind and high-handed. *And I wish I didn't fantasize about her. Frequently.* "This was really stupid. I know nothing about this girl."

"Not true. You know that she lives here, that she owns her own business, and that she believes roses are the most romantic flower in the world."

"Yeah, exactly. Why this fucking computer thought we'd be a match, I have no idea. It probably saw *business owner* on our profiles and was like, *Done. Easy. Match made in heaven.* This place is overhyped and ridiculous."

"It's not like you have to stay that long. Just go have a drink and then—"

"That's not how this process works. You have to stay and have a meal with the person. It's the godforsaken program."

Breaker snorts. "Oh shit, really?"

"Yes, really. Something about how they want you to get to know the person before making a snap judgment and moving on to the next date."

"Makes sense."

"Yeah, for someone who doesn't have to go on the date."

"Dude, stop bitching and just go in there. Jesus, aren't you late?"

I glance down at my watch. Shit, six minutes late. I sigh heavily and say, "I hate you."

"Can't wait to hear all about the date. Have fun, bro."

"Fuck off." I hang up as his laughter booms through the phone.

Now, if I were a true asshole, someone who didn't keep their word, I'd go right past this restaurant, hang out at a bar, and catch the latest Rebels game. But even though that sounds incredibly appealing, I'm not that guy. I can't stand someone up. I would feel way too damn guilty.

So, I stuff my phone in my pocket and wish this night could be over before it begins.

Going In Blind, what a stupid-as-shit concept.

Letting a computer match you with someone without even seeing what the person looks like...seems like reckless behavior if you ask me.

Irresponsible, actually.

And holding them hostage until the meal is over?

Well, guess who's about to annihilate a meal to get the hell out of here?

Me.

I open the door to the restaurant and am greeted by a more-than-jubilant hostess and an entirely too romantic atmosphere. Strings of large bulb lights are draped throughout the space and there's a plethora of hanging plants, the vines dangling just above the tables. The walls are floor-to-ceiling exposed white brick, the intimate tables all have that urban metal feel, and the wood beams that run parallel with the ceiling soften the design.

Sure...the place is nice.

I'll give it that.

But the rest of this concept is stupid.

"Good evening, sir," the ebullient hostess says. "You must be JP."

Of course they know who I am. I'm sure they have pictures of every person who has been roped into a date here.

Tacking on a smile, I nod. "That would be me."

"Wonderful. Well, your date is at the bar. Shall I introduce you, or would you like to introduce yourself?"

I glance over at the bar and see a woman in a purple dress sitting alone. I take in her long brown hair that's loosely curled and draped over her bare shoulders. Hmm…

Maybe this whole thing isn't *entirely* stupid.

"I can introduce myself."

"Wonderful. Have a nice evening."

"Thank you," I say before I make my way through the restaurant. When you sign up for the program, they make you choose a handle, a name to represent you but isn't your real-life name. I went with ManWearsPants, because I was too annoyed to think of anything clever, and the girl I was matched with, well…

"Hello, you must be RosesAreRed," I say as a greeting.

She sets down her half-empty glass and turns around, almost in slow motion. I hold my breath, steeling myself for what this woman looks like, but when her face comes into view, I'm blown away by the familiar dark-haired beauty before me.

Her smile is wide, her eyes are hopeful, and when she flicks her hair over her shoulder and looks me in the eyes…her face falls flat, her mouth turning into a thin, angry line.

"What the hell are you doing here?" she asks.

Oh man, this is fucking awesome.

Kelsey Gardner.

What are the odds?

Sticking both my hands in my pockets, I gleefully say, "I'm your date for the evening."

Glancing over my shoulder, she seems to take a second to comprehend what's happening and then asks, "Are you some sort of stalker who followed me here? JP, this is going way too freaking far. I'm about to go

on a date with someone. I don't want him thinking I'm here with you, so if you'd please leave—"

"ManWearsPants," I say, and her eyes narrow.

With a quick look around, she wets her lips, leans in, and in a tight voice, she asks, "Why did you just say that?"

Oh, it's too fucking cute watching her nose scrunch up in confusion. I was so, so wrong. This evening is going to be so much more fun than I anticipated.

"That's my avatar. ManWearsPants, and you, my irritated shrew, are RosesAreRed, and you can deny it all you want, but this dating program thinks we're the perfect match."

"Well, clearly it was wrong." The shrillness of her voice reaches a pitch nearly capable of breaking the bottles of liquor behind her. She stands from her chair, snatches her purse, and attempts to walk past me when I grab her hand.

"Excuse me, Miss Irritable, but I believe we aren't allowed to leave the restaurant until we share a meal together. It's in the terms and conditions."

Her eyes flash to mine. "You can't be serious."

"Oh, I'm very serious. I believe it's section three, line five where it states the definitive guidelines," I say. "I signed up for this dating app, and I expect to get the full experience." I flash her a grin that I know irritates her more than anything.

"Everything okay here?" the hostess asks, coming up to us.

"Everything is great," I answer.

"No, everything is not great," Kelsey says. "There must have been some mistake with the algorithm and the matching, because I know this man, and let me tell you, I can say with full confidence that we're not a match."

"Oh, how interesting. I don't think we've ever had this happen before."

"Ah, wonderful. So you can imagine how we'd just like to move on from this ill-fated inconvenience and go on our way."

The hostess shakes her head. I can practically hear the agonized inner howling from Kelsey, as if this is her own personal doomsday. "I'm so sorry, but unfortunately, you have to stay and enjoy a meal together. It's part of the terms."

"But I said I know him." Kelsey frantically jabs her hand in my direction.

Point all you want, lady; not going to help.

"And I don't like him. I don't need to have a meal with him to figure that out."

"You wound me," I whisper playfully in her ear. She swats me away with an unexpected flick of her wrist. Whoa, almost got a fingernail to the eyeball.

"Do you see what I'm dealing with? Trust me, you don't want us sharing a meal together, it'll distract the other people around us. All we do is bicker."

"Then we'll give you one of our new private tables in the loft area." The hostess smirks and then nods toward the stairs to the right. "Right this way."

"You can't be serious," Kelsey says.

"Looks like she *is* serious," I say, pressing my hand to her lower back and guiding her forward.

"You're really going to make me have dinner with him?"

The hostess doesn't answer, she just keeps walking, and I keep pushing Kelsey forward, a smile on my face the entire time. Here I thought the night was going to be a complete bust, but it's turned into a night in which I'm very interested in taking part.

"This is ridiculous. I shouldn't be held against my will."

We walk up the stairs.

"This program is a load of crock if you think I should be matched with JP. Did you even do a background check?"

We reach the loft, a private space draped in white linen curtains and twinkle lights. There's one table in the middle, surrounded by an ambiance suited only for intimate lovers, two people tangling in each other's lives with romantic interludes, long, drawn-out stories of childhood, and far-off fantasies of what their future might look like together.

And then there's me and Kelsey, the angry porcupine, rearing up her quills and ready to impale me at her first chance.

This sensual room dripping in fairy-tale potential is about to get a show.

"There's nothing romantic between us, nothing at all. Why is this happening?" she drones on.

The hostess holds out a basket with a sign that so eloquently reads, *Unplug and be present*, and shakes it at us, clearly and wordlessly stating we must deposit our lifelines within.

I plop my phone in because, if anything, I'm an excellent rule follower.

Panic sweeps through Kelsey's eyes as she stares down at the basket. "What if I have an important phone call that comes in? What if I need my sister to fake a broken ankle so I can leave?"

At least she's honest, but it does nothing to dissuade the hostess, and with a feral groan only heard through the depths of a dark, dank night, Kelsey puts her phone in the basket with mine.

Next, we're shown to our table, parallel to a quaint stone fireplace offering an orange glow for a very romantic evening…with the priggish she-wolf.

"Your server's name is Helix. He'll be joining you shortly. Please let us know if you need anything," the hostess says before pulling out both chairs for us.

"Yes, I need to get out of this date. How can you assist me in that?" Kelsey asks.

"I'm sure you two will have a beautiful evening together. Enjoy."

And then she leaves, taking off downstairs and leaving me completely alone in what some might refer to as a dreamy loft with Kelsey.

A fuming, nostrils-flared Kelsey.

A Kelsey who would most likely prefer to share this space with anyone—and I mean *anyone*—but me.

She raises her hand and points at me, her finger shaking as she speaks through clenched teeth. "You did this. You planned this whole thing, didn't you?"

"What? You've lost your mind if you think I have time in my day to figure out what kind of cheesy dating app you're on, infiltrate the app, and then somehow compromise the system so you and I are forced to have a date together."

"I knew it." She throws her hands in the air. "God, and you play the fool so well, when in reality, you're a conniving birdbrain with nothing better to do than provoke people in your path."

I take a seat at the table, pick up the napkin in front of me, and rest it across my lap. "Firstly, I said I didn't have time to do all that. Secondly, *conniving birdbrain* is an insult I'm going to have to store away for later. It's a good one."

"Eww, don't try to be charming with me." She takes a seat as well, albeit reluctantly, and folds her napkin over her lap too. She drums her fingers on the table and takes in the lights around us. "What a wasted room."

See, I knew she'd think that. Do I know this girl or what?

I lean forward and say, "You know, you could try to make the most of this and attempt to be pleasant."

Her eyes shoot to mine. "Why, JP? I thought men and women who work with each other can't be friends."

Touché.

"Not saying we have to be friends, but you could at least not act like an uninspiring wench."

"Do you expect me to have a conversation with you?"

"That's what normal people usually do when they share a meal together. Unless there's a new trend I'm unaware of."

Just then, Helix comes up the stairs with glasses of water balanced precariously on his tray. After he sets them on the table, he stuffs his tray under his arm and says, "Good evening. Our hostess has informed me that we have a happy love nest up here."

The deadpan look on Kelsey's face almost makes me fall out of my chair in laughter, but I hold it together in fear of what would happen to me if I did laugh. After all, there are two knives on this table.

"We're in a bit of a rush, so if you don't mind, we'd like to order, eat, and then get the hell out of here."

"Jesus," I whisper. "Don't be rude to the guy."

Kelsey lets out a slow breath and then plasters on a smile. "I'm sorry. Helix, is it?"

Helix nods.

"You see, when I signed up for this app, I was under the impression that I'd be set up with someone I might actually be interested in. I had all the hope of meeting someone interesting, someone complex, someone fun. I was truly planning on making a deep connection tonight." Her eyes snap to mine. "And when I say deep connection, I mean mentally…not physically."

I just grin.

"But you see, Helix, instead of meeting someone who could have the potential to sweep me off my feet, I was matched with this insolent, vexatious human who thinks more highly of the hangnail on his finger than the people around him. Unfortunately, I work with him and I know enough about him to understand that there's nothing—and I mean absolutely nothing—we have in common. Therefore—"

"That's not what the readout on your profiles says." Helix clutches the tray tightly.

Kelsey blinks. "Excuse me?"

"I heard there might be some trouble up here in paradise, and sometimes, when that happens, we print out the reason the computer connected you both. Would you like me to read it to you?"

"No," Kelsey says.

"Yes," I say at the same time. "I would love nothing more than to hear why Kelsey and I are suited for each other." I cross my ankle over my knee as I scoot back my chair and prepare myself for what I can only imagine will be an absolutely enlightening experience for me and a horrific experience for Kelsey.

From his pocket, Helix pulls out a piece of paper and clears his throat. "You were one of our highest matches in the system with a ninety-seven percent probable success rate."

HA!

Steam flies out of Kelsey's ears as my grin just keeps growing wider and wider.

"RosesAreRed and ManWearsPants." Helix turns to me. "Great name, by the way."

I nod at him. "Thank you."

"Oh my God," Kelsey groans. "There's absolutely no imagination to that name."

"As if RosesAreRed is a poetic masterpiece," I reply. "Might as well have called yourself PointsOutTheObvious."

Kelsey juts her hand at me and looks at Helix. "See what I'm talking about? Insufferable."

Looking slightly weary, Helix takes a step back and continues reading. "RosesAreRed and ManWearsPants are both business owners within the Los Angeles area."

"Whoa, that's a surprise to no one." Kelsey folds her arms over her chest and, honestly, I don't think I've ever seen her this upset. One of the things I've always found interesting about Kelsey is her ability to stay composed, even when under an immense amount of pressure. She never shows emotion, but tonight, I'm experiencing a new side of her. I kind of like it.

"From reviewing their backgrounds, we've established likeness in parent abandonment."

Kelsey falls silent.

"The desire to achieve, and a direct match in fears such as failure, not being loved, and being alone."

Her eyes flash to mine as I quickly look away. Okay, what the fuck is that shit? Sure, we filled out a questionnaire, but what kind of invasive background check was done to figure that out?

"It also determined that where RosesAreRed is very structured and amorous in thought, ManWearsPants can be pessimistic with an apathetic attitude, making these two puzzle pieces fit closely together, creating a continuous balance for a healthy relationship." Helix stuffs his paper back in his pocket and then holds up a pen and paper. "Now, what can I get you two for dinner?"

CHAPTER 3
KELSEY

WELL, HELIX KNOWS HOW TO shut two people up *real* quick.

After we both put in an order for the meatloaf and mashed potatoes—I'm ignoring the fact that we ordered the same thing, thank you very much—Helix took off down the stairs, but not before telling us that the kitchen is short-staffed so the meal might take a bit longer to come out.

Just…great. *Wonder if that's intentional so "dates" have to stay longer.*

An instrumental cover of "Bad Guy" plays overhead as JP and I look everywhere but at each other.

Helix brought in the truth bomb and completely obliterated the evening.

Even the nonstop annoyance from JP has shut down as he twirls his water glass on the table.

The silence is deafening.

Uncomfortable.

And even though I can't stand sitting across from him at the moment, I can't handle the silence. It's more painful than not talking.

"So…do you often eat meatloaf?" I ask, unsure of what else to say.

When he looks up, his brow lifts in this Regé-Jean Page sort of way, like a fishhook grabbed it, tugged it up, and left it there. And does it take me straight back to a scene in *Bridgerton* that had me melting into my couch? Of course, but does it ease the protective ice shield that has formed around me because of this unfortunate evening? Not even a little.

"Are you attempting conversation with me?"

"You can't possibly expect me to sit here in silence for God knows how long."

"I don't know, watching you squirm from a lack of conversation seems enjoyable."

"Why are you an ass?"

"Couldn't you tell from the rundown Helix just gave us? Abandonment issues and false façades are high on that list for defense mechanisms. Doesn't take a psychologist to figure that out, babe," he says.

"Doesn't give you an excuse to act like an asshole. I grew up without a dad and you don't see me parading around with an indignant attitude."

He laughs so loud it startles me backward. "Did you completely forget the 'I hate JP Cane' one-person show you just put on for the restaurant staff?"

"Well, pardon me for being flummoxed when I found out you were my date for the evening. In my head, I was picturing this night going a tad differently."

"I see. And how did you picture it going?"

I take a sip of my water. "Not like this."

"You said that, and given we have a long dinner in front of us, why don't you educate me on how you thought tonight would pan out?"

"I'm not sharing that with you. You're just going to make fun of me."

"Why would I do that?"

"Because you're an oppressor of hopes and dreams."

"How little you know me, Kelsey."

I eye him for a few seconds and then ask, "So if I tell you what I thought would happen tonight, you're not going to make fun of me?"

"You know, it might behoove you to get to know me. Then you might not have such a low opinion of me."

Doubtful.

"Fine," I say, chin held high. "But if you make fun of me, I'm throwing my water in your face."

"That's fair." He nods at me. "Go ahead, light me up with your fantasies."

God, I really despise him.

Clearing my throat, I say, "Well, I signed up for this program because I heard great things about it from Noely Clark."

"Noely, one of the hosts from *Good Morning, Malibu*?" he asks.

"Yes. I interviewed her and her husband for my podcast—"

"You have a podcast? What's it called?"

Feeling shy, because I know he's probably judging me, I say, "I do, and the name is irrelevant. I would rather you not listen to it."

"Afraid I might become a longtime listener?"

"Are you teasing me?" I ask, lifting my water.

He holds up his rather large hands. "No, not teasing. Just engaging in conversation."

"Try using less sarcasm in your 'engagements.'"

"Noted." He gestures with his hand. "Proceed."

"Well, I interviewed them for my podcast, and while we weren't recording, she told me all about Going In Blind. Since I'm in the market to settle down with someone…" I pause to assess his expression, and when he doesn't crack a smile, I proceed. "I thought I'd give it a try. I heard nothing but good things, so when I was getting ready, I was actually kind of nervous. I assumed I'd be meeting someone interesting, someone like-minded, someone I matched well with. You can only imagine my disappointment when you turned out to be ManWearsPants."

He lifts his glass casually and, with his eyes locked in a deep stare on me, takes a sip of water. There's something enigmatic but also annoying about the Cane men. They have excellent self-control, particularly at curbing their initial reactions to things. They're generally subtle with their movements, showing great restraint. I've seen it in Huxley and now in JP.

"Disappointment, indeed," he says. "I'm sorry if I've ruined your evening."

"Ugh, don't do that."

"Don't do what?" he asks, remaining stoic.

"Play the bruised ego card. You and I both know there's nothing about this scenario that hurts your feelings. You're thriving off the fact that we were matched merely because it's ruined my evening and hopes for a possible match."

"I don't thrive off that," he says. "I find it somewhat comical, sure, but I do kind of feel bad for you."

"I don't need you feeling bad for me. Save your pity for someone else."

"I don't pity you. There's a difference. If I pitied you, then that would mean I have a low opinion of you, and that's not the case. I just feel bad that you consider your evening ruined by my presence."

"Why do you have to say it like that? Like you're the victim."

"Trust me, babe, I'm never the victim." He shifts in his chair, and I can tell the easygoing, teasing JP is gone—especially since Helix laid out our backgrounds for each other—and in his place is a guarded man, one I haven't seen before.

"I was just expecting something else," I say, folding my hands in my lap. "I was excited to meet someone new."

Once again, JP studies me, intent, his eyes blazing over me, practically eating me alive as they roam from my eyes to my mouth, to my chest...

Finally, he says, "I'm here because of a bet."

My gaze flashes to his. "What?"

He holds up his hand to calm my simmering rage. "Before you think I intentionally came here to ruin your night, that's not the case. The fact that we're here together, sharing a meal, is pure coincidence. But the reason I signed up for this program is because I lost a bet to Breaker."

"What kind of bet?"

"We were playing one-on-one basketball. Our egos got the best of us and we decided whoever lost had to follow through on whatever the other person chose. It was a tied game. I was ready to force Breaker to go to some baking class I knew he'd absolutely hate, and he apparently had plans for me to do this. I lost, he told me what I had to do, and here I am."

"So, you're here because you lost a bet?"

"Yes."

"What if your date wasn't me? What would you have done then?"

"Attempted to enjoy the evening. Not sure where your disdainful opinion of me started, but I'm a pretty good guy. Sure, the thought of not following through on the date tonight did cross my mind, but I knew I couldn't do that. So, my plan was to try to strike up conversation, enjoy a meal, then end the night with a wave. I planned to spend the rest of the evening in my pool, naked on a raft, staring up at the stars."

My treacherous mind conjures up an image of just that, JP naked on a raft, floating in a pool, his wild tattoos on display.

It's, uh…it's a pleasant visual.

"But now I'm here with you, suffering through this conversation and begging the kitchen staff to hurry up with my meal so I can go back to my house." He smirks and asks, "What do you plan on doing after this?"

Asking Lottie where Huxley got that new "toy" so I can ease the tension that has built in my shoulders from this evening.

"Probably folding and ironing laundry while watching a new rom-com on Netflix."

"Let me guess—it's a flick about two people meeting, falling madly in love; then the guy does something stupid, the girl gets mad, they break up only for him to make a grand gesture to win back her hand, and then it's sealed with a happily ever after."

Chin held high, I say, "If you must know, yes, that would be the general idea."

He snorts. "You really believe life is like that?"

"I'd like to believe there's some validity to those stories. If anything, they give me hope for the kind of life I could have."

"They're far-fetched fiction. Life doesn't revolve around the movie star falling in love with the lonesome construction worker and giving up everything to live in a quirky town."

"You know, JP, just because your life doesn't work that way, doesn't mean others don't. Look at Lottie and Huxley, for instance. Their love story reads heavily like a romantic comedy, with all the twists and turns that a passionate love affair can offer."

"They ran into each other on the sidewalk and struck up a deal to help each other. That doesn't really scream romance to me."

"It's a classic trope."

"A *what*?" he asks, his face twisting in confusion.

"Ugh." I roll my eyes, girding myself to educate this man on the simple pleasures of the romance community. "A trope is a plot or theme that helps tell a story. For instance, if I were to label Huxley and Lottie's romance, I would easily call it 'enemies to lovers' since they hated each other, with a smattering of 'fake fiancée' and a touch of 'billionaire.' All wildly popular."

"'Billionaire' is a trope?" Both his brows raise now in suspicion.

"A very popular one."

"So, let me get this straight—you think that your life is going to be some sort of rom-com with these *tropes*?"

"No, but I was hoping for better company than the one currently present," I snap at him, taking another sip of my water.

"What's wrong with the present company? We're having a healthy conversation."

"This is what you consider healthy? I'm on the verge of either shooting my water up your nose or roundhouse kicking you to the ground. How does that scream healthy conversation?"

His lips press together, and then after he casually leans back in his chair again, he says, "Seems to me like you need to go to some anger management classes."

I wonder if I can get away with forking JP to death.

"That's the dumbest movie ever."

"Excuse me?" I ask, my eyes nearly popping out of their sockets. The audacity of the man.

"You're telling me, out of all the movies in the entire world, your all-time favorite, the one you can watch over and over again is *Sleepless in Seattle*?"

"Yes. *When Harry Met Sally* is a close second."

"Meg Ryan fan, are we?"

"How can you not be a fan of her delightful charm?"

"I mean, she's fine, but I'm not going to seek out a movie because she's in it."

"Well, you should. Maybe you could learn something from watching her movies, become more desirable to be around."

He smooths his hand over his jaw and says, "Haven't had any complaints about my company being desirable."

I roll my eyes and, because our food still hasn't arrived, I ask, "So, what makes *Sleepless in Seattle* so far beneath you?"

"It's unbelievable."

"How so?" I ask in shock.

"Well, besides the fact that a child not only purchased a plane ticket by himself, but he flew across the country with no parental guidance, found his way to the Empire State Building, and reached the top without one person questioning him? Yeah, that would never happen. But also, because Meg Ryan is a clear stalker in this movie."

"She's not a stalker. She's merely curious."

"Be curious about your neighbor, not some questionable father all the way across the country."

"His story touched her."

"He's a forlorn father trying to find some ass through a radio show."

JP claps. "Job well done, Tom Hanks. You were able to sweep lonely and desperate women off their feet from miles away."

"Oh my God, you're…you're gross."

"Gross?" he asks, his hand landing on the table. "How am I the gross one? I'm not chasing tail across the country, using my son as bait."

"Um, Sam Baldwin had no idea that's what was happening. If you recall, he was absolutely distraught over his son's disappearance."

"Okay, sure, he pulled his hand from under his woman's shirt long enough to realize his son was missing. Great parenting. But put all of that aside, and you really think they would've fallen for each other? They caught one glimpse of each other and then all of a sudden, they were at the top of the Empire State Building, and in love? There's absolutely no believability to their relationship. If that movie had an epilogue, it would show them awkwardly realizing the next morning that they live over three thousand miles apart, he lives on a houseboat, and they have absolutely nothing in common other than idiotic spontaneity."

I stare at him, my body thrumming with irritation. The back of my neck feels like it's on fire, my palms are so sweaty I have to restrain myself from wiping them on my dress, and my jaw is clenched so tight that my cheeks are hurting.

"Are you done ripping apart my favorite movie?"

"I think so." He smiles.

"Good. Now, *Rotten Tomatoes*, tell me your favorite movie."

"Why, so you can pretend you don't like it and attempt to give it the tongue-lashing I just unleashed on your favorite movie? I'm good, thanks."

"How do you know I'm going to be negative about your favorite movie? I might like it."

"How do I know you're going to be negative? Because for the past five minutes, I've watched you mentally plot my death. My guess is when we're done with this dinner, you're going to push me down the stairs on our way out, tumbling me into a coma."

Wrong. It involves a solid twenty minutes of forking…and not the sexual kind!

"You know, if I'm going to get caught, planting my knife in your chest might be more satisfactory."

"Jesus," he says, horrified.

Embarrassment falls over me. The knife might have gone a bit too far. "You're right, that was uncalled for. I think the trip down the stairs is more my style."

He chuckles. "Glad I don't have to whisk your knife away when you're not looking."

"Don't be so dramatic. I don't look good in orange. Committing a crime is not for me."

"So orange is not the new black for you?"

"No." I cross my leg over the other and ask, "So, what's your favorite movie? You owe me this much."

"I owe you nothing."

"JP, this has been an uneventful evening that I'm begging to end and you've made it that much more unbearable. Please, delight me with your nonsensical movie choice. Or I'm going to start guessing."

"That sounds more appealing. Start guessing."

Heaving a heavy sigh, I compose myself and ask, "Is it porn?"

"Come on, I have more class than that."

"Debatable, but I'll rule that out just for now. Hmm." I make a show of tapping my chin. "Based on your disdain for romantic comedies, I'm going to lean more toward some blood-and-gore action flick. And since you try to hold the high-and-mighty card, I'm going to guess your favorite movie is something like *Braveheart*."

"Nope." He shakes his head.

"*The Godfather*?"

"Not even close."

"Eww, is it *Rocky*?"

"That would be laughable."

I fold my arms and really study him. "Umm, *Saving Private Ryan, The Green Mile, Philadelphia.*"

"Are you just guessing Tom Hanks movies now?"

"Just checking, seeing if any of those sparked any interest. I can see that they didn't. So now I'm going to go the less prolific route and say *Step Brothers, 40-Year-Old Virgin, Billy Madison.*"

"All funny, but no."

"Ugh, I don't know. Give me a hint. Who stars in it?"

"Julie Andrews."

"Julie—what? Julie Andrews as in *Mary Poppins* Julie Andrews?"

He nods.

"You're messing with me."

"No. What's wrong with Julie Andrews?"

"Nothing, I just…I don't know, I was thinking you were going to say someone like Liam Neeson, Sam Elliott, or Jeff Bridges. You know, all rough and gruff, ready-to-seek-revenge actors. Not Julie Andrews, with her blond pixie haircut."

"What little you know of me."

"You're not kidding, your favorite movie has Julie Andrews in it?"

"Yup." He smirks.

"What is it?"

"Isn't it obvious?"

"Not even in the slightest. It's truly more confusing than anything. So, I'm at a loss. The only Julie Andrews movies coming to mind are, well, *Mary Poppins* and *The Princess Diaries,* and I think I'll fall out of my chair if any of those are the answer."

"Nope, neither of those classics."

"You've watched both of them?" I ask, still in disbelief. This is a side of JP I never expected. He's one of three brothers.

"Of course I have. *Mary Poppins* is wholesome, and I once dated this girl who was obsessed with Anne Hathaway and made me watch every movie of hers. *The Devil Wears Prada* was a complete nightmare, by the way. What kind of shit ending was that?"

"I thought you didn't like romantic comedies?"

"I don't, and that movie is one of the main reasons."

"Okay, so if it's not one of those...what is it?" I laugh. "Can't possibly be *The Sound of Music*."

"Why do you assume that?" he asks, looking entirely too serious.

No.

That can't be it.

The Sound of Music? No freaking way.

"Uh, because it's a musical and, excuse me if I'm wrong, I don't really see you as a toe-tapping, musical kind of man."

"You know, you really shouldn't judge people based on the little knowledge you have of them." He adjusts the cuffs on his sleeves and says, "For your information, *The Sound of Music* is my favorite movie. It has everything you need, a hot nanny ex-nun who can sing, a grumpy, Nazi-fighting hero, beautifully composed music, betrayal, and suspense."

I'm stunned.

In disbelief.

Sure, it's an okay movie, but a favorite?

"Why don't I believe you?"

He shrugs. "That's on you if you choose to believe me or not."

"If I had my phone, I would text Huxley right now and see if that's the truth."

"When you get your phone, have at it. He knows I love watching Maria twirl around on a mountaintop. One year, for Halloween, I dressed up as Maria, and another year, I was Baron Von Trapp. And then Maria again, because the costume was too good to only wear once."

"I still...I don't believe you."

"Suit yourself. But I'll tell you this, I own the cassette tape, the CD, the

VHS, the DVR, the Blu-ray, and a digital copy of *The Sound of Music*. Not to mention, I have a treasured signed autograph picture from Julie Andrews. I keep them all in a fireproof safe in my house in an undisclosed location."

"Okay, now I know you're lying."

He just shrugs, which is such an infuriating response. It's like he doesn't even care enough to come up with something proper, just offers a know-it-all shrug.

And, no, I don't believe him, not for one second. There's no way after the prolific criticism he had about *Sleepless in Seattle* that he can sit back and say *The Sound of Music*—a love story in its own right—is his favorite movie. Nope, he's just trying to provoke me and I'm not going to fall for it.

Nice try.

———————

"Doe, a deer, a female deer—"

"Will you knock that off?" I ask as our food finally arrives. "God, just eat your food and be quiet so we can get the hell out of here."

"Aren't you a pleasant dinner companion?"

"You've been nonstop singing, humming, beat-bopping songs since you brought up *The Sound of Music* and I'm about to lose my mind. I'm going to have 'How do you solve a problem like Maria?' stuck in my head for eternity."

"Could be worse."

"How could it be worse?" I ask.

"Could be a completely inappropriate song. Something along the lines of…" He leans forward and in a seductive voice, says, "My neck, my back, lick—"

"Okay, I got your point," I say, holding my hand up.

"Have you heard that one?"

"Everyone has heard that one," I say while sticking a forkful of meatloaf into my mouth. The most delicious meatloaf I've ever had. So good that I would actually consider coming on another date with JP just to have this meatloaf... Yeah, suffer through another night of this, that's how good it is.

"Have you ever entertained such an adventure as that song suggests?"

My cheeks heat up immediately as I stare at the swirl of garlic in my mashed potatoes. "I don't see how that's any of your business."

"It's not, but we have to kill the time somehow, so I'm going to assume from your bothered answer, that would be a *no*."

"As if you've done something like that."

He delivers that rakish brow once more. He doesn't have to say anything, that one expression says it all. He has licked from well, you know...

"I've done pretty much everything, Kelsey, and I've delivered...every single time."

"Uh-huh, I'm sure," I say sarcastically.

Ignoring me, he continues, "I always make sure my girl comes, even if I don't."

"That's great." I offer him a closed-mouth smile.

"I've even faked it a time or two, just to get the hell out of there, you know?"

My fork pauses midway to my mouth as I look over our water glasses and right at his smirking face. "There's no way you fake it. You can't fake sperm."

"Girls don't check the condom, unless that's something you do."

"Eww, no, gross. Please change the subject; I hardly see how this is an appetizing conversation."

"Sex is always an appetizing conversation."

"Yes, well, not the details of you acting like you fake it and what's in or not in your condom."

"I'm not acting like I fake it...I do."

"Okay, JP." I give him a thumbs-up. "Good for you on your accomplishments."

His lips quirk to the side before he lifts his fork to his mouth. *That's right, eat up so we can get the hell out of here.* Honestly, conversation with this man has been one failure after another. I felt hope with the movie topic, but that burned down really quickly with him tearing apart *Sleepless in Seattle*. And I would never admit this to him, but now I'm wondering... how was that boy able to just fly across the country like that?

"Fuck," JP whispers as he grips the edge of the table. His fork is resting on his plate and his head is down as if he just hurt himself.

And because I'm the person that I am, I ask, "Are you okay?"

He lifts his head slightly so I can see his teeth roll over the bottom of his lip. "Mmm," he groans.

"Did you bite your lip? You know, I do that sometimes. It might develop into a canker sore, so be mentally prepared for that."

His head falls all the way back now as he leans backward in his chair, hands still on the edge of the table while he manspreads. "Fuck...yes."

Wait, hold on. What is happening?

He shifts and clenches his fist as he wets his lips. "Yes, baby, right there...mmm, you feel so good."

My expression falls.

My nostrils flare.

I fold my arms over my chest.

Could he be any more immature?

"Are you really doing this? Are you really doing the scene from *When Harry Met Sally*?" I ask.

"Fuck. That mouth of yours. Yes, suck me deep."

Oh dear God.

My face flames as I lean forward and tap the table. "Hey, yoo-hoo, you can stop that now. I get your point."

But he doesn't stop. Not even a little.

Nope, he continues to moan, to groan, to bite on his lip...move his hips.

"Yes, baby, your pussy is so fucking good. Uhhhhh, yes, fuck, I need to pump harder."

"No, no, that's okay, no pumping necessary," I say, but my mind starts to visualize and my neck starts to sweat.

You are NOT getting horny from this, you ARE NOT!

"Shit…" He slams his fist on the table and I watch in absolute horror—and secret suspense—as he moves closer to the table, his eyes still shut, his head bent down. "You're going to come, I can feel it, but not yet, not until I tell you," he groans.

I wet my lips.

Cross my legs.

Look away, only for my eyes to look back at him.

His hand reaches out and grips his cloth napkin. He crumples it in his fist. "Not yet, baby, don't you fucking come, not until I give you permission." His head falls back briefly. "Ahh, fuck, good girl. Hold it."

I lightly pat around the base of my neck with my napkin when he's not looking. Did they turn off the AC or something? What's with the pressure cooker up here?

"Jesus, your pussy is so good, so good. Yes, fuck me like that. Keep going, baby." He slams his fist on the table again and groans so loudly that it feels like a gallon of lava is pouring down my spine.

I bite the inside of my cheek, trying to distract myself, but it's no use. A dull throb pulses between my legs, my palms are sweating, and my gaze doesn't leave him as he grips the knife in front of him, pounds it into the table, and moans so loud, I KNOW the people below us are wondering what the hell is going on.

"Mother…fucker," he shouts. "Come, baby, come on my greedy cock." And then…he grinds down on his teeth, his neck veins bulge, and the most guttural sound falls past his lips.

Oh.

My.

God.

My tongue tingles. My cheeks are on fire. A light sweat glistens on my forehead. Did he actually just come? Because…I mean, that was so convincing, so sexy, so—

"Uh, everything okay up here?" Helix asks from the stairs, startling me right out of my chair and onto the floor with a loud plop.

Jesus Christ, Kelsey, get up.

Humiliation consumes me while I scramble to my feet, press down on my dress, and straighten my spine. "Yes!" I shout. "Everything is… Yes. We're fine. Nothing going on up here. Just, uh, chatting and whatnot. No need to worry about us. Yup. Nothing freaky happening."

I glance over at JP, who's smirking, fork in hand with a giant piece of meatloaf on the tines. He tips the fork to Helix and says, "My compliments to the chef." And then he takes a bite.

Meanwhile, my randy and ready body is over here, sending an SOS to the universe, saying, "I'll have what HE'S having."

––––––––––––

"Are you really not going to talk to me for the rest of the evening?"

Whispering, I ask, "Do you realize how embarrassing that was?"

"Yeah, really embarrassing for you. Helix saw you turned on, nipples hard, ready to go. Not sure if he was ready for that."

"I was NOT turned on," I say, even though I think we all know that's a complete lie. "You're acting like a child."

"Or am I just trying to loosen you up? Christ, woman, take a chill pill."

"Don't tell me to loosen up. I'll loosen up when I want to loosen up."

He nods, lips locked in a way that communicates exactly what he's thinking—*She's crazy.*

"Well, guess what, I'm only crazy because you're making me crazy."

His brow pulls together. "What?"

Wait…huh?

"I didn't say you were crazy."

"Then what did you say?"

"Nothing." He raises his glass. "But now I'm thinking you're crazy."

I groan and rest my arms on the table, crossing them in front of me. "Ugh, this night will never end."

"Instead of complaining about it, you could ask me another question, you know?"

"That doesn't sound appealing."

"Fine, I'll ask you a question." He clears his throat obnoxiously. "So, tell me, Kelsey, what are you looking for in a man?"

"Not you."

"Your flushed cheeks from moments ago beg to differ."

I swear I feel steam blow out my nose.

Smirking, he adds, "You know, we can either sit here in silence, which I know makes you more uncomfortable and chattier and will cause you to divulge information you probably don't want me knowing. Or you can control your babbling by answering a simple question."

Why is he right?

Just add it to the list of infuriating things about the man.

"Ask me something else."

"Okay, what do you find attractive in a man?"

I roll my eyes heavily. "Let me guess—if I don't answer this question, you will find one eerily similar to ask?"

He grins. "Yes, and I'll keep going from there."

I dab at my mouth with my napkin and then set it back in my lap. "Fine, you want to know what I want in a man? Well, firstly, someone who doesn't annoy me; secondly, someone who doesn't purposely lie—"

He slides his hand on the table and says, "Kelsey, from the tone of your voice, it almost seems like you're suggesting that I annoy you and purposely lie."

"How did you ever figure that out? Wow, JP, you're a genius."

"Jesus," he mutters. "You're ripe tonight. You've always been decently chill, but tonight, you're on another level."

I set my napkin on the table and fold my arms as I lean back. "Yes, because I thought tonight was going to be different. I thought…" In a wistful tone, I continue, "I thought I was going to meet someone I could actually date. I thought this was the start of something new, something exciting. I was excited to go on a date, but that's not what tonight has been. It's been disappointing, and a giant ball of irritation. So, excuse me if I'm not the delightful company *you* expected."

"You're really not. I might ask for a refund. Hypercritical fishwife isn't what I call a good first date or a match, for that matter."

"*Fishwife?*" I ask.

"Yup. Already called you a shrew, thought *fishwife* would be a good second option."

"Yeah…well, you're a…you're a…"

"A what?" he asks, his grin growing even wider.

Think, Kelsey, think of a good name.

"A shortsighted boob."

He tosses his head back, laughter erupting from his lips. "That's the best you could come up with? *A shortsighted boob*? Shit." He wipes at his eyes as I grow more furious by the second. "I think I might get that printed on a T-shirt. *You're a shortsighted boob.* Jesus, that's good."

I stare at him as he continues to laugh, then chuckle, then laugh again, and when he finally calms himself down, I ask, "Are you finished?"

"I think so." He gives his eyes one more swipe. "Oh man, any more of those golden insults you have stored away?"

"I don't know. Do you have any other names to call me other than *fishwife*?"

"Sure do…uptight gorgon."

What the hell is a *gorgon*? Doesn't matter, it's a hideous name, doesn't fall off the tongue.

And to hell if I'm going to let him get away with calling me…*that.*

My eyes narrow. "Half-cracked ignoramus."

"Fastidious wench."

My jaw clenches. "Cynical ninny."

He cracks a smile. "Pretentious strumpet."

The sound of Helix climbing the stairs momentarily distracts me before I say, "Callous cockhead."

Now he's full-on smiling. "Simpering concubine."

"*Strumpet* and *concubine* would allude to me being loose with my legs, and I can guarantee you right now, there's nothing loose about my appendages."

"Uh…everything okay?" Helix asks, stepping up to the table.

"Maybe you should be loose, have someone fish that pole out of your ass that you seem to be clenching." JP crosses his arms, looking like the casual butthole that he is.

"Would you guys like the check?" Helix asks.

"So, I have a pole up my ass because I'm not fainting at your feet over your nonsensical drivel and squawky singing?"

"Squawky?" JP asks, insulted. "Try again. There's nothing squawky about my singing."

"Yeah, I'll just, uh, go grab that check. I'm thinking dessert isn't a thing tonight." Helix takes off while JP and I share an unwavering stare-down.

"I've heard cats in heat sound better than what I've had to suffer through tonight."

"You're so full of shit." He tosses his napkin on the table. "I saw you bobbing your head."

"Oh, you're cute thinking that was bobbing, more like twitching from how horrendous you sounded. You sure know how to make someone's muscles fire off in revolt."

"Is that supposed to be funny? Because it's not."

I clutch at my chest. "Have I hurt your man feelings?"

Helix approaches again and sets the check on the table. Both of us reach for it at the same time.

"Let go," JP says.

"There's no way in hell I'm letting you pay for this meal," I counter. He might have ruined this night, and I'll forever have "Doe, a deer" stuck in my freaking head, but to hell if I'm going to let him pay.

Ohhhhh no.

"Over my dead and squawking body will I let you pay."

"Here are your phones," Helix says, sounding nervous. He should be. Shots have been fired, our voices are raised, we're engaging in the stare-down of a lifetime, and with one wrong move, this powder keg of a date will explode. "I'll just set them down here." He slowly places the phones on the table, careful not to disrupt anything, and then cautiously backs away.

Smart, smart man.

"Fine." I let go of the check but reach into my purse to pull out a few twenties. I set them on the table. "There, paid my half."

"Pick that fucking money up right now. You're not paying."

"Why not? I can afford it. Your brother pays me pretty well."

"This isn't a money thing."

"Then what is it?" I counter. "A pride thing?"

"Yeah, I always pay for a goddamn meal when I take someone out on a date."

"Well, you didn't take me out on a date, as this was an unfortunate coincidence. This was a loathsome, mind-numbingly pitiful tryst. Trust me, if this was a real date, it would not have gone like this."

"If this was a real date, I would've bent you over this table and spanked your ass for the way you've spoken to me."

My eyes widen. "Excuse me?"

"You heard me." He picks up my twenties and stuffs them into his pocket before pulling out two, one-hundred-dollar bills and dropping them on the table. There's no way dinner cost that much. Not even close.

Always trying to show off. Ugh, pretentious prick.

Everyone, please offer JP applause: he has money, good for him. Clearly, he wants to make a show of it.

But back to what he said. "That's outrageous behavior. No one spanks women these days."

He stands from the table and buttons his suit jacket. "Clearly you haven't been with the right men."

He walks over to me and holds out his hand to help me up from my chair. I smack his hand away and stand myself.

"I've been with perfect gentlemen, thank you very much."

"And there's your problem," JP says, leaning in. "A perfect gentleman isn't going to make you come the way I can."

He's so close I can practically feel the heat coming off his body. It warms me and simmers at the base of my stomach, causing a flash of heat to pulse through my body for a mere second, reminding me of that initial attraction on the day I met him. But just as fast as it arrives, it flits away.

"Don't flatter yourself, JP." I start to walk past him, but once again, just like in the conference room, he pauses me with a hand on my hip. He leans in close to my ear.

"I don't need to flatter myself when it's facts. If you were in my bed, you'd forget your name, your cunt would be begging for my cock, and your voice would be hoarse from crying out *my* name repeatedly."

I hate to admit it, but I can see it.

I can feel it.

What it would be like in his bed, him hovering over me.

He's demanding.

Controlling.

Doesn't let up until every last inch of my body has nothing left to give.

Even whispered, there's demand in his voice, and I can feel how it would be.

But that doesn't mean I want it.

There's a difference between romance and good sex. Good sex lasts a night, while romance lasts a lifetime.

But before I can respond, he steps away from me. We both make our way down the stairs, my legs wobblier than expected.

We bypass the hostess, who asks us how our dinner was, JP holds the door open for me, and when we're both on the sidewalk, JP closes the distance between us and puts his hand on my hip once again.

"Tonight was an absolute succubus of valuable time. I hope it never happens again."

"You and me both," I say, holding my head high. "You were unpleasant and a self-assured ass. I would rather stick my head in a gas station toilet than go on another date with you."

"The pleasure was not mine, babe. Hope you come down with a bad case of the toots later."

I gasp and look him in the eye as he smiles. "Yeah, well…I hope your penis gets stuck in your zipper." I make a step to walk away when he grips my wrist, brings it to his lips, and to my horror, places a kiss just on the inside of my wrist. His lips pause for only a breath, but it's just enough time to cause my stomach to flip-flop, a demoralizing feeling.

No, body, we don't like him.

Don't you dare get sucked in by his flippant charm.

"If only my penis got stuck between your legs instead." He lets go of my wrist. "Don't trip on your way home."

And then with one hand in his pocket, he takes off in the opposite direction, swagger in every step.

God, he's infuriating.

"Hope to see you never," I call out, for unknown reasons. Because I will see him again, in the office, because that's the kind of luck I have.

Sighing, I reach into my purse for my phone so I can call an Uber when my hand connects with some paper. Confused, I open my purse and find the three twenty-dollar bills I left on the table.

The motherfucker!

MEANT TO BE PODCAST
KNOX AND EMORY

Kelsey: Welcome, listener, to the *Meant to Be Podcast*, where we talk to madly-in-love couples about the way they met. Knox and Emory, thank you so much for joining me today. Please, let's get down to business. Tell us, how did you two meet?

Emory: College, our junior year.

Knox: She was a transfer student from California.

Emory: It was his last year at Brentwood before he was drafted to play for the Chicago Bobbies.

Knox: Technically, we met at a baseball party. She showed me her boob.

Emory: That is not how it went. We were drunk, I was looking for my friends, and I asked him for help. We went into his room, I fell, and my boob popped out.

Knox: I was enamored with the nip slip.

Emory: I was horrified the next morning. We went on our merry way until he spotted me lost on campus. He said—and I quote—he never forgets a good pair of tits.

Kelsey: Oh my God. Ha-ha-ha.

Knox: I don't. And I never did. The rest is history.

Emory: The rest is not history. He spent months attempting to win my affections in the most ridiculous ways possible.

Knox: And I won her over.

Emory: Only to break up for eight years. But then…we found each other again.

Knox: I wasn't letting her go that time. I put a ring on it and then…the rest is history.

CHAPTER 4
JP

"THERE HE IS, CASANOVA HIMSELF." Breaker takes a seat in my office and smirks at me. "How was it? Love at first sight?"

I unbutton my suit jacket and take a seat in my office chair. The moment the elevator doors opened, I spotted Breaker waiting with a to-go cup of coffee in hand, looking for one person: me.

His text messages last night went unanswered.

I ignored him as I said hello to our receptionist.

I didn't bother making eye contact with him when I was grabbing my own cup of coffee from the break room.

And when he barged into my office right after me, I chose to not growl in frustration at his persistence.

But now that he's sitting across from me, staring me down, looking for a recap, it doesn't seem like I have a choice but to tell him about last night's disaster.

From the inside of my suit pocket, I pull my phone out and set it on my desk before leaning back in my chair. "Last night?" I steeple my fingers together. "Well, when I first saw my date, I actually hoped it would go well, but that thought quickly vanished when she opened her mouth."

"Oh shit, did she have a screechy voice?"

I shake my head. "No, she let me know how much she hated me."

Breaker's brow draws together in confusion. "What do you mean? Did she know you?"

I slowly nod. "Oh yeah, she knew me."

"How? Did you go out with her once?"

"Nope." I shake the mouse on my desk, waking up my computer. "My date was Kelsey."

"Kelsey?" Breaker asks in disbelief. "As in Lottie's sister?"

"Yup."

"Oh, fuck." Breaker busts out in a long, drawn-out laugh. The sound fucking irritates me. "Dude, what are the chances?"

"Pretty good, apparently."

"Let me guess—she walked out of the restaurant when she saw it was you?"

"Nope. Because of the program's rules, you're forced to eat dinner with the person they set you up with. And because we showed signs of a full-out medieval battle, they put us in the private loft, away from everyone else."

"And how did that go?"

"Not great." I open my inbox and am flooded by emails.

"But you said you were excited at first. Why?"

"Because it was Kelsey," I say casually. "I knew her, so I didn't have to try to get to know a stranger when I was already not in the mood to be there. Didn't think it would be uncomfortable, plus...she looked hot." I shrug. "But all of that washed away the moment she begged me to leave."

"Which she wasn't allowed to do, and I'm sure that only made her even angrier. She has the same fiery spirit as Lottie."

"Yeah, and it showed. When I say she was unpleasant, I'm not kidding. We ended up fighting the entire time and, sure, I didn't help matters. At the end of the night, we went our separate ways."

"And how do you feel about that?" Breaker asks.

"Relieved," I answer. "It was fucking exhausting having dinner with her. Sure, I like some quick-witted repartee here and there, but when I got home, I felt drained."

Breaker is silent for a moment as he studies me. I'm sure he's looking for some sort of tell that I'm lying. He's wondering if Kelsey and I did hit it off and we're secretly dating now.

Could not be further from the truth.

"Why don't I believe you?" he asks.

Here we go.

"Dude, trust me when I say—" I stop speaking, my eyes falling on an email from Kelsey.

Subject line: I'm coming to your office.

I barely have time to open it before the door to my office flies open and Kelsey steps in. The expression on her face reads irritated, and the way her hands clench at her sides makes me feel anxious. The surprised look in her eyes when she spots Breaker completely changes her demeanor in seconds.

"Breaker, hi." She smooths her hand over her hair. "I, uh, I didn't see you there. Sorry about barging in."

Breaker, of course, smiles, showing off his freshly whitened teeth. "Hey, Kelsey, heard you had quite the night last night."

Kelsey's murderous eyes flash to me. "You told him?"

"Well, he's my brother, and he was the one who forced me to go on the date, so it's only natural that he'd ask me how it went."

Composing herself, Kelsey turns to Breaker and asks, "Would you give me a second with your brother?"

He smirks and stands. "Of course."

Before he can walk away, Kelsey adds, "And I would appreciate your discretion in this matter."

Breaker pats her on the shoulder and says, "I understand the need to not be attached by name to him. I wish I wasn't either."

Wow, what a brother.

He takes off and closes the door behind him. I turn my attention to Kelsey, who closes the distance between us and takes a seat in the chair Breaker just vacated.

"To what do I owe the pleasure?" I ask her.

"After last night, I figured we need to talk about how to handle this."

"Handle what?" I pause and tilt my head to the side. "Oh, hell, did you fall in love with me last night and now you're trying to figure out how to muddle through work while harboring these intense feelings about me?"

Her face falls flat only for her top lip to curl into a sneer. "If any revelation happened last night, it most certainly had nothing to do with love and everything to do with this extreme distaste I have for you."

"Ooh, distaste. That's a new one." I lean my forearms on my desk. "Please do elaborate."

"This isn't funny, JP."

"Didn't know I was laughing."

Her eyes narrow and she speaks through clenched teeth. "You don't have to laugh in order to make a laughing matter out of something that's incredibly serious."

I pick up a pen off my very untidy desk, a desk that I know drives Kelsey nuts. The tension in her expression is from our conversation, but the death grip she has on the chair's armrests is undoubtedly from the rumpled reports on my desk, the askew pen jar that's tipped over, and the unconventional way I have my computer tilted.

"Okay, tell me why our situation is incredibly serious, because unless I missed something, nothing, and I mean nothing, happened between us last night. Well, nothing that requires this level of psychosis."

"JP, we went on a date last night."

"Not by our choice." I click the pen open and then shut.

"But it still happened. We shared an intense meal, and then after, when we were leaving, you said...you said some things."

"Oh...the whole 'If you were in my bed, your cunt would be begging for my cock' part?"

She swallows, her cheeks heating. "Yes, that part."

"It was just basic facts. Nothing to make note of."

"Well"—she smooths her hands over her well-pressed, possibly steamed skirt—"it was inappropriate, and we need to set some ground rules here."

"This should be good." I lace my hands together behind my head and say, "Lay it on me—what are the ground rules?"

"Well, for one—"

"Real quick, I just need to put this out there—your reaction is completely ridiculous and over the top, but you know, to each their own. Your feelings are your feelings…all that bullshit." I gesture to her. "You may proceed."

Her nostrils flare, and I realize it's a small tic of hers when she's upset. "As I was saying, our first ground rule is we don't speak of last night, ever. I didn't tell Lottie and I would appreciate it if you didn't tell anyone else."

"Am I that repulsive?"

"Yes."

I chuckle because I thought she was going to say *no* to that and come up with some long-winded explanation, but got to give the girl credit for her honesty.

"I also don't want people thinking I get involved with any man who crosses my path or that I'm trying to climb the corporate ladder by spreading my legs."

"Don't worry, your sister covered that one."

Her eyes narrow and she points her finger. "That was not how that went down and you know it."

"You're right, that was uncalled for. Sorry." If anyone pursued that relationship, it was Huxley, because he couldn't seem to keep his hands off Lottie.

My apology seems to satisfy her because she continues, "So we don't talk about last night, ever. Act like it never happened."

"I wish it didn't." I smile at her, which only makes her grind her teeth together. Jesus, talk about uptight. Could she relax for like a second?

"JP, I need you to say you're never going to talk about it."

"Christ." I roll my eyes. "I'm never going to talk about it."

That appeases the gremlin inside her.

"Second ground rule—there will be no more inappropriate behavior."

I kick my feet up on my desk and lean back in my chair. "Not sure what you're alluding to with that ground rule."

"The way you speak to me and the little touches need to end."

"You act as if I'm grazing your hand when I walk by or sliding my hand to your lower back...or gripping your thigh while at the conference table. Correct me if I'm wrong, but that has never happened."

"It, uh...it hasn't. But you know, the things you say aren't appropriate for a workplace, so that needs to stop."

"The 'cunt calling out for my cock' thing was outside of work."

"You've said more than that while at work, and don't deny it."

I have.

"Okay, your wish is my command, babe."

"And none of that." She points her finger at me again. "None of that *babe* stuff. I'm Kelsey, you're JP, and that's it. Nothing else. I'm not your babe."

"Just a term of endearment, but sure, *Kelsey.* That's how I'll refer to you from now on, unless you wanted something more along the lines of...*fishwife?*"

Let's pause here for a moment. I'm not a complete asshole...*all the time.* I'm really not. But Kelsey just has the best reactions, and I can't resist. She's so goddamned gorgeous, and it's fun to rile her. To ruffle her feathers.

"You do realize you're the absolute worst to have a conversation with, right? Like...the absolute worst," she says, her face wincing with irritation.

"I only seem to receive that sort of feedback from you, which makes me think it's a *you* thing, not a *me* thing."

She pinches her brow and I swear she silently counts to ten. "And thirdly—"

"A third ground rule? Was not expecting that. Total plot twist." I lean back in my chair again. "Please, continue to pleasure me with your commands."

"I'm talking to Huxley and asking him if I can fall under his management because our working relationship is volatile."

"Ooh, you see, I was with you on points one and two, but unfortunately, your line of work falls under my line of work; therefore, that makes you my employee. Huxley isn't going to bother taking on another task when his plate is already full. He also doesn't take too kindly to people telling him what to do, even if you're his future sister-in-law. And if you do approach him, all he's going to do is pull us into a conference room and ask that we work things out... in front of him. Now, given the restrictions that ground rule one presents us, you're not going to be able to tell him the truth as to why you don't want to work under me anymore, and therefore have no validity behind your case. Also, you're only going to paint yourself as confrontational since everyone else that does work with me has given me nothing but rave reviews. So... if you want to embarrass yourself and shine a spotlight on your difficult disposition, by all means, approach Huxley, but if you want to remain in his good graces, I would suggest you drop ground rule number three."

The tension in her jaw is visible from where I sit. I know this isn't what she wanted to hear, but it's also true. If anything, Huxley is a businessman first so he can remove emotion from business, which is why we're so successful... something Kelsey needs to learn.

"Then maybe Breaker could do it."

I chuckle. "Managing a certified organizer doesn't fall under his scope of responsibilities. He's the numbers guy. Organizing and managing the different properties isn't what he does. Hate to say it, *Kelsey*, but you're stuck with me."

She crosses her arms at her chest and mutters something under her breath.

I move closer to her and say, "I didn't quite catch that. Can you repeat it?"

She looks me dead in the eyes and says, "I despise you."

"Now, now, now, is that something you should be saying to your employer?"

She stands from the chair, grumbling some more, and then puts her manicured finger on my desk. "From here on out, we adhere to the two ground rules. Do you hear me?"

"I do." I smirk. "I hear you quite well."

"And we'll only talk to each other when we need to, and about business only. When Huxley and Lottie invite us over, I want you nowhere near me. Don't even think about talking to me. Do you understand?"

"I'm practically shivering in my shoes."

"JP, I'm being serious. Do you understand?"

Whatever caused this much animosity toward me must really be affecting her because I'm not sure I've ever seen anyone this worked up before, let alone Kelsey.

What's behind this anger?

They always say there's a thin line between love and hate—could it possibly be love?

I hold back my chuckle. Hell, if she heard what was going on inside my head right now, she'd have me hung up by the balls.

I think there's one thing clear, though—she wants nothing to do with me. This entire conversation has made that crystal clear.

Smiling up at her, I say, "I understand you. And I look forward to our newly established working relationship where we don't ever mention the hot date we went on or the way you shivered when I talked about your cunt, or how you secretly love it when I call you *babe*."

There…just one more jab for the road.

She tosses her hands up in frustration, turns on her heel, and charges out of my office, slamming the door behind her.

That went exceedingly well.

CHAPTER 5
KELSEY

Kelsey: Welcome, listener, to the *Meant to Be Podcast*, where we talk to madly-in-love couples about the way they met. Pacey and Winnie, thank you so much for joining me today. Please, tell us how you met.

Winnie: Where to even begin? It's all kind of whimsical if you think about it.

Pacey: I thought she was a murderer.

Winnie: Stop it. No, you didn't. Well, I guess you did, but that's not the start of it. I was driving to Banff in honor of my late mother and got lost in the mountains. It was one of the worst storms I've ever seen and my car got stuck in mud. I had no reception, so I decided to go find help. That's when I stumbled upon the cabin.

Pacey: I play hockey for the Vancouver Agitators, and every summer, a few of the boys and I drive to Banff for some relaxation. It was our first night there and Winnie came knocking on the door.

Winnie: I was soaking wet, and the minute the door opened, a flash of lightning lit me up from behind.

Pacey: It was absolutely horrifying.

Winnie: As a group, we went back and forth, attempting to show each other that they weren't the murdering types and I wasn't the murdering type. Pacey was really quiet at first. Eli Hornsby, a defenseman for the Agitators, was the one who welcomed me into the house and gave me a place to stay for the night. But the next morning, Pacey was the one who helped me find my car.

Pacey: I thought she was beautiful when she was all wet, but the next morning, I couldn't take my eyes off her. And I knew I needed to spend every spare moment I had listening to her stories and enjoying her company.

THREE WEEKS LATER...

"Wow, sis…that's some dress," I say as Lottie steps out of her bathroom.

"Hux got it for me. Is it too…booby?"

My eyes fall to her very prominent cleavage, and I wince. "I mean, it's really booby, but you also look hot. The red is perfect for your skin and that red lip color is such a great match. Now I feel like a fuddy-duddy in my dress."

Lottie has this hourglass shape that any woman would kill for. Hips and tits, that's her. I might have a good rack, but I am also more petite than she is. My curves on the bottom half aren't like hers. And this siren-red form-fitting dress she's wearing shows off every single curve. And despite the hem falling to her calves, it's still one of the most revealing yet exquisite dresses I've ever seen.

"Stop it. You look beautiful. I think the yellow was a perfect choice and it goes so nicely with your fresh caramel highlights."

"You think so?" I glance at myself in the full-length mirror positioned in front of Lottie and Huxley's bed. We all know that mirror isn't there for checking out outfits. I adjust the delicate straps on my shoulders and smooth my hands over the beautifully expensive silk fabric. The apron neckline cuts just low enough for a decent show of cleavage, while the flowy long skirt has a slit to just above my upper thigh, making my short legs look longer in my heels. "God, why am I so nervous?"

Lottie flips her hair over her shoulder and then slips on a pair of nude heels. "Probably because you asked a man on a date to a work event and you're worried about it."

That's very true.

Edwin is his name.

He's a computer programmer who works remotely for a medical tech company. He loves to cook, go to comic book conventions, and is quite educated on different types of birds. He's really nice, and we've been on three dates.

This will be our fourth.

We didn't meet through the Going In Blind app. After my date with JP, I didn't want to take any chances on whom they'd match me with. But instead, we were both at a coffeehouse, working. He spilled his coffee and I helped him clean it up. We started chatting, and well…that's that. Some of the greatest love affairs start because of spilled coffee, and this very well might be one of them.

And the best thing about Edwin is that he's not JP. He's nothing like JP. He's quieter, reserved, with thick-rimmed glasses and a mess of curly blond hair. He told me he can't grow a beard, so he doesn't even try. And he's slimmer, whereas JP obviously puts time in at the gym. Oh…and not even one tattoo.

Everything I need in life. *Why on earth am I even comparing him to JP?* JP is a work colleague and nothing more. He's irrelevant.

"I'm a bit nervous. I like this guy. We've only been out three times, and sometimes when he talks about birds, it can get slightly boring, but he's so kind and he doesn't try to poke my buttons."

"The antithesis of JP."

"Exactly," I say while exhaling. "Not that JP and I were ever an item, but after the night we don't talk about…which, you didn't tell Huxley, did you?"

"No."

"And you're not mad that I'm making you keep it a secret? It was your fault I told you since you kept pestering me."

"I know." Lottie turns toward me, clutch in hand now. "And I like having a secret from Huxley. Makes me feel naughty. And if he ever finds out…ooh, I can't wait for the punishment."

I roll my eyes and, standing from the bed, straighten out my dress, shimmying the fabric down my legs. Lottie looks at me and smirks. "What?" I ask.

"Not only are you going to make Edwin fall to the floor, but JP is going to be all over you."

"No, he's not. He has barely even looked at me during the last three weeks."

"Doesn't mean he doesn't think about you."

"Will you stop it with that? He never even liked me…ever."

"That's not what I heard. When he first met you, you were all he could talk about. But you were the one who put up the wall."

"Because I work for him."

Lottie gives me a look. "And I worked for Huxley."

"Yeah, well…you apparently have no morals, but I do."

She chuckles just as there's a knock at the door. "Come in," Lottie calls out.

The door pops open and Huxley steps in. He's wearing a black three-piece velvet suit with a black tie, his hair is slicked properly to the side, and his beard is trimmed just enough to not be messy, but still thick enough to make a mark. He exudes confidence as he approaches Lottie, his eyes locked on her and only her as he adjusts the expensive watch on his wrist.

Without saying anything, he closes the space between them, wraps his arm around her waist, and brings her up against his chest. I watch as he grips her chin with his forefinger and thumb, forcing her mouth toward his, and she gives in willingly. Quietly, just above a whisper, he says, "You. Are. Exquisite. I'm going to peel that dress off you tonight, spread your legs, and make you come on my tongue."

I softly clear my throat, attempting to clue him in that I'm standing right next to my sister.

He doesn't apologize. He simply presses his lips to Lottie's and moves his hand down to her ass and grips it tightly. "Fuck, babe, you look so good."

"Well, what a lovely night for a gala, don't you think?" I say, standing there awkwardly.

"Mmm, I could easily stay home and sit on your face, if you want," Lottie says.

And that's my cue to leave.

"I'm just going to…uh…yeah, I'm going to meet you guys downstairs."

I scoot past them and their wandering hands, hoping they realize they're my ride to the event and that we need to leave in five minutes.

As I make my way down the stairs to the entryway, I can't help but feel a bout of jealousy. Lottie is so in love, more in love than I've ever seen her. She's not only infatuated with Huxley, but he's infatuated with her. Possessive of her. Worships her. And, yes, I'm all about independence and women running the world, but there's something to be said about breaking the glass ceiling during the day and coming home to a man who'll do everything in his power to remind you exactly who you belong to.

Lottie has that with Huxley.

Will I ever have that?

Edwin flashes through my mind as I walk down the stairs. He might not be as power hungry and domineering as Huxley, but he has traits that excite me. For one, we have a nice time together. For another, we can enjoy a simple conversation.

And the kiss we shared the other night when he walked me back to my apartment was...nice.

Sure, my shoes didn't fly off when our lips met, but I also didn't hate it.

If I've learned anything from my podcast, it's that sometimes the type of passion Lottie and Huxley have for each other doesn't happen right away, but needs time to grow. Edwin and I are still in the learning phase of our relationship. There's so much more time to grow when it comes to passion.

When I reach the bottom step, I head toward the bench in the entryway, but just then the front door opens and JP walks in, momentarily stopping me.

He's dressed in a navy-blue suit and black button-up shirt, of which he's left the top two buttons undone, and his tie is draped over his neck, loose and messy. His hair curls over his forehead in just the right way that my eyes are drawn toward the thickness of his brows and the darkness of his lashes.

When he spots me, a smirk barely crosses his face as he adjusts one of the cuffs of his shirt.

Not saying a word to me, he heads to the stairs, grips the railing, and shouts up to Huxley. "Dude, the van is here. Get your ass down here."

To my dismay, because I'm curious, I ask, "Wh-what are you doing here?"

He turns around and starts buttoning his shirt. "What do you mean *what am I doing here*? Same reason you are."

"But...don't you have your own transportation?"

"Don't you?" he asks.

"I got ready with Lottie."

"Well, I just moved in across the street and figured it would be more eco-friendly to all ride together. Any other questions?"

That makes me shut my mouth very quickly.

He moved across the street? How come Lottie never said anything to me? And which house did he move into? From memory, I can recall two that are across the way. A white one that's bright and cheery, and an all-black house. Black windows, black siding, black roof. My guess is… that one.

I keep my gaze averted, but out of the corner of my eye, I catch JP adjusting his tie and making loops just as Huxley and Lottie come down the stairs, hand in hand, looking pristine and polished. I thought Lottie might have makeup smeared across her face and Huxley's hair would be a total mess.

When they reach the bottom, Lottie pats JP's shoulder and says, "Hey, neighbor," and then walks up to me. Giving me a once-over, she says, "Doesn't my sister look beautiful tonight?"

Oh God, Lottie. Why?

She looks over her shoulder at JP, who gives me the briefest of glances before saying, "I've seen better."

Huxley smacks JP on the back of the head and mumbles something under his breath I can't quite hear. Then he turns to me and says, "Kelsey, you look stunning. I'm sure Edwin will be very happy to have you on his arm tonight."

That pulls JP's attention. "Edwin? Is that your latest attempt at love?"

"That is none of your concern," I say while taking my sister's hand, more for support than anything. I wish she had told me we'd be riding with JP, because I wouldn't have gotten ready with her.

Hell, that's probably why she didn't say anything. When our eyes connect, I can see the apology in them.

"I hate you," I mutter to her.

"I know," she says back, and together, we walk out the door to the van that's parked out front.

It's one of those super fancy electric vans that celebrities use when going to the Met Gala so their dresses aren't wrinkled. It can also double as an office on wheels, which is often what the boys use it for when they need to be driven around town and get work done at the same time.

The driver holds the door open for us and I step in first, followed by Lottie. We maneuver to the very back and take our seats.

"You should've told me he was coming tonight," I whisper. Huxley is talking to JP at the front door of the house. From their mannerisms, it seems as though Huxley is lecturing JP about something. Hopefully how rude he just was. If I've learned one thing since Lottie started dating Huxley, it's that I earned another person in my corner. Huxley will always stick up for me.

"I didn't want you to not get ready with me because he was going to be here. This is our first fancy gala together. I didn't want him to ruin it."

"Well, he did. I mean…*he's seen better*, what kind of comment is that?"

"A stupid one, because that's what he is, stupid. He clearly has feelings for you and doesn't know how to manage them."

"Oh my God, don't give me that crap. We're not in elementary school. He can act like an adult man."

"I'm not taking his side, just trying to offer up some sort of explanation as to why he's acting like a tool. I've seen him when he's relaxed and you're not around, and he's really nice, easygoing, and fun. Sure, he teases a lot, but that's sort of his way. I think if you got to know him better, you'd see the same things."

"I don't need to get to know him better. What I know is enough."

The boys walk onto the van, joining us, and they take the two captain's chairs in front of us, but not before Huxley gives Lottie one of the most consuming glances I've ever seen.

Listen, I don't have a crush on my sister's fiancé, I really don't, but I have to say, the way he looks at her is incredibly sexy. So sexy that at times, I notice how attractive Huxley is. I know, I know, I shouldn't be thinking about my sister's fiancé like that, BUT…ugh, the way he looks at her.

I'm knocked out of my inappropriate thoughts when the driver shuts the door and we are on our way.

"How long is the drive?" Lottie asks.

"Twenty minutes," Huxley answers. "It's at the River Estate."

"Edwin is meeting you there?" Lottie asks.

"Yes," I answer. "He'll be a touch late, but he'll be there. He actually had to rent a suit for the event because he didn't have one. It was cute, and I helped him pick one out online."

"What self-respecting man doesn't own a suit?" JP asks.

My eyes flash to the back of his head. "Someone who works from home for a living and doesn't go to events that require a suit." My voice is laced with attitude and for very good reason. I don't want JP picking on Edwin. Sure, I can handle his snark, but I'm not sure Edwin has a thick enough skin to handle it.

"Did your date have a dress?" Lottie asks, taking the attention off me. "Or did you have to buy her one?"

JP turns in his chair and says, "Genesis has multiple dresses, but I still bought her one anyway."

Wait…what? JP is dating someone? When did this happen? I mean, not that I really care, but I didn't think he was the dating type, unless…

"Did you hire her to go on this date as well?" I ask.

Not sure why I'm poking the bear, but the question flies out of my mouth before I can stop it.

"Interested in my dating life?" JP asks with a wiggle of his brows.

"No, I'm not. Not even sure why I asked that. Probably just to goad you."

"Well, for your information, I've been dating Genesis for about two weeks now. She's the vice president of Mecca Tech."

"That's nice," I say, looking out the window. "I hope you two are very happy together."

"We are, thanks."

"She only just kissed him the other night," Huxley chimes in.

"Dude," JP bemoans, which of course brings a smile to my face.

When I glance at Huxley, he sends me a wink. I knew I liked him for more than one reason, besides loving my sister.

JP once again turns in his seat, and as if he needs to save face in front of me, he says, "We're taking things slow."

"I didn't ask." I hold my hands up, smiling. "But you know, Edwin and I have shared more than one kiss."

His eyes narrow. "And were those kisses any good? Seems like a guy named Edwin kisses more like a cow licking a salt block than with desirable affection."

"He kisses just fine." Slightly sloppy, but JP doesn't need to know that.

"Why don't we talk about something else?" Lottie suggests. The tension is rising, therefore Lottie swoops in with the need to defuse it. I'm usually that person, but I'm in the trenches, grenades being tossed around, and I'm sitting back, knocking them right back at the thrower. "Uh, how about the wedding? We haven't talked about that much. Huxley and I decided on a beach wedding."

"You did decide on the beach?" I ask, facing my sister now. "That's so exciting. When did you decide?"

"Just now...upstairs. Huxley went by the cove and restaurant you and I looked at the other day and he really liked it."

"Isn't it breathtaking?" I ask Huxley.

"It is." His eyes connect with Lottie. "I could envision marrying Lottie there, making her officially mine."

His eyes sear her with love and I inwardly groan as I go back to staring out the window. They're exhausting to be around.

Lottie was never the romantic between the two of us. She's been the one searching out success, looking for validation in her work. I happened to stumble upon my business while seeking out love. I was the one who read all the books about romance, watched all the movies... Hell, I started a podcast based on love.

And yet, I'm loveless, and my sister is consumed by it.

Where's the luck there?

Hint—there's none.

Just wait, Edwin and I will get there. Slowly but surely, we'll get there.

The van door opens and cameras immediately start flashing.

Tonight's gala is supposed to be a star-studded event, full of high-society members and a few celebrities. All proceeds benefit the Children's Hospital, and just to get through the doors, it's five thousand dollars a head.

Cane Enterprises paid for my ticket and Edwin's without blinking an eye.

And the River Estate is a gorgeous mansion in the epicenter of Beverly Hills. It's one of the largest properties in the area, with a sprawling circular driveway, towering palm trees lined up along the pavement, and a grand entrance to the estate fit only for royalty.

Huxley is the first to exit the van and, as talked about prior to arriving, Lottie will follow behind him, and they will walk the red carpet, hand in hand. JP and I are to follow, separately.

Lottie offers me a wink before moving by me and heading out of the van. Together, they walk down the carpet, pulling the attention away from who's left. Just the way I like it.

JP gets out next and buttons his suit jacket once he exits.

I take a deep breath and then make my way out, but just as I reach the second step, my heel catches on something and my body falls forward.

Oh God, no.

Cameras flash, I lose my balance, and just as I start to plummet forward, a hand closes around my elbow and steadies me so I don't fall.

My eyes quickly land on JP, who smiles thoughtfully. Under his breath, he says, "Easy there, killer. Wouldn't want to make a spectacle on your first red carpet."

And I don't know what throws me off more, his kind gesture of helping me or the soft tone of his voice that rolls over me as he helps me all the way out of the van.

Either way, color me shocked. Given the tumultuous nature of our relationship, I would've thought he'd have stepped to the side and let me land flat on my face, only to gather the cameras around me to take pictures.

Look, folks, come closer, come closer, see how she missed that step completely? Notice the gravel stuck to the side of her cheek. Oh, oh, wait, yes, zoom in; she bit her tongue on the way down, attempting to hold back a slew of curse words I've heard her say before. Be alarmed; she says fuck.

"You okay?" he asks, his voice growing close to my ear.

"Ye-yeah." I stumble over the words that seem to be getting lost in my throat. He's right next to me, shoulder to shoulder, still holding my hand. Anyone who isn't privileged to our hostile banter would assume we're a couple. Which we very much aren't.

"You sure? You seem unsteady," he says, still holding my hand as we walk toward the entrance. Thankfully, thanks to Lottie and Huxley, not too many cameras are paying attention to us.

"Just a little shaken."

"Here, come this way, then," JP says, ushering me around the gauntlet of photographers to a back entrance where a few cars are parked, most likely ready to sneak people in and out.

When we reach the door, JP opens it for me and we're greeted by a doorman.

"JP Cane," JP says.

The man doesn't even bother looking at the clipboard in his hand, he just offers us a curt nod and then lets us in the back entrance.

Once inside, we pause a few feet away from the door and I lean against the wall, composing myself.

"God, I almost fell flat on my face." I press my hand to my chest, taking a deep breath. JP is adjusting his tie when our eyes connect. "Thank you for helping me."

"You're welcome," he answers calmly. Sweetly.

Are we in some sort of alternate reality? Because…this is a different side of JP, one I didn't know existed. He's being…nice. There's no snark, there's no insult, no teasing. He's being normal. Did I actually trip and, instead of being steadied by him, fall into some sort of black hole?

"That could've been embarrassing," I say, patting down my dress and checking to make sure everything is in place.

"I've seen worse. You probably would've just fallen to your knees, a boob would've popped out, and then it would've been blurred in photos. Not a big deal."

"Uh, that would've been mortifying to me."

"Seems like a fun Friday night to me," he says with a reassuring smile. He's not trying to set me off; he's just trying to help me forget. He takes a step forward, leaving little room between us as he reaches up and tucks a strand of hair behind my ear.

His fingers linger.

My pulse escalates.

And oh my God, why am I reacting to his touch, to his proximity?

Clearing my throat, I say, "Well, I know that must have been painful for you. Helping me, that is."

His eyes study me and I can feel myself wilt under the steely gaze of his green eyes. Just like Huxley's, they're hungry, unmistakably intense, and there's nothing I can do to tear my eyes away as my core temperature spikes. His cologne—serving more as an aphrodisiac—swirls around me, and when he takes another step forward, my mouth goes dry. "You might think I don't like you, Kelsey," he says with a shake of his head, "but that's not the case at all. I actually—"

"There you are," calls a feminine voice from down the hall. "I saw your brother come in but I didn't see you. Got a little worried you were going to stand me up."

JP looks to the left, where a beautiful blond in a brilliantly sparkling gold gown is standing, looking nervous but also genuine at the same time.

"Hi," she says to me. "I'm Genesis."

"Oh, hi." I wave while JP puts some distance between us, and from the corner of my eye, I catch him pull on the back of his neck, his veins straining. "Genesis, it's nice to meet you. I'm Kelsey."

"Kelsey, as in the sustainable organizer Kelsey?"

I smile politely. "That would be me."

"Wow, I'm really impressed with your work. JP was showing me the kinds of changes you've made in the office the other day."

I glance at JP. "You were?" That's…shocking, to say the least. I didn't think JP even cared what I did in the scope of my job. In all honesty, I assumed he thought it was just a bunch of wasted time and resources from the way he approached managing me. From the more efficient filing, to the cans of water in the break room, I didn't think he cared.

"Oh yes, he talks about it all the time. He's very impressed by you."

Okay…

Okay, everyone.

Let's all take a collective breath, because I truly, truly think I'm in a different world right now. What on earth is happening?

JP Cane talks about me all the time? Better yet, he's impressed? That's not like him, some might even say quite off-brand for him. Impressed? No, more like irritated by my presence, right?

"You know what"—JP steps up next to Genesis and puts his hand on her back—"I think I have to greet a couple of people. Genesis, do you mind coming with me?"

"Not at all." Genesis loops her arm through JP's. "Kelsey, I'd love to talk to you more; please find me this evening."

"Sure." I smile. "Enjoy."

Together, I watch them walk away, down the hall and toward the party.

What the hell was all that about?

It almost seemed like JP cared about me. Like he didn't want to see me fail, like he actually thought highly of my talents.

Maybe I'm just delirious. There's no way JP has any kind feelings toward me.

None.

The door to the side entrance opens again, and this time, a familiar face smiles at me.

"Kelsey," Edwin says right before pushing his glasses back up his nose. "Boy, am I glad to see you. Did you see all the cameras out there?"

I chuckle and nod. "Yeah, I almost fell on my face in front of them."

"That would've been a travesty."

"Tell me about it."

He walks up to me and I half expect him to reach out and at least give me a hug, maybe a kiss on the cheek, but instead, he pats me on the shoulder. "That's a nice color dress."

A nice color dress? That's all he can say about my appearance? I spent a good two hours getting ready today. Curling my long thick freshly highlighted hair was the main time suck. And then meticulously making sure I picked out the perfect lingerie that would accentuate this dress, to make my breasts look amazing, and leave no question if there's a panty line.

Hint—there isn't.

And the compliment I get is *nice color?*

That makes me feel...sad.

Growing up, I didn't have the highest self-esteem when it came to my body, because I was always compared to Lottie, the goddess with curves. I've tried hard to make myself feel beautiful, and it's been a journey. And my insecurities coupled with my inability to be in a relationship have taken their toll on me.

Tonight, with JP's comment and now Edwin's...my insecurities are tickling the back of my mind, telling me I'm not good enough.

CHAPTER 6
JP

"DID YOU HEAR WHAT I said?" Genesis asks, tugging on my arm.

"Hmm? What's that? Sorry." I clear my throat. "It's loud in here."

"It is," she softly says. "But I can't help thinking that you've been distracted all night."

Because I have been.

I've been distracted by glimpses of a yellow dress sweeping through the crowd. A yellow dress that I can't seem to get out of my head ever since I first caught sight of it this evening. A form-fitting creation that wraps around her waist but drapes down to her ankles, and the delicate straps that hold up her mouth-watering tits, and that slit...fuck. I lied. Kelsey looked—*looks*—stunning in her dress. Why on earth I said otherwise... well, my fucking stupid defense mechanism.

Don't say you like someone, because then you'll never get hurt. Fucking idiotic.

But, yeah, I haven't been paying attention to Genesis because someone else has completely captivated me. And I hate that.

Fuck do I hate that she has control over my head tonight.

After the "ground rules" she set, I chalked up any chances of becoming close with Kelsey to absolutely zero. And sure, did I assist in that zero percent chance? Of course I did, and I'm not going to pretend I didn't. I use instigation as a defense technique, to guard myself. Kelsey is no exception.

She's the first girl I've had more than one night's interest in. From the moment I met her in the conference room with Lottie, when they were pitching their organizing services, I felt the need to get closer to her. To find out who this strong-willed, intelligent woman is, what makes her tick, what brings her joy...who brings her joy.

And I've tried everything you could think of to break down her walls.

I've attempted friendship, which was a complete shitshow.

I've tried flirting. I was knocked down a peg or two rather quickly.

I tried sarcasm, wit, and well...that didn't go over well either.

On *the date*, I reverted to my last resort, poking her with annoyance. I think we all know how that ended up—a follow-up the next day with ground rules on how to stay the hell away from her. Instruction received.

I'm not one to push against the tide; I know when I'm simply wasting my time, so when I met Genesis at a meeting at Mecca Tech and we got on well, I didn't hesitate to give dating a shot. She's smart and beautiful, and we seem compatible.

When Kelsey's working at Cane Enterprises, I've behaved professionally, kept my eyes down unless asked a direct question, my heart guarded, and avoided inhaling Kelsey's flirty perfume.

It's worked.

All of it.

Until she walked down those stairs tonight.

Until her hand landed in mine when she exited the van.

Until I helped her into the back entrance of the estate and caught a rare glimpse of her vulnerability, something she keeps very well hidden.

Now, I'm a desperate, needy asshole all over again.

"Sorry, Genesis," I say softly. "Work events are always stressful. Even though it's supposed to be a fun night out, I still have eyes on me at any given time." Very true—I'm always stiffer at work events.

Cane Enterprises is always under scrutiny because of how powerful we've become. Our competitors would like nothing more than to see us crumble and fall.

"I can totally understand that. The pressure of being one of a few female vice presidents in the tech world is intense. Feels the same way, everyone is waiting for me to make a mistake."

"Sorry for interrupting," a waiter says, coming to stand before us. "But they're calling everyone to their assigned seats as dinner is about to begin."

"Of course." I nod at the man and then offer my arm to Genesis. She takes it and together we walk into the ballroom of the estate.

The room is bustling with Beverly Hills elites dressed in their finest. From Tom Ford suits to obscure designer gowns, the glitter and the glam of the evening almost overshadow the cause, the reason why we're here. Typical for most events in this part of town. You pay a fee to attend, and then the rest of the night, business is conducted, gossip is spread, and deals are made with a discreet handshake.

But not this event. It's one of the reasons why my brothers and I attend. Right after dinner, they remind guests why we're all here by showing a very poignant video. A video about where your money is going, whom you're helping, and why it's so important. You not only leave feeling fulfilled, but you leave educated and with a slightly lighter wallet.

After receiving our table number from the door attendant, we weave through the golden ballroom, which is decked out with low-hanging chandeliers over every long rectangular table. Each table is decorated with low-profile lush centerpieces of white lilies, complete place settings, and gold serviettes that match the gold in the room and the golden swirls in the cream tablecloths. An exquisite, intimate dinner that provides the opportunity for attendees to communicate easily across the table.

"What table are we again?" Genesis asks.

"Table two," I answer. "It'll be up front. They always stick us up front."

We're stopped by a few attendees who shake my hand. I introduce Genesis, she hands out her card, and when we finally make it to our table, I'm ready to drop the smile for a second and just breathe.

That's until I see that the only place setting available is directly across from Kelsey and her date.

Fucking great.

I scan the table, and when I see a smirking Breaker glance up at me, I wonder how much of this seating arrangement was because of him.

"Seems like we're right over here." I direct Genesis to the table and pull out her seat for her.

For a brief second, my eyes connect with Kelsey's, but she quickly looks away and adjusts the silverware in front of her. Well, seems like the moment we had at the back entrance is gone. Probably better off since she's with her—wait, is that her date?

A gangly man with glasses and frumpy hair is perched next to her, fidgeting and pushing up his glasses every few seconds. He looks very out of place, rather uncomfortable, and his ill-fitted suit practically swallows his neck in his seated position.

This is Edwin?

This is the guy Kelsey has been seeing?

I think I know enough about Kelsey to know this guy—just from appearance, yeah, I'm judging—is an absolute dud.

"Genesis?" Edwin says as his eyes connect with my date.

Genesis glances across the table as I take a seat and then audibly gasps. "Edwin, oh my gosh. Wow, how are you?"

Kelsey and I exchange confused glances.

"You two know each other?" I ask Genesis, who's now leaning over the table to reach out and take Edwin's hand. He grips it tightly.

"I'm great," Edwin responds, both of them ignoring me. "You look... wow, you look stunning."

I catch Kelsey's reaction to the compliment. A turned-down brow and an insecure look in her expression. *What's that about?* Surely she knows she's gorgeous.

"Thank you. You've grown out your hair. I always thought you looked exceedingly handsome with longer hair."

I clear my throat rather loudly and repeat my question. "You two know each other?"

"Oh, sorry, yes." Genesis releases Edwin's hand and turns toward me. "Edwin and I attended UCLA together. We were in the same study group all four years. We spent many late nights studying together."

"Remember that one night in the library when we snuck ice cream in our backpacks?"

Genesis laughs. "For how smart we are, that was really dumb. There was ice cream all over our books."

"How were we supposed to know we were going to be stopped by Professor Harkin for half an hour?"

Genesis chuckles. "I can still remember the look on your face when you pulled your notebook out of your backpack, drenched in strawberry shortcake ice cream."

"Thank goodness you were a better notetaker than I was so I could copy your every page."

"Well, anything for you, Edwin." She winks, and I can feel my irritation start to climb. "What are you doing here in LA? I thought you were up in San Jose?"

"I was, but three months ago, I moved down here to be closer to family."

"Edwin, you should've called me."

He blushes, actually freaking blushes. "I wasn't sure you'd want me to call you."

"Are you kidding me? Of course, I would've wanted you to call me." And then, they fall silent as they stare at each other from across the table.

Sparks fly.

Just like that, the air is thick with an intimate history.

And I can honestly say, without a doubt, this doesn't look good for me or Kelsey.

———————

"Oh my gosh, I completely forgot about that," Genesis says, cutting her salad into more manageable bites. "The baseball team had no idea you could actually hit a ball, let alone off their best pitcher."

The now very lively Edwin dusts off his shoulders. "Sometimes the nerd can play a little sport too."

"And get the ladies," Genesis says with a wink.

Kelsey pushes her salad to the side while I dab my mouth with my napkin, not sure how to contribute to this conversation.

All I can think of is how athletes usually don't use the phrase *play a little sport.*

———————

"Wow, I am so impressed with you right now, Edwin." Genesis smiles brightly.

"Impressed with me?" Edwin says, pointing the tip of his fork at his chest. "You're the one who's the vice president of Mecca Tech."

Genesis waves him off. "But you've changed the medical field in the best way possible."

"What did you do?" Kelsey asks, attempting to butt into the conversation. But like every other attempt, she's brushed off.

"I thought about you, the night I got my award," Edwin says. "I considered calling you."

"You should have. I would've answered in a flash."

A flash, huh?

Well, she takes at least a few hours to answer my text messages.

Not sure why I divulged that deprecating information, but there you have it. Clearly, I'm not as important as Edwin.

———————

I take a very large bite of my dessert as Genesis laughs so loud I feel like stuffing her half-eaten piece of bread into my ear to drown out the noise.

"The pants are in the oven, oh my God." Genesis waves her hand in front of her face, warding off her tears of laughter.

The joke isn't that funny.

The pants are in the oven being the punchline…honestly, I don't even get it.

And from the looks of it, neither does Kelsey, who's mindlessly sipping her water, looking around the ballroom.

"I knew you'd like that one," Edwin says. "You've always had a great sense of humor."

"You always know how to make me laugh," she replies.

Jesus Christ.

Barf.

———————

"Wait, so Christie and Matt broke up?" Genesis asks. "I thought they were meant to be together forever."

Clearly, they weren't.

"Christie was cheating on Matt," Edwin says.

Ooh, now…this is some juice I can get on board with. Let's dive into the specifics.

"What?" Genesis asks. "But she told me Matt was the best she'd ever had."

"It was with her strength coach," Edwin says.

"Wait…Strength with Sven? Him?" Genesis asks. When Edwin nods, she slaps the table.

"Have you seen his Instagram? He has a 'fans only' page."

Which could probably mean one thing: poor Matt's penis was eclipsed by Sven's most likely mammoth of a cannon.

I'm not particularly thrilled about being ignored this entire night, but the gossip about Matt and Christie has at least captured my interest for a second. Don't know the people, but their adultery gossip is more entertaining than Edwin's lackluster jokes.

Doesn't seem like everyone is as keen on the Matt-and-Christie drama though. When I glance over at Kelsey, I spot her leaning on the table, her chin in her hand, looking wearier than ever. I'm trying not to let this girl get in my head again, but I actually feel bad for her, seeing her so bored.

Seems like there's only one solution to this unconventional evening, one solution that will make this situation slightly more bearable...

"Why on earth would you switch seats with Edwin?" Kelsey asks through clenched teeth. Not sure I've ever seen a woman so perfectly poised and ballistically heated at the same time.

Well...I thought this was going to be a good idea. Once again, I'm proven wrong.

"I switched with Edwin so at least we didn't have to hear about the old UCLA days anymore," I answer while leaning back in my chair and staring around the ballroom.

The presentation about the Children's Hospital just ended, and for a second, I thought that was going to be our out, that once the lights turned back on, I would be able to sneak Genesis away and bring her attention back to me. Once the presentation was done, however, Edwin leaned across the table and started rambling on about the coffee shop they used to go to all the time.

Fucking boring shit.

I couldn't sit through it anymore, so I switched seats with him, which he gladly jumped on. And now that I'm sitting next to Kelsey, I'm wondering if that was a good idea after all and if I shouldn't have just stuck out the monotony of traveling down memory lane with Genesis and Edwin.

Didn't anyone ever teach them ignoring their dates is just fucking rude?

But, no, now I'm stuck with a prickly, unappreciative woman who barely looks my way.

Here I was, trying to be a Good Samaritan, help a damsel in boiling distress, and come to her rescue, maybe give her someone to talk to, but clearly, she'd rather stare off into the distance and listen to a reminiscing Edwin than talk to me.

If I were a better man, I'd sit in silence with her.

But I think at this point, we all know I'm not going to allow that attitude to slide.

Leaning in close to Kelsey, I whisper, "Do you actually like that guy?"

The chill ice-queen façade around her warms—only slightly—as she shrugs and casually examines her nude manicured nails. "I thought he was nice."

"Is that what you're looking for? Nice?"

"I'm not looking for an asshole, if that's what you're asking," she says while giving me a once-over.

"Are you calling me an asshole?"

"If the shoe fits, JP."

I lean in so only she can hear me when I say, "The shoe absolutely does not fit. If you actually got to know me, you'd see that I'm more than what you assume of me."

"I don't agree. You can't seem to take anything seriously, which I think is obnoxious, you're messy, something I abhor, and you see the glass as half-empty, rather than half-full." She crosses one leg over the other and rests her hands on her lap.

Well, isn't she just a fucking ball of fun?

"I see," I answer. Not the definition of an asshole, but it would probably be asshole-ish for me to point that out.

She has me all wrong. Sure, my desk is messy, but that's the way I fucking like it. And I might be obnoxious, but I can't help the way I seek attention. It's in my bones and I shouldn't be chastised for that. And the glass half-empty? That's called being a realist.

I'm not going to parade around thinking the world is made up of puppy-and-kitty parties where fanciful Parisian desserts are served and romantic comedies blast on repeat as background music.

Sorry.

I've been through too much shit growing up, being sucked into a profession I never asked for and ending up stuck with no way out, to sit here and say, yes…I'm living a glass-half-full life.

I might have money, but what they say is true—money can't buy happiness, and that's the most honest thing I've ever heard.

I'm not sure how she developed such a low opinion of me, but it seems to have stuck with her.

Okay, I know…I know, I was kind of a dick on our surprise date, but what was I supposed to do, sit back and let her act like it was the worst thing ever that she was paired with me? A guy has to save his dignity somehow.

Just then, Edwin stands from his chair and takes Genesis's hand in his. Turning to Kelsey, he asks, "Would it be all right if I took Genesis out for a spin on the dance floor?"

Hell, the fucking balls on this man.

Here I thought he was a bit cowardly with a penchant to touch his glasses every six seconds, but then he goes and pulls this stunt. Takes a massive amount of douchery to do something like this. I didn't know he had it in him.

"Of course." Kelsey kindly smiles, but that smile is quickly wiped away when the happy "couple" turns away and heads to the dance floor.

"Oof, that has got to sting," I say.

"Uh, he stole your date, so I'm not the only loser here."

I shrug. "I wasn't too attached to her. Honestly, I just brought her because my brothers said I should have a date."

"Then how come Breaker didn't bring anyone?"

I glance over at my single brother, who's entertaining a circle of women. "Because he's able to pass off the appearance that he's with someone, when really he isn't. Younger brother showmanship type of stuff."

She folds her arms over her chest and says, "This night is stupid."

"Tell me how you really feel."

"I'd rather not."

"Why not?" I ask. "We're both here, have been ditched by our dates. Might as well delight in each other's company."

"There's nothing delightful about your company."

Jesus, she's snappy. Good comeback, though. Got to give credit where credit's due.

"So, what was so delightful about Edwin's company? Before he lit up with an onslaught of memories, he seemed like a bit of a bore."

"He wasn't boring," Kelsey says. "Just different."

"Different? How so?"

Warming up a bit more, she answers, "Well, he likes birds, and I found that fascinating. Not the bird facts, that actually was a bit rough at times, but that he was so in tune with nature that he could recognize specific bird chirps of each species."

"Is that how he lured you into his bed? Chirping and flapping his arms?"

Kelsey's eyes dart to mine in a deathly stare. "For your information, we never went to bed together. Just a kiss. And he's not a geek who speaks bird to unhook a bra. He just likes to tell stories."

"Gathered that from the mundane conversation he shared over the table."

"As if Genesis was any better," Kelsey snaps. "What did you even see in her?"

"Stature," I answer honestly.

"Eww, that's repulsive."

"At least I was with someone for a purpose. You were with Edwin because you were desperate."

She gasps and now fully turns toward me. "I was not desperate. I'm trying to find my soulmate, you know, someone to fall in love with, not that you could ever relate to that kind of emotion with that cold, lifeless heart of yours."

I press my hand to my chest and say, "Lifeless, not so much. There's quite a steady pulse beating through my soulless veins. Cold, though, now that's an accurate description." When she turns away, I push her a little more and ask, "What did he think of your dress?"

She glances at me over her bare shoulder. "What do you mean?"

"When Edwin saw you tonight, did he wax poetic about how you reminded him of his favorite chickadee perched amongst a field of flowers?"

"He did not." She lifts her chin.

"Okay, so then what did he say?"

"Why does it matter?"

"Because you say you're looking for love. A simple reaction to your appearance tonight would warrant you an answer on where he stands with you. What did he say? A simple *you're beautiful*? Maybe a shy… *wow*?"

Her clenched jaw works back and forth as she stares at the dance floor. "He said I was wearing a nice colored dress."

"And?" I ask.

"That was it." She picks up her glass of water and takes a sip.

"Wait, that's *all* he said? That you had on a nice colored dress?"

She carefully sets down her glass and I can see her bitter movements, the way she clenches her fists, and the longing in her eyes as she stares at each couple on the dance floor.

I don't know how long she took to get ready tonight.

I can't imagine what she went through picking out the perfect dress.

Nor could I imagine the excitement she felt about her date seeing her—because she's a vision.

But I've watched Kelsey for several months now, and I know when she's annoyed, and probably when she's hurt. So I'm sure about one thing—the time she spent getting ready for tonight was enough time to warrant a better reaction than *nice colored dress*. And it makes me feel even shittier for telling her I'd seen better. *Shit.*

CHAPTER 7
KELSEY

I WISH HE'D LEAVE ME alone.

I wish I hadn't been left here at the table, with JP as the only person to talk to.

Hell, I wish Edwin had an ounce of self-awareness and didn't leave me hanging, especially since I was the one who brought him here.

But that's not my luck, is it? And, of course, during the presentation, I got a text from Lottie, who has been MIA this entire party. She and Huxley were headed back to the house. This was followed by an eggplant emoji and three squirting drops. She also trusted Edwin would drive me back to her place to pick up my car.

If only she knew.

"I asked you a question," JP says next to me.

Lost in thought, I say, "Uh…what was the question?"

"Edwin, all he said was that you had a nice colored dress?"

Oh, yes, we're still on that.

"I don't want to talk about it."

He pauses and I can feel his eyes on me. In fact, they haven't left me since he switched seats with Edwin. His green irises, focused completely in my direction, like a nagging mother, tapping me on the shoulder every few seconds with questions I don't want to answer. Shouldn't he be looking toward the dance floor to reclaim his date? His beautiful, sweet date… who definitely seems more into Edwin than JP. *So, so weird.*

"Fine, then…" He holds out his hand. "Come dance with me."

I glance down at his large palm and long fingers and then back up at him. "Excuse me?"

Leaning in close, his cologne soft and seductive as it swirls around me, he says, "Dance with me."

Okay…

Dance with JP. I can list more than enough reasons why I don't want to do that.

One—being held by him is at the very bottom of things I want to do.

Two—I can't imagine a scenario where I don't accidentally knee him in the crotch for something annoying he'll say while we dance.

And three—his cologne is far too enticing at the moment. I like the smell of it, which would possibly make me think positively toward him, and I don't want that. I want to forever think he's the worst.

But…

Pride is a funny thing.

I came to this gala with all the intention of getting lost in an evening with a nice guy. I assumed we'd talk about the different nests each one of Edwin's favorite birds make, I would have a few glasses of champagne and hope that maybe…just maybe, Edwin would have enough confidence in himself to try to at least push me against his car and make out with me.

I think we all can agree that such imagined events won't be transpiring tonight. I don't want to be the girl that was ditched at the event. I don't want to be the girl in the *nice colored dress*, and I don't want to leave this evening feeling like I was the last girl picked…if that makes sense.

I want to feel valued, and even though taking the hand of JP Cane would be like conducting a waltz with the devil, I'm desperate.

"You know, it would be rude to say no," he says. "When a man offers a dance, it's the polite thing to do to take his hand." When I don't say anything, he adds, "You can't possibly just sit here like a wallflower the rest of the night."

My eyes flash to his. "Wow, you sure know how to woo a woman."

He smirks. "Thank you."

"That wasn't a compliment."

"Felt like one to me."

Could he be any more infuriating?

Wait, don't answer that. I'm sure he can.

Ugh, God, I can't believe I'm doing this.

I place my hand in his and watch as his face lights up with a rakish grin. "Good choice, Kelsey."

Remember what I said about the whole "kneeing in the crotch" thing? Chances have just increased.

He's the first to stand from his chair, and then he helps me up and ushers me to the side so he can push our chairs in.

For some reason, it feels as if every eye in the ballroom is on us as we slowly weave through the crowded tables. *Why couldn't the dance floor be at the front of the room where we are, rather than at the side?* He stops to shake hands with a few people, a gallant businessman working the room. He keeps his hand on the small of my back while he speaks, never neglecting to introduce me and what I do.

It's…a kind thing to do. The right thing to do. *Professional.* I'm sure business etiquette has been drilled into him from a young age, so it's only second nature to conduct himself in this way. It has nothing to do with me.

"Sorry," he whispers into my ear as we make our way closer to the dance floor. "It's impossible to walk anywhere in these events without getting stopped."

"Don't flatter yourself. The need to talk to you is out of obligation. These people don't actually like you." I really want to bite my tongue. Clearly Edwin dissing me has affected me more than I thought. *Or maybe, I don't want to look like a loser in front of JP.* If anything, watching him network the room has been a great lesson for me. He has the sort of business acumen I admire. *But…I need to remain unfazed.*

His nose moves close to my ear as his hand is at my back, guiding me. "Mmm, I love it when you talk dirty to me."

"You're obnoxious."

"So you've said before."

"Just reminding you."

We're nearly clear of the tables now, and he smooths his hand over my back, ushering me ahead of him. "Don't need a remin-*ooooof*!"

JP exhales against my skin, like a gust of very strong wind. There's a loud crash and then a horrifying thud.

I turn just in time to see JP's body bounce off the dance floor, his arms clutching his stomach, his long legs stretched out.

"What on earth—"

"Mother...fu—" he starts to say but stops himself. Eyes wincing with an immense amount of pain, he takes a few deep breaths, and just when I think he's about to unleash a plethora of swear words, the room falls silent. All eyes are on us.

He groans.

Winces in pain once more and then lets out a loud...forceful reaction...

"Golly...goodness," he groans.

Golly goodness?

No *motherfucker?*

No *holy shit?*

No *fuckety fuck fuck?*

Just a simple classic George Bailey from *It's a Wonderful Life* "golly goodness."

I snort.

My hand covers my face and I attempt to hold back the laughter that's bubbling up inside of me.

If I know one thing about JP Cane, it's that he's not the "golly goodness" type.

He's the guy that whispers the words *throbbing cock* in your ear, repeatedly, just for the hell of it.

Unsure of what to do, I consider bending down to ask him what happened, when an old man behind JP stands shakily from his chair. That's when I see the pushed-out chair in the walkway. Oh no, JP must have been struck solid while walking by. With the tip of his black cane, the old man taps JP on the leg and says, "Watch where you're going, son."

With no regard for what he caused, or even a hint of an apology, the ballsy old man hobbles away, muttering something about people getting in his way.

A waiter quickly helps JP to his feet, lifting him under his arms. A few of the men who were just shaking his hand come to ask if he's all right, but all I can focus on is the way JP is staring at me as if I'm the one who knocked him out with a chair.

"I'm good," he says, dusting off his suit.

"Are you sure?" one of the waiters asks. "I can get you some ice."

"Not necessary. I think the only thing bruised here is my pride. Wasn't expecting a seventy-year-old man to take me out like that."

Another snort.

Another glare from him.

"I'll be good." He shakes off the waiter and closes the space between us once again, takes my hand in his, and leads me to the dance floor.

I'm still chuckling when he pulls me close to his body, his hand on my lower back, his other holding our palms closely together. With his mouth right next to my ear, he asks, "Did you find that entertaining?"

"Very much so," I answer as he pulls me in tighter. My chest is pressed against his, our legs tangling, and I honestly can't tell where I begin and he ends. Our bodies fuse together, like magnets, drawing in, pulling, with no release.

It's unexpected.

It's damning.

It's not a position I want to be in with JP, but it doesn't seem like one I can get out of.

"So, me getting hurt and humiliated in front of the masses, that's comical to you?"

"A little slapstick humor never hurt anyone. But it wasn't what happened to you; it was your reaction." I laugh softly as he moves me around the dance floor. We're slowly swaying to the music, an instrumental version of Taylor Swift's "Wildest Dreams," but the way he's twirling me makes the room a blur, and I can't focus on anything but us and only us.

The stillness in his breath as we float over the parquet floor.

The tight grip he has on my hand, guiding me to our next move.

The gentle whisper of his words in my ear as he speaks just low enough to keep our conversation private.

"And what about my reaction made you chuckle?" He releases me, twirls me out so my dress floats against the whoosh of wind, then yanks me back close to his chest. My breath catches in my lungs and my eyes widen from the elegant dance move I wasn't expecting.

When I don't answer right away, he lowers his lips closer to my ear and says, "I'm waiting, Kelsey."

Waiting.

He's waiting for…oh, an answer to his question.

What's happening to me? One spin around the dance floor and I can't seem to keep my mind straight.

My brain feels foggy, disrupted, disoriented. His warm palm slides to the spot just above the curve of my ass and all I can think about is…are people watching? Do they think we're a couple? Is he going to lower his hand any farther?

I wet my lips and focus on the conversation. "Correct me if I'm wrong, but *golly goodness* doesn't seem like something that would ever come out of your mouth."

"You'd be correct about that," he answers, and then, to my utter surprise, he braces himself and dips me. My startled gasp makes him smile as he lifts me back up. "What did you expect me to say, though? That old fucking bastard just Tonya Harding-ed my ass, nearly cutting my dick off with the edge of his chair. I didn't think *motherfucker* was appropriate for the setting."

The music slows, and so do we. It almost feels as though he created his own dance to this song, and he led me through it with precision and grace, something I didn't think he had in him.

"Well, it was funny, is all," I say, my ability to come up with a witty response completely gone as his hand slides up my spine. The music switches to another slow-paced song, and when I think our dance is over, he doesn't let go. Instead, he continues to move us around as two cellists take centerstage and play "With or Without You."

It's beautiful, the deep glide of the strings weaving through the gold room as the chandeliers dim, setting more of a romantic mood. I've been so irritated by Edwin and Genesis that I've completely neglected the romance of the night—not that there's any romance between me and JP, but the ambiance offers a stunning setting for a first kiss.

"What are you thinking about?" JP asks. "I can practically see the wheels in your head turning."

"The ballroom is beautiful. I'm finally taking a moment to appreciate it."

"It is," he says softly. "The food, the décor, the band. It's the same every year, and even though it benefits the children, I know a lot of couples come to this event just for the experience."

"I can see why. It's all so whimsical."

"Is this what you envisioned the night being like?"

I shake my head gently. "No, I didn't envision being ditched by my date, then finishing the night dancing with you."

"I meant with the décor, the feeling, the mood. I know being here, in my arms, with the one person who repulses you the most wasn't at the forefront of your mind."

The way he said that, the dejection in his tone, actually makes me feel bad. He might annoy me and he might irritate me, now more than ever, but if I strip away his defense mechanism of acting like an ass, I know there's a good man under that sarcastic wit.

"You...you don't repulse me, JP."

"Not looking for a pity comment, just looking for an answer to my question."

But he doesn't repulse me. He might not be my favorite person, but repulse? I mean, if he repulsed me, there's no way I'd allow him to hold me as close as he is. I wouldn't be getting lost in his delectable scent, a scent that I know will cling to me for the rest of the night.

But he's a prideful man, and I know he's not one—in a serious moment—to fish for compliments.

"I didn't know what to expect about the event. I figured it had to be nice for such a steep price. But this, the almost *Great Gatsby* feel, this is what movies are made of."

"None of the donations go to the actual event. This event is put on by a society who chips in their own money. It's another reason why we love it so much. It's a true fundraiser. Very little business occurs here."

"Is that why you brought a date?" I ask, truly curious about him and Genesis.

Not that I'm the expert on JP Cane, but he just doesn't seem like the dating type to me. He seems more like the guy who's in and out of bedrooms every other night. The guy that never settles down, flirts shamelessly, and has no need for a companion other than himself.

"Genesis and I met a few weeks ago. She's smart, someone who can hold an intelligent conversation, and when we went out, I had a good time. I thought this would be a good place to take her, let her mingle with some people, make connections. Didn't expect her to mingle with your date, though."

"Yeah, me neither," I say softly.

JP pulls away just enough that our eyes meet, his light green ones to my hazel. "Listen, Kelsey, he's—"

"Excuse us. Sorry to interrupt," Edwin says as he walks up to us, Genesis at his side. "I hope it's okay, but I think we're going to head out." Edwin thumbs to the door behind him. "Genesis has a headache and I figured I'd take her home."

My stomach drops. He's leaving the party with someone else?

Sure, the sting of seeing him talk to someone else the entire night was a direct hit to the ego.

Watching him dance with someone else was drink-worthy.

But seeing him leave...

JP's arm stiffens around me as he says, "Sure thing, thanks, man."

"You don't mind?" Genesis asks. I can't even look at them, because from the corner of my eye, I can see Edwin's hand laced with Genesis's.

"Not at all," JP answers, his voice even.

"Okay, well...thanks for a good night," Edwin says before patting me on the shoulder and taking off.

That's all I get.

A pat on the shoulder.

I expected this night to go so differently. I thought that maybe Edwin and I could get to know each other a little more, become more comfortable with one another, maybe kiss again.

But he's taking another woman home.

And that's an absolute gut punch.

My feet stop moving, and my grip loosens on JP.

"Head held high," he whispers as he spins me around. "Don't let him see you upset."

"But I am."

"I know." JP's mouth is now touching my ear as he speaks softly. "But give them a few more minutes and then I'll get you out of here."

My lip trembles and I can feel my eyes start to well, and just when I think a tear is going to fall, JP grips my hand tighter, spins me out, and smirks at me, before pulling me back in. It's just enough to forget for a moment that, once again, romance isn't in the cards for me.

"Good evening, Mr. Cane," the driver says as he opens the back door for us.

After Edwin and Genesis took off, we spent another five minutes on the dance floor before JP escorted me toward the back of the ballroom and sent a quick text. He then led me to the bar, where he handed me a heavy glass of wine and said we weren't leaving until I finished it.

It took me no more than a minute.

With a wine belly and heavy heart, we made our way to the front of the mansion where JP's driver just happened to be waiting. I'm not sure if Huxley set it up that way or if JP's driver can drive at lightning speed, but I didn't have to hang around the event for longer than I needed to.

JP helps me into the car and then slides in beside me. We both buckle up, and when the driver sits in his seat, JP says, "My house."

I don't have it in me to discuss the details, to consider if JP has any idea what's going to happen tonight, so I lean my head to the side and look out the window.

The dark starry sky looms over us as we drive through rows and rows of impressive houses. And with every gated home that we pass, I can't help but wonder if the people who live inside that home are actually in love, or if they live in a world where ditching a date for someone else is the norm.

God, I expected so much more from Edwin, the bird-loving prick. He was so…nice. A bit of a nerd, but definitely someone I thought I could trust. Sure, we only went out for a few weeks, but I feel like I'm a good judge of character.

But Edwin's actions reflected something I'd almost expect JP to do. And yet, JP was the one who made sure I didn't look foolish, the one who carried me around the dance floor, and the one who made me forget, even if it was momentarily.

There seems to be some good in him after all.

"He's an idiot," JP says as the car makes a right-hand turn and Huxley's house comes into view.

"What?" I ask.

And instead of turning right into Huxley's circular driveway, we turn left, to a large looming gate that opens as we approach.

JP is silent for a moment, and when the car is parked, he holds his hand up to the driver and opens the door himself. Once outside of the car, he dips back in and holds his hand out to me. Disoriented, I take it and he helps me out of the car. The moment he shuts it, the driver takes off, leaving me alone under the stars with JP.

Together, my hand still in his, we stand in the driveway, the darkness of the night enveloping us. "Edwin," JP says. "He's an idiot."

"He's not an idiot; he was just—"

JP lifts my chin, forcing me to look him in the eyes. This time when he speaks, it's more authoritative. "He's an idiot, Kelsey. Do you know how I know he's an idiot?"

From the sincere look in his eyes and the firm grip he has on my chin, I'm rendered speechless. I feel captured, captivated, and looped into this unexpected whirlwind of a night with JP. And I don't know how to handle it.

JP takes a step closer and says, "Edwin is an idiot because he didn't appreciate something other than the color of your dress. What he should've said the moment he saw you was how fucking breathtaking you look, how the yellow in your dress makes the gold in your eyes sparkle even brighter. He should've lifted your hand and pressed the lightest of kisses to your knuckles, just so he could claim you in front of everyone around him. His eyes never should have strayed from yours. And when he lowered your hand, he should've taken one more step closer to you, leaned inches from your ear, and said how intoxicatingly beautiful you smelled."

My lungs have seized.

My legs have melted, like ice cream on a scalding day.

And my hand laced with JP's trembles in his grasp.

What...what's he doing?

Why is he saying these things?

What's his end goal?

The romantic in me would love to believe he means what he just said. That he *thinks* those things about me. But sadly, I suspect there's only one end goal when it comes to JP and a girl, late at night, standing outside his house. I'm confident I know what he expects. And I'm not blind. I can understand the appeal. He's an extremely handsome man, after all. He can pull you in with one look, one flash of his rakish eyes. You can *feel* his gaze.

Just like I can feel it now.

The flash of his eyes to my lips.

The dip of his tongue over his lips, wetting them. Preparing.

The step he makes to close the space between us one more time.

It's all there, the signs.

And I might be sad. I might feel distraught, but I know one thing—a night in JP Cane's bed is not going to help matters.

So, I release his hand and take a step back. "JP, I'm not going to sleep with you." The words fly out of my mouth in a flurry, making it clear where I stand.

His compliments, his kindness aren't going to factor into my decision.

And when I look him in the eyes, to hold strong, I'm not met with his usual smirk or flirtatious expression, but rather a scowl. His dark thick brows are pulled together; the softness has morphed into a stern, almost insulted gaze.

His lips twist to the side in a mock snarl, and when I think he's going to say something, his hand drives through his thick hair as he turns away.

"Yeah," he says on a huff, his back turned toward me. "Let's get you back to your car."

One hand still in his hair, he walks toward the gate of his driveway, not even bothering to wait for me. I hurry behind him as he opens an undetected single-person gate hidden in the bushes. He holds it open for me, and right before I walk through it, I stop and stare up at him.

"You can't be mad at me for not wanting to sleep with you, JP."

He stares up at the sky as he lets out a heavy breath. "Just walk through the gate, Kelsey."

Irritation is steaming off him, and even though I have this need to push him, to make him understand my reasoning, I can see that's only going to make him madder. Keeping my composure, I walk past him, through the gate, and then together, we walk across the street to Huxley and Lottie's house, where once again, JP opens a gate for me and takes me right to my car.

"Do you have your keys?" he asks.

I hold up my small clutch. "In here."

"Good." He steps back and sticks both hands in his pockets.

He doesn't say another word, and I can't help but feel that I did something wrong. He was gallant and kind, which I truly appreciate, but it should be okay for me to use words—*not my body*—to thank him.

"JP—"

"Have a good night, Kelsey." He takes another step back and I realize he's not going to leave until I get in my car and start it, another gentlemanly act that I didn't expect from him. This entire night has been incredibly unexpected and I'm not sure I'm capable of sifting through it all in my head, not when I'm exhausted and mentally spent.

Thankfully, I really only had that one glass of wine, so I'm good to drive. I unlock my car and get in. I consider saying something to JP. *Thank you*, maybe, but when I turn to roll down my window, he's already walking across the street to his house.

Well, I guess that's that.

With a heavy heart, I start my car and drive back to my small studio apartment.

MEANT TO BE PODCAST
RATH AND CHARLEE

Kelsey: Welcome, listener, to the *Meant to Be Podcast*, where we talk to madly-in-love couples about the way they met. Rath and Charlee, thank you so much for joining me today. Please, tell us how you met.

Charlee: First, can I say how much I love this podcast? I can't believe you are actually having us on the show. Gah, I listen to it every week. Rath thinks I'm a lunatic, of course, when I gush over every couple, but he's also one of the biggest grumps you could imagine. I had to bribe him with sexual favors to get him here.

Rath: Charlee, filter.

Charlee: He's really worried that I'm going to say something that embarrasses him, which, sure, is probably the truth because I don't know when to stop talking. Ask me a question and I just let loose. But, yeah, I told him I would do some favors under his desk while at work—

Rath: For the love of Christ, Charlee.

Kelsey: Oh, please, tell me more about these favors.

Charlee: Well, he really likes it when you tickle—

Rath: We bumped into each other at an office supply convention. I needed an assistant. She drove me insane with her incessant jabbering. Somehow, I fell in love, we got married, end of story.

Charlee: Isn't he just so charming?

CHAPTER 8
JP

"HEY." THERE'S A KNOCK AT my door. I lift my head to see Huxley poke his head in. "Conference room in ten."

"Got the eleven fucking memos you sent already. I'll be there."

"Just making sure."

"I'm a grown-ass man, Hux. I know how to schedule my damn day." I turn back to my computer and click through the annoying emails I've put off answering all morning.

When my door shuts, I heave a sigh of relief, until I realize Huxley never left, but rather let himself into my office. He occupies a seat across from me and crosses one leg over the other.

"Mind telling me why you've been such a bastard lately?"

I press my fingers into my brow, attempting to massage the impending migraine away.

"How about you go back to your office and leave me the hell alone?"

"You see, I would do that, but we have a meeting in ten minutes and I can't have you acting like a dick in there."

My eyes snap up to his. "When have I ever been a dick to people in the conference room?"

"Uh, all fucking week. Not to mention, you've been stomping around here with a chip on your shoulder. Everyone's aware of your mood and there have been rumblings that people are uncomfortable."

"Oh, well, Jesus Christ, I should just slap on a happy face, then, shouldn't I? I wouldn't want to cause a stir in the office. Heaven forbid someone should have some fucking feelings in this place."

"Dude," Hux says, sitting taller in his chair now. "What the hell is going on? You've been like this ever since the fundraiser. Is this about Genesis?"

Of course, he'd go there because I haven't spoken a goddamn word to anyone about that night. Neither Huxley nor Breaker saw how the old man took me out. Neither saw how I danced with Kelsey and held her so close to me that, and how, for the first time since I met her, I felt something click inside my head, that where I was, what I was doing, was actually right.

I didn't say anything, because the night didn't end the way I wanted it to.

There was no intention of taking her inside my house.

There wasn't even a thought of taking her to my bedroom.

My only purpose at the end of the night was to make sure she understood how fucking beautiful she was. How I hadn't been able to take my eyes off her and couldn't fathom how stupid her date had been in leaving her, missing his one chance at having her. I wanted her to know that, in my eyes, her smile had outshone all the radiance of the room, and that she was easily the most captivating woman in there.

I didn't want her to leave thinking she wasn't valued, that she was disposable.

I meant what I said, Edwin was an idiot. An absolute fool.

Genesis is beautiful and smart. But she has nothing, and I mean absolutely nothing, on Kelsey.

And I wanted to show Kelsey that. But Kelsey didn't take it that way.

No, she saw me as a man acting kind to have a chance at lifting her skirt.

She saw me as nothing but a man with an agenda that involved the bedroom.

She could not have been more wrong.

Insult eclipsed me.

I shut down.

And there was no coming back from it.

I've been a bastard ever since.

When I've seen her in the office, I've avoided her. All correspondence has been through email, and I've canceled two meetings with her so far, blaming some media bullshit that I made up.

"Yeah, sure, this is about Genesis," I answer.

Huxley studies me and is about to say something when Breaker comes into the office and says, "There you are. Hux, I need your signature on a few things before the meeting."

Eyes on me, Huxley stands and says, "This isn't over."

The fuck it's not. In my eyes, this conversation is dead at this point.

I wave him away, and when the door shuts, I let out a heavy breath and push back from my desk. I turn toward my window and lean back, staring out over the lines of palm trees along the streets.

I don't think I've ever been in this kind of funk, one that has taken over just about every aspect of my life. Sleep evades me. Working out has become more of an escape from frustration rather than enjoyment. And my nights out with friends have turned into nights in, vibrating with anger as I pace my house, only to end up in my workout room, where I slip on a pair of boxing gloves and repeatedly punch my bag until my knuckles can't take the abuse anymore.

Just...fuck, how could she think that all I wanted was to fuck her?

Am I really that much of an asshole that she'd confuse my intention with a bargain? My kindness, my compliments, in exchange for the spread of her legs?

I can be a dick.

A prick.

An absolute asshole.

But I'm not that man, the one who takes advantage of a woman who's clearly not in the right headspace.

I stand from my chair, pull my suit jacket back on, and stick my phone in my pocket before heading out of my office door. On the way to the conference room, I pop into the kitchen and grab a can of water—we just started carrying water in aluminum cans, thanks to fucking Kelsey and her sustainability initiatives—and then head into the conference room. I take a seat on the left-hand side.

Just as I pop open the can, one of the chairs to the right of me swivels around and, lo and behold, Kelsey's face comes into view.

Fuck...

"JP," she says with a smile that barely reaches her eyes. I can tell a polite smile from a genuine one, and this screams, *I'm smiling at you because I have to, not because I want to.* "I wasn't aware you were going to be in this meeting."

"Yeah, well, Huxley sent me eleven messages saying my attendance was required."

"Do you have any idea what it's about?"

"Nope," I snap.

"Oh...okay." She fidgets next to me and heat crawls up the back of my neck.

Fuck, I can smell her sweet, flowery scent that seems to follow me everywhere I go. I don't know if it's my mind playing tricks on me, but I swear, I smell it everywhere I go, and it's more prevalent than ever right now.

"Did you, uh, did you see my designs for the Anderson building?"

"Yeah," I answer.

"Did you like them?"

"Seemed like everything else you've turned in. Unless I'm mistaken and you used something other than bamboo storage."

I don't bother to look at her, but from the corner of my eye, I can see her mouth turn down in a frown.

"JP, if there's something I did—"

"You know, I have some emails to answer," I say, pulling out my phone and tapping away on it.

Instead of going to my inbox—because there's no way in fuck I'm answering any emails right now—I scroll through Twitter, checking out what all the trolls have to say about the Vancouver Agitators and their recent playoff loss. Talk about a weak showing. Not sure they even decided to show up.

"I know you're ignoring me," she says, clearly not getting the hint.

Keeping my eyes on my phone, I say, "Kelsey, I have better things to do with my life than to ignore you. You're not that important."

I can feel the sting of my words as they fall off my tongue, and yet, I don't stop them.

I don't even bother to look at how they affect her.

I don't need to.

I know Kelsey will take offense to such a sentence, and yet, I still said it.

Yup, really living up to that bastard persona.

Thankfully, Huxley walks in at that moment, along with Breaker and Lottie. I expect maybe a few other employees to join us, but when Huxley shuts the door and takes a seat, I realize this is it.

Just us five.

Not so sure I'm going to like this.

I swear to fuck if this is some sort of attitude intervention, I'm going to have a Hades-inspired conniption, flames and all.

"We got some news yesterday." Huxley looks over at Lottie and my heart sinks. Holy shit, are they pregnant?

I sit a little taller in my chair.

Attempt to put on a happy face.

"Are you pregnant?" Breaker asks.

Huxley's eyebrows knit together. "No, why would you think that?"

"Uh, the way you looked at Lottie, the fact that it's just family in this room, and the inconspicuous meeting invite."

All facts.

"Do you really think I would use company time to announce something like that? That would be a private affair, not something we'd do in the conference room at work."

Huh...also facts.

"Plus, there will be no pregnancy for at least another year. I need a killer honeymoon and babies aren't invited," Lottie adds.

Well, there goes the pregnancy guess.

"Then why are we here?" I ask.

"Because what I have to say can't be said outside of these walls. It's highly classified; therefore, we're the only ones who are allowed to know at the moment."

"Just spit it out," I say. "Enough with the dramatics."

Huxley shoots me a withering glare, but luckily for me, I couldn't care less about his menacing scowl.

"We got a call from William Edison, our realtor. We won the bid for the historic Angelica Building in San Francisco."

Oh shit...

Kelsey looks around for answers. "What's the Angelica Building?"

"It's one of the most prominent apartment buildings in San Francisco. Currently completely empty because it needs deep renovations. It was put up for sale a few months ago, but instead of simply submitting an offer, we had to submit with accompanying plans as to how we'd preserve the building during renovations," Huxley says.

"The building is beautiful," Breaker adds. "Sits just beyond the Bay and has panoramic views and some of the most intricate marble work I've ever seen."

"So why is this a secret?" Kelsey asks.

"Because before the news breaks, we want our team to go in, assess, and then draw up plans on how we're going to proceed. Once the press finds out, it'll be very hard to get our work done in peace without restoration groups knocking at our door, telling us how to do the job." Huxley presses his palm to the table surface. "We have two weeks before the deal is announced. I want plans drawn up and contracts made before those two weeks are up."

"I'm sorry," Kelsey says, glancing around the room. "How does this pertain to me?"

"We want your input on sustainability for the building. We're already in talks with a solar panel specialist to see what our options are for energy, but when it comes to building materials and organization, we want your input as well. Which means you're going to San Francisco tonight to meet with Edison and the team."

"Oh." Kelsey blinks a few times. "Okay. Sure, not a problem."

"And JP will be going with you."

And there it is.

I knew that was fucking coming.

Even though I knew it was coming and I know the reasoning behind it, I still say, "Why do I need to go? I believe this is something Lottie and Kelsey can handle themselves. I'm not her babysitter."

"Uh…I have a bunch of wedding planning meetings scheduled." Lottie winces. "I don't think I can reschedule anything. I wasn't aware I had to go with Kelsey."

"You aren't required to go," Huxley says, keeping his eyes on me. "Sustainably Organized falls under JP's management, which means he'll be going." The steeliness in his voice would scare any other employee, but it washes right over me. His intimidation tactics are useless on me.

We stare each other down, the tension growing in the room, and I wait for Breaker to jump in, to say something, but when the room remains silent, I know there's no help coming my way.

It's pointless.

They're going to gang up on me and then I'll be headed to San Francisco with Kelsey, the person I most want to avoid.

But being the people pleaser that she is, Kelsey chimes in and says, "If JP is busy, I can go on my own. I'm sure I can handle this."

"The fuck you can," I say before I can stop myself. All eyes fall on me, perhaps shocked at my obvious anger. Shit, that was harsh. I attempt to tone it down. "There's more to it than just walking around an office. Hate to say it, but you're not sufficiently educated to handle this on your own. This is more like a job for Huxley, given the logistics of it."

If looks could fucking kill, I would be six feet under right now.

But all care has left my body.

I can't seem to scrounge up one ounce of giving a fuck.

Speaking in a clipped tone, Huxley says, "I have to be at the wedding planning meetings with Lottie."

"You've had no problem flying back and forth before."

"What do you not understand about this being your responsibility?" Huxley asks.

"I never asked for this responsibility," I say and then motion to Breaker. "Why doesn't he go?"

With a confused look on his face, Breaker tilts his head and asks, "Why the hell would I go when Kelsey works with you? I have no fucking clue what you guys are doing over there with the buildings and all the environmental changes happening in this office. All I know is that my water comes in an aluminum can now and I like it." He leans close and asks, "Dude, what the fuck is going on? You love San Francisco, and this is your job, so why don't you want to go?"

Great question.

Can't tell him the real reason.

This conversation is already humiliating enough, and I don't need to add to that humiliation.

Nope, I need to come up with an excuse. Something good.

Something that will require my attention in Los Angeles.

"I can't go," I say, as if it's the most preposterous suggestion. "I have… things to do. Important things." Christ, that's not exactly what I was hoping to say, but then again, kind of drawing a blank here. I have no things. I basically sit on my ass waiting for my brothers to tell me what to do because that's how much I despise this job. "Things that can't be rescheduled."

"What kind of things?" Breaker asks skeptically. He's onto me.

"Important things," I repeat.

"But what kind of important things? Give us an example."

Huh…

Umm…

Mentally taps chin

What could be so important in my otherwise boring life that could prevent me from flying up to San Francisco with Kelsey?

Nothing.

Absolutely fucking nothing.

But that doesn't prevent me from continuing the farce.

"Appointments," I answer. Vagueness is the way to go. "The kind of appointments I don't care to discuss in front of the ladies."

There. That should work.

Man troubles.

It's written in bro code that when a man says he has an appointment he doesn't want to discuss in front of the ladies, that it should be kept hush-hush and talked about later when female ears aren't around.

"An appointment you don't want to talk about in front of the ladies?" Breaker asks. "Like…are you having man troubles, dude?"

God, I hate him.

Now what the fuck do I say?

If I confirm I might be having man troubles, Kelsey and Lottie will

ASSUME I have man troubles, and there's nothing troubling about my manhood. Everything is in healthy working order.

But if I say no, then that exposes me and I'll have to go to San Francisco.

So…pride or giving in?

Save my self-image or spend two weeks in agony with Kelsey?

Fuck…this is a hard—

Pinning me with a stare, Huxley says, "Tell me right now something is wrong with your dick or you're going to San Francisco."

Shit.

Nothing is wrong with my dick.

I don't want anyone thinking there's something wrong with my dick because, yes, I'm shallow, thank you very much.

And Huxley fucking knows it.

"That's what I thought. You're going."

Fuck.

So much for being able to think on my goddamn feet.

"You leave tonight. I had Karla call ahead to the penthouse. It's already been cleaned and stocked with food."

The penthouse?

No fucking way.

Okay, sure, I have to go to San Francisco, but the penthouse? Has he lost his goddamn mind?

"Do you really think the penthouse is necessary? A simple hotel room will do, don't you think?"

"What's the penthouse?" Kelsey asks.

"Housing the company owns," Huxley answers. "And, yes, the penthouse is necessary. You will be much more comfortable there. We've already set up a car service, and Karla is working on scheduling meetings with our architect and contractors. If we're sending you up there, we want to make the most of our time. The trip will last two weeks."

"Two weeks?" I shout. "You want us to be up there for two weeks? I thought we just had a two-week limit to turn things in." *It shouldn't take that long.*

Huxley's jaw ticks, his frustration coming to a boiling point as his forehead starts to turn a dangerous shade of red. He's frustrated with me, but who the fuck cares? He wants me to share a penthouse with Kelsey for two weeks, the one person I don't want to be around? Is this some sort of scheme by the engaged couple to get two singles together? When have we ever forced two employees to share the penthouse before...for two weeks?

Never.

In a firm voice, Huxley says, "You will be there for two weeks. I expect to receive daily reports on all decisions. And while you're up there, make sure you set up meetings with the mayor. You're the media relations for this company, after all, JP, the face. Don't forget it."

As if he'd ever let me.

Pushing away from the table, I stand abruptly and ask, "When does the plane leave?"

"Six sharp. Don't be late."

"Wouldn't dream of it." I move past everyone, straight out of the conference room, and toward my office.

This is bullshit.

There's no need for us to be in San Francisco for two weeks, sharing a place. It's like he's purposely trying to make my life a living hell. But that's how it's always been—Huxley gets what he wants.

Starting this business was his idea. I jumped on board because, frankly, I didn't have anything better to do with my life, but when responsibilities started to roll out, it was as if Breaker and Huxley just came up with jobs they wanted and gave me the leftovers. Does it look like I want to be the face of the company? The guy who talks to the media and waves his hand about and cuts ribbons?

Fuck no.

There's no purpose behind it.

Nothing.

I don't feel fulfilled when I go to work.

And now, this…I'm a fucking glorified babysitter.

I reach my office, but when I go to shut my door, I'm quickly stopped by my brothers, who apparently have been hot on my heels during my retreat.

I don't bother arguing with them to leave me alone, because there's no point; they won't give me privacy. I take a seat on my couch and spread out, ready for the lecture.

Breaker shuts the door and then joins Huxley, who's standing in front of me, hands in his pockets.

"What the actual fuck was that about?" Breaker asks.

"Me?" I point to myself. "You don't think you could've told me that in private? You know, so we could discuss it without the girls being there? Instead, you just gave me a sentencing and went on with your life."

"*Sentencing*?" Huxley asks. "I fail to see how spending two weeks in a penthouse in San Francisco, one of your favorite cities, is a sentencing. I assumed you'd appreciate the break from LA."

"Not when I have to spend it babysitting someone," I say.

"It's not babysitting," Breaker says. "You'd be helping Kelsey and taking on one of our most prestigious renovation projects. This is fucking huge, man."

"Not to mention, we're working with a new set of contractors in San Francisco because that's who was available. They know how much we're worth and they know the importance of the project. We don't need them taking advantage of Kelsey, who isn't experienced in this at all."

"You don't think she can stand up for herself?" I ask. "Because I have it on very good authority that she knows how to put a man in his place."

She's only done it half a dozen times with me.

"It's not that she can't handle herself," Huxley says. "Because if she's anything like her sister, then I know there's a solid fighting spirit in her. But this is about headlining the process as an owner, making sure things are done the way we want them, and assisting Kelsey with her initiatives. We have one shot at impressing the historic societies in a city we love. If we can make good on this building, think of all the other buildings we could help with."

"If it's that important, then you fucking do it."

Huxley's jaw tightens even more. "You know I can't. I have commitments with Lottie, and even though this company means everything to me, she means more. You're the one who represents Cane Enterprises, you're the one who works directly with Kelsey, and unless you can give me a specific—and I mean very specific—reason why you can't go up there tonight, then you're leaving in four hours."

I look away because fuck...I'm frustrated.

Because I don't have a good reason other than Kelsey hurt my man feelings and I haven't been able to get over it.

Because I don't want to be around her.

Because...shit, because I think I like her, and I don't know how to navigate those feelings, feelings I've been suppressing for quite some time. And because she wants absolutely nothing to do with me, it makes navigating those feelings that much more difficult. She thinks of me as a player, a man who seeks his own pleasure, nothing more.

Spending two weeks with her in the penthouse is going to be absolute torture.

I'll be surrounded by her heady scent, subjected to her nighttime wear, forced to share meals... It'll be like having a live-in girlfriend without the girlfriend part.

But I have no excuse.

No out.

So, might as well stop fighting it and go fucking pack.

"Well, then, I guess I'm leaving in four hours." In silence, with their eyes watching my every move, I shoot up from the couch and make sure I have everything I need before walking past my brothers and out of my office, straight to the elevator where…of course, Lottie and Kelsey are talking.

Great.

I stand a good five feet away, but their conversation is loud enough for me to hear.

"I'm sure it won't be that bad, as there are two large rooms separated by a living area and kitchenette. So, don't worry. Hey, remember the time we went to San Francisco with Mom?" Lottie asks. "She took us to that dim sum restaurant and we ate so much that the owners took a picture of us because they'd never seen two girls consume as much food as we did."

Kelsey asks, "What was it called again? Dim Sum Star?"

Jesus, how long does it take for an elevator to get here? And clearly, Kelsey's not happy with the plan to share the penthouse with me either. *Don't worry, Kelsey; I know how you feel about me.*

Lottie nods. "Yup. It was so good. And, of course, the Ghirardelli store. You have to go. Oh, and hey, kind of convenient that Derek will be up there, right?"

Derek?

Now my ears are turned in their direction. Who the hell is Derek?

"Oh yeah, you're right. This trip already sounds better."

"Want me to text Ellie and see if he'll meet you for dinner? I mean, it's kind of perfect that the timing's matched up."

Ellie…there's only one Ellie I know and that's Dave Toney's Ellie. Dave Toney is one of our business partners. Ellie and Lottie have grown close. Which means…Derek must be Derek Toney, Dave's younger brother.

Is Lottie trying to fix Kelsey up with Derek?

"Might be nice to have something to do at night," Kelsey says.

Well, Jesus fuck, I'll be there. It's not like you're going to be banished to an island all alone.

Then again, why would she consider me a decent companion? The *obnoxious asshole.*

"I'll set it up," Lottie says. "Ellie was telling me that Derek is a total foodie. I'll bet he takes you somewhere that will blow your mind."

"Which means I need to pack some dresses for a date or two," Kelsey says with excitement.

Fucking...great.

Just what I need, to stay in the penthouse for two weeks while Kelsey goes out on dates with *Derek.*

This is going to be a fucking fantastic trip.

CHAPTER 9
KELSEY

Kelsey: Welcome, listener, to the *Meant to Be Podcast*, where we talk to madly-in-love couples about the way they met. Rowan and Bonnie, thank you so much for joining me today. Please, tell us how you met.

Bonnie: I was in a towel, and he was a voyeur in my kitchen, waiting to catch a glimpse.

Rowan: Jesus. That's not what happened.

Bonnie: Were you or were you not in my kitchen uninvited?

Rowan: I was in me maw's house. She neglected to tell me two lasses were renting the cottage.

Bonnie: Still, you were there and I was in a towel. I tried to shoo him away with a broom, but he wouldn't leave.

Kelsey: A broom, always a good weapon.

Bonnie: Not for a stubborn Scot.

Rowan: Want to talk about stubborn? Shall we talk about your laundry list of stubbornness?

Bonnie: Not necessary, dear. Back to the story—of course I thought he was attractive, I mean, look at him, how could you not? But, man, was he grumpy.

Kelsey: What were you doing in Scotland?

Bonnie: Oh, my friend and I took a job with Rowan's mom. They needed someone to watch over their coffee shop, and housing was included. We both needed a change of scenery, so we jumped on the idea. We were hired. But I wasn't prepared for the kind of repairs the coffee shop needed, nor the challenging glare from Rowan with every step I took.

Kelsey: So, you two were enemies to lovers, then.

Rowan: Aye. Very much enemies.

Bonnie: Until I wore him down with my American accent. He won me over with his cake.

Rowan: That I did.

Lottie has always talked about flying in Huxley's private plane. She's told me the wonders of not having to go through the same routine as flying commercial and dealing with crowds of people. She's talked about the service…the bedroom in the back, but nothing she told me would have prepared me for this flight.

Because this, my friends, is bougie.

This is easily the fanciest thing I've ever done in my life.

Cane is printed on everything. The seats, the stationery…the napkins, even the apron the flight attendant is wearing.

And these seats—my God, I could get lost in one forever. I'd buy this seat alone, sell everything else in my tiny studio apartment, and live in this seat. I'd do everything in this seat. I'd sleep, eat, I'd even sponge-bathe myself.

I've already texted Lottie good luck to the flight staff in removing me from this plane.

Oh, and the staff. They call me Miss Gardner and they have my favorite seltzer on hand, which I of course indulged in. As well as these fresh-from-the-freaking-airplane-oven cookies. I had three.

THREE!

And we're talking the size of my fist. Three large chocolatey cookies that tasted like success.

Needless to say, I've been enjoying myself despite the brooding, in-a-constant-state-of-annoyance JP.

He didn't speak to me when we arrived at the hangar. He didn't say anything when we both sat down, and when the flight attendant asked him if he wanted a cookie, he said *no* but added another finger of scotch to his drink.

His loss, because these cookies are phenomenal.

"Can I get you anything else, Mr. Cane?" Ronda, the lovely flight attendant, asks.

"I'm good," he says, staring out the window.

She then turns to me. "Miss Gardner, can I grab you another cookie?" She winks, as if we both know I really want another one.

And I do, but three is pushing it. Four is out of line.

I press my palm to my stomach and say, "I don't think I should."

She gently rests her hand on my shoulder and says, "How about this? I'll pack some up in a bag for you to take with you."

Don't mind if I do.

"You're an absolute angel, Ronda."

She gives me a pat and then retreats to the back of the airplane.

I glance over at JP and watch him casually lift his glass to his lips. Even though there was a seat right across from me, he chose to sit on the other side of the plane. If his outrage in the conference room didn't clue me in on his displeasure with this trip, then his obvious seat choice has.

"You know…you could be a little nicer to Ronda," I say, because why not poke the bear even more?

"I'm perfectly pleasant to her," he says, keeping his eyes on the window.

"I haven't heard any *pleases* or *thank yous* from you. Politeness goes a long way, JP."

"Are you the polite police now?"

"No, but I do think we need to hold each other accountable for our actions and, frankly, I don't think you're being very kind at the moment."

He slowly moves his head to the side so he's looking at me through his dark-framed aviators. "Have I told her to fuck off? Have I tripped her on purpose? Did I punch her at any point in time?" When I don't answer, he continues. "Didn't think so. Now, get off my back."

God, he's being so…nasty. What's his deal?

"Well, you could stand to be nicer to me, that's for sure. You know, we have to spend two weeks together."

"I'm well aware of my sentencing."

"*Sentencing?*" I say with a gasp. "That's what this is to you? A sentencing? Because, to me, it seems like a once-in-a-lifetime opportunity to help restore a building to its glory days while making it modern and sustainable."

JP smooths his hand over his jaw and says, "Of course you'd put some sort of fairy-tale spin on it."

"It's not a fairy tale. This is a huge opportunity."

"I'll tell you what this trip is going to be, Kelsey. We're going to have to share a penthouse for two weeks, which I know won't be big enough to stay out of each other's hair. You'll follow me around to different meetings, I'll get to hear you say the same spiel repeatedly about how using bamboo organizers is so much healthier for the earth than the plastic ones, and you'll get all excited about everyone else's excitement. Meanwhile, I'm counting down the minutes until I can return to my normal life in LA."

When he turns back to the window, I say, "Or you can use it as a chance to get to know me better. You know, the option to be a friend is still there."

"Why the fuck would you want to be my friend?" he asks.

"Why wouldn't I?" I ask, feeling affronted all of a sudden.

"I'm an obnoxious asshole in your opinion. You think I'm some sort of sycophant who preys on women when they're at their lowest. Why would you want to be my friend?"

"When have I ever said that?"

"You didn't have to," he answers.

"What the hell are you talking about?"

His eyes shoot to mine and he says, "The night of the gala. You assumed I was trying to take you to bed. Couldn't have been further from the truth."

I pause and allow my mind to rewind back to that night. We had a nice time dancing, Edwin left with Genesis, and I was feeling out of sorts, like I wasn't good enough. JP took me back to his place...*and said so many kind words that I've banished from my mind.*

Until now.

"What he should've said the moment he saw you was how fucking breathtaking you look... He should've lifted your hand and pressed the lightest of kisses to your knuckles, just so he could claim you in front of everyone around him... And when he lowered your hand, he should've...leaned inches from your ear, and said how intoxicatingly beautiful you smelled."

Because they'd seemed so out of character for JP, I'd largely ignored how I'd reacted to them. What I had recalled was *where* he'd had his driver take us.

"But you took me back to your place. If you weren't trying to do that, then what were you doing?"

"Being nice," he wails. "Something, apparently, you don't think I can be. Your opinion of me is so low that you believe only the worst."

"But..." I chew on my bottom lip, trying to figure out the details.

"Just forget it, Kelsey."

"No, JP, let's talk about this."

"I don't want to be on this airplane right now, so do you really think I want to talk about that night? I don't. So, fucking drop it."

And then he turns away from me, shutting me out.

The rest of the trip is spent in silence. I can't be sure what he's thinking about, but his words are playing on repeat in my head.

Your opinion of me is so low that you believe only the worst.

Have I always gotten along with JP? No.

But I wouldn't say he's the worst human I've ever come across. He's temperamental, doesn't seem to have the most impeccable conversational skills, and loves to drive people nuts, but I wouldn't say he's the worst.

I see good in him.

I see how he helps others.

I see the way he knows everyone's name in the office, how he says hi to them, how he gets people coffee just out of the kindness of his heart.

I see the compliments he tosses around, the good-natured comradery he creates, and the smiles he puts on faces.

I see the love and respect he has for his brothers, even when they're fighting.

So why didn't I see that the night of the gala?

I glance over at him.

Did I really make him feel that way? But then I consider his comments from a few hours ago when I suggested I could do the job on my own. There had been…disdain in his voice.

"The fuck you can. There's more to it than just walking around an office. Hate to say it, but you're not sufficiently educated to handle this on your own." Something tells me that his reaction wasn't completely about my professional skills, but more to do with his feelings about me.

How did this go so wrong?

"What room do you want?" JP asks once we're done touring the penthouse. And I use the word *touring* loosely. JP tossed his arm around, telling me exactly where "everything" was while I gazed at the luxurious suite I'd be living in for the next two weeks.

The exterior walls of the penthouse are made up entirely of floor-to-ceiling windows, offering a breathtaking view of the San Francisco Bay and the Golden Gate Bridge. The floors are beautiful gray-stained wood, accented with plush rugs and pristine white furniture. There are pictures of buildings on the walls and I recognize a few that I've visited in LA. These must all belong to Cane Enterprises. And the kitchen…oh, it's beautiful, with state-of-the-art appliances, marble countertops, and a kitchen island that seems bigger than my entire apartment combined.

Two weeks here will be no problem.

If only my company was more agreeable.

"I don't mind. Whichever is fine," I say, especially since both rooms are the same, from what JP said. If one was bigger, I could clearly take the smaller room.

"Just choose one," he says in an exasperated tone.

"Fine, the right one."

"Good." JP rolls his bag across the wooden floors and calls out, "Ronda ordered us dinner. Should be here any moment. Just start eating whenever you want." And then he's down the hall and out of sight.

Well, I guess that's that.

I roll my suitcase in the opposite direction, toward my room. I'm determined to not let his bad attitude affect me.

When I reach my room, I set my purse down and flop back on the king-sized bed, which is decorated in white linens and soft gray pillows. A girl could seriously get used to this. Now I kind of know how it felt to be Lottie when she first moved in with Huxley. Too bad for me, this is only for two weeks.

I reach for my purse and pull out my phone. I press on Lottie's name and put the phone on speaker, listening to it ring.

"Gah! Did you make it to San Francisco?" Lottie says when she answers the phone.

"I did and, oh my God, Lottie, this place is so beautiful. I can't get over it."

"I'm so jealous. I told Hux when you two are done there, we need to at least take a weekend trip, because he was showing me pictures of the penthouse and it looks like a total dream."

"It is. I can't wait to see what kind of views I have in the morning."

"And the flight was good?"

"As good as it could be."

"Turbulence?" she asks.

"Well, not turbulence with the plane, more like turbulence with JP. He's really not happy with me."

"I gathered that. Did he say why?"

Your opinion of me is so low that you believe only the worst.

"He did and, honestly, Lottie, I feel sick about it."

"What happened?"

"Well, you know how Edwin and Genesis went off with each other the night of the gala?"

"Ah, yes, and you haven't heard from him since. A real winner, that one."

"Yeah, well, I didn't really tell you what happened after."

"What do you mean you didn't tell me—oh my God, Kelsey, did you sleep with JP?"

"No!" I nearly shout and then realize I might be too loud. I bring my voice down while I stand from the bed and start to unpack and organize my things. "We didn't sleep together, but he did take me back to his place, and when I say *his place*, I mean the driveway. That's as far as I let it go before I told him I wasn't sleeping with him."

"Did he ask you into his house?"

"No, I kind of…you know…assumed that he wanted to sleep with me. But he was just being nice. I inadvertently insulted him and now he pretty much hates me. He barely talked to me on the airplane, and has retreated to his room, where I'm sure he'll stay the entire night."

"So, you're in an uncomfortable situation, then?"

"Correct." I carry my toiletries to the bathroom and line up everything in a row in order of how I use them. "I really want to enjoy myself here. We've rarely been able to travel, let alone in a lavish way, but things are weird with him and I don't know how to make it better."

"JP is an odd one. He's very sarcastic, and sometimes, it seems like he doesn't take things seriously, but there's a darker side to him, too, a side he doesn't talk about much. Even Huxley was saying how JP can be very closed off. I think you struck that dark part and maybe the only way to fix things is to apologize sincerely."

I sigh and lean against the bathroom's honeycomb-tiled wall. "I think you're right."

"I know I am. Oh, and hey, I talked to Ellie. Derek would love to meet up while you're in San Francisco. He's going to check his schedule and will let you know when he's available."

"Okay, yeah, cool." My stomach lurches and I can't be sure if it's from needing dinner or the looming conversation I have to have with JP. Either way, it's not a good feeling. "I should go. Dinner will be here soon."

"You got this, sis. Show them what the Gardner sisters are all about."

It'll be fine.

Just lightly knock on his door and if he happens to snap at you like a beast, just know it has everything to do with what you said to him, and nothing to do with him...

Taking a deep breath, I lift my knuckles to his door and give it a quick knock.

I press my lips together as I wait for his response, but when I hear nothing, I knock again and ask, "JP, are you in there? Dinner is here."

I wait for a few breaths and then he finally calls out, "Eat without me."

I was afraid he'd say that.

That's why I devised a plan to get him out of his room.

"Okay, but, uh, I think I broke the oven and it sort of smells like gas so do you think you could help me with that? Then I'll leave you alone."

Between you and me, I didn't even touch the oven, but I figured a gas leak might get him moving.

And lucky for me, I'm right.

The doorknob tilts down and then the door opens, revealing a bare-chested JP, wearing only a pair of shorts.

Well, uh…would you look at that?

An expansive chest of thick pecs that connect to his prominent collarbone, and sculpted arms that are peppered in ink. Below his pecs are a row of what I can only describe as unattainable abs that ripple into an edged Adonis belt where his shorts hang dangerously low.

I wasn't, uh, I wasn't expecting him to answer the door like this, hence why I haven't said anything. Or why I can't seem to find my words.

"Kelsey…the oven."

"Right," I say, stepping to the side. "The oven. Gas. It smells like gas."

JP moves past me and I watch his backside retreat into the main living space.

I'm not one to dismiss the truth, even if it pains me. And the truth here is that JP is gorgeous, especially with his shirt off. The kind of man that you see walking down the street and all you can do is stop and stare to take in everything about him. With his shirt off, not only do you get glimpses of JP's tattoos, but you get a whole show.

Mentally cries God, he's sexy.

Ahh, did I just think that? No, he's not sexy. He's just…someone to look at that's easy on the eyes.

Not sexy. Nope. Just…attractive. That's all.

Okay, moving on.

"What did you do to the oven?" he calls out.

This is where I have to play defense because the moment he knows I was lying, he'll make a run for his room and I'm going to have to block him. I prepared for such an event by rolling up my sleeves and removing my socks so I don't slide along the floor. The sweaty grip on the bottom of my feet has already occurred, so I believe I'm ready.

I walk into the living area, staying close to his hallway to perform a blockade, and in a very dramatic voice, I say, "I lied."

His head snaps around and his eyes meet mine. "You lied?" he asks with a tilt of his brow.

"Indeed." I hold my chin up even higher. "The oven story is a farce. I never even touched it."

"Jesus Christ," he says, and just like I predicted, he starts moving in my direction.

Man your position!

I back up into the mouth of the hallway and extend all limbs out, creating a wall with my body. If he wants to get to his room, he has to get through me first.

Which, I'm aware he probably has an entire person's weight of muscle on his body over me, but I'm scrappy and I know how to cling to someone like a spider monkey.

"What are you doing?" he asks as he stops a few feet in front of me, seeming to realize I'm a force to be reckoned with.

"Stopping you from retreating to your room. What does it look like?"

"It looks like a pathetic attempt to get in my way. With one push of my pinky, I will have you flat on your ass."

"I'm much stronger than I let on. Try me." *There is no way he'll touch me.*

Boy, was I wrong.

He steps up to me, presses his pinky to my chest, and gives me just enough of a nudge to throw me off-balance.

TIMBER!

Because my arms and legs are fully extended, I have nothing to grab and, before I can even think about a counterattack, I'm falling on my ass with a clunk.

Man down.

Heat washes over my cheeks when I look up at JP, just as he starts to step over me. I might be embarrassed by my pitiful attempt to stop him, but I'm not giving up. Ohhhh no. I will not go down without a fight.

This man will talk to me if it's the last thing I do.

I twist my body so my stomach is pressing against the ground, extend my arms out, latch on to his leg, and pull myself closer, hanging on for dear life.

"What the fuck?" he asks, staring down at me. He shakes his leg, attempting to rid himself of me—as if I'm an inconvenient piece of toilet paper that's stuck to his shoe. Too bad for him, my grip is strong. "Kelsey, what the hell are you doing?"

With my cheek pressed against his leg, the bottom of his shorts tickling my nose, I say, "You're not getting away from me, sir. No way. You will talk to me."

"Let go." He places his hand on the wall for balance and shakes harder.

"Never!" I cry out. "If you want me off you, you're going to have to pry me off."

Bad choice of words, because the next thing I know, he reaches down and plucks at my fingers.

I swat him away.

He swats at my hand.

I swat back.

He swats again.

I open my mouth and start chomping at his hand to scare him away.

That does the trick because the swatting ends and I resume my lethal grip.

"Kelsey, seriously, let the fuck go."

"You have no idea who you're dealing with. I have no problem claiming squatter's rights on your leg. I have nowhere to be all night. It's just you and me, bub, so it's your choice. You either come talk to me, or you spend your evening with me attached to your foot."

He looks down at me, looks up at his room, and then, to my chagrin, he starts dragging me along the floor. He can't possibly be serious.

"JP, I demand you stop at once."

He doesn't. He keeps walking, me dragging behind him.

"Stop this insanity," I call out. "Just talk to me."

Drag.

Drag.

...drag.

Frustration consumes me, my ears heat to boiling levels, and I can feel the anger start to take over. I tried to be nice about this. I attempted a smooth conversation. Yes, I had to resort to becoming an actual ball and chain, but now...oh now, I'm getting upset.

Keeping one hand planted on the leg that's dragging me, I reach for his other leg but miss by a long shot. In a horrible attempt to grasp anything so I don't lose him to a full-out sprint when he shakes free of me, my fingers curl around the fabric of his shorts.

I don't really register that I have shorts in my hand. All I know is that I have a hold of something and it's time to pull.

That's exactly what I do.

I yank on his shorts so hard that he stumbles forward, and because I'm holding on to his other leg, he can't catch his balance.

Ladies and gentlemen, this is where things go terribly, terribly wrong.

It happens in slow motion. I'm unable to completely process what's going to occur as everything else fades away and the only sound is the long, drawn-out noise of JP saying, "What...the...fuuuuuuck?"

It was never my intention to anger him more, nor was it my intention to cause him to fall.

But I accomplished both things…while pantsing him at the same time.

Yup, just like that, with a slight yank, those elastic-banded shorts of his slide right off his narrow hips and down his legs, causing him to stumble even more.

I cry out in horror because, good God, there are loose shorts in my hand.

Which only means…

Please let him be wearing underwear. Please let him be wearing underwear.

He dances above me, attempting to gain balance.

I squeeze my eyes shut out of pure self-preservation.

I twist.

He turns.

He jumps.

I clutch.

And then, with a big crash to the floor, he falls on top of me, pillowing my face with what I can only assume is his stomach.

"Jesus fuck," he says.

I open my eyes and come face to face with man scrotum.

A man's freaking scrotum!

"Ahhh!" I scream and swat at his leg. "Your penis is on my face. Your penis is on my face."

"I know. Fuck," he yells, attempting to get off me.

"Where is your underwear?"

"I don't wear underwear at night."

"Dear God! It's on my nose! Your genitals are resting on my freaking nose!"

"I fucking know!" he yells back. "But I can't get up because you're still holding on to me."

"I've been tea-bagged," I cry out in horror, his penis still rubbing along my nostrils.

"Let the fuck GO, KELSEY!"

As if I finally realize what's happening, I release all my limbs and he climbs off me. I scramble up against the wall and hold my hand—still clutching his shorts—in front of my face.

"I've been defiled."

"*You've* been defiled?" he retorts. "I'm the one who's been stripped bare." He yanks the shorts from my grasp and I hear him scurry around, putting them on. When I think the coast is clear, I part my fingers to see if he's decent.

I'm met with a very angry stare. Menacing, to be precise. Some might actually say...*gulp* sinister.

I attempt a smile, but it falls flat.

I lift my finger to speak, but he cuts me off.

"Let's get one thing straight, Kelsey. I'm not here to be friends with you, nor am I here to try to solve any sort of complex you might have about not being liked. I'm here to do a job and I'd prefer you just leave me alone." He turns away, pushes his hand through his hair, and mutters, "Christ," right before he slams his door.

Well...that didn't go as planned.

Lottie: How did it go? Are things good with you two?

Kelsey: I tricked him with a gas scare, got him out of his room, then flung my body onto his leg. He proceeded to drag me across the penthouse. In my attempt to stop him, I yanked his shorts down, tripped him up, and his penis landed on my face. To sum it up, I would say things are not going well.

Lottie: His penis was on your face? Call me crazy, but that's a typical Friday night for me and Hux. Seems like things are going swimmingly.

Kelsey: I hate you.

CHAPTER 10
JP

"YOU KNOW, MAYBE WE SHOULD discuss what we're going to say in the meeting," Kelsey says as she fidgets next to me in the car.

Last night was…hell, I don't even know how to describe what happened last night. If I wasn't so irritated, I might have actually found it comical. But my irritation turned into anger as I lay in bed, because for the fucking life of me, I couldn't escape the feeling of her exasperated breath blowing on my nuts. That breath was the most action I've received in *months*.

It tingled.

Felt good.

And before I knew it, I was jacking off in the shower over the goddamn fact that she breathed on my scrotum. I'm so desperate *and* horny that I actually liked it.

Let me tell you something, the stark realization of that—of understanding that you're such a lonely bastard that a woman's breath on your junk gets you horny—is incredibly unsettling and, frankly, pathetic.

And yet, there I was last night, hammering away on my dick because, if I didn't, I wouldn't have been able to get any sleep.

I woke up this morning, unable to think any less of myself.

In an attempt to lift my self-esteem, I went to the gym, stared at myself in the mirror while doing bicep curls and listening to Adele—"Easy on Me"—and recited affirmations in my head.

You are strong.

You are handsome.

You're not a pathetic loser who jacks off to a simple exhalation.

Once I repeated that mantra over and over in my head, I went back to my room, opened my computer, and donated ten thousand dollars to a pigeon rescue, because in all honesty, I doubt many people care about pigeons at all.

From the combination of seeing my biceps work in their pure form, Adele's uplifting voice, my affirmations, and a solid donation...I felt better about myself and felt confident I could face this day head-on.

That was until Kelsey appeared from her room wearing a skintight pencil skirt, which hit just above her calves, and a black sleeveless turtleneck. She smelled like a goddamn angel sent from above and looked like hell on heels with her voluptuous hair in waves hanging loosely over her shoulders.

Fuck.

Me.

The memory of *the exhalation*—that's what we'll call it now—came roaring back to life, and I had to turn away to hide any impending excitement.

You are strong.

You are handsome.

You're not a pathetic loser who jacks off to a simple exhalation.

That was on repeat the entire morning while I moved around Kelsey, grabbing coffee and a protein bar while she made herself scrambled eggs, whole wheat toast, spinach, and oddly...black beans. I've never seen anyone work so cleanly in a kitchen, nor have I seen someone set out a complete place setting—placemat included—for breakfast. It was hard not to watch.

After her breakfast spectacle, we made our way to the lobby, where a car was waiting for us, and now we're making our way through rush-hour traffic in San Francisco.

"Did you hear me?" Kelsey asks, poking me.

I glance at where she poked me in the arm and then back at my phone.

She huffs in anger and turns toward me, swatting my phone out of my hand. It falls to the floor of the car with a clunk.

"Hey—"

With her red-painted nail, she points very closely at my face and leans in. "Listen to me, Jonathan Patrick Cane—"

"That's not my name."

"I don't care if your name is Junior Pooper, you're going to listen to me." *Don't laugh at Junior Pooper, do not laugh.* "I'm sick of you ignoring me. Let's call last night what it was, a total miss on my end. I'll take the blame for how things…panned out, but now you're just being cruel."

"I'm not being cruel. I just don't have anything to say to you."

"You always have something to say to me. Always. From the moment I freaking met you, you've had something to say. You've never stopped talking, nagging, prodding. You're constantly in my ear chattering about utter nonsense, and now, all of a sudden, you're going to stop? When we have to spend two weeks together?" She shakes her head. "Oh no, that's not how this is going to work. I would rather spend two weeks in a penthouse with you constantly aggravating me with your nonsensical drivel than this silent treatment you've decided to try out. You might not think it's cruel, but it is. It's not fair to me. You won't even let me apologize."

"Apologize for what?" I ask.

"For my presumption the night of the gala. What I said was out of line, JP." She rests her hand on my arm. "I'm sorry. You were right, you were being nice and I took it the wrong way. I never should've made that kind of assumption about you. I'm sorry."

Well…the apology is nice. Glad to see she doesn't believe I'm a complete asshole. But going back to the playful banter, the "nagging," as she put it, I'm not sure I can do that. I don't think I have it within me to control myself.

Messing around with her has been a turn-on. Even when we're in full-on disagreement, I love seeing the spark in her eyes, the way she huffs and puffs and tries to get her point across. I love hearing her reasoning and watching as her chest gets blotchy with irritation. It's hot.

And now that we're close to each other, there's no way I'll be able to keep my hands off her. I know it. Especially after last night's humiliating revelation.

No.

You are strong.

You are handsome.

You're not a pathetic loser who jacks off to a simple exhalation.

"Thank you for apologizing," I say while fishing around for my phone. Once I find it, I go back to my emails.

"Uh...that's it? Nothing else?"

"What else do you want me to say?"

"I don't know—make a joke about how I tickled your balls?"

The driver's eyes flash to the rearview mirror quickly before focusing on the road again.

Wanting to clarify things, I lean forward and say to the driver, "She didn't tickle my balls. She breathed on them."

"Not on purpose!" Kelsey practically shouts as she leans forward as well, gripping the driver's seat. "He fell on my face."

"After she pantsed me."

"It's not my fault you weren't wearing underwear. How was I supposed to know that?"

"Either way, you shouldn't have been pulling on my shorts, unless... that was your plan all along. Trying to get me naked to sit on your face." I lean back and slowly clap. "Wow, Kelsey, job well done."

Her head whips toward me and her nostrils flare. Ahh, there they are. I missed them. "You know damn well my intention wasn't to get you naked to sit on my face. I couldn't imagine a more grotesque situation."

"Didn't seem to mind it last night," I say, going back to my phone. She swats it out of my hand again. "Hey, stop doing that."

"I did not enjoy your balls on my face. I specifically remember screaming and telling you to get off me."

"Yeah, as you held me down."

She turns back to the driver, who has remained silent this entire time. What I wouldn't pay to be inside his head right now. "I did not hold him down. I was flustered and didn't know what was happening. When I realized what was on my face, I got up immediately. I just want you to know I'm not the kind of girl who enjoys balls on her face."

"Such a shame," I say.

She growls out a frustrated noise and folds her arms over her chest as she sits back in her seat. "Why do I even bother talking to you? You're so infuriating."

"Beats me. You're the one who didn't want the silent treatment, so this is your choice." I locate my phone and, when she goes to swat it again, I hold it close to my chest. "Nice try."

Just then, her phone rings in her purse and she quickly brings it into view. She glances at me. "It's Huxley."

"Put it on speaker."

Looking at me with murder weapons as eyes, she says, "I swear to God, JP, if you bring up the balls-on-the-face thing with him, I'll legit haunt you in your sleep. Do you understand me?"

"Sure," I say, even though I wouldn't say anything to the boys. I didn't tell them last night what happened, didn't think it was appropriate.

Putting on a smile—as if he can see her—she answers the phone, "Good morning, Huxley."

Wow, what a transformation, from a she-devil to Delightful Diane. Who knew she was capable of such a metamorphosis?

"Good morning, Kelsey."

"I have you on speakerphone so JP can hear you. We're on our way to the meeting right now."

"I take it you two have settled in since the activities of last night?"

"Oh my God, JP," she says, looking at me. "You told your brother that your penis landed on my face?"

Oh, Kelsey...

He was not talking about *that*.

I can't hold back my smile. I held it together with *Junior Pooper*, but this, nope, I have to smile, because she just gave herself away.

"What?" Huxley growls.

Kelsey's eyes widen as her cheeks flush to a gorgeous shade of pink.

"I didn't tell him anything." I smirk. "But you just did."

"Oh, dear God," she whispers.

"What's going on? JP, if you fuck with her, I'm going to—"

"No, nothing happened," Kelsey quickly says. "It was just a, uh, scramble, and then we tripped on each other, and I really mean that, not like, *Oops, I tripped and fell on his penis, my bad.* I swear, this was just an unfortunate incident and it was quickly rectified with screaming, yelling, and swatting. There's no funny business between us."

"She's correct," I say. "Nothing is going on, and trust me, nothing will be going on. You don't have to worry about that."

"Good. Kelsey, you tell me if he does try to make a move."

I roll my eyes. I was the innocent in all of this. I didn't ask her to strip my pants off and breathe on my scrotum...

Oh, hell.

Her hot breath...dancing across my nuts...

You are strong.

You are handsome.

You're not a pathetic loser who jacks off to a simple exhalation.

"He's been nothing but professional. Don't worry. Just forget I even mentioned it. Anyway, we're on our way to the meeting."

"Good. Edison will meet with the both of you, along with our general contractor, Regis. He's new, JP. I've heard mixed reviews on the man, so keep an eye on him."

"Then why the hell did you hire him?" I ask.

"Time. Darius couldn't squeeze us in. But Regis has done beautiful work around the city, so that's why we hired him."

"Has everyone signed an NDA?" I ask.

"Yes. Edison has some details to go over before you walk the property. Since he has experience in renovating historic buildings in the area, I asked him to be a voice while going through the plans. He has no problem doing that. Did you get the renovation plans that I emailed last night?"

"Yes," I answer. "I'm assuming you sent them to Regis as well?"

"Correct," Huxley answers. "Kelsey, I sent them to you as well. I want you to insert your input like you have for the rest of our buildings. I know this is new to you, starting from scratch, but I think it's important to have you there to oversee our plans for sustainability. Karla also scheduled meetings for you around town with the other buildings that we own, did you see that?"

"I did. I'm assuming you want me to walk through them, speak with the office managers, and organize like I've been doing in Los Angeles?"

"Correct. You have a busy two weeks. Hope you're up for it."

"I am," Kelsey says with excitement.

"JP, plan a meeting with the mayor. Tell him exactly what we plan on doing. He's been wary of us coming into his city, but if he sees what we stand for, it might help for future bids. When I said we were lucky to get the Angelica Building, I wasn't fucking lying. If done right, this could be huge for us. We've been involved in restoration for a few years now, but nothing of this magnitude. Mixing the old with the new could put us at the top of the game."

"Well, I'm excited. I think it's an awesome plan, preserving the brilliance of the old-school architecture, but also combining today's trends to help with costs, as well as making positive changes to help our environment. It's a worthwhile combination," Kelsey says. "I've been doing research on the structure and identity of the Angelica and I already have a ton of ideas. I can't wait to walk through them all."

"Good. Do you two have any questions?"

"I don't think so," Kelsey says as she looks over at me. I just shake my head. "Seems like we're good. Thanks for calling, Huxley."

"Anytime. If you need anything, ask JP. That's why he's there, to help you out."

"Okay, thanks."

They exchange goodbyes and then she hangs up the phone. She crosses one leg over the other in that skintight pencil skirt, turns toward me, and says, "Hear that, JP? You're here to help me out."

"Your point?" I ask with a brow raised in her direction.

"Which means...no more ignoring me."

"If you have something productive to say or a well-thought-out question, I'll be more than happy to be at your service. Anything other than that...just move along."

"Mr. Edison will be right with you," the receptionist says as we both take a seat on a terribly stiff couch.

Kelsey glances around, but I keep my eyes trained on my phone. "This place is...interesting," Kelsey says. "Is that a chair in the shape of a hand over there?"

"Yup," I say without having to look up. I know exactly which chair she's talking about. I sat in it once and it was incredibly uncomfortable. "Edison believes he has a refined palate when it comes to interior design. When in fact, he has zero taste. Wait until you see his desk. It's one giant Rubik's Cube."

"That's...interesting."

"One way to put it."

The door that I know leads into Edison's office opens, and the balding tubby man waddles over to us. Dressed in a pair of brown-and-orange plaid shorts and a green suit jacket, he reads more like an absolute imbecile than a serious real estate agent. But he's completed some important business deals for us, so we keep coming back, despite his eccentricities.

When he looks up and spots me, a large smile spans across his face. "JP Cane, you old bastard. How the hell are ya?"

He also has zero decorum.

Standing along with Kelsey, I walk up to him and shake his hand. "Edison, good to see you. I see you're still unable to match a pair of slacks with a suit jacket."

He lets out a boisterous laugh and says, "Not all of us want to be caught up in a sea of black suits. Some of us like to be memorable."

"Memorable, indeed," I say with a smile, internally hating myself.

This side of me? It's the fake business side. It's the reason I'm the "face" of the company, because when push comes to shove, I can slap on a smile and lay on the charm. I have...charisma, and it has definitely been needed to clean up Huxley's messes caused by his *inability* to mask his irritation. I'm the one clients and partners want to take out, because I know how to have a conversation that's equal parts business and fun. And yet, Kelsey thinks I'm an asshole.

Holding his hand past me, Edison says, "You must be Kelsey Gardner."

"Hello," Kelsey says politely while shaking his hand. "It's nice to meet you, Mr. Edison."

"Edison is fine, dear. No need to add the *mister* in front of it. I'm sure JP could regale you with stories of how such a formal title would not suit me and my personality."

"I could, but I'll save you the embarrassment," I say, patting him on the back.

"A kind man." Edison gestures to his office. "Please, come in. Regis said he'd meet us at the Angelica."

I place my hand on Kelsey's lower back for some reason—who fucking knows why. I expect her to pull away, but when she doesn't, I continue to guide her until we're in his office.

And what an office it is. I've never seen anything like it. An interesting and bold combination of gaming and nerdery with posters of Zelda on one wall and the periodic table of elements on another. Walking into his office, you wouldn't think a real estate agent—the top in the city, to be precise—worked here. Not that I'd expect him to have pictures of buildings lining his walls, but there's a giant whisk—about three feet long—hanging behind his Rubik's Cube desk. What's with the whisk? Did he just like it and decide to hang it up? Is there sentimental value to the whisk? Did he win a whisking contest and that's the prize?

In the sitting area, there is a set of purple armchairs and a polka-dot loveseat surrounding a coffee table fish tank…with no fish in it, but rather, floating eyeglasses. See what I'm talking about?

Weird-as-shit office.

I watch Kelsey as she takes in the space.

"Can I get you a drink?" Edison asks as he sits down in the chair closest to Kelsey. He watches her with delight as she continues to find new things about his office.

"I'm good," Kelsey says after a few seconds.

"I'm good as well," I say.

"Edison, your office is so unique."

"That's a nice way of putting it," I say, causing Edison to laugh. "More like a garage sale for misfits."

"Hey now, you said you liked the Zelda poster," Edison says with a pointed look.

I chuckle. "I did. The teenage boy in me was jealous when I saw it."

"Never too old to be prancing around the forest." Edison claps his hands together. "Okay, we should get to work, or else that brother of yours is going to have a conniption that we didn't accomplish anything."

"Can't have that." I dramatically roll my eyes.

"First thing's first...Regis isn't going to like working with Kelsey."

Uh, that's not what I was expecting him to say.

"Why the hell not?" I ask as I see Kelsey shift uncomfortably next to me.

Edison crosses one leg over the other and says, "I've worked with him a few times. He's a great guy, does amazing work, but when it comes to renovations, he has a certain esthetic. He likes things done his way, and sustainability isn't in his wheelhouse."

"Did Huxley know this when he hired him?"

"I warned him. He said you'd be able to handle it."

"Of course he did." I lean back on the couch, draping my arm behind Kelsey, and say, "What kind of trouble are we talking here? How much grief will this cause?"

"Enough to make you want to go back to Los Angeles." Edison cringes.

"Fuck," I mutter.

"Hold on, it might not be that bad," Kelsey says. "I can be quite agreeable and accommodating. I think we need to give Regis the benefit of the doubt first. He doesn't know what my plans are and I don't know what his plans are, so maybe we go into this blind and just see how it goes."

Spoken like a true rookie.

Regis stares, unblinking.

It doesn't take a mind reader to know exactly what he's thinking.

He DESPISES Kelsey.

Let me paint a picture for you.

Regis Stallone, born and bred Italian, straight from New Jersey with a heavy accent and a no-bullshit attitude, is decked out in worn paint-splattered jeans, a Henley top, construction vest, and a dented construction hat. His mustache has more character than the two assistants he brought along with him, and the tape measure that he keeps snapping up and down is his frustration meter. The more he opens it and snaps it shut, the closer and closer he's getting to lashing out.

Kelsey, charming, yet naïve Kelsey, in her high heels, pencil skirt, and skintight top, has come in hot with design ideas that have been approved in previous buildings of ours but, from the look on Regis's face, have no business being tossed around in the Angelica. Which, according to Regis, was designed to proclaim its intricate architecture, not save the earth.

Then there's me and Edison, standing between them, watching them volley ideas back and forth. Currently, we're on the topic of windows.

"Do you realize how old these windows are?" Regis asks. "These are casement windows, very rare. You can't possibly replace them."

"But don't you see? They can't even swing all the way open due to building code, and because they're original to the building, they don't have any insulation, meaning they have zero energy efficiency."

"You can't possibly be proposing to remove all of them?"

Kelsey nods with gusto. "I am. I've already written it in my notes."

Regis grows even more furious. "And what do you suppose you do with the windows? Toss them in a landfill? How sustainable is that?"

Ooh, he has Kelsey on that one.

"Actually," Kelsey says while flipping her notepad around, "I was going to suggest that we refurbish them and use them throughout the building. Since they're looking to make this into apartment buildings, you can fashion the old windows as room dividers in the individual apartments, or in the common spaces, like in the laundry room. I'd never suggest we toss anything into a landfill. As a matter of fact, I believe I'll talk to Huxley about an approval process. Nothing is tossed without our permission."

Okay…okay. Point for Kelsey.

"Do you understand the cost of replacing all these windows? These casings aren't standard size."

"Do you understand the type of impact we'll have if we do change them? The energy costs for the entire building? Actually, can you add installing a geothermal system for heat to your list? That will definitely cut costs on energy."

"And where do you suppose we dig for a geothermal system? If you haven't noticed, we're in the middle of the city. Jesus Christ." Regis then looks at me and says, "JP, a word." He walks away and I know I'm about to be on the receiving end of a rant. Just what I fucking want.

I start to walk after him when Kelsey tugs on my hand. "When he's done having a word, I'd like to have a word as well."

"About what?" I ask, noticing the trend already. Middleman. Fucking perfect.

"About what he's going to complain to you about. I need to know what he's saying about me."

"Paranoid much?" I ask.

"You know it's about me." Her eyes grow worried. "And if someone's trying to get me fired, I'd like to know why."

"I think you know why." I move away from her and join Regis in the other room.

But when he starts talking—I mean yelling—I know I won't need a second conversation with Kelsey, because given how thin these old walls are, she'll hear everything.

"You can't be fucking serious with this sustainable crap," Regis starts. "This is a historic building, so you can't strip it down and make it modern. Activists for the historic buildings in this city will have a field day with this, and I'm telling you right now, if I hadn't signed an NDA, I'd be headed to one of their meetings to let them know the kind of asinine ideas that woman out there has."

I put on my "face of the company" pants and gently say, "I understand your concerns about the integrity of the building, Regis. And we're just as concerned as you are. Preserving the history within these walls is just as vital to us as it is to you. But you need to know something. Kelsey is my colleague, and I will not tolerate you talking about her like that. She deserves just as much respect as the next person you work with. In addition, she's right. If we're going to open this building up to the public for the first time in over thirty years, we need to do it right. We need to make sure we meet today's needs with yesterday's intricate designs. Compromise, man, okay?"

"There's no possible way we can do a geothermal heating system. I'll cave on the windows if they're being utilized elsewhere, but the heating system can't physically be done."

"Okay, then maybe we can come up with another solution. I know this is our first time working together, but this isn't Kelsey's first time working with us. We value her opinion and ideas and I need you to do the same, or else we'll have to find someone else who can see our vision." I grip Regis on the shoulder. "And you won't want to miss out on working with us, especially with the kinds of plans we have for the future. Got it?"

Regis's mustache twitches as he nods. He's capitulating, but I know it's only temporary. The next two weeks will be a living nightmare when it comes to managing this man. This is why Huxley is in charge of this shit.

We move back to the living room. Kelsey is standing by herself, while Edison is off in the corner, talking quietly on the phone. When she looks up and makes eye contact with me, there's relief in her expression. There's no doubt she heard that entire conversation and it looks as if we'll need to figure out how to make these walls a lot thicker.

"I think we've done enough talking for today," I say. "We've walked the building; we've taken notes. How about you both write up your ideas according to Huxley's plans, how we can get it done, and then we can reconvene sometime in the next couple of days?"

Regis sticks his pencil behind his ear and then shakes my hand. To my surprise, he does the same for Kelsey.

I might hate this goddamn job, but it sure as hell looks like I'm good at it.

The car door shuts behind me and Kelsey quickly swivels in her seat, gratefulness spread all over her face.

"JP, I can't tell you how thankful I am that you stuck up for me when speaking with Regis."

I stick my phone in my suit pocket and buckle myself in. "It was no big deal."

She rests her hand on my thigh, drawing my attention. And because I'm a weak man, my mind goes right back to yesterday. My junk on her face…

Her breath…

Jesus Christ, man!

"It was a big deal to me, JP," she says. "I know the last thing you probably wanted was to play the middleman between me and Regis, but I heard what you said to him and it truly meant a lot to me. I'm not sure you know how important it was that you did it."

"Seriously, Kelsey, it was no big deal."

"No, you need to hear this." She pushes her hair behind her ear, exposing the column of her neck. I fight the urge to curl my fingers around her nape and bring her in closer. "You set the tone. Moving forward, hopefully, Regis will know that you honor my ideas. You established this is teamwork and not just a project run by men. I owe you, JP."

"You owe me nothing," I say, looking out the window now. Kelsey has been working with Cane Enterprises for several months now, and she's proven herself to Huxley, Breaker, and me. She works hard and she's knowledgeable, not a lofty plant hugger without specific and wise goals. Cane Enterprises has a reputation—is respected for quality—and there's no way in hell we'd align ourselves with anything or anyone we didn't believe saw our vision. Today wasn't about simply "saving" Kelsey, but ensuring we have a team that works cohesively. Surely, she knows that by now.

"If it was Huxley or Breaker, they would've done the same exact thing. We protect our company; you're a part of that; therefore, I protected you today. Don't think anything of it."

"Okay, well, for what it's worth, thank you."

Quietly, I say, "You're welcome."

CHAPTER 11
KELSEY

Kelsey: Welcome, listener, to the *Meant to Be Podcast*, where we talk to madly-in-love couples about the way they met. Arlo and Greer, thank you so much for joining me today. Please, tell us how you met.

Greer: Do you want to tell the story, or do you want me to?

Arlo: I don't think you want me to tell the story.

Greer: Probably not. You'll most likely include details that I don't want everyone to know.

Arlo: Details like…the kitchen island?

Greer: Okay, okay, keep your mouth shut, mister.

Arlo: Why don't you tell her about the stink smell…or the chipmunk voice…or the blue pee?

Greer: I assure you, Kelsey, all three of those items aren't related in any way to the kitchen island or anything sexual, for that matter. He's referring to the pranks I pulled on him.

Kelsey: Pranks? Oh, please, tell me more.

Greer: It all started when I was hired to teach English at the school Arlo was teaching at. He didn't want to hire me because he thought my way of teaching was too progressive for his stuffy, old-school mentality.

Arlo: She used CliffsNotes and movies to portray the written word.

Greer: Oh my God, do we need to get into this now?

Kelsey: So, I can see you guys hit it off really well at first.

Greer: Not even close. He was a hot prick in a cardigan. We hated each other. That's where the blue pee comes in. Sort of pranked him a bit to get back at him.

Arlo: I seriously thought something was wrong with me. Blue pee isn't something a guy should ever see in the urinal.

Greer: But then, he made this gesture—he dressed up like Jay Gatsby on my 'dress like a literary character' day and…well, it was the first step in the direction of falling for each other.

Arlo: It was hard not to try to impress her or to keep away from her, for that matter. And when she went out on a date with someone else, I knew I was being a complete fool and, if I didn't snatch her up right then and there, I'd regret it forever.

Greer: I'm glad he did, because I've never been more madly in love.

Mom: How is San Francisco, honey? I haven't been in years. I'm quite jealous.

I read my mom's text message and smile as I lie on my stomach on my bed and text her back.

Kelsey: It's beautiful. I haven't been able to explore yet, but soon. Just walking around, though, smelling the ocean, feeling the breeze. Makes me want to move up here.

Mom: Oh no, you don't. No daughter of mine is moving away from me.

Kelsey: Funny you say that after you were begging Lottie to move out.

Mom: Move out, yes. Move away, no.

Kelsey: Ahh, I see.

Mom: And how is living with JP?

Kelsey: Can you not fish for information? I promise you, nothing is happening between us. Which reminds me, I left my food in the microwave. I need to get it.

Mom: But he's so handsome.

Kelsey: Bye, Mother.

I set my phone down on my bed and head toward the kitchen, but pause. I look at myself in the mirror and scan my outfit. Joggers and a white tank top with no bra. Semi revealing, but not revealing enough, plus JP isn't home. He went out somewhere. Nothing to worry about.

I'm not going to change clothes to retrieve my food from the microwave.

I head out of my room and down the hall to the kitchen, debating if I should start a new show—such a commitment—or find a movie that appeals to me—also a commitment. If I choose a show, that means I have something to watch for—

"Errrrrrrrm."

I pause.

What was that?

I don't move.

I hold my breath, waiting to hear the noise again.

The way the building is mapped out, you wouldn't hear the penthouse on the other side, and I know I'm alone because JP said he was going out. So, does that mean…? Is someone in here?

My heart pounds wildly in my chest as I creep forward, listening, waiting...

"Urggghhh."

There it is again.

This time, the sound sends a chill down my spine, and the hairs on the back of my neck rise.

That isn't a normal building creaking sound. That's a sound that comes from a human. Or a suffering animal.

Or a suffering human.

Something is suffering.

Creeping forward, I try to stay as quiet as I can so I can locate the sound.

"Uhhhhhhhrrrrrr."

My head snaps to the right, down the hallway toward JP's room.

Since the only light on in the main living space is in the kitchen, I can see that there's no light showing through the crack under JP's door.

So he's definitely not home.

Which means...there's either a murderer in there, a suffering animal, or a ghost.

I shuffle to the kitchen, keeping my eyes on his door the entire time as I haphazardly reach for a wooden spoon from the utensils crock on the counter. Spoon in hand, I creep toward his hallway, only to stop when I hear the noise again.

"Frrrrrrrreeeerm."

Oh God.

Oh God.

OH GOD!

I can practically taste my heartbeat as I move closer. My pulse zaps against my neck, stiffening my shoulders. Why am I doing this alone? I should wait for JP to get home.

"Uhhhhhh."

I squeeze my eyes shut and nervously run in place, my feet lightly padding on the floor.

Turn around, you idiot, this is how people in scary movies die. They investigate the sound. But just like every other moron in a scary movie, I don't run to my room and call for help. I don't even grab a freaking knife.

Nope, manned with a wooden spoon—the worst it can do is toss a salad—I slide closer and closer to his room until I hear it…a constant pumping sound. Like…oh God, like someone is getting stabbed.

"Fuuuuuu."

Stabbed!

They're getting stabbed in his room right now. Wait…what if JP is getting stabbed and I'm just standing here, outside of his door with a wooden spoon, doing nothing? What if he came home without me knowing and was attacked?

My nipples grow hard in fear.

I nearly choke on my saliva.

And before I can stop myself, I pull down on the doorknob, then kick the door open and accompany it with a warrior scream that nearly deafens me.

"EEEEEEE AHHHHHHHHH!" I yell, wielding my spoon at the air.

"What the fuck!" JP's voice calls out.

My eyes land on the bed, where he pops up, completely and utterly naked…and holding a pillow in front of his crotch.

What is…?

Oh no.

Oh God.

OH, DEAR HEAVEN.

That wasn't a suffering animal.

Or a suffering human.

Or a ghost.

Or a stabbing.

That was…

Oh, sweet lord, that was JP jacking off.

The spoon falls from my hand as I quickly cover my eyes and spin away.

"Oh, wow…sorry. You're, uh, you're home, having private time." Eyes still covered, I head in the direction of the door, but run right into the wall, banging my nose and forehead on the hard surface. "Oh, fuck," I say as I feel around with my other hand, trying to find the doorway.

I turn, spin.

Lose track of where I'm going.

And before I know it, my hand is caressing a very stiff body.

"Ahh," I yell again, dropping the hand covering my eyes only to find my other hand passing over JP's nipples. "Oh shit, sorry. That's your, uh, that's your man chest. Your nipple. I was just rubbing your nipple. Not on purpose. Not because I wanted to."

"Kelsey, what the fuck are you doing in here?"

"Great question." I offer him a thumbs-up. "And I have an equally great explanation. You see, I went to grab my dinner when I heard this noise. I thought it was a ghost or a murderer, or even a suffering animal, like a squirrel caught in a wall or something like that. You never know in these old buildings. Anyway, I thought I'd check it out, and then when I got closer, I thought you were being stabbed. It really sounded like a stabbing, not that I listen to stabbing noises, but, you know, the movies prepare you for such sounds, so I came in here, attempting to scare away the stabber."

He stares at me, his face falling flat. "With a wooden spoon?"

"I didn't say I was being smart about it. I was just trying to be a hero without a plan. I see now that maybe that wasn't the best idea."

"You should've fucking knocked. Jesus." He winces, and because I can't help myself, I glance down at his pillow and then back up at him.

"Did you get to finish?"

"Does it look like I got to finish?"

"Well, I don't know. Maybe you were in the middle of coming when I came in." I reach out and touch the tip of his nipple—still not sure why. "Your nipple is hard."

He takes a step forward, closing the space between us, and pokes my nipple, dead center.

"Ow," I complain, covering my nipple.

"Your nipple is hard. Does that mean you're coming as we speak?"

"Don't poke my nipple like that. It hurts."

"It didn't hurt."

"Yes, it did."

"No, it didn't."

"YES, it did!" I say as I reach out and poke his nipple the same way he poked mine. He doesn't even flinch. So, I do it again. And again. And—

He pokes my other nipple.

A gasp pops out of me as I cover that boob, too.

The actual audacity of this man.

"I can't believe you poked both of my nipples."

"You poked mine," he says, standing there in a face-off, testing me.

"This isn't a tit-for-tit type of thing."

"Is this something you do often to know the rules about it? Barge in when someone's jacking off and then start poking their nipples?" He pokes my hand.

I grow angrier and poke him back.

He pokes me in the chest.

I poke him in the abdomen.

He swats my shin with his foot.

I cry out in shock and then swat at him with my foot, followed by a poke.

He fakes to the right and then pokes me on the left.

"Urgggh." I release both my breasts and go in for a double poke, but he's just swift enough to poke me in the nipple one more time before stepping away. Before I know what I'm doing, I run at him at full force and tackle him to the ground, his pillow falling to the side, me falling on top of his stomach, straddling him.

And like the casual ass that he is, he puts his hands behind his head and stares up at me.

"If this is what you wanted, babe, you should've just asked."

My teeth grind together and I say, "I was trying to save you."

"Likely story."

"I was," I say, more irritated. "I said I owe you, and that's what I meant. I was throwing my body at your attacker."

"You were throwing your body at me."

I growl and then poke him again.

He pokes me back, this time, lifting my breast while he does it.

"Stop that!" I yell.

"You stop it."

"I did stop."

"No, you started it again."

"Because you're irritating me."

"Because you interrupted my man time."

"Your *man time*?" I pause, letting his words sink in, and for some reason—maybe the way he said it, the words he chose—they hit me in a way I wasn't expecting. I start to giggle.

Then giggle some more.

Then snort.

Then chuckle.

A laugh...

"What's so fucking funny?"

"You said *man time*."

"So? What do you call it?"

"Not *man time*." I laugh some more, the obnoxious, nervous, but also can't-control-it laughter.

That causes him to laugh.

Smile lines crease his eyes. Joy overtakes his expression. And then, we're laughing together, to the point that I roll off his stomach and fall to the ground. I catch him pulling the pillow back over his crotch so I don't see anything as his chest moves up and down with laughter.

After what seems like forever, I turn toward him and say, "I'm sorry I interrupted your *man time*. Next time, can you attempt to not sound like a suffering animal?"

He passes his hands over his eyes. "I'm never going to be able to come again without worrying what I sound like. Thank you for that."

"You're welcome." I sit up and say, "I think we needed this."

"You walking in on me jacking off?" he asks with humor.

"No, not that per se, just a moment of levity to break up the tension."

"Trust me, babe, the tension is still there since you didn't let me come. Probably worse than ever."

I wince. "Well, then, let me let you get back to your...man time." We both stand, him still covering himself. "Try not to be so loud this time."

"Yeah, trust me, I'll be putting a goddamn sock in my mouth from now on."

"Whatever gets you off."

We both smirk and then I leave before I burst into another fit of laughter.

"How was the rest of your night?" I ask when JP walks into the kitchen the next morning, freshly showered and dressed in a suit and tie, an outfit I see him in regularly. For some reason, his choice of clothing feels different today.

Maybe because of what happened last night. Walking in on him during his "man time." It was kind of sexy, knowing that he was doing that while I was in the penthouse. That he didn't care that I was nearby. I thought about it all last night. Did he want me to hear him? Was he taunting me? That would be true to his personality, to do something like that.

"The rest of my night?" JP asks, briefly looking over his shoulder as he gets his coffee. "Explosive."

I swallow hard.

Explosive, as in…

"Well, that's good to know."

He turns and leans against the counter as he brings the mug to his lips. "Is it good to know?"

"Sure, everyone deserves…relief. I interrupted the process, so I'm glad you got to finish."

"Seems like an odd thing to say to someone."

"Yeah, I was just thinking that." I push my plate to the side and sit back in my chair at the dining room table. "I honestly wasn't sure what I was going to say to you this morning. That was the best I could come up with."

"It was weak."

"I know. Maybe this is why I'm still single, because I have weak repartee."

"Nah, that's not it."

"Oh? Do you have a theory about why I'm still single?"

He slowly nods while lowering his mug. "Trying too hard."

"How am I trying too hard?"

"Because you're always looking for the next date. Why not sit back and wait for something to happen? You never know, the person you're meant to be with might be right in front of your face."

I roll my eyes. "I've tried the waiting game. Nothing has happened. Maybe I should start walking around neighborhoods like Lottie did."

"Could help." He smiles and then takes a seat at the table. "Maybe if you stop looking, it'll find you." Then he shrugs and says, "Plus, you're hot. It's not like you don't arouse interest."

"I have none, JP. Edwin was the best I could do."

"Edwin was a tool." He rotates his mug on the table. "There has to be something you're more interested in than finding love."

"Well, I do have this podcast, but it's focused around love."

He chuckles. "What's it called?"

"*Meant to Be*. I interview couples on how they met and found love." Sheepishly, I shrug. "I guess I just love love. I enjoy origin stories, meet-cutes, and the different ways people find each other. It's fascinating to me. I also like taking aquatic classes."

"Aquatic classes?" he asks. "Tell me more about that. Like, aerobics in the water?"

I nod. "Yeah. I'm easily the youngest in the class, but that doesn't bother me. I just like working out in the water and the music they play is old-school love songs. So, it works for me."

"Do you wear a one-piece?"

"Of course."

He shakes his head. "Such a shame."

"I'm not about to work out with a bunch of old ladies in a two-piece. I have a respectable one-piece."

"Color?"

"Red."

"Nice." He takes another sip of his coffee. "What's your plan for today?"

"I was going to finalize my ideas for the renovations. Maybe go for a walk. I have meetings lined up for tomorrow, but nothing today. What about you?"

He checks the expensive matte-black watch wrapped around his thick wrist and says, "I have a meeting in about thirty minutes that I have to run to. Want to meet me for lunch?"

"Oh, uh, sure," I answer, caught off guard. Meet him for lunch? As in… just the two of us? That doesn't seem like him. Then again, I think last night might have broken the ice for him. *For us.*

He was brooding on the plane to San Francisco.

But I apologized for the gala.

He defended me to Regis.

And we broke the tension.

Maybe this is the next step.

He taps the table with his knuckle and rises from the chair. "I'll text you the time and place. See you later, Kelsey."

"Bye," I say with an awkward wave, watching him walk away.

Huh…

Maybe this trip won't be as bad as I first thought.

"Pickle-flavored chips? I don't know about that," I say as I stare at the bag of chips JP insisted on sharing.

He reaches for the bag, pops it open, and tilts it toward me. "Try one. I promise you'll like it."

"And what if I don't?"

"Then you need new taste buds."

"You aren't always right, you know," I say while taking a chip.

"Most of the time, I am. And I'm right about these chips." He takes one as well, and together, we place them in our mouths. The heavenly, seasoned chip introduces my tongue to a world of flavors. Like tasty fireworks blasting off in my mouth.

And damn it…he's right. They're good.

They're really good.

Some of the most flavorful chips I've ever had.

"What do you think?" he asks.

Not wanting to hand him the satisfaction of me liking them, I just shrug and say, "Eh, they're okay."

The corner of his lip twitches as he whispers, "Liar." Then he pulls the bag closer to him and adds, "If they're just *okay*, I guess I'll eat them myself."

Should've seen that coming.

I groan and hold out my hand. "Fine...they're really freaking good and I want more, please."

That causes him to laugh. He hands me the bag and I take a nice fistful of chips for my plate. "See, always right," he says.

"And humble, too." I pop a few more chips in my mouth. "So, what was today's meeting about?"

He sighs and says, "Just a meeting with Edison. We went around and looked at some other buildings Huxley wanted me to check out."

"Anything good?"

"Not really. Not worth our time."

"How can you tell if it's worth your time or not?"

He brushes his hand with a napkin, cleaning the heavy pickle seasoning from his fingers. "Location is always the first thing. The purpose of the building—will it be worth the time and energy we put into it to make money? And then, of course, renovations. There was also no character to these buildings. They were just kind of there. We've made plenty of money on generic buildings, you've seen them around LA, and we have a few in New York City now, too. They've done the job, but now we're more interested in unique buildings."

"Passion projects?"

"Sort of," he answers. "Huxley really wants to expand, hence why he partnered with you. Sometimes I think nothing will be good enough, that he'll constantly keep pressing to be the best, but I'm not sure what the best is."

"Meanwhile, your workload is filling up."

"Exactly." He glances out the window of the sandwich shop and says, "I'm surprised you met up with me for lunch. I thought you hated me too much to do such a thing."

"I don't hate you. Hell, I thought you hated me. I was surprised that you asked me to lunch. Wasn't sure if it was a ploy to do something else."

"Like what?" He chuckles.

"I don't know, plant some sort of chip in my bedroom so you knew what I was doing at all times."

"Jesus." He laughs. "What kind of psychopath do you think I am?"

"Apparently, a creepy one. I don't know. It's just nice that you're talking to me."

"I've always talked to you, Kelsey; I just vary the tone."

"No, you were doing the silent treatment there for a bit."

"Because you pissed me off," he counters. "I was being a nice guy that night and you treated me like I was an insensitive asshole."

"I know, and I'm sorry. I think I was just thrown off by that entire evening, and I wasn't in the best frame of mind. Can I ask, what were your intentions for that night? You asked me to dance, why?"

"Because." He pops another chip in his mouth and chews. "I wanted to make sure that you had some fun. Getting run over by an old man wasn't the plan. But at least that brought you a little joy."

"And then Edwin and Genesis took off. Reminds me of *When Harry Met Sally*—you know, when they go on a double date and their dates go off with each other. That was us."

"You lucked out, then. I was much better company than Edwin. Better to look at, too."

"Ah, there's that humility."

"I'm humble. I'm just showing you that I know my worth. Nothing wrong with that."

"I suppose not." I finish my last chip and ask, "So when we got back to your place, what was your intention?"

"To kick you to your car and send you on your way. I had a date with some chocolate-covered cherries that night and the hell if I was sharing with you."

"Stop; no, you did not."

He holds his heart. "Swear by it. I went back to my house, sat in my empty living room because I didn't have any furniture at that point, and ate five chocolate-covered cherries while I scrolled through Twitter."

"I'm having a hard time believing you. You don't seem like the kind of guy who kicks back with a box of chocolate-covered cherries."

"Well, I am," he says. "They're my kryptonite. I'll do anything for them and I have a pantry stocked with boxes. Queen Anne's, to be precise, because I know that was your next question."

"You're serious?"

"Yes. Don't believe me? Text Huxley."

"I'm not going to bother him with that."

"Fine, I will." He pulls his phone from his pocket and starts typing away. He presses *send*, and then, with an air of arrogance, he takes a sip of his drink. His phone soon buzzes on the table. He doesn't look at the answer. He simply unlocks the screen and turns it toward me.

JP: Sitting here with Kelsey. She doesn't believe I'm obsessed with chocolate-covered cherries. Set her straight.

Huxley: He has at least thirty boxes in his pantry. It's an obsession.

I glance at JP, who smirks now. "Told you."

"Wow…that's something I never would've guessed about you."

"Sometimes you have to get to know someone first, Kelsey, before you start trying to put them in a lane in your mind. There's a lot you don't know about me. Stick around. I'm sure you'll find out more."

"Yes, I probably will. Just like I found out you don't mind masturbating while other people are home."

With a grin, he winks. "Precisely."

"What are you up to tonight?" Lottie asks over the phone as I finish my nighttime skincare regimen.

If you were wondering, I wash my face, pat it dry, apply my nighttime wrinkle-free serum, followed by moisturizer, and then lock it in with a touch of rose oil. I follow up the whole process by applying lotion to the rest of my body.

"Nothing special. Spent dinner on my own again, second night in a row. JP had a meeting with someone, so I just ordered some cauliflower mac and cheese and called it a night. I'm planning to read a book in the living room because the skyline at night is so beautiful. I want to soak it in as much as I can."

"Sounds…riveting. Here's an idea—when he gets home, why don't you try to walk in on his man time again?"

Yeah, I told her about the other night. I had to. She's my sister. But I didn't tell her about the lunch, because I didn't want her getting all weird about it. It was a simple lunch, nothing too crazy, nothing to talk about.

"I'm never going near that room again."

"Come on, after that nipple poking, you can't tell me you're not interested in seeing what it's like to be kissed by JP. Now is the time. You guys are alone, together, might as well test it out."

"Have you hit yourself on the head? That isn't what we're here for and there's no way I'm going there."

"Are you saying you don't want him? Because I don't believe that. The Cane brothers are another breed, and it's clear there's chemistry between you and JP. Find out how hot it could be between you guys."

"JP doesn't want me in that way. There was nothing sexual about the nipple poking. If there was the slightest bit of sexiness to that, he would've attempted something when I was sitting on his chest. And, also, sure, I think he's hot, but I don't want to go there with him. I'm not looking for a one-night stand. I'm looking for love."

"If he's anything like Huxley, you won't want it to be one night."

"He'll want one night. You know he doesn't do relationships and I don't even know why we're talking about this, as nothing is happening between us. That whole ordeal in his room was an accident. I have no intention of furthering any sort of physical touching."

"Okay, but tell me this—how did it feel poking his nipple?"

Oddly good.

And after the initial shock of him poking me wore off, I kind of liked it.

The playfulness.

It was a different side of him, and I appreciated it. But I need to put a stop to Lottie's incessant need to get me to think of JP in another way.

"It was simple. It's not like some magical spark erupted between us. It was brief and awkward and we didn't talk about it after. I'm telling you, nothing is going on, so just drop it."

"Ugh," she groans. "Why are you ruining my dreams?"

"Your dreams? What on earth do you mean?"

"Brother-brother, sister-sister couples."

"I feel like you didn't say that in the right order."

"You know what I mean," she huffs. "It would be so cool if, as sisters, we dated brothers."

"You're not just dating Huxley, you're marrying him. Which, by the way, how was the floral meeting?"

"Boring," she says. "Huxley insists on the best for our wedding and I keep telling him it's not necessary. He told me today he wants to fly in some Italian designer to make my dress. I told him he was nuts and that I could just go to some boutique here in LA. You should've seen the disgusted look on his face. As if the thought of having to shop for my own dress is so far beneath him. The thing is, Kelse, I just want to be married; I don't care about all the fanfare."

"But it matters to Huxley, right?"

"Yes," she drawls. "Which means I should just go along with it. You know, he was never this flashy when we first started our whole relationship farce."

"Uh, I beg to differ. Do you not remember the designer clothes and expensive lingerie he forced you to wear? People didn't even see your lingerie, and yet, Huxley insisted you wear what *he* chose, and nothing cost less than one hundred dollars apiece."

"Ah, I guess you're right. Which reminds me, how are you liking those nighttime rompers?"

"Oh my God, Lottie. I love them so much. They're so comfortable. I brought them with me to sleep in."

"Wait…that's what you took to sleep in while you're there?"

"Yeah, why?"

She laughs. "Okay, sure, Kelsey, nothing is going to happen between you and JP."

"I brought a robe to go over it. Listen, I'm not going to sacrifice my comfort because it may be considered indecent. I don't plan on walking around in them. I'll always have a robe on."

"If you say so. But let me tell you this: you have that date with Derek in a couple of days. If you're in any way involved with JP, please don't hurt Derek's feelings. Ellie would kill me."

"You know I wouldn't do that. I'm actually excited about the date. I brought a few dress options for that night. You can help me pick one."

"Okay, good. Oh, hey, Huxley's giving me bedroom eyes, so I should probably go."

"Shocking—you two are going to have sex, what else is new?"

"You sound jealous."

No, just horny.

"Have fun, sis. Good night." I hang up the phone and then go to my room to pick up my book, a rom-com about three siblings who go back to their hometown to throw an anniversary party for their parents, but then all hell breaks loose when their personalities clash and their love lives are tested. I've heard nothing but great things about it.

I head back to the living room. I switch on the light, illuminating the space...*and* the man standing there in nothing but a pair of sweats, a glass of water in his hand.

"Jesus HELL ON EARTH!" I scream as I stumble backwards. "JP," I huff out. "What the hell are you doing, standing in the dark like that?"

The lightest of smirks pulls at his lips. "Just grabbing some water." His eyes scan me, taking in my robe and bare legs. "What are you doing?"

"I was going to read out here and enjoy the skyline. God, when did you get home?" I attempt to calm my racing heart as I make my way to the couch.

"About ten minutes ago. Didn't feel like saying hi to you."

"Well, aren't you kind? You were just going to wait around in the dark to scare me?"

"How was I supposed to know you were going to read in here? Seems kind of weird to me if you plan on reading a book while enjoying the skyline because you can't do both at the same time."

"Yes, I can," I say with a tilt of my chin. "Every so often I can look up from my book and enjoy the scenery, and then go back to reading."

"The book can't be that good if you're looking up from it."

I take a deep breath and slowly let it out. "Is there a reason you're sticking around and not retreating back to your space?"

"Question for you."

"Oh, please delight me with your inquiry," I say, folding one leg over the other.

His eyes stray to my legs for only a moment before he shifts on his feet. "Friday night, I've been invited to the mayor's house for a ball. Wasn't sure if you wanted to tag along."

He's asking me out again.

Well, not asking me out, like on a date, but asking to spend more time with me, and I'd be lying if I said it doesn't thrill me that he wants that.

But...hell. I'm busy Friday night.

"Friday night?" I ask and wince. "That's when I have that date with Derek. I don't want to stand him up."

JP's face tightens as he asks, "Date, huh? Still going out with that guy?"

"Well, seeing as though I'm currently in the dating ring, I would say yes. But if this is a work thing, I can see if Derek can reschedule."

"It's not. Go on your date. Find love. I'm sure he'll be the man of your dreams." From the clipped tone, the way he's ducking away from the conversation, it's clear he's flip-flopped from the "warming up" JP back to his grumpy persona.

"You don't have to be a dick about it, JP."

"Didn't think I was being a dick."

I grip my book tighter. "Your sarcasm is unmistakable."

"I'm sorry you see it that way."

"I don't see it that way, JP; that's how you're acting."

"What do you want me to do? Throw a party for you because you finally have a date?"

"Hey," I say, feeling insulted. "Don't throw that in my face."

"Throw what in your face?" He pushes his hand through his hair and I can see how his muscles contract with his annoyance. Well, guess what? I'm annoyed, too.

"The fact that I don't get many dates. Using the word *finally* in your sentence was a low blow."

"Jesus Christ, are you going to pick apart every sentence I say to you?"

"No, but if you're going to be rude to me, then I'm going to point it out."

"I'm not being rude. Christ, stop being so sensitive."

"Me, sensitive?" I ask, pointing at my chest. "How am I being sensitive? You're the one whose mood swings like goddamn Tarzan on a vine. For Christ's sake, I can't keep up with you. Just moments ago, we were cool, and now you're being mean. Is this because I can't go with you to the ball? Newsflash, JP, people need some notice."

"Don't flatter yourself," he says and turns toward his bedroom.

"Why are you like this?"

"Like what?"

"We were having a nice time. We had a great lunch, we were communicating well, and now you're dismissing me."

"How do you want me to act? Do you want me to gush over your date?"

I want him to be normal.

I want him to not push me away.

I want him to...to... God, I'm so irritated that I can't think straight.

I just want to make him understand. When I don't answer, he starts to walk away again, but nope, that's not a choice I'll give him.

We *will* be talking about this.

And we'll be talking about this now.

I toss my book on the coffee table in front of me and walk up to him. I grab his hand, pull him to the couch, and force him to sit down.

"What the hell are you doing?"

No answers. He doesn't deserve them. I push him back against the cushion of the couch, straddle his lap, and take a seat.

"Uh, Kelsey..."

"I'm not getting up until you change your attitude." There, deal with that!

"Is this another attempt to trap me again?"

"Yes. And don't get any funny ideas. I'm not trying to do anything... sexual, but knowing you, this position is satisfactory to you, therefore, this is where I'll sit, on your lap, until you can talk to me without a sarcastic tone in your voice."

"Might take a bit," he says, sipping water from his glass.

I steal the glass from him and set it on the end table. I push him back on the couch with my other hand.

"Man, I didn't know you were a dominatrix. That's a hidden gem."

"Shut up," I say. "God, you're so annoying."

"And yet, you choose to be in my company."

"I choose peace and that means getting you to stop being a dick. So… tell me something about you."

"What?" he asks, a question on his brow.

"Tell me something, anything. We're getting to know each other right now. Call it a company get-to-know-you. Oh, hey, okay…how about two truths and a lie? You know, that icebreaker game."

"Does it look like I'm the type of guy who plays that sort of game?"

"Humor me…please," I beg.

His eyes scan me and I can see him waffling between saying something snarky and giving in to my pleading. If he says no, I'm just going to continue begging him. I want to make things at least okay between us, for the sake of our working relationship.

I wait a few more breaths and then finally…

He heaves out a heavy, "Fine," and then scratches the side of his jaw. "Two truths and a lie…okay. How about this? I once went scuba diving with whales. I think I have the greatest job in the world. And winter is my favorite season."

"Well, that's easy. Scuba diving with whales seems like a rich-person activity, so that's true. You clearly love your job, so…winter isn't your favorite season, which makes sense since you're a born-and-raised California boy."

"*Errrrr*, wrong," he says, making a buzzing sound.

"Really? You never went scuba diving with whales?"

"No, I swam with whales. In Mo'orea, an island of French Polynesia to be exact. It's a sanctuary for humpback whales. One of the best vacations of my life."

I growl out in frustration. "JP, if you're not going to take this seriously—"

"Who says I'm not taking it seriously?"

I attempt to get off his lap, but his hands clamp down on my thighs, holding me in place.

"I told two truths and a lie."

In utter disbelief, I say, "So, you're telling me you hate your job?"

"Yes. I am," he answers matter-of-factly.

"Wait... Are you being serious? You hate it?"

"Yes. I hate my job."

"But...you make it seem like you enjoy it. I'm confused. You have your own company with your brothers, you get to work with them day in and day out, you have your own schedule, and you get to stay in places like this." I gesture around the room. "What can you possibly hate about all of that?"

He shakes his head and says, "Yeah, didn't think you'd understand." He goes to move me, but this time, I'm the one who stays put.

"Hold on." I press my fingers to his chest. "You're being honest, you hate it?"

"How many times do I have to say it?"

"I'm sorry," I reply. "I'm just confused. You've been very convincing that you enjoy what you do. Why do you hate it?"

"Let me ask you this—what do you like about your job?"

"Well, besides the obvious of having my own business and the complexities of experiencing the growth and downfalls, I love it because I feel like I'm helping make this world a better place to live. There are studies that go into detail about the therapeutic process of organizing spaces and how it can act as a calming technique for people who have to live and work in that space. And on top of that, I'm spreading the word about sustainability, which alone makes this job all worth it."

"You feel like you're making a difference."

I nod.

"That's where I fall flat. I don't think I'm doing anything in this damn life of mine that's worth something. Sure, I have money, more money than any of us or any lineage to follow could spend in a lifetime, and it just keeps coming in, multiplying. There's no stopping it because there's no stopping my brothers. They want to take over the world and I'm only really along for the ride."

"But you're not money-greedy humans. You donate a lot of money to organizations throughout LA. You're leaders in real estate when it comes to best business practices—minus Huxley's 'fake fiancée' thing with Lottie—but you're honest men, trustworthy. You're not hurting anyone."

"Yeah, but we're not helping anyone. We're only helping ourselves."

"That's not true," I say. "Lottie specifically asked Huxley why he kept working when they first started seeing each other. He said he had all the money he could possibly need, but he continued because if he didn't work, if he didn't expand, then the people who relied on him couldn't afford a life for their families. He keeps working so his employees can keep working."

"And Huxley can say that, because it's true, but my job doesn't warrant the accolades Huxley and Breaker receive. I'm just the public relations face. Hell, some days, I have nothing to do. The only reason why you work with me is because I'm the one who could handle the additional workload, which is barely anything since you pretty much do everything on your own. I get a paycheck, but for nothing."

"Some people would be pleased with that, you know, especially your paycheck."

"Yes, but when you have to live up to your brothers' reputations, it's brutal."

I subconsciously rub his chest and say, "I can understand that." I attempt to get off his lap again, since he's talking—finally—but once again, he keeps me where I'm at. Okay, not ready to let go just yet, that's fine. "Then, can I ask you, what is it that you want to do?"

He shrugs. "Still trying to figure that out."

"Would you leave the company?"

He shakes his head. "No, my brothers depend on me. They're very private people and trust practically no one. If I left, they'd have to take on my job responsibilities. They wouldn't hire someone outside of the family for that."

"That doesn't make sense, though. You're not happy."

He shrugs. "Maybe that's my life. Unhappy."

"That's not fair to you."

"Well, Kelsey, sometimes life isn't fair."

There's the pessimist.

"You don't have to put yourself in purgatory in order to help your brothers. I'm sure if you spoke to them, they'd want to know that you're not happy."

"You'd think," he mutters and then blows out a heavy breath. Now he attempts to move me, but like this push-and-pull game we've been playing, I'm the one to stay put this time.

"I still need to do two truths and a lie."

"Right." He settles back into the couch and waits. I can see that his mood has shifted again—actually, I'm not sure it was ever not sour. But instead of being a grump, he talked to me. Looks like I have so much more work to do. "What are your two truths and a lie?"

In a cheery tone, I say, "Since you asked."

He rolls his eyes again.

"Let's see. I like to collect magnets. I've always said I'd collect a magnet from every new place I visit, but I haven't been many places, so it's a sad collection. I have a plant in my apartment that I've had since college. His name is Boris and we have a mutual understanding that I'll always water him and he'll never die on me. And I plan the color of my underwear for each day of the working week. Weekends are a free-for-all. And before you ask, Monday is red. Tuesday is pink. Wednesday is black. Thursday is green, because I once heard green is for Thursdays, because that's when you make the money, when you should work the hardest. And Friday is white."

He's silent. Blinks.

And then scratches the side of his jaw. "All three were in-depth. Frankly, it's disturbing how easily you rattled those off. Makes me believe you're some secret operative."

I wiggle my eyebrows. "Better watch your back."

He gives my answers some thought. "The first one seems like something you'd do, but you only have like...five magnets."

"Four, to be exact. But it's a collection nonetheless."

"And a plant named Boris feels on-brand for you, but so does the underwear, but my guess is you messed up the days of the week so instead of Friday being white, it's actually black, because that's a typical date night."

My jaw falls open as I stare down at him. "How the hell did you guess that?"

"You might be able to think quick on your feet, but I can smell bullshit from a mile away. You're a romantic on a dating journey and I'm assuming, given your innocence, wearing black on Friday, date night, is daring for you. Just makes sense."

I fold my arms over my chest now and ask, "Okay, so what's the order of the rest of my underwear?"

He pauses for a moment and then holds his fingers up. "Monday is white, to start the week off on a fresh note. Tuesday is pink because you seem to be the type of girl who would have a lot of pink underwear so it fits in on a Tuesday. Wednesday is red for hump day. Thursday...well, that's the wild card. I kind of believe the whole green money-making thing, so I'm going to say that's right. And then black on Friday. The weekends are probably when you wear fun underwear. Like some pink thong with a heart." When I don't say anything, he says, "I'm right, aren't I?"

I slip off his lap, and he actually lets me this time. "Unfortunately, you are."

He chuckles, and even though it annoys me that, apparently, I'm so predictable, I'm glad that he's found something humorous.

"But I do want you to know that I'm not that innocent."

"Sure." He gets up from the couch and smooths down his shorts before picking up his glass of water.

"I'm not." I stand as well. "I've done plenty of noninnocent things in my lifetime."

He turns. "Like what?"

Yeah, Kelsey...like what?

How come nothing is coming to mind? I do plenty of things that wouldn't be considered innocent.

"Face it, you're as innocent as they come."

He starts to walk away, so I shout, "Vibrator."

The corner of his lip quirks up when he faces me again.

I straighten my robe, clenching it tighter. "I have a vibrator. There, that's not innocent."

"What kind of vibrator?"

"You know...the kind that vibrates," I say, hating myself. "It's pink."

"Of course it's pink." He chuckles. "Not innocent, Kelsey. Just about every woman has a vibrator. And from my guess, you probably use it every Wednesday to go along with your red underwear."

God...why is he right again?

He reaches the kitchen and refills his water. "Face it, you're as innocent as they come. If your day-of-the-week underwear doesn't say it, then your inability to tell me—in detail—the kind of vibrator you have is."

"It's pink." I throw my arms up. "What else do you want from me?"

He grips the kitchen counter and his eyes connect with mine, his dark brows shadowing his light-green eyes. "Pulse rate, settings, girth, length, and attachments. I want to know if you were too scared to even look at vibrators with a clit stimulator, so you just went with a common stick."

My lips rub together.

"That's what you got, wasn't it?"

"What does it matter the kind of…er, pulse rate it has? I masturbate, so, therefore, I'm not innocent."

He drags his hand over his face and then moves toward his bedroom. "Okay, Kelsey."

"Hey," I call out, but he doesn't stop. I've been known as innocent my entire life and I've really attempted to break through that label—as I don't like it—but I can't have him thinking that. So, I untie my robe and drop it to the ground. "Would you call this outfit innocent?" I ask.

"A robe is innocent," he says, not turning around.

"I'm not wearing a robe."

He pauses and then slowly turns. I'm wearing my black lace romper. It's a tank top with a deep V neckline, cinched at the waist, and then the attached shorts have high slits that blow open from the lightest of breezes. It's the most comfortable piece of clothing I have and, yet, also the sexiest.

There's a deliberate once-over, his eyes traveling from my toes, up to my legs, my waist, and then they pause at my chest, where I know my cleavage is giving him quite the show. When his eyes meet mine, he wets his lips, his expression resembling more that of a big-bad-wolf type than a simple acquaintance.

"Why the hell are you wearing that?" he finally asks.

"This is what I wear at night. It's just one of the many pieces of lingerie I have in my dresser."

"Well, I suggest you go change," he says, before turning around again.

"Excuse me?" I ask, walking after him. "What do you mean, I should go change?"

"It's indecent, Kelsey."

Indecent?

This is indecent?

Coming from the man who's walking around the apartment without a shirt and in only a pair of shorts. I've been kind to keep my eyes north, but we all know JP doesn't wear underwear with those shorts and, yes, I can see…things. So, if this is indecent, what the hell is he?

"Is there some sort of acceptance of a double standard in this penthouse that I'm unaware of?" I ask. "Because I'm pretty sure I'm more covered up than you."

He keeps walking, ignoring me.

So, I pick up my pace, and when I've closed the distance between us, I pull on his shoulder so he's forced to face me. But he spins so fast, I'm caught off guard, and he pins me against the hallway wall, one hand on my hip, the other still holding his water glass. He props it against the wall.

Like scalding lasers, his eyes fixate on me.

"Wh-what are you doing?" I ask, a hitch in my breath.

"You're tempting me, Kelsey, and I don't take too kindly to it."

"How am I tempting you? I'm just…I'm showing you I'm not the innocent peasant girl you think I am."

He lowers his body to set his water on the ground and when he comes back up, his chest is so close that I can feel the heat coming off him. It wraps around me in an unexpected grip. The hallway fades to dark, the sparkling skyline a distant memory as he lowers his face so we're eye to eye.

The hand pinning me against the wall has slipped past one of the flaps of my romper so his palm is directly on my flesh, his thumb at the very end of the juncture of my thigh. The small barely-there touch causes the air to seize in my lungs.

"You could've chosen any pajamas to bring with you, and you bring this." The backs of his fingers run along the neckline, to just above my cleavage. "So, unless you plan on bedding someone while you're here that I don't know about, you brought this specifically knowing you'd be spending nights in the same penthouse as me."

"This has nothing to do with you and everything to do with comfort."

His hand slides farther under the slit on the side, his fingers now curling around my waist, imprinting themselves on my skin.

"So, you're telling me, if you were sharing a penthouse with Huxley instead, you'd have worn this?"

"No," I say before I can catch myself. Shit.

The truth of the matter is…I wouldn't have worn this around Huxley. When I've stayed the night at their house, I wear something respectful because I'm not about to prance around in this romper near my soon-to-be brother-in-law. That would be…weird.

But did I really wear this because of JP?

No. I wore this because it's comfortable.

"I mean…I wouldn't wear this around him because—"

"Because he's not single." JP's other hand caresses up my side, and I nearly slide down the wall from the touch. God, it's been so long.

So long since a male has touched me. Having JP, this incredibly sexy man, come near me has me losing all sorts of intelligent thoughts.

"You wore this to tempt me, admit it." He leans his head forward so we're cheek to cheek and moves his hand to my shoulder to one of the lace straps. He toys with it, his fingers delicately smoothing over the intricate lace. "It's why you keep coming after me to talk, because you want this, Kelsey."

"I don't," I say, my voice coming out all breathy.

He tugs on the strap, moving it toward the end of my shoulder. "You're a fucking liar," he whispers into my ear, right before he tips the strap over my shoulder so it falls down, the fabric around my breasts barely hanging on.

I should move away.

Tell him to stop.

But…I don't.

Because I know, deep in my soul, that even though JP isn't the man for me, because he's not a relationship kind of guy, I can't help my attraction to him. I can't help but fall under his spell.

And I can't help but want more.

More in this moment.

Keeping his mouth at my ear, he gently runs his finger over my collarbone. "You're glistening, Kelsey. Your breath is uneven, your body is yearning for more, and I know for a fucking fact, that if I spread your legs, I'd find a wet cunt, begging for me."

I squeeze my eyes shut, processing his words, words that have never been spoken to me before.

Ever.

In my entire life.

And yet, they strike me so deep in my soul that I can feel just how penetrating they are. I know he's right. I know he'd be happy if he pressed two fingers inside of me.

"Tell me it's the truth."

Never.

I won't give him the satisfaction of knowing that.

I can't.

He'd hold it over my head for a lifetime.

So, I keep my mouth shut.

"Is that how you're going to be, Kelsey?" he asks, his nose now dragging over my cheek. "You're not going to be truthful?" His fingers shuffle down my chest, to my nearly exposed breast. I hold my breath as he dances them over the loose fabric, my mind screaming, pleading for him to pull the fabric down, to lift my breast into his mouth.

"Your nipple is hard." He makes the briefest pass over it with his thumb—so brief that I barely feel it—but it's enough to cause the lightest of moans to pop out of my mouth. "Mmmm," he hums into my ear. "That's what I fucking thought."

Then he takes hold of my hand and slides it under the loose fabric at my hip, bringing it to just above my pubic bone.

"Tell me this, Kelsey, do you have your vibrator with you?"

I nearly choke on my own saliva as I shake my head.

"Big mistake," he says. He shifts my hand lower until my fingers slide along my crease.

"Fuck," I whisper.

"*Fuck* is right, babe," he says, then passes his hand over mine and directs me to massage my clit. Unable to control anything at this point, I allow his hand to move mine. I spread my legs. "That's right, make room. Tell me—how wet are you?"

On a heavy breath, I say, "Really wet."

So wet.

Enough that I could spend no more than a minute getting myself off.

His voice, his hands, his possessive actions, they're all setting me off, prepping me for what's to come next.

And I want whatever it is.

He nibbles on my earlobe—*yes, just like that, more of that*—and a breathy moan falls past my lips. I want more. His hands on me. His mouth on me. His—

He pulls my hand out of my shorts and pins it against the wall.

My eyes fly open, and when he pulls away, he looks me in the eyes and says, "I told you, you were fucking lying." And then, with his heated chest pressing against mine, he sucks my fingers into his mouth. He runs his tongue along the digits, licking my arousal, and then quickly releases them with a pop.

Oh my God!

He pushes away, leaving me like a puddle on the wall.

"Lie to me again, and you won't like what happens next time." He licks his lips, my taste wet on them, and then he grabs his glass and walks back to his room, shutting the door behind him. *Holy. Fuck.*

Slowly, I slide down the wall until I'm sitting on the floor. I attempt to catch my breath as my heart beats wildly and my clit hammers with the need for release.

What…what was that?

I stare at his door and attempt to make sense of it all, but all my brain can come up with is…my body wants more.

My body wants *him*.

My body wants to charge through his door, strip down to nothing, and let him take charge.

I move my strap back up onto my shoulder and attempt to stand on wobbly legs. Using the wall for assistance, I walk back into the living room and grab my items before heading to my room, absolutely shook. I won't be reading tonight.

My body might want him, but I know for certain, my heart doesn't.

And his heart doesn't want me.

I've seen the roulette of women on his phone, so I know I'm just a speed bump in his pursuit of pleasure.

He's not for me. He's the type of man who can deliver an orgasm that you'll remember for the rest of your life, but he'll break your heart in the long run.

Lust is an addiction.

But for me, love wins over lust, and I'm searching for love…

Kelsey: Lottie, things are not going well.

Lottie: What do you mean?

Kelsey: You have to swear you're not going to tell Huxley.

Lottie: Of course I won't. It's a form of foreplay, keeping innocent things away from him. Drives him nuts. So, please, more secrets.

Kelsey: JP almost made me come.

Lottie: WHAT?

Kelsey: I know. God, too much backstory, but before I knew what was happening, he had me pinned against the wall, forcing me to massage my clit. I did it and then he sucked my fingers.

Lottie: What in the holy hell is happening over there? Plus, Huxley did that to me once, when we hated each other, remember? I told you about it. It's the sexiest thing ever.

Kelsey: I nearly came when his mouth pulled on my fingers. Why…why is this happening?

Lottie: I told you not to wear those pajamas.

Kelsey: That's not helpful. Lottie, I know he's not the guy for me, I know this deep in my soul. But, God, I couldn't have stopped myself even if I'd wanted to tonight. He has this control over me and I find myself just slipping into his touch. I completely lost who I was in that moment.

Lottie: You say that as if it's a bad thing.

Kelsey: It is. I don't want a one-night stand. I want to find love. JP is not a man who offers orgasms and companionship.

Lottie: How do you know that? Ever ask him?

Kelsey: Are you insane? I would never ask that. Plus, he's all about one-night stands. Everyone knows that. I'm an easy grab for him. We're sharing a place, alone… It was bound to happen.

Lottie: I think there's more to JP than you know.

Kelsey: There is, but when it comes to relationships, trust me, I know. *deep breaths* I just need to refocus. I got sidetracked there for a second and, sure, it was nice, but I have that date with Derek on Friday. I need to focus on that.

Lottie: Yes, but remember what I said—if there's any inkling that you might be starting something with JP, don't go on the date with Derek. I don't want you hurting him.

Kelsey: I know. I promise, nothing is happening between me and JP. It was a momentary lapse of judgment. I'm glad I talked it out. Now I can move on. I feel better now.

Lottie: Are you sure?

Kelsey: Positive.

CHAPTER 12
JP

STANDING AT THE KITCHEN COUNTER, a cup of coffee in hand, I lean against the cabinets, wearing only a pair of sweats as Kelsey comes strolling in. Her makeup's done, her hair expertly styled and hanging over her shoulders, and she's wearing a pair of high-waisted black business pants and a white blouse with a white camisole underneath. And to really fucking kick me in the goddamn dick, she swiped on a dark red lipstick I know matches her panties.

She looks fucking delicious, and even though she claims she's not tempting me, that red lipstick says differently after the conversation we had last night.

Hell…I lost control. I keep telling myself I need to avoid her. That was the plan when I first showed up at this penthouse, but she's gotten under my skin. When she apologized, it actually meant something to me. It's why I asked her to lunch. I reasoned that if I start showing her a gentler side of me, she might actually think differently about me. And, fuck, it was working, but last night, when she said she was still going on that date, all hell froze over.

It might have been stupid of me, but I kind of thought that if I opened up—got her to *enjoy* my company—she wouldn't go on that date. I thought she'd go to the ball with me instead. One lunch out isn't going to change her mind, though.

And then she went and sat on my goddamn lap. All control flew right out the floor-to-ceiling windows. I was just grasping on to anything that would keep me from stripping her down and burying my head between her legs.

It was downhill from there. How I ended up pushing her against the wall and digging my fingers into her velvety skin, I have no idea, but watching her cool, well-put-together façade combust was one of the sexiest things I've ever experienced.

I left her in the hallway, the taste of her on my tongue, and retreated to my bedroom. I then released the pent-up energy in the shower. Fuck, she tasted magnificent, and I have no clue how I walked away from her after having her on my tongue like that. I wanted more. I wanted to get down on my knees and worship her.

And now, this morning, seeing her dressed up for work, everything that happened last night is at the forefront of my mind.

"Morning," I say as she steps into the kitchen.

She looks up from the bracelet she's attempting to fix on her wrist.

"Good morning," she says softly.

I set my coffee down on the counter and reach out to help her. "Let me," I say softly, taking the small clasp in my hand.

"Oh…thank you," she says, clearly stunned by my gesture. Don't blame her. When she said I had mood swings like Tarzan—I think that's how she put it—she wasn't wrong. I've been up and down. I blame it on my inability to control my daily simmering anger. Anger over losing my father—*my best friend*—anger over my job, and anger over the fact that I like this girl, I really fucking do, and I can't get her to look at me the way I want her to.

I take my time fastening the clasp, and once it's on her wrist, I pause for a second, letting my fingers drag over her skin, and then I go back to my coffee.

Her eyes flash to mine and she slowly takes a step back. I nod toward the oven. "Your breakfast is warming in there."

"My breakfast?" she asks, confused. "Did you order in?"

"No." I reach for my protein bar. "Woke up early, couldn't sleep, so I cooked your breakfast that you like, beans and all."

"Why…why would you do that?"

Because I want you to think I'm a good guy despite how I act.

I want you to see that I like you, but am afraid to tell you because there's a great possibility you will laugh in my face.

I want you to give me a chance.

To date me…

"You know, Kelsey, a simple *thank you* would be just fine." With protein bar in hand, I consider going back to my room to eat but, hell, she smells good, and I'm a glutton for punishment. So I take a seat at the dining room table where I've already set up a place setting for her.

I hear her move around the kitchen, grab her breakfast, and when she turns to sit at the table with me, she notices the placemat. Once again, those hazel eyes of hers flash to mine.

Before she can question me, I say, "I was bored this morning."

Nervously, she takes a seat and sets down her plate. After she fixes her napkin on her lap, she glances up at me and says, "Thank you for breakfast."

"Sure," I answer and kick my feet up on the chair next to me. I can feel her eyes still on me when I'm opening my protein bar. When I finally look up, I ask, "Can I help you?"

"I'm just confused, is all. It seemed like you were mad at me last night and now you made me breakfast… I don't know how to process this."

"I wasn't mad at you last night."

"You threatened me."

"Jesus Christ." I roll my eyes. "That wasn't a threat, more like…a warning."

"So, you warned me last night. And if that's the case, then maybe I should warn you."

This should be good.

"Okay, what do you need to warn me about?"

"Well...you shouldn't be walking around without a shirt on."

"Uh-huh," I drag out. "And what's going to happen to me if I do?"

She stabs a forkful of eggs. "You don't want to know."

"I do, actually. I really want to know."

"Fine." She shrugs. "If you walk around without a shirt on, I will too."

A loud laugh escapes me. "And you consider that a punishment?" I glance down at my bare chest and back at her. "My shirt is off now, so please, Kelsey, go ahead and punish me. Strip out of that starchy blouse of yours. Show me the good stuff."

"Ugh." She rolls her eyes. "Why are you so insufferable? I'm just trying to make things comfortable for us, but you're either angry, teasing me, or...well...you know."

"I don't know. Please finish that sentence."

She pins me with a glare. "You're...well, touching me intimately."

"That was barely touching you last night. And correct me if I'm wrong, but you seemed to like it...a lot."

"I was faking it."

That makes me nearly spit out my coffee. "Babe, I tasted you off your finger last night. You can't fake that."

"Don't call me *babe*." She scoops up some beans. "Can we just be friends?"

"What did I tell you about workplace friendships?"

"That was some load of bullshit. I'm friends with Huxley and Breaker. So don't tell me I can't be friends with you. You just don't want to be friend-zoned because you want in my pants."

I smirk at that. "I do want in your pants."

Her eyes flash to mine as her cheeks blush. Flustered, she says, "Well, that's not an option for you. So, why don't we just put that behind us and move on? We can be friends. It's simple. We just need to do friendly types of things."

Interested, I ask, "Okay, what are friendly types of things?"

"I can't think of anything off the top of my head, but—oh, we could go sightseeing."

"Why does that sound not the least bit interesting to me?"

"It's totally a friend thing to do. You've been here before, clearly, so why don't we do that after I'm done with my last meeting? You could show me around. I can take pictures in all the obvious places. It could be fun and we could get to know each other."

"It doesn't sound fun to me."

"JP!" she shouts, surprising me. "Stop being difficult, and for the love of God, just go sightseeing with me. Good God."

Chuckling, I nod. "Okay, no need to get all riled up. We can go sightseeing, but I'll tell you this—I'll be a bastard the whole time."

"It wouldn't be an evening out with you if you weren't." She dabs her mouth with her napkin. "My last meeting is at two today. After I get back, I'll change, and then we can hit the town. How does that sound?"

"Like a nightmare." I tilt my coffee cup toward her. "Can't wait." Then I stand from my chair and, with coffee cup and protein bar in hand, I head toward my room, only to stop midway. "Kelsey?"

"Yes?" she asks, fork poised near her mouth.

"Just so you know, you can act like we're friends all you want, but know this…I can still taste your sweet cunt on my tongue."

And then, with a smile on my face, I turn away from her and head into my bedroom. This is exactly what I needed, some more alone time with her. *Now, let's see if I can keep my sarcasm toned down when that happens.*

"This place is so cute," Kelsey says as she walks next to me, taking in everything around us.

"It's hemorrhaging tourists," I say.

"Which is exactly what we wanted, right?"

"What you wanted. This is not my idea of fun in San Francisco." I dodge a couple who are sharing a soft pretzel.

"Ooo, they have a carousel. Let's ride it."

"You're out of your goddamn mind if you think I'm going to ride a carousel."

She gives me a playful grin and then pulls on my arm. "It'll be fun."

"Kelsey, I'm serious, I'm not riding that thing."

She gets us in line and I attempt to leave, but she loops her arm through mine and surprisingly holds me in place.

"Loosen up. This is what friends do—silly things like this. You can take a boomerang of me on a horse."

"What the hell is a boomerang?"

"On Instagram," she says, as if I'm an idiot.

"That clarifies nothing."

"It's what we did in front of the *Full House* houses."

Yes, we were those people. We searched them out, the Painted Ladies to be exact, and we stood in front of them while taking weird back-and-forth pictures. From there, we stopped by the actual house from *Full House*, where I took a dozen pictures of Kelsey posing. She forced me to take a picture with her, which she texted to me, saying how adorable we look as friends.

Fucking…great.

After that, we came down to the pier, where we are, as you know, currently in line for the carousel.

"How many times have you been up here? San Francisco, that is," she asks.

"More than I can count," I answer.

"Have you ever been to Pier 39?"

"A few times. Took a date here once."

"Oooo, a date," Kelsey says in such an annoying tone. "Tell me more. I didn't think Jack Parker dated."

"Not my name."

"A solid guess." She smirks.

"It was a few years ago. We went out for fun and ended the night in my bed. Worth the inconvenience of coming down here."

"Let me guess—since I won't be ending up in your bed—this isn't worth the *inconvenience*?"

"There's always time for that to turn around," I answer honestly.

"Not happening." She pats my forearm. "But nice try. So, tell me, have you ever had a girlfriend?"

"Yes," I answer.

"Care to elaborate?" she asks as we take a few steps forward in line.

"Not really."

"Oh, is it one of those stories where she was the one and only girl to break your heart?"

We keep slowly moving forward as the carousel loads up. "No, actually. I was the one who broke her heart."

"You were?" she asks. "Was she in love with you?"

"Yes," I answer.

"And you weren't?"

I shake my head. "I wasn't. And I didn't think it was fair to keep dating her if I knew the feelings weren't going to grow in that direction, so I broke up with her. She threw a milkshake in my face and then stormed away."

"Oh my God, she threw a milkshake in your face? What flavor was it?"

I chuckle. "Why does that matter?"

"Can't be sure, but you know, details make a story."

"I believe it was vanilla, another reason why I knew we weren't supposed to be together. Vanilla milkshakes are boring."

"Hey, no, they're not. They're the original. You're not going to get another flavor without them. Don't knock the vanilla milkshake."

"Is that what you order?"

"Of course not." She flips her hair over her shoulder. "Strawberry is obviously what I get." I chuckle, and we make it to the front of the line, just to be stopped because the carousel is full. Kelsey turns toward me and leans against the gate. "What's your milkshake order?"

"Chocolate."

"Could've guessed that. You're so predictable."

I scoff at that. "And strawberry milkshake wasn't predictable? All you have to do is say hi, and everyone knows you're a strawberry milkshake girl."

"Nothing wrong with that. So, this girl threw a milkshake in your face when you broke up with her. Was there anything that happened after that, or was the milkshake where it ended?"

I wince and smooth my hand over my jaw. "We had breakup sex that night, but after that, it was over."

"Oh, Jean-Pierre…"

"Not my name."

She snaps in disappointment. "Still, sex after you broke up with her? Kind of skeezy, don't you think?"

"Never said I made the best choices," I say unapologetically.

"How long ago was this relationship?"

"Eh, like two, three years ago. I think she's engaged now. At least that's what I surmised when she 'accidentally' texted me a photo of her engagement ring. She said it was meant for someone else."

"Oh, surrrrrre," Kelsey says, dragging it out, which makes me smile. "That's what they all say. She sent you that picture on purpose to try to make you jealous. Were you? Jealous, that is?"

"Not in the slightest. Honestly, it's shitty to say, but I'd kind of forgotten about her until that text."

"And since then, you've been a lone wolf?"

"Yeah, nothing wrong with that."

"Not saying there is," she says as the carousel slows. I pull out my wallet to pay for the ride—a ride I didn't think I'd be going on—and grab a ten-dollar bill to pay for the both of us. "Just fascinating. I, on the other hand, am single because…well, apparently I'm unlovable."

"You know for damn sure that's not the truth," I say as I hand the attendant our money and he opens the gate. "What do they always say… you just haven't found the right person yet?"

"But do you truly believe that?" she asks as she hops up on the carousel and finds a blue horse. I take the yellow one next to her and straddle it, feeling like a complete idiot. I'm a grown man riding a yellow horse. This is incredibly off-brand for me.

"Sure," I answer offhandedly, because I really don't know what I believe when it comes to that kind of shit.

"That's not very convincing."

"I don't know what you want me to say. You're hot, so there's instant attraction. In the work environment, you're cool, professional, and obviously know sustainability issues front to back. Having spent more time with you recently, I've learned that you always want to get your way, in a…pestering, control-freak way, and I'm seeing more she-devil behavior that I'm not sure many people know is there. But there's got to be someone out there who likes that kind of thing." I shrug.

I like her, even when the she-devil comes out. Regardless, I'm drawn to her.

"Wow," she says, smiling. "What a lovely picture you've painted of me."

The bell rings and the carousel starts moving so she drops the conversation, pulls out her phone, and starts snapping pictures.

"What do you plan on doing with those pictures?" I ask her as the carousel picks up speed.

"Blackmail, of course." She smirks and then takes a selfie of the both of us.

"I'd expect nothing less."

"JP, put it on."

"If you think I'm wearing that, you've lost your goddamn mind. I've already ridden the carousel, taken those stupid boomerang things on a trolley, and pretended to hold Alcatraz in my hand. I draw the line at wearing a goddamn bib at dinner."

"You're being a snob."

"Because I don't want to wear a bib?"

"Precisely." She gestures to the restaurant. "It's part of the experience."

An experience I didn't want. She chose where we were going to eat and, of course, she picked the popular tourist attraction, the Crab House, which, granted, I heard has amazing food. But the vibe is not me. I don't do plastic bibs.

"I'm good with missing out on the experience."

"Joo-Joo Poo-Poo, put on the bib."

"Is Joo-Joo Poo-Poo supposed to be a guess of my name?"

"Yes...is that not correct?"

"Not even close."

"Damn, I would've absolutely snorted all over this table if it was."

"Attractive."

"Here we are," our waitress says, setting down a giant—and I mean giant, baking-sheet-sized—skillet of two cooked crabs and a plate of fries between us, along with melted butter in ramekins. "Enjoy."

"Wow, that's a lot of crab," Kelsey says. "But I've worked up quite the appetite." And before I can even consider picking up a fry, she snaps a leg off a crab and smiles at me.

Uhh...

The crunch, the ninja-like way she just did that, the satisfaction in her face...makes me think I should be scared for my life.

"What's wrong?" she asks with a smirk.

"It's startling how quickly you snapped off that leg."

"Let that be a reminder to you, JP. Don't cross me."

"Clearly." I reach for the crab and, gently, because I'm not some sort of barbarian, remove a leg and pull out the meat. When I dip it into the butter, I watch it drip, and drip...and drip.

Fuck.

When I glance up at Kelsey, she's just smiling at me with that knowing grin of hers. She lifts up the plastic bib and wiggles it at me.

"Just give it to me," I say, snatching it from her grasp, causing her to tip her head back and laugh.

I fix the bib around my neck and scoot my chair closer to the table.

"Oh, don't you look adorable?"

"If you take a picture, I'm going to—"

She lifts her phone and smiles just as I see her finger press against the screen. "Oops, too late." She smiles again and stares at the screen. "Ooo, this might be my favorite of the night. It's a keeper."

"Teasing your boss isn't in your best interest."

"You're technically not my boss as you just oversee things. If we want to get down to the nitty-gritty, my boss is Huxley, as you've pointed out to me, and I'm sure he'll give me a raise once he sees the 'data' I've collected tonight."

Unfortunately, I think she's correct.

"I'll still report insubordination."

"Good luck with that." She winks and then rips loose another crab leg. "Now, will you please tell me why this place isn't suitable for you? Clearly, the crab is delicious, the views are amazing, the attire...top-notch. How could this not appeal to you?"

"It's gimmicky."

She rolls her eyes. "Just what I thought, you're a snob. Don't hate on a place that does it right for the people who come to visit. This is fulfilling dreams for me right now. Eating crab by the pier, boats just outside the window in the Bay, the old subway tile from floor to ceiling, and the simple dining room tables that aren't quite nautical but offer nautical vibes. This is everything. So, excuse me if I find this completely fulfilling. Now if only the grump sitting across from me would lighten up."

"This just isn't my ideal night."

"Uh-huh. You say that as if you have an ideal night in mind."

"I do." I pop a fry into my mouth, and my answer causes her to grow a curious look.

She leans forward, her hand supporting her chin as she says, "Oh, please, do tell."

"I don't have to tell you," I say. "I'm going to show you."

"Show me?"

I nod. "Tomorrow night, when you're done with your meetings. I'm showing you what my ideal night in San Francisco is."

She spreads her hand on the table and in a dramatic tone, she asks, "Wait, so this friendship we're developing, it isn't just a one-night thing?"

"This isn't a friendship; it's a...short-term companionship."

She laughs out loud, and the addictive sound draws the attention of the tables around us. "Wow, no wonder you're in charge of the media for Cane Enterprises. You sure know how to spin things. Okay, I'll bite. This short-term companionship, it's going to continue tomorrow?"

"Yes," I answer, taking another fry. Have to admit, this shit is good, despite the goddamn bib. "And I'll show you exactly what a night out on the town is like."

"Bet it won't be better than tonight."

"Guaranteed it will be."

"Listen, Julian Prince..." She pauses with a wince, waiting to see if she's correct. I just shake my head, and her shoulders droop. "I gathered damning evidence of you on a carousel and wearing a bib. Nothing is going to beat this."

"That's what you think," I say before grabbing another crab leg.

"Okay...admit it, this is good," Kelsey says around her mouthful of ice cream.

When I first met Kelsey, I thought she was this hot uptight organizer with a dream to fall in love. But I now realize that she had maintained her guarded, professional façade even when we were hanging out with Huxley and Lottie at their house. But slowly, as this night has unfolded, I've seen her relax more and more. She's now talking to me with ice cream on her lips and fudge on the corner of her mouth.

It's...hell, it's endearing.

She's dropped that shield of perfection and I like this side of her. Sort of unpredictable, and a whole lot relatable.

"Come on." She nudges me with her elbow and I decide to give in.

"Yes, this is good."

"Ha, I knew it." She holds her fudge-covered spoon in the air. "I knew I'd get you."

"You didn't get me, Ghirardelli did."

After we had dinner, Kelsey demanded that we head up the hill to Ghirardelli to get dessert. It was a bit of a hike, so by the time we got there, dinner was partially digested and we were ready to dig into dessert.

We decided to share a classic hot-fudge sundae. We found a table in the middle of the busy restaurant. Where I would've rather walked around outside to eat, she once again wanted the full experience. So we're crowded around a round bistro table with a marble top, people all around us, enjoying their sundaes just as much as we are.

It's chaotic.

It's loud.

And I hate to admit it, but it's the perfect ending to our evening.

"Oh my God, look over there, that couple is making out."

"What?" I ask.

She points with her spoon. "Right there, in the corner. What do you think—first date?"

"Do you do that on a first date?" I ask her. "Because from what I recall of our first and only date, you were pricklier than that."

"Because I was expecting to meet the man of my dreams, and instead it was the man of my nightmares."

I clutch my heart. "You wound me, Kelsey."

She nudges my shoulder playfully. "But look at us now, living out a short-term companionship. Miracles do happen."

"Don't let it get to your head. We're barely a short-term companionship."

"I don't know, you agreed to a second outing with me, so it seems like we're committed to each other. If that doesn't smell of short-term companionship, I don't know what does."

"Christ, you're incessantly annoying tonight."

"Just a dash of what I have to deal with when I'm hanging out with you."

And witty.

I scoop up another spoonful of our sundae but focus more on the ice cream than the fudge. I've noticed Kelsey is very much into the fudge and figured I'd let her have more.

See, I can be a good guy.

"So, you never answered the question. Is that what you do on a first date? Make out in the corner of a chocolate store so romance voyeurs like yourself can watch the sideshow of lip-locking?"

"Maybe when I was twenty-one I would've been more likely to make out in a restaurant, but now that I'm a respectable lady in her mid-twenties, I have standards. I expect a good meal, great conversation, and then, if I've been dazzled by the end of the night, I'll lean in for a kiss."

"Dazzled, huh? What does it take to dazzle you?"

"Taking notes?" she asks with a raised brow.

"Yes, on how to do the opposite, you know, because if I'm not annoying you, then what am I actually doing with my life?"

Her face falls flat, and I chuckle. "Well, if that's the case, I'll be keeping my dazzling to myself." I nudge her under the table with my foot. "Just tell me."

She studies me for a second and then says, "Well, first of all, he can't be full of himself. He needs to have a level head, and be a good listener, but also not be afraid to talk about himself. Family is important to me, so I want to know that he's close to his family. Hmm, what else? Oh, a self-deprecating story is always good, because then I know he doesn't take himself too seriously. I also like little touches here and there, but nothing too over the top. I like to know that he's interested without crowding me. And of course, interesting questions, a conversation that just flows. Also, I'm super into a good smile, kind eyes, and a man who pulls a chair out for me. A gentleman."

I slowly nod. "There was a column I used to read, called 'The Modern Gentleman.' He always said to open the door for your girl, but as she walks through that door, be sure to run your hand along her ass so she knows who she belongs to. Is that what you're looking for?"

She blinks a few times and then turns her attention to the sundae. "I mean, I wouldn't be mad about it."

I chuckle. "I'm going to take that as a *yes*. You know, that's a pretty high standard you're requiring a man to live up to."

"Should I feel guilty about that?" she says in challenge.

Not even having to think about it, I shake my head. "No, I don't think so. Why settle when you know what you want? Although, don't you think you were settling with Edwin?"

"Edwin was clearly a momentary lapse of judgment. Frankly, I blame you for Edwin."

"Me?" I point to my chest. "Why do you blame me? I didn't force you to go out with the dweeb."

"He wasn't a dweeb, he was just…dweebish."

"If that makes you feel better, sure. But not sure why you're blaming me."

"Because, that dinner we had at the blind date restaurant was atrocious. It made me think I had to lower my standards."

"It wasn't *that* bad," I say.

"You weren't the one who was there to meet someone. You were there to fulfill a bet. I was honestly excited. It might have seemed entertaining to you, but it was more disheartening to me."

Now that actually makes me feel bad. I never thought about it that way, and before I know it, guilt consumes me.

"Sorry, Kelsey," I say, looking her in the eyes. "I was an idiotic, prideful man that night. You wounded my pride when I first showed up, and I didn't shake it off. I tried to bring you down with me. I shouldn't have done that."

She pauses, her spoon midway to her mouth as she says, "Wow, uh… thanks, JP." She grins while bringing her spoon to her mouth. "Carousel, pictures, bibs…and an apology. Dare I say, this might be one of my favorite nights ever? A vast improvement from the blind date restaurant. This whole 'short-term companionship' thing is actually rather enjoyable."

"Glad I could make it up to you."

"You did…Josiah Phoenix."

"Close."

Her eyes widen with excitement. "Really?"

I laugh. "No."

"Ugh." She pushes me. "That was just mean."

"I found it entertaining." I exchange a smirk with her, which to my goddamn delight…she reciprocates.

———

"Can you roll me to my room?" Kelsey asks as she collapses to the floor of the penthouse and takes off her shoes. "I don't think I can move another inch."

She then lies on the floor, fumbles with the waistband of her jeans, and undoes the button before groaning in relief.

"Wow, this is a sight to see."

Blechhhh.

She covers her mouth from the very unladylike burp that just erupted out of her. She glances at me, shock registering across her face, before she asks, "Did you happen to hear that?"

"Babe, the doorman thirty stories down heard that. It rattled the very floor I'm standing on."

"Don't be dramatic."

"I think San Francisco will be reporting an earthquake on the Richter scale."

"Stop it."

"I actually feel nauseated from the aftershocks."

She swats at my legs, and I laugh as I reach down and grab her by the ankles.

"What are you doing?"

"Pulling you to your room... Wait... Nothing going to come out of the bottom end, is there?"

"Eww, do you really think I would do that?"

"Well, honestly, I wouldn't be able to tell you, because the girl I once knew as the tight-lipped perfectionist just unbuttoned her jeans in front of me and let out a monstrous belch, so...I can't be sure what might happen next."

She drapes her arm over her eyes as I continue to pull her. "This is why I'll never find anyone to love me. I'm a closet gross person."

"No, you're not...you're just normal."

She peeks past her arm and says, "You're just saying that so I don't actually fart while you're pulling me."

"I'm really not. It's nice to see that you're not always so stuck-up."

"Stuck-up? That's preposterous."

"Only someone who's stuck-up would use the term *preposterous,*" I say as I reach her bedroom. I open her door and drag her in. I consider leaving her on the floor but, bending down, I pick her up. She squeals in surprise before looping her arms around my neck.

"What on earth are you doing?"

"Tossing you on your bed," I say as I throw her, but to my chagrin, she doesn't let go of my neck, so instead of me watching her flop onto the bed, we collide in a fit of limbs on the bed. "Jesus Christ," I mumble into the comforter. "You were supposed to let go."

"I just ate a whole crab, half a plate of fries, half a sundae, and had to unbutton my pants in front of you when we got home. What on earth makes you think I want to be tossed around?"

"So, this, me pressing into your stomach, is better?"

"Could be better positioning."

"Let go," I say.

"Oh, right, yes." She unloops her arms from around my neck and I lift off her. "Now, would it be too much to ask of our short-term companionship to have you strip me down and put my pajamas on?"

I glare at her. "Babe, if I'm stripping you down, I'm sure as fuck not putting anything back on you."

She rubs her stomach. "Oh yeah? You'd want a piece of this?"

"Oddly, I find it intriguing."

"Standards, JP...standards."

I shrug. "I have none." I walk toward her bedroom door. "Are you going to be able to manage on your own?"

She heaves a large sigh. "I believe so. It might take me a hot second to gather myself but, yes, I'll persevere."

"Okay, then...good night."

"Good night...Jordan Preston."

I grip the doorway and look over my shoulder. "It's Jonah Peter."

A slow, sexy smile passes over her lips before she says, "Good night... Jonah."

"Good night, Kelse."

Breaker: Are you dead?

JP: You know damn well I'm not dead and you know damn well I don't want to talk about it.

Breaker: Dude…a carousel? A bib? Kelsey texted Lottie, who showed the pictures to Huxley, who clearly sent them to me. She really has you by the balls, doesn't she?

JP: I said, I don't want to talk about it.

Breaker: No way in hell am I going to let you drop this. What the hell is going on?

JP: Absolutely nothing.

Breaker: Did you go out on a date tonight?

JP: No, we went out as short-term companions.

Breaker: Is that what the kids are calling it these days?

JP: Unless you have something productive to talk about, you can go to hell.

Breaker: I'm being serious. You've crushed on her ever since you met her, so what's going on? You trying to start something?

JP: No. It was a simple outing. We have nothing to do here, so she asked me to do touristy things with her. I did. That's it. When we got back to the penthouse, she burped, and I had to drag her by her feet to her room because she was so full. Trust me, nothing is going on.

Breaker: But do you want something to happen?

JP: Why are you acting like a gossiping mom right now?

Breaker: I just worry about you. You've been different lately. I want to make sure you're okay.

JP: If I've been different, it has nothing to do with Kelsey.

Breaker: What does that mean?

JP: Nothing. Don't worry about it. Listen, I'm tired and I have an early meeting tomorrow with Jeremiah over at The Wharf.

Breaker: Okay, but you know I'm here for you if you need to talk. Huxley might be occupied, but I'm not. You can rely on me.

JP: Thanks. I'm good, though.

Breaker: Good. Also…if you have feelings for her, man, go for it.

JP: Get a life, Breaker. Night.

CHAPTER 13
KELSEY

Kelsey: Welcome, listener, to the *Meant to Be Podcast*, where we talk to madly-in-love couples about the way they met. Huxley and Lottie, thank you so much for joining me today. Please, tell us how you met.

Lottie: It's about freaking time you have your sister on this podcast. We should've been your first couple.

Kelsey: You weren't a couple when I started this podcast.

Lottie: That's an annoyingly good point, but still, took you long enough. We, by far, have the most interesting story out of anyone out there.

Huxley: Might want to tone it down a bit.

Lottie: Huxley is nervous he'll lose credibility if we tell our story, but I told him, it just shows how you're a really good business-man. Isn't that right, snookums?

Huxley: Laying it on thick, are we?

Lottie: The listeners need to know how in love we are.

Huxley: You never call me snookums.

Lottie: What I call you isn't probably podcast-approved.

Huxley: You call me by my name.

Lottie: Really? Because I think I call you "oh God" more often than not.

Kelsey: And this is precisely why I haven't had you on the show. This was a bad idea.

Lottie: No, it wasn't. We're in love. We're getting married. Don't turn off the chat. Kelsey, don't turn it—

"Are you almost ready?" JP calls out from the entryway.

"Yes," I yell. "Sheesh, give a girl a second."

"You've had multiple seconds."

"I got home like a minute ago."

"Try ten minutes. You just had to change. What are you doing in there?"

"Putting on deodorant." I swipe my armpits one more time, cap the deodorant, then grab my purse and head to the entryway. "God, do you want me to smell?" I ask just as I look up to find JP posed against the front door.

Holy…moly.

I'm not sure I've ever seen the man look this casual, but it's doing all sorts of bubbly, warm things inside my stomach. Decked out in worn and torn jeans, a black shirt, and a hooded black leather jacket, he's oozing with sex appeal. He tops off the look with a backwards hat, and I feel my insides quake. Not to mention the thick hair peppered on his jawline or the deep color of his lashes making his eyes seem impossibly greener.

"What?" he asks when he catches me staring.

"Uh…sorry, just don't think I've ever seen you this casual before."

He glances down at his outfit and then back at me. "Did you expect me to dress up for you? This isn't a date."

Well aware this isn't a date.

"I know that," I snap at him and put my purse over my shoulder. "But pardon me if I'm a little stunned to see you in a hat. Didn't know you owned one."

"I'm pretty sure every male owns a baseball hat."

"Well, it looks odd on you." It doesn't, it looks really good, but there's no way I'm going to say that.

"Well, jeans look fucking weird on you," he shoots back.

"Really?" I ask in an insecure voice.

He rolls his eyes. "No, but see how it's unkind to say people look weird? A compliment would've been good."

"You want me to compliment you? When this isn't a date? I thought this was a short-term companionship. If that's the case, I tease my friends, and therefore, I'll say you look weird in a hat because I'm so used to Mr. Businessman. But if you truly need to know, the backwards hat suits you."

"I want to say there's a compliment in there, so I'll take it."

He starts to walk away, but I hold out my arms and ask, "Care to toss a compliment my way?"

His eyes roam over my simple jeans and off-the-shoulder sweater before he says, "I can smell your deodorant, and it doesn't smell like BO. Good job."

I feel my face fall flat. "That's your compliment?"

He opens the front door for me and asks, "Have a problem with that?"

"It's not even a compliment; it's just pointing out the obvious." It's about as good as being told the color of my dress is nice. Or *I've seen better.*

I start to walk past him, but then he grips my wrist and leans into my ear. "Kelsey..."

His voice drips like honey over my exposed shoulder. I swallow tightly and nod. "Yes?"

His body moves against mine, my side to his chest as he whispers, "I like how white your shoes are."

And then he lets go of me and shuts the penthouse door behind us.

He glances back at me with a smirk as we head for the elevator. I jog after him and give him a push.

"What?" he asks. "You wanted a compliment."

"Yeah, well, don't do it like that."

"Like what?"

"You know…all seductive."

His brow raises, nearly touching his hat. "You thought that was seductive? And from the blush on your cheeks, it seems you liked it."

"That's makeup," I say, patting my heated face.

It's not makeup.

That's all me.

If I'm going to be truthful, last night shook me.

I had a great time with JP. Of course, I had to battle his bad mood from time to time, but I also watched him comply with my demands on many occasions. He was out of his comfort zone, and yet, he kept up with me and never truly complained. I had a lot of fun. And then, when we got home and he dragged me by the ankles to my room, *and* told me his real name…

Ladies…listen, I've never in my life had such a wave of butterflies erupt in my stomach. Like a swarm of them, all fluttering at the same time. It was overwhelming.

I spent the entire day today thinking about it, thinking about him, and by the time I was headed back to the penthouse, I told myself to get it together. Yes, JP is hot. Yes, he has this alpha-like attitude that's appealing to me. And, yes, he opened up last night and had fun with me, but… there's one thing I need to remember.

One important thing.

He doesn't do relationships.

He's not the type of guy who settles down, wants to settle down, or even wants a girlfriend. That was evident in our conversation last night.

So, before my heart starts skipping a beat every time I hear him breathe, I need to remind myself that he's not the marrying type. He's not long-term. *He's not what you're looking for despite how much he makes you mentally faint from just one wink.*

"Doesn't seem like makeup," JP says as the elevator doors part and he walks in.

"Are you a makeup aficionado now?"

"I know some things about the stuff." He presses the *lobby* button.

"Oh yeah? Do you wear blush, JP?"

"Only when it's caught on the collar of my shirt." He smirks and I hate him for it.

But also...God, he's so hot.

Attempting to move past this topic, I clear my throat and ask, "So, what's planned for the evening? All you said was dress casual. Should I know anything else?"

"Just leave it to me."

"That's what you keep saying, but I need to tell you, I'm a bit worried."

"Why? You know I wouldn't let anything happen to you," he says so earnestly that I truly believe him.

"I know that," I say, feeling shy about the confession. "But, you know, it's always nice to prepare oneself for what's to come. So, what should I prepare for?"

"Prepare yourself to have a good time," is all he says as the elevator slows and the doors open. He steps behind me, places his hand on my lower back, and guides me out to the front of the hotel, where the doorman opens the door for us.

"Mr. Cane, Miss Gardner. Have a good night."

"You, too, Tim," JP says before he leads me to our waiting car and opens my door for me.

It takes me a moment, but when I'm settled in the back seat with him, my mind whirls with thoughts. Stupid thoughts.

Annoying thoughts.

He opened doors for me.

He touches me.

He couldn't possibly be doing the things I said I look for on dates...
right?

Oh my God, Kelsey, are you hearing yourself?

*This is exactly why you don't get involved in stupid short-term compan-
ionships—or friendships with men—because you're such a stupid romantic
that you think everyone is trying to date you.*

This is JP we're talking about. The man is a flirt. He's also very attentive and a gentleman by nature. During meetings at Cane Enterprises,
before any of this insanity even started, he often held open doors, or
helped me out of cars. This is nothing new. This is JP just being JP.

"Want to tell me why your jaw is clenched like that?" JP asks as we
start making our way through town.

"Is it clenched? Oh...I don't know. I'm not mad or anything, if that's
what you're thinking. There's nothing to be mad about, or irritated at,
right? Just two short-term companions going somewhere unknown,
that's all."

He eyes me suspiciously. "You're acting weird."

"Am I?" I wave my hand in front of my face. "Maybe it's hot in here.
Are you hot? I'm wearing a lightweight sweater but it still feels hot. Are
you hot?"

"I'm fine," he says, looking disturbed. I don't blame him. I'm internally
freaking out and externally starting to project it. "But we can turn up the
AC."

"No, that's fine. No need to get crazy or anything."

He pauses and then turns toward me. "Kelsey, do you not want to do
this?"

"What? No. I mean...yes."

"Yes, you don't want to do this?"

"No. Yes...urgh. I want to do this. I'm sorry; I'm just...awkward.
Ignore me while I gather myself and try to act like a normal human for

you." I give him a brief smile, then look out the window, squeeze my eyes shut, and attempt to steady my heart.

Get it together, Kelsey.

So what if he took pictures on a carousel with you yesterday, told you his real name, touched you in the lobby...

This means nothing.

Absolutely nothing.

My phone buzzes in my purse and I'm grateful for the reprieve. I fish it out and glance at the screen.

Lottie: Dinner tomorrow night with Derek at the Crab House on Pier 39. He thought it would be the perfect place for a date. Meet him there at seven. Don't be late.

I smirk.

The perfect date—seems like a good date to me. Maybe Derek and I have something in common.

And just like that, the anxiety and tension that was knocking me in the chest with every breath I took is quickly wiped away. That's right, I have a date tomorrow, a very real date. With a guy who, by all standards, is quite a looker. Lottie sent me a picture of him the other day.

Blond hair, has that whole..."I own a boat" look. Which I'm sure he does, given how he's in the same realm of business as Dave and the Cane brothers. Graduated from Yale and has a golden retriever named Freddie. Doesn't get better than that, right?

"You're smiling like a madwoman now. Should I be worried?" JP asks, snapping my attention back to the present.

"No, not at all. Just excited about our evening out, of course."

"Okay, you sure? Because I feel like you've run through a gauntlet of emotions in the last five minutes."

"Positive. There will be no more erratic emotions from here on out."

"Why do you have tears in your eyes?" JP asks when we step up to the restaurant.

I turn toward him and ask, "How do you know about this restaurant?"

"Uh, you and Lottie talked about it in the elevator. Said how your mom took you here. Are you...not cool with that? We can go somewhere else. I've never tried this place, but I knew dim sum was a must in San Francisco, so I thought you'd want to go here."

My lip quivers.

A tear slides down my cheek.

And I'm left speechless as we stare at each other, on the sidewalk, outside of Dim Sum Star.

"Kelsey..."

"I'm sorry." I wipe at my tears. "This was very thoughtful, JP. I didn't think you were paying attention to that conversation."

"I pay attention a lot more than you think," he says before taking my hand in his, giving it a squeeze, and walking us to the door. Before he opens it, though, he quietly says, "If you need another moment, let me know."

I shake my head. "No, I'm good." I smile. He takes that as the green light, opens the door for me, and leads me into the restaurant.

And, oh my gosh, it looks exactly the same.

Plain beige walls, dingy blue carpet, and flimsy partitions that separate tables and rooms. It's absolutely perfect. Just as I remembered it.

The worldly smell of some of the best food I've ever had assaults me with memories.

I turn to JP and say, "It hasn't changed one bit, which makes me wonder..." I turn toward their wall of pictures and walk up to it. My eyes scan the many faces until they land on two very familiar expressions. My eyes well up all over again and I quickly take my phone out of my purse. I'm about to take a picture when JP plucks my phone from my hands.

I turn to protest, but JP nods at the picture and says, "Point at it. I'll take your picture with it."

I do just that. Then I take a few pictures, including one of just the picture to have it, and then send them to Lottie, while JP examines the two innocent girls with full bellies in the frame.

"Nice braces."

I chuckle. "Thank you."

"And that Minnie Mouse shirt…wow. You know, I might have asked you to hold my hand if I knew you back then."

"You think Young JP and Young Kelsey could've been more than short-term companions?"

He pauses to think about it and then shakes his head. "Nah, I was too much of a dick, always causing trouble. With those braces and that shirt, you'd have seemed far too innocent for me."

"Hey, what did I tell you about my innocence? Do I need to prove you otherwise again?"

"Please, prove that again. Wouldn't mind sneaking another taste of you," he says, before pulling me toward the hostess.

I don't have time to respond to his blatant flirting—that's flirting, right?—because we're ushered through the restaurant until we're shown to a seat by a window that gives us a great view of bustling Chinatown.

Before I can reach for my chair, JP pulls it out for me and then takes a seat across from me. When I glance in his direction, he just gives me a shrug and picks up his menu, placing it in front of his face.

Don't overthink it, Kelsey. Just have fun.

My phone buzzes and I say, "I bet that's Lottie texting back; can I look at it?"

"You don't need my permission. Have at it. Hey, do you know if this tea is any good?"

"Uh…I don't think I've had it before," I say and then pick up my phone and read the text message.

Lottie: OMG! He took you to Dim Sum Star? Why did that just make my heart flutter? How did he know?

I glance up at JP, who's immersed in the menu, so I text back.

Kelsey: Heard us talking about it. Thought I'd want to revisit it.

Her response is immediate.

Lottie: Umm…is he thoughtful?
Kelsey: I think he's just trying to show me he's not the asshole I've claimed he is.
Lottie: He's definitely not, with that kind of dinner surprise. Well, have fun. Don't get the tea, remember, Mom gagged on it.

Oh, that's right.

"Don't get it," I nearly shout while holding my arm out to him.

He peeks over the menu, his dark brows pulling together.

"Jesus…don't get what?"

My cheeks heat up as I realize how insane I must have just sounded. "Uh, the tea. Lottie just reminded me that Mom got it and gagged on it. So, maybe skip the tea."

"Okay." He eyes me weirdly. "Are you sure you're okay?"

I offer him a smile. "Just fine."

"Okay," he drags out.

We spend the next few minutes deciding what we want to order. They no longer cart the food around but bring the items you choose. We pick out a few dishes that we're both interested in and then, once our waitress heads back to the kitchen, I take a sip of my water.

"So, this is your ideal night out? Chasing after a girl's dream restaurant?"

"No. Getting dim sum in Chinatown is a must."

"Don't you think…that's slightly touristy?"

"Probably," he answers. "If I was taking you out, you know, on a date, I would've taken you to the Parkside Club."

"What's that?" I ask.

"A restaurant at the top of the Parkside Building. We own it."

"Naturally." I laugh.

"Brilliant chef who makes the best fucking dumplings you'll ever have. He started his culinary journey in Chinatown, actually. Huxley found him and offered him a job that he couldn't refuse. Not many people can afford to eat at the Parkside Club, but those that do, eat well."

"Well, you know, you could've taken me there."

He shakes his head. "Nah, the vibe wouldn't have been right. Formal attire is required and the place is stuffy as shit. Here, we get to relax." He says that as he slouches in his chair.

"So, then who would you take to the Parkside Club? A special date?"

He adjusts his hat on his head and says, "I've only gone with my brothers. Haven't taken anyone. Like I said, food is fucking good, but it's stuffy. I'm not about to take a date there."

"But I thought you said this wasn't a date? Maybe you should've taken me there."

"And miss out on the opportunity to see you cry over a picture of yourself with braces? Fuck no."

I laugh. "Ah, yes, a dream moment, I'm sure."

He taps the side of his head. "Filed that away for safekeeping."

"I'm sure you did." I lean on the table and ask, "So, what did you do today?"

"Nothing special," he answers. "Answered a laundry list of emails from my brothers, worked out, did some visits."

"What kind of visits? Conjugal?"

"What?" He laughs. "Who the fuck would I be visiting in prison?"

"I don't know your life. Could be anyone."

"That fucking brain of yours, there's something wrong with it. No, I just visited with some nonprofits in the area."

That perks me up. "Really? Which ones?"

"If you must know, you fucking nosey thing"—that makes me smile—"I met with a foundation that saves pigeons and then stopped by an animal shelter."

"You just casually went and saved animals today. Is that what you're telling me?"

"I didn't save them but, you know, grew some connections." He shrugs. "Then went back to the penthouse, where I took a shower and got ready. If I knew you were going to take forever to get dressed, I would've spent more time in the shower."

"Oh yeah, doing what?"

He raises a brow, and that's all he has to say.

"Ah, I see. The old scrub and tug, huh?"

His head falls back and a very sexy rumble of laughter falls out of him. "Yeah, something like that. What about you, how were your meetings today?"

"Fun," I say with a smile. "I met with Dena over at the South building. She was the sweetest, and we spent all morning walking through the building and seeing where we could make changes. She's very excited about all the plans we mapped out."

"Dena is chill; I like her."

Just as my belly rumbles, the waitress approaches with our food, so conversation is put on hold as we make room for the dishes. Pork and chive dumplings, shrimp dumplings, Shanghai chicken bun, vegetable spring rolls, and sauteed asparagus. It smells amazing.

We both pick up chopsticks, prep them, and without saying a word, we dig in.

We stand on the sidewalk outside of Dim Sum Star, waiting for the car to pull around, when I say, "You know…I remember it being a lot better than that."

JP pats his chest as he lets out a quiet burp. "Fuck…I need something to remove the taste of that chive dumpling from my mouth."

"I'm sorry. Are you going to be okay?"

"We'll see, won't we?" he asks.

Like rabid animals, we dug into our dishes, each pulling dumplings from the steaming baskets and placing them on our plates. Our first bites were ravenous. Our second…quizzical. Our third…worried. Silently, we tried another item, and another, until we both looked up at each other, grabbed our water glasses, and attempted to wash down the peculiar taste.

There was no use, our taste buds were tainted, and it wasn't a pleasant experience after that. We ate the food because neither of us wanted to waste it, but when they asked what else we wanted to order, we raised our hands with a polite "No, thank you," and then JP paid the bill.

The driver pulls up, and JP steps to the door, opening it for me and, just like the other times, once I'm in, he follows right behind me. Calling to the driver, he says, "Twentieth Century Bakery, please."

Then he pulls out his phone and starts typing away on it.

"What, uh, what's at the Twentieth Century Bakery?"

"Something that will hopefully appease our stomachs." He finishes up on his phone and then relaxes into the seat. "Hell, Kelsey, that shit was terrible."

"I know. I have no idea how Lottie and I ate as much as we did the first time we went."

"Kids don't have proper taste buds, that's why. I should've thought about that."

"Well, the sentiment was there, and I appreciate it." I reach over and squeeze his forearm. "Thank you."

The corner of his mouth tips up. "You're welcome."

"So, this bakery place, does it have a seating area?"

"Yes, but we'll get our dessert to go. We have a bit of a drive to the next stop and a reservation we can't miss."

"The next place?" I turn more toward him. "Tell me more."

"Nope." He shakes his head. "That's a surprise."

"That's annoying."

"Is it?" he asks. "Or is it fun?"

"Annoying."

He chuckles. "Yeah, I'd be annoyed too, but remember, this is my night, not yours; therefore, we do it my way."

"Ah, yes, which reminds me." We're stopped at a light, so I unbuckle my seatbelt momentarily, scoot closer to JP, and hold my phone out in front of us for a selfie. "Smile, short-term companion."

He wraps his arm around me and holds me close as he smiles that wicked smile of his, and for a moment, I almost forget to take the picture. For a moment, I get lost in the feel of his arm holding me close, of his cologne curling around me, and the warmth of his body.

But the car starts moving again, so I snap the picture and hurry back to my side. "I should've taken a picture of us at Dim Sum Star."

"A memory we don't need reminding of."

We spend a few more moments driving through town; then the driver pulls up at the curb and JP says, "Wait here." He hops out of the car into this old corner building that looks positively charming from the outside. Through the large glass windows, I see him pull out his wallet, hand someone some money, and then thank them as he walks back toward the door with a cake box and two waters.

The moment he's back in the car, he says to the driver, "All set."

The driver nods and starts moving the car again.

To my surprise, JP scoots into the middle seat, buckles up, and then hands me a water and a fork. That's when the delicious sugary smell from the box hits me.

"Um, whatever you have under there smells amazing."

"That's what you said about the dim sum."

"Is this going to taste like the food from the Dim Sum Star?"

He shakes his head and pops open the lid, revealing a beige-colored cake. "Not even close. This is my favorite dessert in the Bay Area. Nothing beats it. A honey cake from Twentieth Century Bakery. Guaranteed, you won't find anything better."

"I'll be the judge of that." I dip my fork and cut off a large piece from the side, and then bring it to my mouth, which waters. "Oh God," I awkwardly moan as I chew. "Wow...okay...wow, this is..."

"Phenomenal," he says while taking his own bite.

"Yup, that would be correct. This is phenomenal. Mmm." I lift another piece. "Is it weird to say I love you right now?"

"After the meal we just suffered through? No. Eat up, babe. This will make up for all those chewy dumplings you just consumed."

"They were quite chewy, weren't they? Not this, though, this is like a sugar cloud in my mouth."

"Sugar cloud, huh?" he asks.

"Yup. Seriously, this is amazing. How did you find it?"

"Trial and error. I like to find something special in every city I go to so if someone asks me what they should try, I can give them something good to get. This is on my list. It's a must-have when you come here."

"Do you have a list of these places?"

He nods, to my surprise. "I keep notes in my phone."

"Really?" I ask. "That doesn't seem like something you'd do."

"Why not?"

"I don't know." I take another bite. "Your attitude comes across as too cool, too accomplished to do something like taking notes in your phone of good food places. I'd never have guessed that."

"There's a lot you don't know about me, Kelsey. That's just one thing."

"Apparently. What else are you hiding?"

"You'll see," he answers.

"Does this have anything to do with where we're going?"

"Yup." He wiggles his brows and takes another bite. "And when you compare our nights out, I don't think the main course should be taken into consideration. We had a shit dinner because of you."

I chuckle. "That's fair, the main course was on me. But this dessert, I don't know. Not sure if it beats the sundae at Ghirardelli."

"Fuck off, it easily does."

That makes me laugh hard. "Protective much?"

"Yes, because they sell the damn products in the store so you can make your own Ghirardelli sundae at home—"

"They don't sell the atmosphere, though, and that makes it taste better."

"You make no sense," JP informs me, and I laugh some more. He points his fork at the cake. "Now, as for this cake, you can try to make it, but I guarantee, it won't taste anything like this, even if you ask for the recipe. They actually have a recipe book you can buy. But it still won't taste the same. This cake takes years to refine, and that, you need to appreciate."

"But we're eating it in the back of a Tesla. Not sure about the ambiance."

He scowls at me. "If anything, you should appreciate the atmosphere more because we're eating in an electric car, driving around like goddamn earth liberators. If you're really lucky, I'll give you this box when we're done so you can recycle it."

"Wow, you really know the key to a woman's heart."

"See…better. You even admit it yourself—I'm unlocking your heart."

I roll my eyes. "I was being sarcastic."

"And I choose not to take it that way." He smirks.

"Do you always have to be right?"

"Yes. Glad you're finally seeing that."

I open my water and say, "Does this place we're going to have alcohol?

Because I'll need it if I'm sticking around with you for the rest of the night."

"There's alcohol. Trust me, I wouldn't leave myself stranded and alone with you without it."

My lips flatten and he chuckles. "You're such an ass," I grumble.

"I know, babe." He winks. "But admit it, you like it."

"I don't."

He tips my chin up with his finger and whispers, "Liar."

Eh...he very well might be right about everything, because even though he does drive me nuts, I sort of like it. I fall in line with his teasing and...oh God...am I starting to crave it?

No, that couldn't possibly be true, right?

He dips his fork into the cake and takes another bite, his eyes on me the entire time.

Huh...maybe I am.

"What are you doing?" JP asks, tugging my arm.

"Sending my sister a pin location of where I am."

"Why the hell would you do that?"

I stuff my phone in my purse and pause on the dark sidewalk. We ate half of the cake in the car and I honestly could've kept going. I didn't think it would settle well in my belly if I ate more cake and then had alcohol right after. Not a good thing at all. So, I controlled myself and focused on my conversation with JP, telling him all about where I'd seen my business going when I first started.

He sat there and listened the entire time, occasionally brushing his hand against my leg. I couldn't figure out if he was doing it on purpose or if it was because he was still sitting in the middle seat when we were done with the cake. Either way, every light pass, every small touch, was like an ember starting to flame and burn harder, stronger.

"Why would I send a pin to my sister? Uh, have you looked around us? I'm in a dark alleyway where there are no lights on, and I'm with a man."

"A man you know."

"But do I know you, JP?"

"Enough that you should be conscious of the fact that I'd protect you over...whatever the hell is playing in your head."

Arms crossed, I jut out a hip and say, "Okay, if someone came up to us right now and said they were going to take me away to their lair, what would you do?"

"What kind of fucked-up fairy tale are you living in?"

"Just answer the question."

"Jesus." He drags a hand over his face. "I'd tell him to get the fuck away, and if he didn't, I'd probably introduce him to the ten years of boxing lessons I've been taking."

Dear heavens, he boxes? That's hot.

My eyes go to his chest. Hmm, that would explain some of those ripped muscles.

"Is that satisfactory to you?" he asks.

"I believe so." I loop my arm through his and lean in close. "Now, where the hell are we going?"

"Over here." He leads me down an alleyway to a metal door. He raps on the metal and after a moment, it opens. A large burly man with a curly mustache steps into the alleyway with us.

He lifts a clipboard to his face and asks, "Name?"

"Jonah Cane," JP answers. *Jonah Cane.* I like that, too. Especially since I feel like I'm seeing him as Jonah right now, not his Cane Enterprises persona of JP.

The bouncer makes a scratching mark on his clipboard and opens the door for us.

"Down the hallway, first door on the right. Wait to be seated."

We head down the hall, and I quietly ask, "Do you often use your first name?"

"Sometimes," he says.

"Do you like it if people call you Jonah?"

He glances down at me. His eyes fall briefly to my lips but then tear away and focus on the dimly lit hallway in front of us.

"Is there an answer to that?" I ask as we reach the door on the right. He doesn't answer, but instead knocks on the door, and this time, when the door opens, a cacophony of conversations and soft music filters out into the hallway.

"Cane?" the attendant asks.

"Yup," JP answers.

"Right this way."

Clutching tighter to him, I ask just above a whisper, "Did you take me to a sex club?"

He chuckles but doesn't answer.

The room is filled with people; every table is occupied, everyone with drinks in their hands, their faces lit up by a simple short table lamp in front of them. The walls are covered in red velvet, the ceiling sprinkled with bulb lights, and there's a raised stage at the very end of the room, covered in the same lavish red velvet with old-time lights that line the bottom of the stage.

What on earth is this place?

The hostess—I'm assuming that's who she is—walks us to the only empty table in the room. Right at the front. "Hilary will be here momentarily to take your drink orders."

"Thank you," JP says. He pulls my chair out for me, takes my hand in his, and helps me as I take a seat. Then he slides his chair right next to mine. Talking quietly in my ear, he asks, "What do you want to drink?"

"Uh…not sure," I answer as chills from his soft voice cover the back of my neck.

"Wine?" he asks, his lips dangerously close to my ear. "Or something stronger?"

"What, uh, what are you getting?" I ask.

"Scotch."

"Nice order, a little strong for me, so a glass of cab would be fine."

Hilary arrives just at the right time and takes our order before setting a bowl of trail mix in front of us. I glance around the room. The people at the other tables are all quietly talking to themselves, and I honestly can't tell what's going to happen on that stage.

I lean in toward JP and ask, "Seriously, where are we?" When I turn my head, our noses nearly touch as I whisper, "Is this a sex den?"

He chuckles. "Would you be mad if it was?"

Would I be mad? I honestly don't know.

"It would be different. I've never been to one. Is that what this is? Is that what you like to do in different clubs, go to different sex dens? I mean, the red velvet says it all. Oh God, and we have front-row seats. We'll see things."

He chuckles and drapes his arm over the back of my chair, casually crossing his ankle over his knee. "Would you like to see things?"

"I'll be honest. When you suggested I was innocent, I'd have to say, this is exposing some innocence, because I really have never done anything like this before. And I am nervous. Are they going to have sex? Like, strip down in front of us? Oh God, am I going to be turned on? Are you?" My eyes flash to his, which are truly smiling. "Do you get boners here?"

Leaning in close, he presses his mouth to my ear and says, "This isn't a sex den, Kelsey. Nor a sex club, or anything to do with sex. So, rest that little innocent heart of yours."

Hilary drops off our drinks, offers us a wink, and says, "Enjoy the show."

"The show?" I ask, so freaking confused.

JP lifts his tumbler of scotch and takes a sip, and then turns his attention to the stage as the curtain opens and the crowd erupts into loud cheers.

"Ladies and gentlemen," a voice says over the loudspeaker. "Please stay seated, holler at your own will, and bring your hands together for the incomparable, the magnificent, the hottest ass this side of San Francisco." More uproarious cheers. "Mrs. Frisbee Lane."

Frisbee Lane?

Is this a comedy show?

A one-person monologue?

A—

My thoughts cut off the moment a very tall, very beautiful human struts out onto the stage, dressed in full drag, with a wig that rivals Marie Antoinette, an ass bigger than a Kardashian's, and nails longer than my hand.

"Good evening, my beautiful babies," she says into a microphone.

"Oh my God," I say quietly with glee as I turn toward JP. "Did you bring me to a drag show?"

He just smirks and sits back.

"We have quite the evening planned for you tonight. But before we get started, some quick reminders. Let the lip-synching be handled by the professionals, please refrain from bringing down the morale—you know us bitches love the drama, but not when we're performing—and of course, as always, tips are appreciated." She presses her hand to her chest. "I'll be your emcee tonight, Mrs. Frisbee Lane. If you're interested in tossing your frisbee down my lane after the show, my bartenders will take your number, and I'll call you later, darling." More hoots and hollers. "Now let's get this night started with a club favorite. Put your hands together for Winter Lips."

The lights dim, and I can't help it, I place my hand on JP's leg and say, "I can't believe you brought me to a drag show. This is…this is so freaking amazing."

From his pocket, he pulls out a wad of cash and holds it in front of me. "Have at it, babe. Tip well."

And once again…my heart skips a beat.

"I'm so jealous of Fifi Heart's cleavage," I say as JP opens the waiting car door for me. Before I get in, I turn to him and press my boobs together. "How do I get that kind of lift?"

"You have plenty of lift. Now, get your ass in the car."

"Not like Fifi," I groan as I take a seat in the car and buckle up. "You saw it, her cleavage was kissing her chin."

JP shuts the door behind him and buckles up, as well. "You're perfect just as you are, Kelsey," he says as he leans his head back and closes his eyes.

"Are you falling asleep on me?" I poke him in the arm. "You can't fall asleep."

He turns his head and smirks. "Just taking a second. Can you stop jabbering for a hot minute?"

"Well, excuse me if I just bore witness to one of the greatest shows of my entire life. I'm still reeling."

"Greatest, huh?"

I nod and twist my body so I'm facing him. "JP, that was so much fun. And I never thought sliding money in between fake breasts could be so much fun, but, God, I feel like a new woman."

"I'm glad you enjoyed it."

"I didn't just enjoy it," I say seriously, pulling his attention. "I honestly think that was the most fun I've had in a while."

And that's the truth.

The minute the show started, I was into it. I've never been to a drag show before, but I'm a firm believer in not missing one episode of *RuPaul's Drag Race*, so I knew what to expect going in. Lord help me, I didn't think it was going to be that amazing. And it wasn't just the show, it was JP, too. He was so relaxed, so…present. He wasn't sarcastic. He was just… smiling and having a great time, while making sure *I* was taken care of. His arm never once strayed from my chair, and at one point, I felt him playing with the ends of my hair as LuLu Lemons lip-synched to "I Will Always Love You."

"Good. You deserve it," he says as he looks away.

I have this weird urge to take his hand in mine, to curl against his side and breathe in this man that feels new, but also…the same. But even though the urge is strong, I know it's not what I should do. I mean, it's definitely not what I should do. I need to remind myself what tonight is all about—JP proving to me that his choices in activities are better than mine.

I can admit when I've been defeated.

And this night blew me away.

"Thank you for tonight, JP."

Still with his eyes shut, he says, "It's not over yet."

"It's not?" I ask, surprised.

He shakes his head. "Nope, just sit back and relax. We'll arrive at our final destination shortly."

Lampposts line the wood-planked pier all the way to where it ends in the middle of the Bay. The deep richness of the midnight sky looms over us as distant lights from the city twinkle behind us. A cool breeze lifts off the water as we walk slowly down the long stretch of boardwalk, the gentle sound of water lapping at the Bay's edge as our soundtrack. Dotted with only a few people, JP and I are almost completely alone.

"I didn't think you were a touristy person," I say in awe as we walk. "Wouldn't this classify as a touristy spot?"

"Pier Thirty-Nine, yes. Pier Seven, not so much. You learn that quickly when you stay here for more than a few days."

"When did you start coming out here?"

"I was often too wired when my brothers went to bed, so I'd go out. They assumed I was hitting the bars, or attempting to hook up with someone for the night, but I came down here, walked to the end of the pier, and just stared out into the dark water."

"What would you think about?" I ask.

"Anything. Everything. Whatever was on my mind at the moment."

"So why did you bring me here?" I ask as we continue making our way down the long stretch. "You don't have anything to think on, do you?"

"There's always something to think about, and I figured you might like it here. If you ever come back, this could be your thinking spot, too."

"I like that a lot," I say as I gently bump my shoulder against his.

He smiles and brings his arm around my shoulder, pulling me into his side as we walk.

"This might be the best place to come after a long day of organizing. Stop by the bakery, get one of those honey cakes, snap a picture of it, and gloat, then come here and eat it alongside the Bay."

"Careful of the birds, they're ruthless during the day."

"Good point."

"You know how I know that?" he asks.

"Please tell me it's by experience."

He nods. "It was a long goddamn day in the conference room with my brothers, I needed some air, so I grabbed some Thai food to go, brought it down here, and started eating. It was slow at first. A random bird here, a seagull there. I flailed a bit, trying to scare them away, but then they started talking...chirping to each other. Saying, *Hey, there's an unsuspecting idiot over there at the end of the pier—*"

"Why do they have a Brooklyn accent?"

"These birds have been places." That makes me laugh, and he continues. "I didn't think much of it at first, when another bird landed in front of me. One off to the side, then one behind me. They swarmed, their numbers outweighing my limbs, and they grew closer and closer until one brave soul pecked me on the leg."

"No, it didn't."

"It fucking did. Right on the shin. I yelled at it, obviously, bent down to check on my shin, and that's when they converged."

"They used a decoy bird on you."

"Precisely. I was a lost man, had no defense. The birds attacked. Feathers were everywhere. Beaks were knocking together, and there was nothing I could do other than toss my to-go box of food as far from me as I could and hold on for dear life until they left me a shaking shell of a man on the boardwalk."

Chuckling so hard, I feel tears under my eyes, I say, "Oh my God, you were almost pecked to death."

"That wasn't even the worst part."

"What was the worst part?"

"When I was screaming at them, begging them to leave me alone, one of them pooped."

"Gah, you were pooped on? They took your food and then did a doo-doo on you? How is that fair?"

"It's not, but, with all of the flapping and flailing, the poop somehow flipped in my direction and landed on my face."

I gasp and cover my mouth. "Oh my God, no, it didn't."

"It did. Bird shit landed on my face. Needless to say, my already shitty day—no pun intended—became an even shittier one."

"I'm surprised you came back here after that."

"Wasn't the pier's fault," he says. "It was mine for naively thinking I could eat a meal in a place where tourists have no concept of not feeding the wildlife, because the more you feed them, the more aggressive they become. A lesson was learned, and whenever I come here now, it's usually just me and my thoughts. Well…now you."

We reach the end of the pier. I walk up to the railing and lean against it, gazing at the waves and the expanse of darkness. The breeze picks up, a chill rushes through me, and before I can cross my arms for added warmth, JP places his leather jacket on my back. I glance over my shoulder and find him in his thin long-sleeved T-shirt. "JP, I don't want you to be cold."

"I'm good; don't worry about me," he says before coming up behind me, putting his arms on either side of me on the fence, and leaning his chest against my back. I'm pinned against the rail. For a moment, I'm stiff, unsure what to do, but when the warmth hits me, I ease into the hold.

"How's your mom? Still enjoying being alone with her man, Jeff, in their house?"

I chuckle. "Yes." Lottie had been living with them, and one of the main reasons she struck up a deal with Huxley in the first place was to give our mom and Jeff some privacy after many years of dealing with us girls. Jeff and our mom have been to many dinners and outdoor parties at Lottie and Huxley's house, and JP and Breaker know them by now. "They're loving it. Currently, they're building a pergola and fighting over what color to paint it."

JP rests his chin on my shoulder, the scruff of his cheek pressing against mine.

Call me crazy, but this doesn't seem very short-term companionship-like, this feels like more, and my romantic heart is trying to make something of it, while my brain is telling it no, no, no, no.

"What color does your mom want to paint it?"

"Black," I answer, leaning more against his chest. "She wants to go with the trends. And of course, Jeff, the traditionalist, wants to stain it, because to him, painting wood is an absolute sin."

"Who do you think is going to win?"

"My mom, of course. She always wins. I'm sure she'll let him win in another way, though. Maybe with some potted plant to decorate the area."

"That's right, he's an avid gardener. Maybe he's putting up a big fight about the color, then intentionally letting her win so she'll allow him to pick the plants."

"Ooo, I never thought of it that way. Knowing Jeff, I could see him doing that."

"When the pergola is done, are they going to have you over to test it out?"

"I'm sure they will. Although, we've been spending more time as a family at Huxley and Lottie's. Mom wants to host a bridal shower for Lottie in their backyard. Being her maid of honor and all, I'll help make that happen. Hey, are you the best man?"

"Breaker and I are sharing the responsibility," he answers. "But since I'm older I get to walk down the aisle with the maid of honor. Lucky you."

"Oh, yes, lucky me. I'm sure you will make some inappropriate comments."

"Wouldn't be right if I didn't." He sighs and then says, "I'm happy for Huxley, though, despite how their relationship came about. Since he's the oldest, I feel like he's always carried the burden of making sure we're all taken care of. When we decided to invest money into a business of our own, he sat us down and said he was setting us up for the future, which he did. Financially, Breaker and I are both set. We don't have to worry."

"But when it comes to happiness?" I ask.

"Still figuring that out." He straightens up and says, "I'm sure you have some early morning meetings. I should get you back to the penthouse."

"Unfortunately, I do."

I turn to face him and just catch the way his face almost falls in disappointment. But he puts his arm around my shoulders again, and together, we walk back up the pier.

"Thank you, again, for tonight. I had a lot of fun."

"I did, too," he says.

"I was kind of afraid when we were told to come up here that it would be awkward and weird. It was at first, but these last two days have been really great. Just what I needed."

"Yeah, about that," he says just as his phone rings in his pocket. Groaning, he takes it out, and I see Huxley's name flash across it before he silences the phone call. But it's only seconds before Huxley rings again.

"Must be important," I say. "Go ahead, answer it. I'll meet you in the car."

"You sure?" he asks.

"Yeah. It's fine." I go to take off his jacket but he holds his hand up.

"Keep it. I'm fine." And then he turns away and brings the phone to his ear. "What?" he answers in an annoyed tone.

As I walk toward the car, I hear a distant "Fuck" slip out of his mouth and my stomach immediately churns with worry.

It takes him about ten minutes before he joins me in the warm car, and when he sits down, I can tell the good mood he was in is gone as he moves his hand over his jaw. I'm afraid to ask, but I know if I don't at least check with him, I'll regret it.

"Everything okay?"

"Yeah," he says through clenched teeth. "Just some bullshit stuff I have to deal with tomorrow."

"Anything I can help with?" I ask.

He shakes his head and looks out the window. "Nah, nothing you can deal with."

And then, that's it.

He shuts down.

What once was a perfect evening quickly vanishes and I don't know what to do. What to say. Or how to help him. Therefore, we drive the rest of the way in silence. And when we get to the penthouse, I hand him his jacket and he tells me to have a good night. Even though JP was fun and mostly easygoing tonight, I'm sad with how it ended. I'm sad he shut down on me, because despite what he's said about friendship between men and women, I felt as though he let me in as his friend tonight. And then, that simply...*vanished*.

CHAPTER 14
JP

I WAS GOING TO KISS her last night.

There was no doubt in my mind that I was going to either kiss her on the pier or at the penthouse. It was going to happen, I was fucking ready, willing, and needy. But then, Huxley's call happened. Regis had gone behind my back to Huxley, saying Kelsey isn't experienced enough for the position. He believes we shouldn't have faith in her and that we should hire someone else. Someone on his team. Huxley told me to set my project straight.

I didn't even want this fucking project.

I blew a goddamn gasket, and even though my phone call with Huxley was only short, I took a moment before getting back in the car. I didn't want to blow up in front of Kelsey. And by the time I got back in the car, the moment was over.

And fuck was I in a bad mood about it last night. Instead of going to bed, I put on some workout clothes and went for a run. When I got back, I thought about checking on her, but by then, it was past midnight and I knew she'd be asleep.

What I would've given to tell her how I've been feeling about her, because, if anything, last night confirmed something for me. The night was perfect because I spent it with Kelsey. I loved hearing her moans of pleasure, her utter delight in the drag show, her obvious love of the beauty that is San Francisco Bay, and her clear enjoyment of being with me, too. So, I was about to tell her everything.

Huxley has the worst timing ever.

I wish I wasn't that person who let small things affect my mood, I wish I could just let them roll off me and enjoy the moment, but that's not me. It's why I woke up this morning ready to make it up to her. I had some bagels delivered, put together a fruit platter, and spent some time making bacon and eggs.

The last two days have been different, and I felt we've connected on another level. I hope she's seen a different side of me, a side that appeals to her. I know she finds me attractive—and I don't say that in a conceited way. I see the way she looks at me, but as she's proven, attraction doesn't mean everything to her. She wants a partner in this life, and unless I show her I can be that kind of man for her, I'm not sure she'll ever give me a chance.

But I'm there. I can feel it. Last night, the night before…I can be the man she needs, and this morning, I plan on driving that home. The Mayor's Ball is tonight, and my plan is to spoil her with a trip to find a dress, to get her hair and makeup done, to make the entire night special, and when the moment is right, I'm going to ask her out. I'm going to ask her to give me a chance. I'm fucking nervous as shit, but I know if I don't ask her, I'll regret it.

I'm in the middle of constructing the breakfast sandwiches when she comes into the living room wearing a pair of tight black pants and a maroon tank top. Fuck, she's so pretty, so pretty it's painful. When she spots me in the kitchen again, she pauses and adjusts the earring she's trying to put in.

"Morning," I say to her, my heart pounding a mile a minute.

She smiles. "Good morning. Did you make me breakfast again?"

"I did." Pride beams through me. "How do you feel about breakfast sandwiches?"

"I feel very positive about them." She walks up to me, her perfume creating a goddamn viselike grip around my chest, constricting it. "Are you feeling better from last night?"

"Yeah." I reach out and take her hand in mine. So soft, so perfect for mine. "Sorry about the way I reacted. Huxley told me some bullshit that I have to deal with tonight and it put me in a bad mood. I shouldn't have responded that way, especially since we were having such a good time."

"What's tonight—oh, you have to go to that Mayor's Ball thing, right?"

"Yeah, I do. Fancy event with a bunch of people I have to talk to." I press our palms together. "But, I was thinking—"

"Do you know what you're wearing?" she asks. "A ball gown, I hope." She wiggles her brows, causing me to chuckle.

"Yeah, it's being dry-cleaned as we speak. I pick it up at noon."

"You must show me pictures when I get back from my date," she says as she releases my hand and walks over to the coffeemaker, grabbing herself a mug.

I can feel all the color completely drain out of my face, leaving me ashen, anguished...shook.

Date...

Fuck, she has that date set up with Dave Toney's brother. I completely forgot about it. After the two nights we spent together, is she still going on that? Hell, a part of me thought that maybe she wouldn't. That maybe she'd set him aside, give me a chance.

Evidently, that was a stupid assumption. *What do you think, dickhead? You're the one who has pushed that your time together is simply a short-term companionship.* She wants long-term love. Fuck.

I grip the back of my neck, this new emotion bubbling up inside me, piercing my chest, constricting my lungs.

"Still, uh, still going on that date?" I stammer out, my mind whirling.

Oblivious to the multitude of emotions racing through me, she starts her coffee pod and turns toward me, her hands on the counter. "Yes, and I'm nervous. What should I wear?"

One of those hideous peasant dresses from Target.

Fuck!

Don't wear anything; instead stay here with me.

Cancel the date.

See me . . . Kelsey.

Fucking see me.

But the confession is lost on my insecure tongue, and instead of voicing what I really want to tell her, I turn away and mumble, "What you're wearing is fine."

Why did I think she wasn't going to go on that date? Maybe because the last two nights, things have almost felt like . . . we've been on dates. Yeah, I told her they were time spent with her short-term companion, but I still thought maybe she felt something, a connection.

Last night I wanted to show her a good time; I wanted to show her that we could have fun together, not just bicker. I wanted to show her I could be someone she could depend on. Someone who fulfills what she's looking for.

The light touches.

The interesting conversation.

The self-deprecating stories.

I fucking tried last night, until Huxley called.

Fucking Huxley. I never should've answered the phone.

"I can't wear this on a date," Kelsey says as if I suggested the most preposterous thing ever. "It's business attire."

"Aren't dates like business at first, though?" I ask as I finish stacking her plate with food. I don't bother taking it over to the table, but leave it on the counter for her and head to the table with my plate.

"Uh, they aren't for me. Not sure how you treat a date, but they're supposed to be fun and exciting, a separate part of your day, something to look forward to. If I wear this outfit, I'll just be reminded of work. Plus, I like wearing dresses on dates."

She didn't wear a dress when we went out.

Because it wasn't a fucking date, you idiot.

Could've been, if you were able to actually tell her how you feel.

"I don't want to be too fancy, though," she continues, really driving what feels like a knife into my back. I know I have no right to feel this way, but I can't control it. All I can think about is how this girl, whom I've crushed on for a bit now, is going out with someone else after I've attempted to show her how I could be someone she might like. "Get this, you're going to laugh." Doubtful. "He's taking me to the Crab House. Can you believe that?"

Yes, I can.

Because the guy seems like a douche.

Because he's not me.

Because he doesn't fucking know you as I do.

He doesn't know that you need someone to push you out of your comfort zone. He doesn't know that you're someone who would enjoy something like a drag show but would never go yourself. He doesn't know that you'd appreciate a quiet walk along an empty boardwalk where you can appreciate the small things like a starry sky and the sound of your feet tapping along the old wood.

"But unlike when you and I had dinner there, I can't possibly order a whole crab, snap the leg off in front of him, and wear a bib."

"Why the hell not?" I ask.

"Because, with you, it didn't matter. I wasn't trying to impress you. I don't want Derek thinking I'm some psycho who likes mutilating sea creatures. I mean, I'm not, but let's be honest, I was sort of putting on a show when it came to snapping those legs. I wanted to startle you."

Mission accomplished, but I also found it endearing. I liked it.

"I think I might just get a salad," she continues.

"That's bullshit," I say under my breath.

"What?" she asks as she grabs her fresh coffee, puts a dab of milk and some sugar in it, and then brings her plate and mug to the table to join me.

"I said, that's bullshit." My tone has an edge to it now and I can see from the way she sits back, eyes on me, that she noticed as well.

"Wait, are you mad?"

Yes.

Irritated, as well.

Also, jealous.

Really fucking jealous.

"Just don't try to be someone you're not, is all." No use starting a fight with her.

"I'm not," she says, mildly insulted.

"You are if you don't get a crab."

"I like salads too, you know?"

"Then why didn't you get a salad when we went to the Crab House?"

"Because I'm more comfortable around you," she shoots back, and that confession nearly brings a smile to my face, only for it to be wiped away as she says, "I don't expect you to understand this since you don't dare date people. You only test-run them to make sure they're good enough for your bed."

Ouch.

And there it is, the way she truly sees me.

"Is that what you really think?" I ask.

"You've had one girlfriend, JP."

"Because no one has been interesting enough for me to consider going any further than a few dates. I was just starting to get to know Genesis before the gala, but we hadn't slept together. Hasn't anyone ever told you quality versus quantity, Kelsey?" I stand from my chair, pick up my plate and coffee, and walk away. If I don't now, I'll say something I'll regret.

"JP, wait. I didn't mean to insult you."

"It's fine, Kelsey," I call out. "Have a good date." I close my door behind me and then slowly slide down it until I'm sitting on the floor. I set my plate and mug down and then grip my hair in my hands, pain ripping through me.

Fuck. I should just go tell her how I feel. I should tear through this door, disrupt her breakfast, and ask her to not go on the date, but to go to the Mayor's Ball with me instead.

But I did already ask her…and she chose the date. I don't think she'll ever see me as someone she wants to know better.

I'm the guy who fucks around, not the settling type. And that's a fucking painful realization.

Before I met Kelsey, she wasn't wrong. As I said to her, though, I haven't found someone I thought I wanted to spend more than a night or three with. There hasn't been an intellectual, physical, or emotional connection. Unlike with Kelsey, where I feel all three. Even though I tease her, purposely aggravate her—because she's fun to fluster—I do respect her. And I want more. I do see her as someone I'd consider settling down with.

I've never had to try hard to get a woman to want me. And the first time I do, I'm rejected.

Can I change her mind? Or is it a lost cause?

"Are you there?" Huxley asks as I sit in my car, staring out the window, listening to his annoying voice through the phone.

"Yes, I'm here," I answer through a clenched jaw.

"Why do you sound short?"

"Oh, I don't know, maybe because I'm in a goddamn tuxedo at this stupid Mayor's Ball, where I have to not only speak with Regis about his stupid bullshit, but also suck up to the mayor."

"This is to expand the business, JP."

"Don't you think we've expanded enough? Jesus Christ, Huxley, we can barely keep up with everything we have going on. You're getting married, and you're going to start a family. Do you really think starting more projects is a smart idea?"

"You thought it was a smart idea months ago, so why am I hearing differently now?"

"I actually didn't say anything in that meeting, if you'd paid attention. You rattled on about new opportunities, Breaker nodded with dollar signs in his eyes, while I sat there, wondering why the fuck we were going to start something new when our plates were already full."

"Then you should've spoken up. We're not mind readers."

"I have spoken up," I shout into the phone, the better part of my cool completely gone. The irritation and annoyance of this morning erupt in one smooth punch to Huxley. "I've said shit to you before, but you never listen. You and Breaker never fucking listen. So here I am, sitting in my goddamn car, waiting to go into this ball to help accomplish your dreams, not mine."

"For the company, JP. Not for me. For the company."

"The company is you, and we're just your minions along for the ride."

"Where the fuck is all of this coming from? Did something happen up there?"

"Of course, that's what you'd assume, that something would happen that would put me in this *mood*, right? It can't possibly be how I actually feel."

He's silent for a second and then says, "I think you and I need to have a meeting."

"Yeah, no fucking thank you," I say before hanging up.

I press my fingers to my brow and take a deep, calming breath.

Chill, man.

It's hard to chill when it feels like nothing is right. Absolutely nothing. I don't feel good in my own skin, like…I don't belong here. Here I am chastising Kelsey for trying to be someone she's not when I'm doing the same exact thing as her.

"Are you ready to get out, sir?" my driver asks me.

For a brief moment, I consider what would happen if I don't go in there. If I don't find Regis and put him in his place. If I don't talk to the mayor about "our" plans. We'd have a tougher time winning bids on any more historic buildings. But that's not that big of a deal in my opinion. But what about Kelsey? What kind of uphill battle will she have if Regis continues to undermine her? Why should I care?

Because you do.

Because you care about her.

Despite the fact that she's on a date right now with another man, I still care about her.

And that's the reason I'm opening my car door, buttoning my tuxedo jacket, and temporarily wiping away the anger in the pit of my stomach, ready to be unleashed.

I let my driver know I won't be long, then stuff my phone in my pocket when I reach the front entrance. No need to hit up the red carpet. I'm not interested in that shit, not when I'm feeling so resentful. Huxley will bitch about it later, since he likes to have us show our faces at events like this, but if he wants it done his way, then next time, he can go.

I slip through the door after getting checked off the guest list and head straight to the massive bar at the back of the ballroom. I bypass the name-card table since I'm not staying for dinner, don't bother shaking hands with the people milling about, and drop my hand on the edge of the bar and order two fingers of scotch. Then I turn around and scan the crowd.

To an outsider, an event like this would seem so glamorous with the designer dresses and the well-pressed suits, but to me, it's just another night in the elite world I live in. There's nothing great that happens for humankind at these events. Instead, hands are shaken, deals are made, and enemies become frenemies for a moment in time as they fake interested expressions for the people around them.

The benefit of these events is for the people solely in this room, and no one else. The mayor isn't here to formulate change; he's here to shake hands with people who can help secure his vote. It's sad, but that's the way the world works, unfortunately.

"JP, didn't think I'd see you tonight," Regis says, standing next to me at the bar. He orders us both a scotch and I let him. "Wasn't sure you attended these events."

Only when forced to.

Thankfully, Regis is making this easy on me, and I didn't have to seek him out.

"When the mood strikes me, I'll put on a tuxedo."

The bartender hands each of us our drinks, and I slip a twenty-dollar bill into his tip jar before turning back around to face the gathering.

Time to get down to business.

"Heard you called Huxley." I sip my drink. I keep my eyes ahead, making sure to give off the vibe that I'm not happy.

"I did," Regis says, not even bothering to hide his arrogance. "I felt like the call needed to be made."

I stick one hand in my pocket. "Why?"

"I felt like you were preoccupied with other things, not seeing the damage her ideas could have to the building."

"And what exactly was I preoccupied with? Because, as I recall, I was present for that entire first meeting, and all I saw from you was misogynistic behavior that will not be tolerated."

From the corner of my eye, I see him shift, and then he says, "You were preoccupied with her. I saw the way you stared at her mouth, got lost in her words, sided with her ideas."

Insecurity constricts my throat. Is that fucking true? I don't recall looking at her a certain way or paying attention to her more. Either way, it's not his fucking place to make that kind of call.

Before answering, I take a sip of my scotch and then turn toward him. He's still facing the crowd and I speak very carefully, so he can hear everything clearly.

"You must be mistaken, Regis, because she's a colleague, nothing more, and unlike some other men, I'm sure someone like you, I have the ability to keep my mind focused on the project and not the woman attempting to use her voice. What you might have seen as affection or one-sidedness toward Miss Gardner was merely the ability to listen attentively to an intelligent woman, a woman who's a partner in our business." I step a little closer. "Did you hear that? A partner. Do you know what being a partner with Cane Enterprises entails?"

I wait for him to answer, but all he does is swallow back his drink.

"Being a partner means we've vetted you. We've made sure that not only are you credible, but we have confidence in putting our name on your brand. Miss Gardner and her business, Sustainably Organized, is a partner. She's fully trusted by all three of the Cane brothers. We've invested in her company to help our company, so any problem you might have with her is a problem with us. Do you understand that?"

He nods.

"And when working in the future with Miss Gardner, you will not only listen to her suggestions, but you will respect them."

He nods again.

"Because if you don't respect Miss Gardner, then your days working with Cane Enterprises are numbered." I grip his shoulder and lighten my voice as I say, "Have a good evening, Regis."

Asshole.

How the fuck did we end up working with him?

As I go to move past him, a large man in an all-black suit walks up to me. There's an earpiece in his left ear, and there's no doubt who he works for. "Mr. Cane, the mayor would like to have a conversation with you."

Perfect. The sooner I can talk to him, the sooner I can get the hell out of here.

The guard walks me past the main ballroom and through a series of halls before opening a rather grand door to the mayor's office.

"He'll be with you shortly." The door clicks shut behind me, and I take that moment to observe the room. It's the mayor's private office. I've been in here only one other time. I know there's a secret door behind one of the bookshelves, and just like the Oval Office, there's a door hidden by the seams in the wallpaper, an entrance only the mayor uses.

In the middle of the room is a large mahogany desk that has been used by every mayor of San Francisco for the last God knows how many years, but the pictures on the credenza behind the desk, those are specific to the one and only Eugene Herbert, the current mayor of San Francisco.

The secret door slides open and Eugene walks through with a large smile on his face and a cigar in hand.

"JP Cane, I'm so glad you could make it." Eugene comes up to me and takes my hand in his.

I offer him a solid shake and say, "Mr. Mayor, thank you for the invite. It's always nice to catch up with everyone." It's painful how fake I'm acting right now.

"You can drop that 'Mr. Mayor' crap." He laughs and gestures to the seating area. I take a seat in a brown leather chair directly across from him. He leans over to the coffee table and opens a small box, offering me a cigar.

I hold up my hand. "I'm good."

"Not sure I've ever seen you smoke, Cane." He flicks open a wooden Zippo lighter and takes a few puffs of his cigar before it's lit.

"Not my thing," I say. "Never was able to get into it. Cough too much."

Eugene smiles and blows a puff of smoke into the air. "Takes some stiff lungs to handle a good cigar. Although, I see you can handle a solid drink. What's that? Brandy?"

"Scotch," I answer. "My drink of choice as of late."

"Ah, how's business?"

"Good," I answer. "Growing, as always."

"I see that." He leans forward and knocks his cigar on an ashtray. "May I suggest why you're here?"

"Please," I say.

"Word on the street is you acquired the Angelica Building."

"That's correct," I answer, taking another sip of my scotch.

"That was a very sought-after building, so I was surprised that a company based in Los Angeles won, given how many local companies were after it."

"We lucked out."

He nods his head. "What are your plans?"

"Currently, those are classified."

He raises his brow as if to say, *Do you know whom you're talking to?* But I know how to play this game, so I'll let him pressure me; he likes power; that's why he's smoking a cigar in his office, attempting to intimidate me.

"You do realize that I'm not an idiot, JP. Now that you've acquired the Angelica, I know you're going to want more once you're done with that building, and I also know that you haven't talked with any of the historical societies in town. Am I correct?"

I nod, giving him a little nibble.

"Cane Enterprises is known for their beautiful buildings around the country, but you're also known for your commercial buildings that are stripped of all character and maximized for profit."

"Smart business choice. I think it's done well for us."

"It might have done well for you in other parts of the country, but not here."

"And that's why we don't have any plans of stripping down the Angelica. We're quite aware of the importance of the Angelica to this city. We also understand preserving history is vital, as well. Rest assured, when we're done with the renovations, not only will the Angelica be brought back to her original beauty, but she'll be fully functioning, more environmentally friendly, and will help the people of this city—if I have anything to do with it," I finish, an idea formulating in my head.

Help the people.

That's exactly what I want to do with this building.

"Well…" Eugene taps his cigar on the ashtray. "It seems as though I'm just going to have to wait and see."

"Correct. But when I say the Angelica is in the right hands, I mean it. Once we're done, you'll seek out more buildings for us to renovate around your beautiful city."

He lets out a hearty laugh and stands. I stand as well. "We'll see about that, JP." He holds his hand out and I give it a shake. "Good seeing you."

"You too…Mr. Mayor."

He smirks and then leads me out of his office.

Since my work here is done, I decide not to stick around, a choice I know Huxley wouldn't be happy with, but I don't give a fuck. I'm feeling like shit, and the only thing I want to do right now is sit in front of a fucking screen and do absolutely nothing.

I wish I could say the last half hour has distracted me from the turmoil that's pulsing through my head, but sadly, it has not, because I know when I get back to the penthouse, it'll be empty. Not a single light will be on, and when I go to her room and knock on her door, she won't be there. She probably won't be home for a while, which can only mean one thing—she's probably bonding with Derek. Having a good time. Getting to know another man.

The drive back is a silent one spent staring out the window. What once used to be my favorite city to visit is quickly becoming my least favorite. Funny how quickly that can change, how a person can remind you of a place, steal the joy right from your grasp.

When I arrive back at the penthouse—a dark penthouse—I change into a pair of shorts, nothing else, and grab a beer from the fridge, my only source of alcohol in the place.

And my phone rings.

I wonder who that could be—hear the sarcasm?

"What?" I answer.

"How did it go?" Huxley asks.

"Don't you have a life?"

"I'm worried about you."

"About me or about your business?"

"Our business," Huxley says. "And I'm worried about you. You sound like you're in a dark place. What's going on? Breaker suggested you have feelings for Kelsey."

Jesus Christ.

I drag my hand over my face. "Are we in some fucking gossiping schoolyard I don't know about? Breaker needs to keep his mouth shut, and I swear to God, if you say anything to Lottie, I'm going to actually murder you."

"I wouldn't," he says. "But is it true?"

"I don't fucking know, okay? I don't fucking know anything. And it's not like it matters anyway. I'm not her type. I'm not someone she'd go for, that's evident, because she's out with Derek Toney right now and he couldn't be more opposite of me. And where the fuck did he come from, anyway? Why is he going out with Kelsey?"

"Lottie set it up," Huxley answers. "Dude, listen, I'm going to send the plane tomorrow. I want to have this conversation with you in person."

"I'm not going to leave Kelsey up here by herself."

"You'll be back. But we have some business to talk about."

"Can you not?" I ask as I press my fingers to my brow. "Please, for the love of God, don't. Not right now." I tip back my beer. "And I'm not leaving tomorrow. Send a plane all you want; I'm not getting on it. Actually, I have to go. I can't fucking deal with this right now."

"JP, whatever the hell is going on, you need to talk to us."

"Yeah, I know, but I can't right now." I shake my head even though he can't see me. "I just fucking can't." And before he can respond, I hang up on him and toss my phone to the other end of the couch. "Fuck," I mutter, sinking into the fabric.

This itchy, uncontrollable, debilitating feeling starts to consume me.

Like I'm caught in a tornado of weary emotion and no matter what I do, I can't get out of it. It just keeps swirling around me. I have no control. I feel like everything is slipping through my grasp.

My sanity.

My job.

Kelsey…

I'm not even sure what I'd do if she looked my way and saw me as more than just JP, how I'd handle the things she needs in her life but, fuck, I want to try. Because when she called me Jonah last night, nothing had ever sounded more right. For a moment, I wasn't just JP, one of the Cane brothers. I was Jonah. A man who likes a woman. A man who's ready for change. *Ready to start my own life…whatever that actually means.*

CHAPTER 15
KELSEY

OH MY GOD.

He's so cute.

Derek, that is.

I mean...really cute.

Thick hair, just short of fluffy, but that's okay. And his style is kind of preppy, but in a cute way, not in a wears-a-cardigan-over-his-shoulders way. His smile is adorable, his eyes are beautiful, and he has a lovely deep voice.

Lottie was right...this guy is a catch.

"I don't think I've ever eaten as much as I have tonight," Derek says, patting his stomach. "I hope I didn't gross you out or anything with the way I took down that crab."

I chuckle. "Not at all. It was impressive." Mind you, I ate the same thing the other night with JP and still had room for dessert.

"Not sure if I should be proud that I impressed you with my eating habits."

"Maybe a little." I wink.

He glances at his watch and winces. "I hate to be that guy, but I have an early morning meeting tomorrow, and I think it's going to take me a long time to walk back to my hotel."

"You're going to walk? I hope it's close."

"A few blocks...uphill. And trust me when I say, I SHOULD walk back."

I chuckle. "Burning some late-night calories?"

"I have to." Since he already paid for the meal, he stands from his chair, and I do the same. Once my things are gathered, I walk toward the exit. He places his hand on the small of my back and guides me down the stairs and out the front door.

Chills run up my spine.

This was a nice date.

There was no arguing.

There was a constant flow of easy conversation.

And even though he's a bit awkward in some ways, he's great in others.

"I'm glad I came out tonight," I say as we reach the pier. I wait for him to take my hand, but when he doesn't, I settle with holding the strap of my purse.

"I'm glad you did, too. Ellie was telling me over and over that I needed to take you out for a meal. I can see why. You're great company, Kelsey."

"Thank you." I smile up at him. "How much longer are you in San Francisco?"

"A week. What about you?"

"Same," I say. "At least, that's what's on the schedule. Who knows; things could change."

"Yeah, doesn't it always seem like the schedule is changing? I was only supposed to be here for a few days, but the time keeps getting extended. This was the first night I've had that didn't involve business. It was a nice reprieve."

"I'm glad I could help with that."

"You did." He sticks his hands in his pockets. "Can I ask you something?"

"Of course," I say with a bright smile, because I have a feeling I know what he's going to ask. He's a bit shy, so his approach doesn't surprise me. My answer will be a yes when he asks for another date. I've truly enjoyed myself tonight. We had some laughs, and even though there were some stutters in our conversation, overall, it was a great night. So, yes, I'll say *yes* to a second date.

"I was curious." He bashfully looks away. "Would you be comfortable with telling me how you like working with Cane Enterprises?"

"That would be great," I answer before I can process his question.

Wait...

What?

Confused, he looks at me with a pinched brow, and that's when I actually register what he asked.

Cane Enterprises.

Working with them.

Oh.

"Errr, that would be a great question to ask," I say, trying to cover up. Not very smooth. "And the answer would be yes. I enjoy working with them a lot."

He nods. "They seem sort of ruthless. Dave was telling me all about what Huxley and Lottie did. It seems they would do just about anything to score a deal, like they don't care about the people around them."

"No, that's not the case at all," I say. "They care deeply about their employees and the work they do. That entire situation stemmed from a momentary lapse of judgment on Huxley's end. He felt awful and swore he'd never do something like that again."

Derek nods. "That's really good to hear. I know Dave can be sort of blind at times when working with other people. He has a heart of gold, and I just wanted to check. I hope I didn't ruin the date by asking."

"Not at all. I actually like that you asked. It shows me that you care about your brother."

"I do. He can be a knucklehead, kind of weird at times, but he's a good man and he's built a solid business. I just want to make sure no one is taking advantage of him."

I smooth my hand over his arm. "That's really kind of you."

He smiles down at me and sticks his hand in his pocket again just as we make it to a row of cabs. "I had a great time, Kelsey."

"I had a nice time too, Derek. I truly did." Such a good time that I hope he leans in and kisses me. I'd totally kiss him back. I think there could be something there between us.

But a kiss would tell me if we have the chemistry I think we have.

I wet my lips as he reaches for a cab door.

Kissing outside a cab, how romantic.

I step in closer to him.

And wait.

Wait for that kiss.

For him to bend over, pucker up, and lay it on me.

But just as I expect him to plant one on me, he takes a step away from me and offers me his hand.

His…hand.

Confused, I take it, and he gives me a solid shake.

"Great meeting you," he says, before letting go and taking another step backwards.

Errr…what's happening?

Where's the kiss?

Or the hug?

Or the offer to call me so we can do this again sometime?

I wait for a few heartbeats, but when nothing happens, I realize this is it. A handshake. That's what I'm getting tonight. A freaking handshake and a *nice to meet you.*

What on earth is happening? This is the end of a business meeting, not a date. Did I miss something? Did I do something wrong? Does he not like me? Self-doubt fills me, causing an ugly set of emotions.

You're not enough.

You're not pretty enough.

JP has said I'm hot twice, but that was clearly just to get in my pants. Derek is backing away after a freaking handshake.

If this was Lottie, Derek would be figuring out a way to stay longer.

My throat grows tight, and before I can make a total ass of myself in front of him, I decide to bid him a goodbye and get into the car, where I can lick my wounds in private.

"Okay. Bye." I wave at him.

"Bye, Kelsey."

He shuts the door with finality and then walks away. Well...

I tell my driver the name of the hotel I'm staying at, then lean back in my seat and stare out the window.

Did I miss something?

I thought we were having a good evening.

I thought we were making a connection. We bonded over *Power Rangers*, for heaven's sake, not something I'd want to bond over, but we had a conversation about them that made us laugh and reminisce about growing up.

He talked about his family. I talked about mine.

He touched my hand several times throughout dinner, and I know for a fact that when I went to the bathroom, he watched me walk away. The girl who followed me into the bathroom shortly after told me the guy I was with had it bad for me, with the way he tracked me all the way to the bathroom.

So, I don't know... Call me crazy, but I guess I read it all wrong. I guess there was something I did wrong that he didn't like. Or maybe...maybe I just didn't impress him the way that I thought I did.

Just like every other man who has taken me out...I didn't make that lasting impression.

I'm not memorable.

Addicting.

I'm not someone a man wants another night with.

I consider texting Lottie, but I don't have the energy to hash out everything, so instead, I stare out the window until I reach the hotel.

I've no idea where JP is right now, probably still at the ball, doing some sort of schmoozing that he's probably hating. Or probably on his way back to a woman's apartment because *she* was too gorgeous to walk away from. *She* will enjoy more than a handshake. And given our strange blowup this morning, why would he want to come back to the penthouse tonight?

But that's probably a good thing.

I don't think I could see anyone right now. I've never felt so unwanted in my life. First Edwin, now Derek. Is there something I'm doing that turns men off?

There has to be.

You're too desperate.

Thank you, JP. That will stick.

Spirit broken, the elevator doors part and I walk down the hotel hallway until I reach the penthouse. When I open the door, I'm met with a dark room, just as I expected. He's not here. I drop my purse on the table in the entryway and kick off my heels. I pick them up from the floor and head to my room.

"Enjoy your evening?" JP's deep voice scares me so much, I squeal and bring my hand to my heart.

I look to where his voice came from and spot him sitting in the chair in the dark corner, a beer in hand.

"You scared me." I catch my breath. "Why are you sitting in the dark?"

"Didn't feel like turning on the lights," he answers without moving.

"Well, it's weird." I reach over to an accent lamp on one of the side tables and switch it on. It illuminates the room so I can fully see JP. He's wearing only shorts again and his hair is a complete tumble of strands, pulled in all different directions.

He lifts the beer to his lips and, before taking a sip, he asks, "How was lover boy?"

"He's not my lover boy." He made that evident enough by offering me a sturdy handshake.

"Date not go well, then?" he asks, clearly in the mood to pick another fight. I'm not falling for it.

"It was great. Thanks. Now, if you'll excuse me, I'm going to bed."

"Did he kiss you?"

"That's none of your business," I say, as I turn back toward him.

He stands from his chair and his face slowly comes into the light with every step forward he takes. Now only a few feet from me, he sets his beer on the end table and stares at me, examining every inch of my face. "He didn't, did he? He didn't kiss you."

I'm not sure if he can see through the brave façade I'm trying to wear, or if he actually sees that these lips of mine are untouched, but he steps even closer and lifts his hand to my face, his thumb pulling on my bottom lip.

"He didn't kiss this mouth, did he?"

I take a step back, still clutching my heels. "Like I said, that's none of your business, JP." Before he can say another thing, I turn away from him and head to my room. I need to get out of this dress and into something comfortable so I can go to bed and forget this entire night. When I reach my room, I set down my heels and twist my arm behind me to undo my zipper. But, for some reason, even though I was the one who got myself into this dress, I can't seem to reach it.

Shit.

But then I feel a strong hand touch my shoulder.

I nearly jump out of my skin as he crowds my back and whispers, "Allow me." His voice feels like ripples of heat caressing my skin. I don't dare move. I don't dare say a thing because, I'm ashamed to say, I'm desperate. Desperate for a man to touch me. *I'm desperate to know that I'm someone who can be treasured the way Huxley treasures Lottie, and how Jeff loves Mom.*

But I think that's why it's been so confusing being around JP. He's sexy as hell, and in the moments we get along, the moments I feel such a deep connection—*as if I'm seeing the real JP*—I'm so tempted to want more. But knowing he doesn't want me for anything more than a sexy night has probably tipped me closer to this edge called desperation.

I'm just a hopeless romantic looking for someone to love her.

The zipper of my dress is gently pulled down until I feel the sides of my dress open. The grip he has on my shoulder tightens.

"What's this?" he asks, his finger tracing over my lingerie. "Did you wear this for him?"

My strapless, black bustier. I didn't, actually. It's something I like to wear every day. Lingerie is the one thing that I splurge on, because it makes me feel special. It makes me feel good under my clothes. It makes me feel sexy, even though my sex life is at an all-time low for the moment.

I spin around and hold my dress up with one hand across my chest. "I did," I answer, lying. I feel like provoking him. Misery loves company. It's a shitty thing to do, but I'm not exactly thinking clearly right now.

"And he didn't kiss you… That seems fucking stupid."

"I never said he didn't kiss me," I shoot back. "You just assumed."

He steps even closer, his hand now curling possessively around the nape of my neck. I have no idea what's happening, what's possessing him to do this, or possessing me to let it happen, but I stand tall—as tall as I can—and hold my chin up high, challenging him.

"I'm not assuming, I know."

"Were you watching us?"

He shakes his head. "I know you, Kelsey. If that man kissed you, you'd have come barreling into this penthouse, happy. But that's not the case, is it? There's a droop in your shoulders, no joy in your smile. The date didn't go the way you wanted it. And now, you're back at ground zero, attempting to find someone else to take you out."

Insult laces his every syllable, and it's like a repeated strike against my heart.

"The date was amazing, actually," I say. "And no, he didn't kiss me, but he was also being a gentleman, something I'm sure you know nothing about."

He propels me backward, and I'm so shocked that I brace my hands on his chest for balance, letting my dress slip to the ground, leaving me in nothing but my lingerie.

"What did I tell you about being a gentleman? I know how to hold a goddamn door open for a woman. I know how to make sure she's well taken care of on a date with engaging conversation. Being a gentleman doesn't mean you don't take what you both want."

"Are you saying you'd have kissed me?"

"I would've done more than kiss you," he says, his voice so dark that I wonder if something happened to him tonight, but I'm so lost in my own world that I don't have time to think about why he's acting like this, what has caused this...*aggression*. "I wouldn't have left you alone in a penthouse with another man, that's for damn sure."

He continues to walk me backwards until my legs hit the edge of the bed.

"I know your MO, JP, your end goal."

"Is that so?" he asks, his hand on my nape slowly dragging forward until his thumb is propped right under my chin, holding me in place. "And what exactly is my end goal, Kelsey?"

"Pleasure," I answer.

"You *would* say that," he says. He pushes me down on the bed and corrals me with a hand on either side of my shoulders. My breath gets stuck in my throat as he lowers his face mere inches from mine. "It's not always about pleasure, Kelsey. It's about the temptation."

"Are you trying to say I'm tempting?"

"Do you want me to find you tempting?"

I wet my lips. My heart hammers so loudly in my chest that I can barely hear myself think. "I just want someone to want to date me, maybe fall in love with me one day." I swallow. "And I think Derek could be that guy."

His brows narrow, tugging together at the center of his forehead. "Bullshit. Stop fucking lying to me and tell me the truth. Your date was barely enjoyable and the fucking douche didn't seize the opportunity to kiss you, leaving you unsatisfied."

"I was left completely satisfied."

"Is that so?" he asks, then lowers his head so his nose runs along my collarbone. A wave of goose bumps springs up on my skin as his breath caresses my chest. "So, you're telling me you wouldn't want more?"

God, I want so much more.

I want to feel something.

I want to know what it's like to be kissed again.

To have a man control me with his hands, with his mouth, with his words.

I want so much more than the date I had with Derek. I wanted him to want more of me. To tell me he wants to call me in the morning, ask me out again.

I want more than a freaking handshake at the end of the night.

But I can't tell JP that. I can't admit to him what a failure the end of the night was, so I keep my mouth shut. His nose rides up the column of my neck until he reaches my ear, where he asks, "Do you want to know what I would've done if I took you out on a date?"

Yes.

Desperately.

"No," I answer. "Because you didn't take me out, JP."

"If I took you out, you wouldn't be home this early. I'd find every opportunity I could to keep you out. I'd extend our night as long as I could until we had no choice but to say goodbye. And when we did"—he nibbles my ear, causing a tidal wave of lust to strike me—"when I said good night to you, it would be by leaning you against my car, stroking your cheek, and then holding you in place as I finally kissed you, the way I'd wanted to kiss you all goddamn night."

"And…and how would you kiss me?" I ask.

"Slowly, at first"—his hand slides to my jaw, just above my throat—"so you get a taste of me, and when I felt that you were comfortable, content, I'd part your lips and demand more. I'd press my body against yours, slip my hand into your hair, just at the base of your skull, and then tangle our tongues, pulling more and more from you until you're absolutely breathless." His nose runs along my cheek. "Just like you are now."

"I'm not breathless. Don't flatter yourself," I say.

His grip on my jaw grows tighter as he asks, "When are you going to learn not to lie to me? If I slipped my hand down your body and between your legs, I know you'd be wet."

I am.

I am wet, throbbing, and so full of need that I can barely process his words.

"Not every woman is won over by what you call charm."

He releases my jaw and sits up from his position, now standing in front of me looking down. His eyes scan my body, wrapped in black lace. That's when I take a second to let my eyes wander his body. Broad, straight shoulders; boulders in his biceps, so thick and veiny, leading all the way down to his impeccable inked forearms; and fingers that seem to curl toward his palm when anger sears through him. His chest is thick, strong, cut, leading down to his abs, which are stacked one right on top of the other. His belly button is the start of the metaphorical arrow that points down to the bulge in his shorts, the very prominent bulge.

He's turned on, just like me.

And instead of listening to his voice, letting him dirty-talk his way over my body, I'm provoking him, pushing him away, making him impossibly angrier.

Eyes on mine, he says, "Touch yourself. Show me you're not wet."

"Why?"

"Because I don't believe you. Show me you aren't won over by my charm."

My teeth run over my lip, my heart wildly beating. I know I'm wet. I know I'm turned on. And I know it's from him.

I move my hand down my body to between my legs. I slip my fingers past the lace and against my clit. My eyes instantly shut from the pressure, and I hate myself for giving up how I feel, for showing him that I'm exactly where he wants me to be.

My eyes fly open as he seizes my wrist, and I find him bent forward, one hand propped on the bed, the other bringing my fingers toward his mouth. He parts his lips, drags my fingers over his tongue, and then releases them.

Fuck, I don't think I've ever seen anything so sexy in my life.

"Fucking liar," he says, tucking my hand back under the lace between my legs. When I try to remove my hand, he keeps me there, pressing his hand against mine. "Why are you lying to me?" I don't answer him, so he says, "I wouldn't lie to you. I'm not concealing how I feel." I glance down at his bulge again, the fabric of his shorts outlining his cock.

"You are by wearing those shorts," I say. I don't know why I say it, maybe because I'm so far gone at this point, but I'm desperate for something, anything.

With his eyes still on mine, he reaches to his waistband, pulls his cock out, and strokes his length right in front of me.

Girthy.

Long.

Promising.

"Is this what you wanted?" he asks. "You wanted this cock?"

Yes.

I also want your lips.

Your hands.

Your body.

"Tell me why you're hard." I attempt to remove my hand from under my bustier again, but he stops me once again.

"Touch yourself," he demands. "I know you want to. I know you need to. Touch yourself, and I'll tell you why I'm hard."

I seal my lips together and slip my fingers along my slit until they press against my clit. With two fingers, I gently massage it while my legs spread on the mattress.

His eyes fall to where I'm pleasuring myself and then back up. He wets his lips and lowers one hand to the mattress, bringing himself closer while he continues to stroke himself.

"That's it, keep touching yourself, Kelsey. Tell me how wet you are."

"Tell me why you're hard, first," I counter.

"I'm hard because of the way you walk through this penthouse, acting as if you don't have any interest in me, but your eyes tell me differently. I'm hard because you have no fucking clue just how alluring you are, how fucking sexy you are. I'm hard because the taste of your pussy is lingering on my tongue, and if I truly had my way, you'd be stripped naked, tied to this bed, waiting for me to pleasure you."

"If you had your way?" I ask, a hitch in my voice. "What does that mean?"

His thumb reaches up and traces my face, down my neck, and across my arm. "You aren't mine." He lets go of his cock and moves me on the bed, making room so he can kneel in front of me. Then he removes my hand from where I'm pleasuring myself and brings his cock to my slit, running it against the fabric. The sensation is absolute torture, feeling him this close, just a miniscule piece of fabric blocking our connection. "If you were mine, there would be nothing between us."

That light pressure, the barely-there feeling of his cock mixed with the erotic nature of what he's doing, sends an intense yearning through me. A need so strong that my mind starts to black out. The only thing it's focused on is relief.

Relief from the buildup.

Relief from this night.

Relief from the tension between us.

He lifts his cock and taps the head right on my clit.

"Fuck," I whisper as I drape my arm over my eyes and breathe heavily.

"You like that, don't you?"

My teeth roll over my bottom lip.

"Tell me you like it and I'll do it again."

God, I hate him... Why is he making me admit things I don't want to admit?

"Say it, Kelsey."

"I...I like it," I stammer, and he taps his dick on my clit a few more times.

My pelvis rises, my skin breaks out in a sweat, and my control starts to slip. And then to my surprise, he pulls the fabric covering my pussy to the side, exposing me, and lets the head of his cock lightly rub against me.

"Oh God," I moan as my legs spread even farther. "Oh yes...JP."

"Fuck, you're so wet."

"More," I beg. I want more.

He glides his cock over my clit two more times, and then with a groan, he pulls away and resumes pumping his length vigorously above me.

"If you want more, you need to fuck yourself," he says, his voice strained. My eyes follow his gestures, the slide of his hand over his thick erection, the veins running down his length, the tension in his chest as he breathes heavily, staring down at me.

It's so freaking hot, so sexy, that my fingers find my clit again and start massaging in fast circles. The first inkling of my orgasm starts to wrap around my muscles, through my back, along my ribs, into my stomach.

"Fuck...you're there, aren't you?" he asks. "You're almost there."

I nod, keeping my teeth clenched as my chest heaves, my fingers moving faster. My eyes stay focused on his hand that's pulling, tugging on his length, the thick veins in his tattooed forearms straining just like the rest of his body.

"God," I mutter as my body starts to seize on me. The overwhelming sensation of pleasure is at its early stages, pulsing through my veins and zeroing in on the spot between my legs. "Yes," I whisper, my eyes shutting as I let myself fall into the hands of my orgasm.

"Look at me," JP says, his voice so commanding that it makes me snap my eyes open. "Look at me when you come."

The tone of his voice.

The meaning behind it…

It's like a bolt of lust zapping right through me. My muscles stiffen, my legs shiver, and my fingers fly over my clit as I moan louder than I can ever remember vocalizing before, and I come, a ferocious orgasm breaking me into a million pieces right there on my bed.

My eyes still on JP, I ready myself to see him come, but to my utter disbelief, he puts his surging cock back in his shorts and then leans down so close that our noses are nearly touching.

"You…you didn't come," I say, breathless.

"Because that's not for you to see, so I'll do that in private. If you want to watch me come, if you want to see my body shake uncontrollably when I think of your sweet fingers gliding over your cunt, then you're going to have to give me a lot more than you gave me tonight." He moves down my body until his head is right between my legs. My breath is so heavy that I can barely register what's happening until his tongue is gliding over my pussy, one smooth swipe before he lifts up, standing straight. Satisfaction on his face, he says, "Next time, you'll be coming on my tongue."

He turns and heads for my door, slipping out before I can say anything.

Breathless, I stare at the door, entirely too turned on—still— wondering what on earth just happened and how we took it this far.

CHAPTER 16
JP

I HAD ONE BEER LAST night, but it feels as though I had twenty. My mouth feels dry, my body is aching, and there's an unsatisfied feeling flooding me. And there's only one reason for this feeling.

Kelsey.

Fucking Kelsey.

I swing my legs over the edge of my bed and rub my palm against my eye as I attempt to wake my body.

Fuck.

Once again, I lost control. Returning to the penthouse, not seeing her there, and having to count down every second until she came back, turned me into a dangerous, jealous man. The moment she walked through that door, I was ready to pick a fight. I was ready to provoke her and no matter what I tried to do to calm myself, I couldn't. That's how I found myself in her bedroom, pulling out my dick, and watching her pleasure herself.

Even this morning, I can still see the look on her face when she orgasmed. I can hear her delicious moans. I can taste her. All three causes for this nonalcoholic hangover I'm experiencing.

From my nightstand, I check the alarm clock for the time. Shit, is it really nine already? Thank fuck it's Saturday and I don't have any meetings. I just have to face Kelsey this morning with no idea what to say.

Am I embarrassed about what happened last night? No.

Am I sure she's embarrassed about what happened last night? Yes.

I don't think Kelsey is the type of woman who masturbates in front of someone, despite the type of underwear she wears. I think her lingerie is probably the naughtiest thing about her.

So, what I should expect from her this morning is an extreme dose of awkwardness with a heavy side of regret. Two things I'm not very good at navigating. I don't necessarily feel those emotions, at least not as heavily as Kelsey, nor would I feel them about a sexual experience. And it makes me want her more. How could I possibly walk away from her knowing what she tastes like? Knowing she wears sexy-as-fuck lingerie? *But she still doesn't believe in me.*

Knowing I can't hang out in my room forever, I slip out of bed and find a pair of shorts to put on so I don't walk into the living space naked. She saw my dick last night, but I doubt she wants to see it this morning.

Dressed, I open my bedroom door and walk down the hallway, scratching my chest, only to stop at the edge of the living room where I spot Kelsey sitting on the couch, rocking back and forth, an iPad in front of her. She's wearing a pair of sweats and a T-shirt and has a worried look on her face.

When her eyes land on mine, fear encompasses them. "What's going on?" I ask.

"Your brother texted. He said he's going to FaceTime us in ten minutes. Is he…is he going to fire me?"

"Why would he fire you?"

"You know, because of last night…" Her voice trails off, and when I don't say anything, she adds, "You know, what we did in my bedroom."

I tug on my hair. "Why the fuck would he know about that?"

"You didn't tell him?"

"I don't tell my brother shit. Plus, that's something I'd never tell him, or Breaker, for that matter. Did you tell your sister?"

"No." She shakes her head. "I was too embarrassed."

See, told you she'd be embarrassed.

I walk over to the kitchen, grab an apple from the bowl, and take a bite. "So, then, there's nothing to worry about. Plus, he'd never fire you over something like that."

"Then what does he want to talk to us about?"

I shrug. "Beats me."

Although that's not the truth, as I'm sure he has some shit to say to me. He wasn't very happy with me yesterday when I hung up on him, so this impromptu need to call feels right.

"Well, I have a bad feeling. I feel like I'm in trouble."

"You only feel that way because you did something you'd never do last night."

Her eyes find mine. "How can you just be so casual about it? I've been up since four this morning unable to sleep. I don't...I don't know what came over me last night. I never should've—"

"No need to hash it out, Kelsey. What happened, happened. Just let it be."

"Let it be? It's not that easy for me, JP. You made me feel—" She catches herself and then takes a deep breath. "That was a wild thing for me to do, especially with a coworker who technically oversees everything I do. Not to mention, I went on a date with another man last night. How on earth is that okay?"

With a crisp snap, I bite off a chunk of apple and chew it thoughtfully. "It's actually just fine. These standards, these rules you seem to be putting on yourself are just that—self-induced rules. You can live your life the way you want. Stop judging yourself."

"Stop trying to act like what happened last night was okay."

"It was okay. We could've done more."

"JP, I'm not that kind of girl," she snaps. She's really worked up. Even though she came last night with her eyes on me, she's anything but okay with it. "I...I don't do those kinds of things, and for some reason, I can't seem to be my normal self around you. I lose my mind and start thinking that it's okay to be sexually provocative."

"It *is* okay for you to be sexually provocative," I say.

"But I don't want to be. I want so much more than sexual gratification." Her voice wavers. "God, I don't know why I'm talking to you about this when it isn't something you understand."

"Because I'm not the relationship kind of guy, right?"

"Right," she says, not holding back. "Last night was probably a silly game to you and I was a pawn."

"You weren't a pawn in my game." My voice grows tighter with irritation.

She folds her arms. "Then what was it? Because I can't think of a good reason why we'd do that."

"I don't know, Kelsey; maybe because there's a sexual attraction between us? Is that too hard to believe? Maybe we were so inflamed with need that we let our will slip last night."

"Well…it won't be happening again," she says, looking away.

"Gathered that," I mumble as I walk over to the couch and take a seat next to her.

Why? Why can't I shift her thinking? Last night was testimony to how good we could be together. *Sexually.* But she's clear on what she wants.

"I don't do those kinds of things… I can't seem to be my normal self around you. I lose my mind and start thinking that it's okay to be sexually provoca-tive… I want so much more than sexual gratification."

And I want to give her so much more than simple sexual gratification. Remorse strikes me, knowing that I put her on the defensive again.

Get a fucking clue, Cane.

"What are you doing?" she asks.

"Sitting in front of your iPad so when Huxley calls, he can see me. Is that a problem?"

"No," she says, leaning back on the couch. I do the same and, together, we sit in silence, letting the time tick by while we wait for Huxley to call.

Unsure of what to do, I offer her my apple, and to my surprise, she takes it. Maybe it's a peace offering, I don't know, but I don't like how angry she is at me, especially since last night, hell...it was probably wrong, but fuck, it felt good. Sliding my cock along her slit, feeling how goddamn turned on she was, it was a high I couldn't kick, and I needed so much more. When I got back to my room, I hopped in the shower and quickly made work of my erection, thinking of her surprised face when she orgasmed. I was done in seconds.

"I'm sorry about last night," I say quietly. "I was in a bad place. I'll be honest, Kelsey. I think you're really hot. I lost control, and I'm sorry if I made you feel uncomfortable."

The apple is halfway to her mouth, but she pauses and turns to me. I hang my head to the side so we're staring into each other's eyes. "No, I'm sorry. I shouldn't have spoken to you like that. I think I freaked out, and rather than acting like a normal human being, I blamed everything on you when I shouldn't have. In the moment, when everything was happening, I wanted it. I wanted it so bad."

That brings a smile to my face and eases the tightness in my chest.

I tug on my hair. "Yeah, I wanted it bad, too. I think there was only one shred of self-control left that held me back from tearing that bustier off and fucking you."

Her teeth roll over her lip and she says, "I would've let it happen."

"Hell," I groan, dragging my hand over my face. "Don't say that."

She chuckles. "I was sad last night. You were right about Derek. He didn't kiss me, and I was feeling really low. I clung to you in all the wrong ways. I should've just talked to you like I'm talking to you now."

I hold my arm out and, to my relief, she moves into my grasp, resting her head on my chest while I hug her closely. "You didn't have a chance to talk to me. I provoked you right away. In all honesty, I was sad you weren't at the Mayor's Ball with me, and I took it out on you. I shouldn't have."

She lifts up. "You were sad about that?"

I nod. "Yeah, I'd had fun the previous two nights and, I don't know, I didn't want to go alone. I forgot about your date, though."

"You should've said something, I would've rescheduled."

I wish you hadn't gone on the date at all.

"Nah, you were excited about it. I should've acted more respectfully, but that's sort of hard for me. I don't make the right choices sometimes, and last night it showed. I'm really sorry, Kelsey."

"Don't be," she says, resting back on my chest. I hold her close, wishing this is what we were normally like, that this was a typical Saturday morning for us. "I think we both treated each other unfairly. I used you because I was feeling empty after that date, and I never should have."

"It really didn't go well?" I ask her, hoping she'll say yes.

"I thought it did."

Damn.

"But it ended…" She pauses and buries her head farther into my chest. "God, this is so embarrassing and I can't believe I'm even considering telling you."

I gently drag my fingers through the long strands as I say, "No judgment here."

She groans and then says, "God, he gave me a handshake last night as a goodbye."

"A handshake?" I ask. Jesus, dude, way to fucking blow it with the most irresistible woman.

"Yes, I was mentally preparing for a kiss, followed up by an *I'll call you,* or *Let's do this again,* maybe even a possible *I can't wait to see you again.* But I got a thank-you and a handshake, and then I was on my way. It was such a letdown because I thought there was chemistry." She shakes her head. "I was so sad when I came home. All I can think about is *What's wrong with me?* What's so horrible about me that I'd pull a handshake out of a man? I mean, not even a hug?"

"Nothing is wrong with you, Kelsey. Trust me, nothing is fucking wrong with you. You're perfect."

She shakes her head again. "I'm not."

I lean away and lift her chin so our eyes connect. "Kelsey, you're fucking perfect," I say again, trying to convey to her how goddamn right I am about this. "Derek is a fool for not kissing you last night. And I'm sorry that he left you feeling anything less than what you truly are. Fuck. I'm so sorry for how I treated you last night."

She shakes her head. "In that moment, I needed it. I needed to feel wanted and beautiful. I'm just sorry I used you."

"You didn't use me, Kelsey. I wanted that just as much as you did. There was no using involved."

She softly smiles. "Well, I guess, thank you." She shrugs and it causes me to laugh. "I know you said we're short-term companions and you will probably deny it until you're blue in the face, but your friendship means a lot to me."

Like a goddamn dagger to the heart. I've been friend-zoned.

After everything we've been through, after last night, after the dates, I'm stuck right there, as her friend.

Fuck.

I continue to stroke her hair, disappointment passing through me. "Yeah, same, babe."

And because he has the WORST timing ever, Huxley calls. Kelsey lifts from my chest, adjusts herself, and then reaches out to the propped-up iPad and accepts the call.

Huxley and Lottie come onscreen and Kelsey quickly waves. "Hi."

"Hey, good morning," Lottie says. "Hope this wasn't too early. I know you had a date last night." Lottie wiggles her eyebrows.

"No, this is fine. Is everything okay?" Kelsey asks.

"She's worried you're going to fire her," I say, causing Kelsey to push me.

"Why would I fire you?" Huxley says, speaking up now. "You're doing excellent work."

"Oh, that's just how Kelsey is," Lottie answers. "She always thinks she's going to get fired. But this has nothing to do with work."

"No, nothing like that," Huxley says. "And for the record, Kelsey, you have nothing to worry about. JP took care of Regis last night."

Jesus Christ, this guy.

Kelsey quickly looks toward me, but I ignore her probing eyes and ask, "So what's the phone call for?"

Lottie loops her arm through Huxley's and says, "Well, while going through all these wedding meetings, we've come to the conclusion that a big fancy wedding isn't necessary. We're getting married in a month instead."

"A month?" Kelsey asks. "Oh wow, that's really soon. Will you have enough time to plan everything?"

"Yes. You'd be surprised how quickly things can get done when the right checkbook is involved," Huxley says.

"It's true. He's been flashing around dollar signs to everyone, and things are getting done. But we're calling because it's going to be a roof-top wedding in Malibu that overlooks the ocean. We're inviting about one hundred people and keeping it pretty small. Don't worry, you each get a plus-one." Lottie winks at Kelsey. "Maybe you can bring Derek. Dave and Ellie will be there."

Fucking wonderful.

"Yeah, maybe," Kelsey says, but her voice is distant.

"Anyway, we'll send the details over shortly. We wanted to call you and tell you the big news. When it came down to it, we just wanted to be married, so we thought this would be a perfect combination for both of us."

"Sounds dreamy," Kelsey says just as a text message pops up at the top of her iPad screen.

My eyes make quick work of reading it before Kelsey can swipe it away.

Derek: Hey, Kelsey, I had a great time last night. Can we please do it again while you're here?

My jaw clenches and sweat breaks out on the back of my neck.

I know I'm friend-zoned.

I know she'll never see me as someone to date.

But fuck…I don't need to see Derek swooping in while things are still raw.

"Are you still going to have a bridal shower or anything like that?" Kelsey asks.

"Um, I think just a lingerie party. Something small. Nothing too crazy. We don't need anything, but I know Hux here would appreciate the lingerie."

Huxley scratches his jaw. "I would."

Bing.

Another text.

Like a moth to a flame, my eyes zero in on the text message.

Derek: And sorry about not kissing you last night. I really wanted to. I just got…

The rest of the text message is hidden, but I get the gist of it. Derek is a goddamn pussy and is now ruining my life by coming in hot with the text messages the next morning.

I don't think life could be any more frustrating.

We spend the next five minutes talking. I'm zoning out the whole time, wondering why this couldn't have been texted or emailed to us. Why this required a FaceTime call. Because now I know that Derek still wants to take Kelsey out, and knowing Kelsey, she's going to be one hundred percent excited about this.

Just as we're about to hang up, one more message comes in.

Derek: I'm free today if you want to have a picnic in the park with me.

Gag me.

Jesus Christ, Derek, give her a chance to respond before you write a fucking novel about how you feel, how you fucked up, and how you want to make it up to her.

"JP, do you still need to talk?" Huxley asks, pulling me from the anger simmering in the pit of my stomach.

"What? Ah, nah, I'm good," I say in the most even-toned voice I can muster.

"Okay." Huxley eyes me. "Text me if you need anything."

"So excited for you two," Kelsey says before we all say bye and she disconnects the call. I'm prepared for her to run off and read her text messages, but instead, she turns toward me and asks, "What did Huxley mean when he said you took care of Regis?"

Of course she'd remember that.

I stand from the couch and say, "Nothing to worry about."

"I am worried," she says, standing as well. "Clearly, it had something to do with me. What was it?"

"He was just being a dick and I set him straight, is all. It's not a big deal so don't make it one."

"You saw him at the ball last night?"

I exhale sharply and go to the kitchen to pour myself a glass of water. "Yes, I saw him there last night. Addressed the issue and moved on."

"What was the issue?"

"Jesus, Kelsey, I said it wasn't a big deal, so just drop it."

She winces from my strong tone. "Okay, I just…I don't know. I thought if I understand what's going on, maybe I can do better."

"You don't need to do better. I told you, you're perfect. Regis was the one who needed to do better." I chug my water and set down the glass before working my way back to the hallway that leads to my room.

"Where are you going?"

"To my room," I say.

"You seem angry again."

Not angry.

I'm hurt.

Disappointed.

Aching for a chance I know I won't get.

"We just don't need to talk about it, okay?"

"Okay," she says, twisting her hands in front of her. "What are you doing today?"

"Not sure," I answer. "But it seems like you have plans."

"Yeah, I guess you saw those messages." She moves her foot in front of her. "What do you think I should do?"

Not come to me for dating advice, that's for damn sure.

"I thought we had a good time, but I felt really let down by him last night. I don't know."

"Seems like you have a choice to make, then," I say.

"But what if it's not the right choice?" she calls out.

"I'm sure it'll be a better choice than the one you made last night," I answer before shutting the door to my room and flopping onto my bed.

Hollow.

That's how I feel, absolutely hollow.

For a brief moment last night, when Kelsey's eyes were on me and she was coming, and then earlier when I had her in my arms, everything felt right. *I* felt right. *Ready.* But now, lying here alone on my bed, knowing that once again what I had with her was a brief intermission during her quest to find Mr. Right, I just feel…hollow.

"Dude, how many drinks have you had?" Breaker asks.

"Not enough," I answer as I tip back another glass of scotch.

When I caught sight of Kelsey dressed in a light blue sundress, hair and makeup all done, her decision was clear—she was giving Derek another shot, and this time, he'll fucking kiss her. So, I went to my phone, asked the concierge to bring up a bottle of scotch and some of those fancy balls of ice, and that's what I've been doing ever since she left.

Drinking.

In my shorts.

I showered because I didn't want to sit in my filth all day, but I did nothing with my hair. I've spent the day so far drinking and watching *Planet Earth* documentaries, letting David Attenborough soothe my massacred soul.

If you're wondering if it's worked...

It has not.

But at least I haven't been entirely alone.

Nope, scotch and the threat of polar bears losing their homes has lived with me through this moment.

That, and my thousands of text messages to Breaker about how we need to do more for the polar bears, which resulted in me donating to the World Wildlife Fund, earmarked to Save the Polar Bear, which of course made me feel guilty that I was cheating on the pigeons. So, I ended up donating another ten thousand to the pigeons.

After I sent him five pictures of pigeons that need to be fostered or adopted, he called me.

"And what's with the pigeon pictures? Should I be worried? Those things shit all over the place, so do you really want to adopt one?"

"*You* shit all over the place," I say. "Don't talk about the pigeons like that. There are thousands of pigeons being euthanized because no one wants to adopt them. No one wants to take care of their vet bills. Everyone wants to be the person who saves the cute kitten with one eye, the dog in a wheelchair, or the rabbit with no teeth. But what about the flightless pigeons? For fuck's sake, who's taking care of them?"

"Hey, JP, dude…are you having a mental health crisis?"

"No," I shout and stand. "I'm not. I'm just a concerned citizen. You walk around these streets, never noticing pigeons, thinking they're just an accessory to a Bob Ross landscape, and then, *bam*, you hear pigeons are being euthanized and the world comes tumbling down around you. Sure, I saved the polar bears today because looking at those emaciated motherfuckers made me physically ill but, dude, I'm going to start a goddamn campaign, and the logo will be a pigeon in flight. And the money will go to saving all the pigeons because no one cares about them. No one thinks they're worth their time. Just because a pigeon might have a fucked-up childhood and can't fly like the rest of the birds, that doesn't mean that the pigeon should be isolated."

"Uh…JP, are you…are you a pigeon?"

"I'm a fucking *man*, you nimrod! Jesus Christ, are you even listening to me?"

"Are you listening to *yourself*?"

"I am. I am listening, and I'm pretty sure I'm the only one who fucking cares about those angelic stout-bodied birds."

"So, are you going to adopt one?"

"What? God, no. Fuck, imagine me with a goddamn pigeon. What the hell would I do with it?"

"I honestly don't know, dude. You sound like you need a hobby or a friend."

"Or a girlfriend," I mutter as I sit back down in my chair.

"A girlfriend?" Breaker asks. "Tell me more about this, because as far as I know, you've never really wanted one."

"Well, you know what, fuckstick? People change. Okay? Why can't anyone see that? People fucking change, and I think it's time that we all sit down, have a glass of wine, and talk about how someone named a freaking pigeon Kazoo and got away with it."

"What's wrong with the name Kazoo?"

"It's such a slap in the face to the pigeon community. Let's name this majestic feathered friend after a simple twenty-five-cent child's toy that gives the vocalist a timbral quality when playing it."

"I love you, man, but I really think you've lost it."

"No." I shake my head. "Nope, I'm seeing things so fucking clearly right now. Like a goddamn crystal."

"It seems like that crystal is foggy."

"Fuck, do you know what I should do?"

"Seek a counselor?"

"I should send an email."

"Uh, what sort of email? You know, sending emails while intoxicated is never a good idea."

"I'm not intoxicated. I'm finally seeing things the way that I should."

"And how is that?" Breaker asks.

"Well, I want a girlfriend, and I need a date for the wedding, so I should send an email."

"Wait, can we go back to this 'wanting a girlfriend' thing? Where's this coming from?"

"Dude, can't you fucking keep up?"

"No, I really can't. One moment you're talking about pigeons, and the next you're saying you're going to send an email about girlfriends. I really think we should slow down, reel it in, and maybe drink some coffee."

I heave a heavy sigh. "Christ, I told you how I like Kelsey, how the urge to be around her is so consuming that I feel like...fuck, I feel like I can't breathe. She's so fucking pretty, and her smile makes me happy, and the way she laughs creates a bolt of lust straight to my cock. And she's so weird and quirky and likes love but is terrible at it for some reason. And fuck is she uptight about things like organization and she loves being right, but I like that about her because she's neurotic and I'm a bit neurotic in my own way—fucking pigeons, you know, man—so I think we'd make a great fucking couple but she doesn't like me and just wants to be my friend because she thinks that I'm just some player who can't commit and, sure, maybe that's in my past, but like I said, people change and I want to change for her, but she doesn't want to see that so she friend-zoned me and she's now going out with Derek, who didn't even fucking kiss her on the first date, what a douche. He shook her hand. Like, dude, have you fucking seen this girl? She's not handshake material, she's marriage material. She's the girl that you take home to your parents. You don't fucking shake her hand at the end of a date; you kiss her, claim her, make her yours. Well, she's going out with him again, so I need a girlfriend, so I'm going to send an email."

"Ah…fuck. And an email to who?"

"To everyone."

"You know, I really think we shouldn't do the email thing. That seems like a bad idea."

"It seems like a great one to me."

"Because you're drunk," Breaker says. "Spending fifty grand on pigeons seems like a good idea to you."

"It was only twenty grand altogether. Fuck, should it have been fifty?"

"That's not the point. I think you should just calm down, take a deep breath, and, JP, if you really like her, I think you should try to date her."

"And how do you suppose I go about doing that?"

"I have some ideas, but I don't think saying them right now is going to help you. Not sure you'll retain anything. I'm going to text you, and you can read it in the morning, when your mind is…fresh."

"I'm fresh as fuck right now."

"It's cute that you think that. Listen, don't email anybody right now. That's a bad idea. Maybe cap that bottle you're drinking from, go get some food, and park it in your room for the rest of the night. You don't want to say or do something stupid. If you really like Kelsey, then let me help you figure out a way to show that."

"Think a pigeon will carry a note to her?"

"Great possibility, man."

I sigh again. "Okay."

"Okay? So, you're going to go get some food, and we'll talk in the morning."

"Yeah."

"And no emailing."

"Right, no emailing."

"Good. And hey, not sure I said this, but good job being a voice for the pigeons, man. You're doing God's work."

I clutch my chest. "Thank you, that means a lot to me."

After some goodbyes, I hang up feeling marginally better. I saved the polar bears and the pigeons and I'm going to win Kelsey. What a productive afternoon.

Pleased with myself, I cap the scotch bottle like Breaker said, pick up my empty glass, and head toward the kitchen. Just then, I hear the door open, and I pause in the hallway, holding my breath.

She's home.

Do I want her to see me like this?

Probably not.

I know I told Breaker I wasn't drunk, but let's call a spade a spade—I'm fucking sitting pretty right now, and I don't need to mess up anything with Kelsey because scotch has been my mistress this afternoon. So, I spin on my heel and head for my bedroom, but I stop when I hear a male voice.

I quickly turn back around. No fucking way did she bring him back here.

I slide along the wall, hoping to stay undetected as I attempt to eavesdrop on a conversation I've no right listening to.

I grow closer and closer. Then I hear Kelsey.

"Thank you so much for walking me up here. You really didn't have to."

Yeah, you didn't have to, fucker. She's more than capable, she's done it many times already.

"I just felt bad, the way I left you last time."

Because you're a moron.

"Well, thank you. I had a nice time," Kelsey says in her sweet voice, and I swear if I hear them kiss, I'll fucking melt into a puddle of despair right here.

"Me too."

I hold my breath.

I wait for the telltale sound of two mouths colliding.

I'm tempted to whip around the corner and watch desperately as they say goodbye.

"I'll call you," Derek finally says, and I can't tell if they kissed, hugged, or shook hands again, but it's nearly killing me.

"Okay, sounds good. Have a good rest of your day."

The door shuts, and I stand there against the wall, unmoving as I attempt to tell myself to move, to get out of here, to not look like a Peeping Tom. But the unknown of whether or not they kissed is keeping me in place, my mind reeling. What is she feeling right now?

"JP?" she asks, looking down the hallway at me plastered against the wall, tumbler in one hand, scotch in the other. "What are you doing?"

Errrr...

What am I doing?

Well, honest truth—trying to decide if I need to finish this bottle based on if he kissed you or not.

But that doesn't seem like a safe answer. Even in my drunken state, I know that's not a safe answer, so I go with the second-best thing...

"Smelling."

"Smelling?" she asks, her face tightening in confusion. "What are you smelling?"

"The wall," I answer, and then to my horror, I spin around, plant my nose right on the wall, and take a big old whiff.

Whoa…why does that smell like kielbasa?

"Why are you smelling the wall?"

Great solid question.

And unfortunately, I don't have a great solid answer to match it.

"Favorite pastime," I say. "Smell a wall in your spare time. Anyway, so you're back from your date."

"Are you okay?" she asks, taking a step closer.

"Fine," I answer, gripping the neck of the bottle tighter. "Just, uh, thirsty." I hold up the scotch. "Going back to my room. Watching a documentary about dying polar bears. Don't worry, I donated to help them…and the pigeons." I swallow. "Anyway, just going to do that. But, yeah, glad you had a nice time and you look…you look beautiful in that dress. But that's neither here nor there. It's just an observation." My throat grows tight. Why is it tightening? Am I…fuck, am I feeling emotion?

"JP, are you sure you're okay?"

"Yeah," I choke out. "Sorry if that *beautiful* comment made you feel weird. I just…I just think that you look really nice. Really pretty. But you know, you're dating Derek. Was his kiss good?" I hold up the bottle. "Wait, don't answer that. I don't want to know. None of my business. I don't want to know. I just…man, those polar bears, they're really thin. You can see their ribs. And I'm going to write a letter to the pigeon place, and tell them they shouldn't name a pigeon Kazoo. He looks more like a Kevin. Just my honest opinion. So, yeah, okay. Well, I'll, uh, see you later."

I turn and practically run to my room. I slam the door and lock it for safekeeping.

Fuck, what was that shit?

Embarrassing, that's what it was.

I set down my scotch glass on my nightstand and pour myself multiple fingers. I can't imagine what she must think of me, but it can't be good. And Derek, fuck, I think they kissed. I didn't hear any lip smacking, but they might be quiet kissers. That motherfucker kissed her before I did and that stings.

I know her better.

We've been acquainted for longer.

I've pined after this girl for fucking months.

And he kissed her first.

I don't even know the fucker, but it makes me so goddamn...sad.

Fuck.

I tip back my tumbler, sucking down some more scotch. I don't like this pain I'm feeling. I don't like these emotions souring through me. I don't like any of it. I want to be numb. I want to not have to deal with these self-deprecating thoughts. I don't want to think about their date, what they did or didn't do, or if she's texting him right now. Or if she's telling Lottie how much she likes Derek, how she wants to take him to the wedding.

The wedding...

I spend the next half hour downing the rest of the bottle until there's only an inch left.

I cry about the polar bears, watching them all over again.

I send an email to the pigeon place, inquiring about Kazoo.

And I text Breaker that I'm a loser who masturbates to exhalations.

And sometime in the night, when I'm just about ready to pass out, I send one more email from my private account.

To: McKayla, Kenzie, Hattie, Eileen, Barbie, Olivia, Betty, Rita, Jessica, Tess, Pauline, Dominique, Miranda, Cara

From: JP Cane

Subject: Be my Date

Hey ladieeees,

Sending a big old cock of an email because, you know…I have a big cock, so this email has to match.

Here's the thing. Hux is getting married to Lulu Lemon and they told me I need a plus-one. Looking for a willing candidate to escort me down the aisle.

All expenses paid. Promises of pleasure.

If interested, hit me up.

I wear condoms still.

K. Bye.

JP

Fuck.

Me.

Ohhhh…fuck.

My stomach rolls, my body heaves, and I'm clutching my toilet, puking for the third time this morning.

Please, Jesus, make it stop. I promise to never drink that much again, just make…the…puking…

Fuck.

My body rears back, my stomach revolts, and once again, I let it rip until there's nothing left inside me.

I slide to the bathroom floor and rest my heated cheek on the cold tile.

If hell was a place, I imagine it being this, over and over again. A hangover with a constant throbbing headache and matching nausea.

I take a few deep breaths as my phone buzzes next to me on the floor. Needing a distraction, I look and see that it's Breaker.

Breaker: Are you alive this morning? You texted me a picture of Kazoo eleven times last night, all in a row. That leads me to believe you didn't stop drinking.

I lean against the wall as I text him back.

JP: I think I used up one of my lives last night. I'm pretty sure I just threw up a boot.

Breaker: What the hell happened to "go get some food"?

JP: Kelsey's date walked her back to the penthouse. I think they kissed. I lost it, man. I told her about the pigeons, rambled about sick polar bears, told her she was beautiful, and then went back to my room where I blacked out. So…yeah.

Breaker: Jesus. So, you didn't listen to me at all.

JP: Nope.

Breaker: So, what are you going to do this morning?

JP: So far, retching. Not sure what the plan is after that.

Breaker: Do you really like her? Like…you want to go for this?

JP: I think after last night's events, if I don't at least try, I'm going to drink myself into an oblivion.

Breaker: Do you have any plans?

JP: Not even one.

Breaker: Okay, first, you need to stop being a dick to her, because that's not winning her over. And start being her friend.

JP: Her friend? I'm already there. She friend-zoned me.

Breaker: Good, because now you can hang out with her without the pressure of sex. Show her that you're fun, that you're a good match for her. You know the attraction is there, but you need to work on the personality.

JP: If you haven't noticed, I'm not very good at controlling my emotions.

Breaker: Not an excuse. Just work harder. If you want her to be with you, you need to show her that you can be the man she wants. You need to woo her.

JP: Woo her? Fuck…don't use that term.

Breaker: But that's the term she'd use. She's a romantic. You have to do things that she'd notice, things that matter. Make her meals, pull out her chair, bring home things that remind you of her. Little touches here and there. And when you're in the penthouse, hanging out, sit close to her. Don't make it sexual, but let her know you're there.

JP: Who made you the expert at this shit?

Breaker: No one, but I'm pretty damn sure I have a better idea than you at this moment.

JP: Fuck…fine.

Breaker: And, for the love of God, don't go out there this morning until you're done puking.

JP: Trust me, I'm smart enough to realize that.

CHAPTER 17
KELSEY

Kelsey: Welcome, listener, to the *Meant to Be Podcast*, where we talk to madly-in-love couples about the way they met. Griffin and Ren, thank you so much for joining me today.

Griffin: Sure. When Ren told me about the podcast, I thought our story was interesting enough to talk about.

Ren: *Interesting enough* is a good way to put it. Tell Kelsey about the curse.

Griffin: *Sighs* I was in New Orleans with my brothers, and it was a drunken night when we stumbled upon a palm reader. Long story short, she did a terrible palm reading, we voiced our opinion, and then—my brothers and I will swear on this—she cursed us.

Kelsey: What was the curse?

Griffin: Broken love. It was intense; the wind swirled and everything.

Ren: We live in a small town called Port Snow, in Maine, and the entire town knew about this curse. The boys were untouchable. And to Griffin's defense, he did lose his wife right after the trip, so he was scared to try to find love again.

Kelsey: So, how did you meet?

Griffin: Ren was looking for a fresh start. She got a teaching job in Port Snow. Came all the way from California.

Ren: I was driving to Port Snow in what felt like the backwoods, and I wasn't prepared for incoming traffic.

Griffin: When she says *incoming traffic*, she means *incoming moose*.

Kelsey: Moose?

Ren: Yup, a moose came out on the road, I swerved and rolled down a hill, and my car got stuck between two trees. Griffin is a volunteer firefighter and pulled me out of my vehicle. I was slightly insane that day and he helped me get to my rental, which happened to be a place his brother owned.

Griffin: Despite her screaming at me and the blood dripping down her head from a cut, I thought she was beautiful. She intrigued me, and it was the first time since my wife passed that I felt attraction. And then, soon after, I believed I could date again. Ren was my miracle.

Kelsey: Aww. I'm so glad to hear that. So, you started dating?

Ren: Not quite. It didn't happen that fast, though, because, you know...the curse.

Griffin: *chuckles* Don't bust my balls about that on a podcast.

Ren: Oh, Kelsey said we have an hour. Trust me when I say I will be talking about the curse for that entire time.

Griffin: Great.

I'd like to say the penthouse is soundproof, that I can't hear what JP is doing and he can't hear what I'm doing, but I think after the whole walking in on him while he was pleasuring himself situation, we know that's not the truth.

For a good portion of the last twenty minutes, I've heard JP throw up multiple times. I'd be concerned that he was sick, but given the bottle of scotch he was holding last night, I know that's not the case.

This means he got completely wasted last night and he's battling the effects of it this morning.

Why did he get drunk last night? Why was he talking about polar bears and pigeons? Well, probably because he was drunk.

He also said I was beautiful, and I'd be lying if I said that didn't make me feel all warm inside. Because it did.

Either way, it kept me up all night, and now, this morning, as I sit on the couch, rereading the same sentence in my book over and over again because I can't concentrate, I'm waiting for him to come out of his room.

My phone buzzes on the coffee table, and I see it's a text from Lottie. Needing the distraction from my thoughts, I pick it up.

Lottie: How was the date last night? Ellie said Derek had a good time. You haven't said much. Not feeling him? Also…remind me to tell you what Ellie told me about JP.

That last part has my attention. I quickly reply.

Kelsey: Date was good. Derek is really sweet. Not sure if he's feeling me. Didn't kiss me again last night, but he did give me a hug. I don't know. It's kind of awkward. What did Ellie say about JP?

Lottie: He didn't kiss you? Sheesh, talk about taking it slow. Oh, she said her friend is a bartender who was at the Mayor's Ball. She served JP a scotch and overheard a conversation between him and Regis Stallone.

The conversation JP wouldn't tell me about. Immersed in my phone now, I text her back immediately.

Kelsey: What happened? What did JP say?
Lottie: I don't have it word for word, but she said JP was incredibly hot when he spoke to Regis. Regis was staring out at the dance floor while JP stared at him. She mentioned his carved jawline and how tense it was as he spoke through clenched teeth. She heard him say that you're a valuable part of the team, and if he fucks with you, then he's done. That's paraphrased. Basically, JP was putting him in his place.

I lean back on the couch, rereading Lottie's text over and over until it sinks in.

He was defending me? I know Regis doesn't like me, but from what Lottie's saying, JP won't settle for that.

Kelsey: Wow, I had no idea.
Lottie: Yeah, and then she heard rumblings later about how JP wasn't taking any shit from Regis. It was the gossip of the party. One of the main reasons no one fucks with Cane Enterprises. So, I guess, consider us lucky. We somehow got on the good side of some of the most powerful men in the country.
Kelsey: I guess so.

The scuffling of approaching feet grabs my attention, and I look up just in time to spot JP appear in the living room, tugging on his wet hair, looking like hell, but clean hell at that.

I set down my phone and say, "Good morning. How are you feeling?"

When he speaks, his voice comes out raspy. "Been better." He winces, as if he has a headache, and asks, "Did you hear me?"

"I did. I'm assuming your trip to the bathroom was a result of the bottle of scotch I saw you with last night?"

His shoulders droop as he walks farther into the living room. "Unfortunately."

Knock. Knock. "Room service," someone calls out from the other side of the door.

"That would be my garbage plate," he says, walking over to the entryway. He opens it and lets the room service attendant wheel in a cart of food.

"Good morning, Mr. Cane. Everything you ordered is here. If you need anything else, please don't hesitate to ask."

"Thank you," JP says as he signs the bill.

When the door is shut and we're alone again, JP rolls the cart into the living room, nudges the coffee table out of the way, and then takes a seat next to me on the couch.

"I ordered you some things, in case you didn't eat breakfast yet." He takes a few tops off the plates and reveals a pile of croissants and a tray of beautifully cut-up fruit, and then he moves a tray of hot water, tea, honey, and jams toward me.

"You got this for me?" I ask in awe.

"You seemed like a tea-and-croissant kind of person. If you don't like it, I can get you something else."

"No, this is…well, this is lovely, thank you."

"You're welcome." He takes the top off his plate and I can't help the queasy look on my face.

"Not to be rude, but, uh…what is that?"

"Hangover cure." He picks up a fork and points at his plate. "Hash browns with refried beans, bacon and steak, eggs scrambled and over easy, drenched in a V8 sauce."

Gags

"Oh…wow, that's, uh, that's something."

He glances at me as he jams his fork into the pile. "Do you want me to eat this somewhere else?"

"What? No."

"I can tell it disgusts you."

"It doesn't disgust me, it's just…interesting. I've never seen something like it before. Two different kinds of eggs, very fascinating. And that V8, it's potent."

The smallest of smirks tugs at the corner of his lip. "I'll eat it in the kitchen."

He goes to stand, but I put my hand on his forearm to stop him. "No, please don't leave. It's fine, really, and I don't want to have you sitting over there while I shove croissants in my mouth. I'd rather not eat alone."

"You sure?" he asks.

"Positive."

"Okay." He moves his fork around his meal and then takes a large mouthful. I just stare as he chews, wondering how on earth he can eat that after the marathon of puking he did in his bathroom.

"That doesn't bother your stomach?"

"Helps it, actually. Something I learned in my college days." He reaches for his glass of water and takes a sip. "Did you not have a hangover cure in college?"

"I didn't drink much. Still don't."

"Ahh, it's because you're a good girl." He winks and takes another mouthful of his food.

"Maybe I am, but at least I'm not puking out my intestines the next morning," I reply.

He smirks. "Not my intestines, but I did tell Breaker I might have seen a boot come out of me."

That makes me snort and cover my nose. "Oh God, I snorted. Ignore that."

"Nah, just add it to your list of good-girl things."

"Do only good girls snort?"

"Yup." He picks up the pepper from the table and dusts some across his plate. I take that moment to steep my tea and prepare a croissant with strawberry jam.

"Are you feeling better, at least?"

"I mean, as best as I can. Sort of embarrassed. Didn't think you could hear me."

"I don't think there's much privacy in these walls, despite how fancy the place is."

"A note to bring up to Huxley when I talk to him next." He lifts his napkin and wipes his mouth.

When I think he's going to say more and he doesn't, I ask, "Are you okay? I'm sure you're sick of me asking that, but it seems as though something was bothering you if you drank that much alone."

His eyes connect with mine, and for the first time since I've known him, I see a hint of shame cross them as he looks down. JP doesn't normally show vulnerability. He'd rather shield it or laugh it off, always presenting himself as the strong, domineering type. But here, on the couch, as he eats breakfast, I can see it written all over his face.

"You must think I'm a loser, huh?" he asks, pushing his food around on his plate.

"Not at all," I say, setting down my croissant and turning toward him. "I'm just concerned. You seem emotionally erratic at times and I wish you'd talk to me about it. I mean, I get that we're not friends, or that you don't want to be friends—"

"I do," he says, surprising me. "I want to be friends."

"What?" I ask, entirely confused now. "But I thought—"

"You thought correctly. I told you we can't be friends and, sure, maybe a part of me still believes that, but I'm also"—he pulls on the back of his neck—"fuck, I have a hard time letting people into my life." His gaze matches mine. "Have, uh…have Lottie or Huxley ever talked to you about my dad?"

"No." I shake my head, feel my pulse pick up.

JP leans back on the couch and stares at the ceiling. "Growing up, being so close in age to my brothers, we were all at each other's throats. Huxley constantly pushed boundaries, and always tried to be the best, the first. Breaker was the easygoing one who just went with the flow. Didn't really care much about anything other than doing the right thing and having a good time. And then I kind of wandered around, attempting to find my place. Never really did. Never felt like I belonged…unless I was hanging with my dad. He didn't get much time off, he was driven like Huxley, but the time I did get with him, he made me feel like I meant something. Like I had something special to offer the world."

"What would you guys do?" I ask. Frankly, I'm so surprised that he's sharing, but I'm also soaking up every ounce of it.

"Go to the batting cages. We'd do five rounds each, grab a lemonade and nachos from the concession stand, then sit at our favorite picnic table and just talk. There were days where we talked for longer, and some days we didn't talk at all. Breaker and Huxley were never that close with Dad. They never came with us, so when he passed away, I suffered from the loss the most." His eyes connect with mine. "I know, ever since losing him, I haven't allowed many people in my life for fear of losing them. It didn't take me long to figure that out."

"Hence why you don't want to be friends."

"Exactly," he exhales. "But with you, Kelsey, it just doesn't seem like I'm able to shake you off, no matter how hard I try. I like hanging out with you."

A smile spreads across my lips. "I like hanging out with you too, JP."

"So, then I guess it's settled." He sits back up, stabs his fork into the middle of his plateful of food, and scoops up a giant mouthful. "We're friends despite the odds of that happening because, you know…I still believe men and women who work together can't be friends."

I roll my eyes. "I'm sure you do, because you can't possibly be wrong about anything, right?"

"Correct." He smirks.

"Okay, so we're friends, which leads me to ask…why did you get drunk last night?"

He glances away and pushes more food around on his plate. "How about we save that question for another day? Let's just focus on the new bond we have."

I don't like pushing whatever was bothering him aside, but I also like this new side of him. He seems more…free, so I'm not going to push it.

"I think I can manage that."

"Good." He sips his water again. "Want to catch a movie today? There's an old-school theater near the Angelica Building that runs old movies. I heard they're playing some sort of rom-com two-for-one special."

I perk up. "Like…two rom-coms in a row?"

He nods. "Yup. I believe it's *When Harry Met Sally* and *He's Just Not That into You*."

I clap my hands together. "Ooo, good ones. And you'd go with me?"

"Wouldn't suggest it if I didn't want to."

"But I thought you didn't like movies like that?"

He shrugs. "I know you like them, so they can't be too bad, right? Plus, reviews say their popcorn is salty and makes your lips burn. That's my kind of popcorn."

"I do love a salty popcorn, as well. Okay, let's do it, but we have to do something you want to do after…that's if you don't have plans."

"My plans consist of hanging out with you, babe."

"Okay." My smile grows even wider. "Then what do you want to do after?"

I watch him chew thoughtfully and then he says, "A touristy thing."

"What? Seriously? But I thought that was beneath you?"

He chuckles. "Hate to admit it, but your touristy outing we had was entertaining. How about a nighttime tour of Alcatraz?"

My eyes widen. "That's way too creepy."

He levels me with a glare. "Hey, I'm going to the rom-com marathon. And you said we could do anything I wanted, so I say we do that."

"As long as you have no problem with me burying my head in your chest the entire time."

"Trust me, babe. No problem with that at all." He smirks and takes another bite of his food.

"Kelsey, you can open your eyes," JP whispers into my ear as I cling tightly to his arm. "It's not like a monster is going to pop out."

"You don't know that," I whisper.

"Babe, open your eyes."

I open one eye and then the other, and the main hall of prison cells comes into view. Because JP can't do anything the "peasant" way, he booked us a behind-the-scenes tour, so we're alone with a tour guide, walking through the eerie halls of Alcatraz. I would've preferred more people.

"See, not so bad," JP says.

Still clinging to him, I look around and say, "I honestly feel like my skin is crawling. Is your skin crawling? There are ghosts everywhere."

"According to legend," Kathy, our tour guide, says, "Alcatraz is one of the most haunted places in the country."

"Oh...lovely," I say, pressing my body closer to JP. "One of the most haunted, can't hear that enough."

"If you want to take a closer look at the prison cells, please feel free," Kathy says, gesturing to the cold steel bars lined up against the wall as she gives us some space.

"Can we get in one?"

"Of course," Kathy says.

"Uh…are you insane? I am not getting in one of those cells."

"Why not?" JP asks. "Once-in-a-lifetime opportunity."

"Never been in a prison cell, never plan on being in one."

JP chuckles and pulls me closer to the cells. I let go of his arm as he steps inside one. "Shit, these are small. You'd have to get creative with how to work with this space." He grips the cell bars and asks, "How do I look?"

"Deranged."

A loud creaking sound echoes through the dank halls, and then in the blink of an eye, JP's cell door slides shut, causing me to gasp and JP to let out the girliest scream I've ever heard.

"Ahhhhhhhhhhhhhh."

From down the hall, Kathy laughs, making us both turn toward her. She presses a button and the cell opens again.

"Jesus…fuck," JP says as he steps out of the cell and glares at Kathy. "I did not pay for the scare factor."

"It's free of charge." She smiles.

"Fuck." He walks up to me and whispers, "My scrotum has shriveled up into my stomach. Won't have balls for days after that."

I cover my mouth and chuckle. "Still loving the idea of being here at night?"

"Slightly rethinking. Didn't know Kathy from *Nightmare Alley* was going to be our tour guide."

"I'm here all night," Kathy calls out, still smiling.

"Jesus Christ, she's in the right line of work." He lets out a deep breath and then says, "I was about to say, that wouldn't be the first time I was behind bars."

"Umm…what's that now?"

He lends out his arm to me and I hang on to it as we walk toward Satan's mistress. "I was in college. Shortly after my dad passed away.

Public intoxication. Some bullshit thing like that. I think I peed on some old lady's tree. She called the cops and I was arrested. Huxley, of course, came flying in like the knight in shining armor that he is and had everything removed from my record, and then threatened to remove me from school if I ever did something like that again."

"Sounds…sad. Seems like you needed someone to care for you. You were going through a rough time."

"Yeah, alcohol cared for me. Alcohol has always been there for me."

"You realize how unhealthy that is?"

"Yup, but never said I was completely healthy. Working on it, though. One day at a time."

"Shall we see the shower room?" Kathy asks when we reach her.

"Absolutely," JP says, leading the way.

We spend the next hour listening to Kathy tell us about the many different inmates who attempted to escape, how they escaped, and the outcome. Despite it being dark, creepy, and not something I'd probably ever choose to do on my own, I actually enjoyed myself immensely. The stories were entertaining, the history unlike anything I've ever heard, and of course, listening to JP ask intense questions was fun, too.

Now that we're on the ferry ride back, sitting outside under the stars, I have a million questions running through my head.

"If you were ever in prison like those guys, would you try to escape? Or would you just suffer in silence, doing what needed to be done in order to leave one day?"

"Depends on the length of my sentence," he says, draping his arm across the bench behind me. "If it was a long sentencing, hell yeah, I'd try to escape. I'd dig a hole like the Anglin brothers, papier-mâché some heads, and work until morning. But if it was like ten years…eh, I'd wait it out."

"I would not survive in prison," I say. "I don't have it in me to be rough and tough."

"Because you're innocent," JP says. "You're too sweet for prison. Me, I could go either way. If I had to hold my own, I would."

"I take it that means you've been in your fair share of fistfights?"

He chuckles. "Not sure I've heard many people call them fistfights—just a fight—and yeah, I've been in quite a few. Like I said, never really felt like I had a place in this world, so I fought my way, trying to find something that mattered to me."

"Have you found anything yet?"

I feel his eyes on me before he says, "I've found a few things."

"Like what?"

"Well, I've found I really like helping people and animals. I want to talk to Huxley about making the Angelica a rent-controlled apartment building. You'd have to fill out an application to live there, make less than a certain amount of money, and if you're a single parent, you're higher on the list of getting a place."

I turn to him now. "JP, that's an amazing idea, but you realize you'd take a huge hit on income. I'm sure you know, the renovations we have planned aren't cheap."

"Sure, we'd take a hit, but we'd also be able to write it off in our taxes, and sometimes, it's not always about the money. I like the idea of being able to help people out. I was thinking, if Huxley says yes, maybe we could start a division in the company, named after the Angelica, that focuses on low-income households, that provides them with not just a roof over their heads, but a roof filled with opportunity. We donate a lot of money to different charities and organizations, but I'd love to do something in-house, something that focuses on helping the people in the cities where we make billions."

"I think it's a brilliant idea, JP."

"Yeah?" he asks, looking insecure.

"I do. Is this something that would fulfill you? I know you hate what you do now, so would this help with that?"

He sifts his hand through his hair as he stares out over the sea of black in front of us. "I really do. I'd actually feel like I'm doing something beneficial. And being the face of that, the face of collaboration—assisting those who need that relief—now that's something I could be happy with."

"When are you going to approach him?"

"When we get back. I still have some things I have to map out and, of course, I need to hit up Breaker for a numbers breakdown. I have a few questions about write-offs for him, as well. And then I'll write everything up, put it in a proposal, and deliver it to him. I know how he likes professional presentations, so I'll make sure it's delivered the way he likes it."

"What if he says no?" I ask.

"Then he's a total self-centered ass, and I'd be set in stone on selling my stock and finding a company or a passion in life that fulfills the need I have. I love my brothers, and I've done everything they've asked of me, and now I think it's time they step back and see what I need."

"Wow, JP, is it weird to say I'm proud of you?"

"Nah, not sure I hear that often, so it's nice."

I lean against his chest and say, "Well, I'm proud of you."

"Thanks, babe."

JP: Where are you right now?

Kelsey: Just finished up a meeting with Regis. I'm pretty sure he sneered at me twice but covered it up with an eye twitch. It was entertaining.

JP: Did he give you shit?

Kelsey: No. He was pleasant and agreeable.

JP: Smart man. Well, I'm on my way to the penthouse. Just got done with an interview with The Gazette. I was going to pick up some pho. Want some?

Kelsey: You don't mind?

JP: Why would I ask?

Kelsey: True. Yes, please. Sounds amazing.

JP: I just get the original. Do you want the same?

Kelsey: Yes, that works. I'm headed back soon. Should I pick us up dessert?

JP: What did you have in mind?

Kelsey: It's going to be a surprise.

JP: Why am I worried?

Kelsey: Because, although innocent in your eyes, I'm still a wild card.

JP: Very true.

I dab my mouth with a napkin and set my container on the coffee table. When JP arrived, we both changed out of our business clothes. He changed into a pair of shorts and nothing else—shocker—and I put on a pair of shorts and a simple T-shirt. I also washed off my makeup and threw my hair into a clip to keep it out of my face while I slurped up noodles.

We decided to turn on *The Office* for background noise while we ate and talked. I found out that Dwight is JP's favorite character, Michael being a close second. And I, of course, being the romantic, said Jim and Pam are my all-time favorites. JP just rolled his eyes at that.

Also found out JP would "bang" Jan easily, have a drunken night with Meredith, and cuddle up to Phyllis on a cozy night. I admitted to having a slight thing for Ryan, and possibly interested in a wild night with Robert California, which of course grossed out JP and ended the conversation.

"I don't think I've ever had pho before," I say. "I've always heard about it and wanted to try it. I hate that I've waited this long. It was so good. Thank you for bringing it home."

JP, who was done about ten minutes ago, leans his head against his propped-up hand and asks, "What's your favorite cuisine?"

"Mexican."

He nods. "Fuck, I could've guessed that. Those tamales your mom makes are fucking killer. And her homemade refried beans. Hell, I'd do anything your mom wanted for them right now."

I smile. "I know how to make them, and it's been said that I make them better than my mom."

JP's eyes narrow. "Says who?"

"My mom."

"Okay, so what do I have to do to get you to make me some?"

"How about this—if you're not doing anything tomorrow night, we can make them together." When he doesn't answer right away, I ask, "Oh…do you have something going on tomorrow? I shouldn't have assumed. You have been spending quite some time with me."

"Kelsey, chill. I'd love to make some tamales with you. I was just thinking about a meeting I have at four, but it shouldn't take long. Should we start at six?"

"That would be perfect."

"I can pick up the ingredients if you want."

I shake my head. "No, that's okay. I'm particular about brands. Trust me, it makes a difference."

He holds up his hand. "Don't want to get in the way of the chef. Just let me know how much I owe you."

"JP, do you really think I'd take your money?"

"No…should I grab dessert?"

I smirk. "I think we're starting a trend."

"Yeah, one that's killing my six-pack." He pats his stomach.

"Doubtful. You still get up early and work out." I point at his stomach. "Let me see."

He slouches in his seat and puffs his stomach out, making a poor attempt at a gut. It's poor because I can still see the outline of his abs.

"Stop that." I poke his belly.

"Don't play with my gut. I'm sensitive."

"Oh my God, that's not a gut. I can still clearly see your abs. Nice try."

"Well, if I keep it up, no woman will want to see me naked."

That makes me actually laugh out loud. "Once again, doubtful. I've, uh…seen enough to know that any woman would want to see you naked."

His brows raise in surprise. "Kelsey Gardner…tell me more."

"Oh, Jesus." I roll my eyes. "This is why I hesitate to compliment you. I knew this was going to happen."

He scoots closer and wiggles his brows. "Were you impressed with my body? How about my penis? Did you like the old log between the legs?"

"Eww, who says that?"

"Who says *eww* when referring to a man's prized possession?"

"Someone who's responding to a person who's being obnoxious, which is you. Your penis isn't a log, it's…a regular penis."

That makes his face fall in disbelief. "A regular penis? You think I have just a regular penis?"

"Well, yeah. I mean, it doesn't have any adornments and, sure, it's well kept, but there's nothing super special about it."

"Um…not to sound like a fucking voyeur here, but I've been in enough gym locker rooms to know my penis isn't regular. Just because it's not pierced doesn't make it ho-hum. There's a lot to my penis that you don't know about. And the length and girth alone are probably better than anything you've had."

"How do you know the kind of penis I've had in my life?" I challenge him, humor in my voice.

"Given how innocent you are, most likely those penises have been regular. Mine is anything but regular."

"Said every man ever."

His eyes grow dark and all humor fades from his face. "Do I need to take my cock out right now?"

"No, that's okay. I can still remember how it felt when you sat on my face. Very…fleshy."

"That's because it is fleshy."

"I always thought penises were supposed to be soft like velvet, you know? I didn't get that from you."

"Where the fuck did you hear that? And what cocks are you hanging out with that are velvet?"

"Ones in romance novels."

He snorts. "If a cock is velvet to the touch, then the man fucking glue-gunned some fabric to his manhood. Dicks are flesh, and when they're hard, they're stiff and veiny. I'm sure you can recall my hard cock. You came in your lingerie, after all." He gives me a pointed look and I can feel my cheeks heat up. Walked right into that one.

"I came because of the work I put in."

"Bullshit," he says. "You came because of the moment you were in."

"Possibly, but we can't ever be sure now, can we?"

"I know for sure. You wouldn't have come like that if I wasn't there, egging you on, telling you how to touch yourself, grabbing my cock, and enticing you."

I just shrug, because I know he's right, but I like pushing his buttons.

"Do I need to show you again? Because I will."

"I know you will, and it's really not necessary. How did we even get on this topic? Weren't we talking about dessert for tomorrow? Let's get back to that. I think it would be lovely if you picked up dessert."

"Who says I need to pick it up…?"

I press my palm to his face and push him away. "It's either dessert we can eat, or no dessert at all."

"I can eat my dessert." He wets his lips.

Oh hell.

"Stop it. You're making me—"

"Aroused?" He waggles his brows at me.

Yes.

"No. You're just…you're making it weird. And I don't want it to be weird between us."

"There's nothing weird about this conversation. Friends can talk about this stuff. Go ahead, tell me the craziest place you've ever had sex."

"Why? So you can just say how vanilla I am?"

"I never said you were vanilla. I said you were innocent. There's a difference. A vanilla person never would've masturbated in front of me."

Once again, my cheeks heat up.

"Well, that was—God, I hate what I'm about to say."

"Just say it. We're buddies now, right?" His one eyebrow raises in question.

"I guess we are." I roll my teeth over the corner of my lip before I say, "Well, it wasn't sex, but what we did was probably my most provocative experience. Which, I still don't understand how that all happened, and I don't care to hash it out. But, yeah, everything else has been pretty bland in bed. Nothing more than that."

"Shame," he says. "If you were mine, we wouldn't just fuck in the bed."

"Oh…I'm sure you have a giant list of odd places you've, uh, you've had sex. So, instead, I'm going to ask, what was your favorite place?"

"Hot tub," he says without even giving it a second thought. "Fucking in the hot tub. Christ, I love it."

"Really?" I ask. "It doesn't get all watery and weird?"

"No." He shakes his head. "There's something about a naked woman in the hot tub, fucking her from behind… Yeah, I love it."

"Oh." I clear my throat. "And, uh, how many times have you done this?"

"Not nearly enough and not with the right person yet."

"How do you know it's not the right person? Clearly, you've enjoyed it."

"Because I know there could be so much more intimacy involved.

I've had just random fucks, but with the right ambiance, with the correct amount of foreplay, I know it could be explosive."

Gulp

Yeah…I could see that.

"What about you?" he asks. "Do you have an ideal situation planned in your head where you'd have the best sex of your life?"

"Not really. I just know that when I find the right person, everything will just click and I won't have to try. I won't have to imagine these romantic situations, but rather just live in the moment and let them happen."

"And you haven't had that yet?"

I shake my head. "No. For a girl who's obsessed with love, it's sad how my love life has turned out."

"Not sad, you're just not settling, and I think that's smart. You will find the right person." He tips my chin with his forefinger. "But in the meantime, unleash the secret you've been holding all night. What's this dessert you got us that you won't tell me about?"

Anticipating his reaction, I can't hide my smile as I get up from the couch and retrieve the bakery box from the fridge.

"Should I be scared by that smile?" he asks when I sit back down across from him.

"Possibly." I flip open the box and reveal the two dollar-sized penis cookies on a popsicle stick. "I bought us penis cookies, covered in white and dark chocolate."

I look up at him and wait, grinning like an idiot. The corner of his mouth ticks up, and then he smiles. He picks up the white chocolate cookie and examines it, twisting it from one side to the other. "I've never had a dick in my mouth, but there's always time to change that." Then he takes a large bite and chews. "Hell, this penis is good."

I snort so hard I feel droplets of snot come out of my nose. *Attractive, Kelsey.*

"And so lifelike." He examines the cookie again. "Now this, Kelsey, this would be average. Your boy…not so much." Then he takes another bite and I can't help but think he's so freaking right.

———————

JP: Do you hear that?

Kelsey: Is someone having sex? I thought the other people on this floor are across the way.

JP: They are. It's not them. It's below us. I just looked. People are fucking on the balcony.

Kelsey: Seriously? Where everyone can see them?

JP: LOL. Oh, Kelsey.

Kelsey: What? That's concerning, don't you think? "Caught with your pants down" is a real term.

JP: But that's the excitement of it all, getting caught.

Kelsey: Let me guess—having sex on a balcony isn't something new to you.

JP: Not so much.

Kelsey: Shocking.

JP: Are you saying I'm a bit of a man-whore?

Kelsey: I don't think we need to label our sex lives. You just have a more frequent one.

JP: Very. Want me to teach you a thing or two?

Kelsey: How did I know you were going to suggest that?

JP: Because I'm becoming a good friend and you know me inside and out.

Kelsey: Sort of. Hell, I think I talk to you more than my sister now. Granted, she's been busy with the wedding.

JP: Do you have any other friends?

Kelsey: Yeah, a few girlfriends, but unfortunately, we've slowly grown apart because of my business. The hustle doesn't allow for many friends.

JP: I get it. Well, you have me now.

Kelsey: I do. And I'm grateful for that.

JP: So…do you want to sit out on the balcony and listen to the fuckers?

Kelsey: …good night, JONAH!

JP: Ooo, say my name again. I like it.

Kelsey: *Sigh*

Kelsey: Thank you for the midmorning smoothie delivery. How did you know I needed this more than anything right now?

JP: Caught a glimpse of you when I was walking through the Angelica with Huxley on FaceTime. Had it delivered right away. You look tired, babe.

Kelsey: The fuckers were really going at it last night.

JP: Is that really what was keeping you up last night?

Kelsey: My mind was racing, thinking about all things business. You know how it goes.

JP: I do. If you want, we can skip the dinner tonight and just hang, or do something else. Not sure what you like to do to decompress.

Kelsey: No, I still want to make dinner, unless you don't want to.

JP: Babe, if I get to spend time with you, I don't care what we do.

Kelsey: Well, okay then…

JP: Was that a weird comment?

Kelsey: It was unexpected.

JP: I just feel my best around you. Sorry if that's weird, but it's true.

Kelsey: It's not weird. Makes me feel like I mean something.

JP: You do, babe. You mean a lot.

"Okay, now add the ice," I say, as my hands are wrist-deep in the masa.

"Sure," JP says, while working around me. The pork has been cooked, I cheated and put it in the crockpot this afternoon, and we already prepared the sauce. I thought it was cute when JP was in awe over the dehydrated peppers and how we rehydrated them and then blended them up.

"And from here, we mix for about ten to fifteen minutes with our hands."

"Oh shit, really?"

"Yup."

"Okay." He maneuvers around and awkwardly stands next to me, but can't quite get the right angle until he finally mutters, "Fuck it," and stands behind me. He reaches around my arms and puts his hand in the bowl, his head right next to mine. "Is this okay?"

His chest is plastered against my back and the rough scruff of his cheek is rubbing against mine, driving my internal temperature up another ten degrees. But I'm not going to make a big deal about it so I nod.

"That's fine. As long as you're comfortable."

"I'm good, babe. What perfume do you wear, by the way? Fucking kills me."

"Dolce and Gabbana, Light Blue."

"Hell, it smells good. Not that I should be saying that while standing next to you like this, but it smells really fucking good."

"Thank you," I say as the hairs on the back of my neck stand at attention.

The last few days have been…comforting. Spending all this time with JP makes me realize that he truly is a good guy. When his mind is clear, when he's happy, he's so open and honest and a good time. He jokes around—like he used to—and I hate to say this, but he sort of makes me feel alive. Like a part of me has been missing and he's woken it up.

I feel excited to see him, thrilled to get a text from him, and count down the minutes until our next planned nondate. Within a very short amount of time, he's become one of my best friends. Never would've expected that.

"This is kind of fun. I feel like a cat, massaging a gut."

My hands pause as I turn just slightly to look at him. "What kind of analogy is that?"

"You know...how cats paw at things." He replicates a massaging motion. "That's what this feels like. Did you not have a cat growing up?"

"I didn't."

"Ah, you missed out," he says, leaning in against me even more. "Shame. You never experienced a sandpaper tongue on the back of your hand. Or the feel of a cat's claw seeping through the threads of your clothing, straight into your flesh. Or the absolute pleasure of sifting shit out of a litter box."

"Yes, an absolute shame," I say sarcastically. "What was your cat's name?"

"Huxley and I called her Cat, because we didn't have any feelings toward her. She was more of an annoying asshole than anything. Always clawed the shit out of us. But Breaker was best friends with the cat. Her name was technically Jiggles. Have you ever watched *New Girl*?"

"Yes, love that show."

"Well, think of Winston and his cat. That was Breaker and Jiggles."

Our hands collide in the bowl, and instead of pulling away or moving, I just let our fingers tangle through the masa mixture. I like it. I shouldn't, but I do.

"I can't see it. Breaker seems so cool and calm. I can't see him fussing over a cat."

JP chuckles. "Man, does he have you fooled. Sure, he's cool and calm, but he's the biggest nerd. Loves data, has autographs from every cast member of *The Lord of the Rings*, and he has been known to dress up a time or two as a calculator for Halloween."

"What? No way." I shake my head. "That can't be true."

"Trust me, babe, he's a nerd. He has a computer at his place that he built on his own."

"Gah, like Henry Cavill?"

"What?" he asks, confused.

"Henry Cavill, he built his own computer and recorded the whole thing. It was hot."

"Wow…man, am I missing the mark on what women find attractive these days."

"Then again, Henry is such a dreamboat. The chin dimple, the seductive eyes, the unbelievable muscles."

"You know, some people have said that I look like a tattooed Henry Cavill."

"Who on earth said that? Someone in your dreams?" I chuckle at my joke.

"Funny. No, it was a girl I met at a baseball game."

"Uh-huh. And let me guess—she asked for your autograph and then was extremely embarrassed that she thought you were someone else, she apologized profusely, you consoled her, bought her a drink, and then took her home that night. Was she one of the hot-tub girls?"

"No," he drags out. "But the rest of that story is scarily accurate."

"Figured. When I was in college, there was this wave of girls who would pull that trick on guys all the time to get free drinks and an easy lay."

"Any guy is an easy lay."

"It was a pickup move. She played you."

"Whatever, play me all you want. I had sex that night."

"As if it's hard for you to find someone to have sex with you."

"You've been difficult," he says, his voice practically caressing my skin. Once again, those goose bumps spread. "But, then again, you friend-zoned me from the beginning, so there was no chance."

"You were off-limits. I didn't have a choice but to friend-zone you."

He pauses, his rough cheek moving across mine as his hands sink deeper into the mixture. "Why was I off-limits?" His lips nearly move against my cheek; I can feel them, they're so close. Just a feather of a whisper away.

And it's frustrating because I shouldn't want his lips near me, I shouldn't be comfortable with him wrapped around me, I shouldn't wait impatiently for him to call me *babe*, but here I am, waiting with bated breath for his next move.

"Because you're Huxley's brother. Because my company falls under your management. Because I knew you were in a different frame of mind than I am."

"And if those weren't factors, then what, Kelsey?"

I swallow hard.

My hands have slowed, barely mixing, and my heart pounds so loudly, it sounds deafening in my ears.

His cologne surrounds me.

His voice rumbles across my skin.

He's deliciously trapped me between him and the counter.

This is everything I could dream up for a romantic moment, and yet, the man who's making me feel, the man who's turning me into a pool of yearning…is supposed to be my friend. He's not supposed to be the one who makes my heart beat faster.

"Hell, I don't know why I asked that," he says, when he pulls his hands from the bowl, mistaking my silence for discomfort. "You have your reasons, and it's great that we have this. You and me, friends. It's been easy."

I don't turn toward him. I can't.

I can't let him see the way he affects me.

I can't let him hear the thick breaths I'm taking, attempting to find that easy rhythm again.

And I can't let him see how my hands are clawing at the masa, begging and pleading for him to come back.

"What can I do to prepare for the next step?" he asks.

I take a deep, steadying breath and slow my racing heartbeat. "You can lay out the husks and grab that spatula. We're going to start spreading the masa on them."

"You got it, babe."

I squeeze my eyes shut. *Keep it together, Kelsey.*

———

"Eating out on the balcony was a great idea," I say as I sip the homemade virgin margarita JP surprised me with.

Virgin, because he said he was backing off on drinking. He didn't elaborate on his decision, but I could see that it was a well-thought-out one and I support him completely.

"But I can't help but wonder," I continue. "Were you hoping for an encore from the fuckers?"

"I mean…a little dinner and a show would've been nice."

I laugh. "Not sure how great of a show that would've been."

"It would've been entertaining, that's for sure. But this is nice, the peaceful night, faint sounds from the streets below, the occasional whip of the wind, amazing food… It's been a great night, Kelse." He rubs his stomach. "Not sure I have room for my dessert."

"Me neither." I lean back in my chair. "I'm grateful for the elastic in my shorts. Is that an unflattering thing to say?"

"Not even a little." He snaps the waistband of his shorts. "I'm just grateful we cleaned up while the tamales were steaming."

"Me too." I let out a low whistle. "I can't believe we only have two more nights here. I feel sad about it. I've grown accustomed to the penthouse and this city."

"What about the company?" JP asks, taking a sip of his margarita.

"That too. Going back to my tiny studio apartment will feel so lonely."

"You can always move into my place. Plenty of room. Comes with access to an elaborate pool…and a hot tub." He wiggles his eyebrows, causing me to laugh.

"Tempting, but I'm sure you're ready to have your life back."

"What do you mean by that?" he asks.

"You know, getting out and about, not always having to hang out with me."

He looks me in the eyes when he says, "I don't *have* to hang out with you, Kelsey. I *want* to hang out with you. I choose to."

A smile tugs across my lips and I look away, hating that his words shoot a thrill up my spine.

"Same, Jonah," I say, testing out his name. When I glance in his direction, his expression is of total awe. I wince. "I mean, JP."

He shakes his head. "Call me what you want. I like both."

"I like your real name. I think it fits you—at least, this side of you. JP is more of the partying playboy guy. But the man I've been hanging out with lately, he's Jonah."

"Yeah." He looks up at me shyly. "I fucking like that a lot."

"I'm glad." I gather our plates and say, "It'll be weird, though, going back to my normal life. I really enjoyed my time here."

"I'm sure you'll be back. We're just starting on the Angelica Building, and Huxley is going to want you to oversee things. This won't be the last time you're here."

"Good. I have so many more dessert places to try. I should start a dessert Instagram. I could call it *Mint to Be*, like a play on words with my podcast."

"Or you could call it *Lick Me Till Ice Cream*."

My eyes level with his playful ones. "That was a JP comment."

"Try all you want. You can't knock that out of me." He winks and stands with me. I grab the plates and he grabs the rest of the tamales and refried beans we didn't eat.

"I wouldn't want you to change. I like you as you are," I say while we walk back into the penthouse and head toward the kitchen.

"Ooo, what movie is that from? I feel like some girl made me watch it."

"*Bridget Jones*," I answer.

He snaps. "That's right. I recall Bridget wandering around onscreen in short skirts, correct?"

"Of course that's the part you remember."

He just shrugs, and together we put away the food and fill the dishwasher with the rest of our dishes. When we're done, I lean against the counter and fold my arms over my chest. "I had fun tonight. You're pretty helpful in the kitchen."

"I make a thing or two."

"Well, I should get to bed, where I can shamelessly avoid any stretchy elastic around my waist so I can better breathe through the tamales I consumed."

"Babe, save the dirty talk for the bedroom."

I chuckle and move past him. "Good night...Jonah."

"Hey," he calls out, causing me to spin around. "I have something for you."

"Please don't tell me it's your penis or something deranged like that."

"First of all, my penis isn't deranged; it's *regular*...remember?"

I laugh.

"And no, I actually have a physical thing for you." He walks toward his suit jacket, which is draped on the back of a dining room chair, and reaches into the inside pocket. He pulls out a small bag and hands it to me. "I saw this and thought of you."

"Oh, it *is* a real thing."

He laughs. "Yes, it is."

I open the tiny blue bag and pull out something long and hard. When I realize what it is, a tsunami of swoon hits me all at once.

"You got me a magnet?"

He sticks his hands in his pockets. "Yeah. I wasn't sure if you'd found one yet. I remember you saying that you get one for every city you visit.

But since we leave soon, I thought it might be a nice memento. But if you already got one, we can just leave it here, or—"

"I haven't bought one yet." I stare down at the magnet. It reads *San Francisco* along the bottom, with the skyline and Golden Gate Bridge at the top. It's cute, bubbly, and colorful, something I would pick for myself. "But this is so perfect." I move my thumb over the lettering.

"Seriously, if you don't like it, I can get something different."

I shake my head and take a step forward so I can press my hand to his chest. "This was so thoughtful and kind." Our eyes connect. "Thank you." I move in closer, loop my arm around him, and give him a hug. His arms fall around me.

"You're welcome. Hopefully, you will have more to add as your business grows." His hand rubs up and down my back.

I don't pull away.

I don't want to.

I grip him tighter instead, pressing my cheek to his chest.

"I really hope so."

And for the next minute or so, we remain like that, hugging each other. From the outside looking in, it might seem awkward, two people simply hugging in the middle of the common space, but right now, it feels right. It feels like I belong here, in his arms, protected by his strength, cared for by his heart. *This. This is what I've missed so much since not having a boyfriend.* Touch. Every time I watch Jeff swallow Mom in a hug, I feel so incredibly grateful to him, because he gave her confidence back in his hugs. Showed her that she was a desirable woman, not a single mom. And the longer you go without incidental touches, something I've gone without for so long now, the more you long for them. Hugs. A brief kiss on the forehead. Holding hands. Fingers stroking your cheek. I miss that terribly. Even though I can't expect JP—*Jonah*—to provide those things, he has been. And I'm going to miss that when I go back to my apartment, back to living on my own.

"You okay?" he asks, probably wondering why I'm still holding on to him.

"Yeah." I nod and take a step back. "That was just really sweet of you." Our eyes connect. "Really sweet."

He awkwardly smiles. "Glad you like it." He thumbs toward his room. "I'm going to go to bed now. Thanks for a great night, babe."

Don't leave yet.

Sit with me on the couch.

Talk to me some more.

Come back to my room, where you can sift your fingers through my hair and let me feel the rumble of your deep voice against your chest…

"Have a good night." I wave.

"Later, Kelse."

And then he takes off to his bedroom, leaving me absolutely breathless. Speechless.

And completely confused.

CHAPTER 18
JP

JP: Dude, I think I did it. I think I "wooed" her.

Breaker: I'll be the judge of that. Lay it on me.

JP: We've spent the last few nights together *as friends* hanging out, talking, sharing meals. We went out to a movie marathon and then did a night tour at Alcatraz. And last night we made dinner together and shared it out on the balcony.

Breaker: Okay, so you've spent some time together. Not sure that's enough.

JP: I saved the best for last. I got her a magnet.

Breaker: That's your best? A magnet? Dude...

JP: No, it was a good thing. She likes to get a magnet from every city she goes to. I remembered her saying that, so I got her a magnet. She was so grateful and she fucking hugged me for a long time.

Breaker: How long?

JP: Like...a minute?

Breaker: Was her cheek on your chest?

JP: It was.

Breaker: Did she cry?

JP: No tears, but I think I was close to getting them.

Breaker: Uh-huh. Any other details you need to divulge so I can make a decision?

JP: She called me Jonah a few times.

Breaker: Wait, you told her your real name?

JP: Yeah. She said the man she's been hanging out with is more of a Jonah, not the playboy JP.

Breaker: I think my heart just skipped a beat.

JP: Yeah? Think she's wooed?

Breaker: I think there's a ninety-nine percent chance that she is.

JP: That's a solid percentage.

Breaker: She really called you Jonah?

JP: Yeah…and I really fucking liked it. Hell, I really like her. If anything, these last few days have shown me how much I care for this woman. Not sure what will happen, but I need to take a chance.

Breaker: I think you have a solid chance. What are you going to do?

JP: Well, it's our last full night here. We leave tomorrow around six, I think. So, I think I'm going to take her to Parkside. I told her about it a while back, how they have the best dim sum, and then I'm going to take her to the rooftop for dessert.

Breaker: Smooth. I like it. After dessert, are you going to tell her how you feel?

JP: Yeah. Call me crazy, but I truly think she has the same feelings for me.

Breaker: I think you're ready.

JP: I know I'm ready. Fuck, I'm excited. I've never felt this way about a woman before.

Breaker: You haven't, at least you've never told me. I can tell… you really like her.

JP: I do. And I don't want to fuck this up. I'd never forgive myself.

Breaker: Well, you'd know if she's ready for you. Do you think she is?

JP: I do. After the hug last night, I think she's ready for me.

Breaker: Then you need to use your words, JP.

JP: What do you mean? We've been talking about lots of things.

Breaker: You need to use words and tell her how you feel. So far, you've tried to show her what you feel. Now it's time to speak, man. Give her your truths.

JP: I will. Fuck…okay.

I walk down the hallway toward the penthouse, feeling nauseated and excited all at the same time. Today dragged on, every minute feeling like an hour. My meetings were mind-numbingly boring. My inbox never stopped dinging with new emails. And when lunch came around, I was hyped up, yet exhausted from my mind constantly wondering about what was going to happen tonight.

But, fuck, I can't wait to see her.

I can't wait to surprise her with plans for tonight.

I open the door to the penthouse, set my wallet and keys on the entryway table, and then call out to her, "Kelsey, are you home?"

"Yes," she says from her room. "Be right out."

There's a mirror in the entryway that I turn to quickly and check myself out.

Hair is in order.

Suit looks good.

Nothing in my teeth.

I turn back around just in time to catch her walking toward me, and she looks fucking stunning. Dressed in a flowy black dress that reaches just below her knees, her hair's curled in waves… My pulse is racing.

"Hey, long day?" she asks while adjusting one of her earrings.

"Yeah, pretty long. What about you?"

"It was okay. Had to have another meeting with Regis. He was slightly more pleasant than usual, but I think that's because he knows we leave tomorrow." She switches to the other ear, playing with that earring now. "What do you have planned for tonight?"

Glad she asked.

"Well, I was thinking—"

Knock. Knock.

I glance behind me. "Did you order room service?"

"No, that's Derek," she says. "We have a date tonight."

And just like that, every ounce of excitement, emotion, and confidence drains from my veins and pools at the bottom of my feet.

As if my heart has been ripped from my chest, being scratched and scarred by my ribs in the process. All my hopes. All my thoughts. All my fucking courage, it's all wiped away. Evaporated. Demolished.

She's…she's going on a date?

This can't be fucking happening.

This has to be a joke, right?

She can't possibly be going on a date with him, not after…well, not after everything.

But to my horror, Kelsey reaches past me and opens the door, revealing Derek on the other side.

Fuck…

"Hey, Derek, just need to grab my shoes. Give me a second."

"Not a problem." Derek turns toward me as Kelsey opens the entry-way closet. "Hey, you must be JP. Nice to meet you. Your brother has talked a lot about you."

He holds out his hand, and because I don't want to look like a dick, I take it in mine and give it a shake. "Nice to meet you," I say, but I barely recognize my voice. It's gravelly, dark.

Fuck, I'm so upset.

So goddamn upset that I can feel my throat start to tighten.

"Okay, I'm ready," Kelsey says.

She's slipping away.

My plans.

My night.

My big ask.

It's all crumbling right in front of me.

I can't feel my feet. My lungs don't seem to have any air in them. And it feels as if a sharp knife is bludgeoning my chest continuously, ratcheting up this overwhelming sense of pain.

"I'll be home later," Kelsey says, her hand dragging over my arm.

Her touch...it does something inside of me.

It reminds me of what Breaker said.

You need to use words and tell her how you feel. So far, you've tried to show her what you feel. Now it's time to speak, man. Give her your truths.

He's not wrong. My tactics have proven to be shortsighted.

And before she can take another step, I ask, "Can I talk to you for a second?"

She pauses, looks over her shoulder, and asks, "Right now?"

"Yes," I answer.

I must look distraught because she tells Derek to give her a second and then follows me down the hallway to my room, where I shut the door. I shed my suit jacket, toss it on a chair in the corner, and pace the room.

"Is everything okay?"

"No." I shake my head. "Everything is not okay." I pause and look up at her. "I'm going to say something that I know you certainly weren't expecting but, fuck, I need you to know."

"JP, what's going on?"

"I like you, Kelsey," I say, just letting it all fly out. "I fucking like you, and I...I want to ask you out on a date, a real date."

Her mouth falls slightly open.

"And I know this isn't the best timing and that this is selfish of me because you're about to go out on a date, but please, please don't go out with him. Stay here, with me, be with me, give me a chance." She doesn't say anything. And I wait as she stands there in shock. "I had plans for tonight. I was going to take you to Parkside and tell you how much I like you and want to be with you. I know that's hard to believe, given your first impression of me, but I swear, Kelsey, I swear I'm fucking ready for something more."

"JP...I...I don't know what to say."

"You don't have to say anything, just don't go out with him. I don't think I could fucking take it. Your last date was when I drank myself stupid. That's how long I've felt this for you. I don't think I could survive tonight knowing he's claiming you as his, holding your hand, making you laugh...kissing you. All I've wanted is to fucking kiss you, to taste your lips, to make you mine. I've wanted this ever since I met you, from the first moment I laid eyes on you, Kelsey. I knew you were special. I knew you were someone I had to get to know, that I wanted to be around. And, sure, I didn't go about it the right way in the beginning, but I've been trying. I've tried to tell you so many times. So many fucking times." I push my hand through my hair. "Please, Kelsey, please just stay here with me, talk this out, give me a chance."

She looks behind herself and then back at me. "JP, I have a date... I don't... I'm not sure..."

Fuck.

Fuck, the pain is searing.

Burning me.

Marking me.

"I'm sorry," I say. "Fuck, this was selfish of me. I'm sorry, Kelsey. I'm fucking sorry." I take a seat on the edge of my bed and bury my hands in my hair.

"JP..."

"Just go. Forget I said anything. Please, I shouldn't have. This puts you in a bad spot. I'm sorry... Just go on your date."

She's silent.

I can feel her eyes on me.

Her indecision weighs heavily on my shoulders, and when, for a moment, I think that she might stay, I hear her first step echo through my room, then another...then another. Trailing away from me, one step at a time, until my door is shut behind her.

Fu-uck.

I suck in a sharp breath through heavy, webbed lungs. It feels impossible to gain much-needed oxygen.

Our last night in San Francisco, and instead of spending it with me, she's spending it with another man.

I've loved learning how she takes her coffee, the special breakfast she has to have in the morning.

I doubt he knows about her day-of-the-week underwear or how she curls her hair when she's in a fun mood, straightens it when she means business.

And knowing what she tastes like when she's wet, aroused, and looking for more? Or how she sounds and looks when she comes? That will be torture for me, going forward.

I've given her my truths. All I've ever wanted since I met her was to kiss her. Impress her.

But in the end, she *will* choose him.

My throat is so tight, I can barely breathe. I feel my frustrations, my emotions bubble to the surface. The urge to call down to the concierge for a bottle of scotch is all-consuming. Just to get lost, forget, to erase this monopolizing pain ricocheting through my chest.

I pull on my thick strands.

Fuck, what do I do now?

Leave?

Chase her down the hall, begging her to stay?

Find the nearest bar?

I can't stay here. I can't wait around, wondering when she'll return. No, I need to get the fuck out of here. I need to get home. I'm a billionaire, so I can fly my fucking self whenever I damn well please. That's what I'll do.

Leave.

Get home tonight.

Go to my safe place, my house, where Kelsey hasn't touched one goddamn thing. Where I won't be reminded of her.

Where I can sink into oblivion.

I glance around for my phone. I need to make the call. I need to pack. Fuck, who cares about packing? I can buy new shit.

I just need to leave.

I just need to—

The bedroom door creaks open. My body stills as my eyes flit to the door. It cracks open some more, and then Kelsey appears.

No air in my lungs.

No blood through my veins.

Nothing is working within me as I sit there, staring…wondering what the hell she's doing.

She shuts the door behind her and walks over to me. Her strides are demure, her body language timid.

Hunched over, I sit up just as she stands in front of me.

"Kelsey, I—"

Not saying a word, she straddles my lap, lifts my chin with her forefinger, and before I can attempt to take my next breath, her lips are on mine.

Fuck…me.

All it takes is one touch for me to break.

I'm not sure what her intentions are, and I don't give a fuck, because she's kissing me. Kelsey is fucking kissing me, and it feels like I just died and went to heaven.

Soft.

In control.

Yearning.

She parts her lips, dips her tongue into my mouth, and then sifts her fingers through my hair.

I snap.

My hands slide around her, one at her waist, the other at the nape of her neck, and I kiss her back with more force. I let her melt into my touch, take control.

She tugs on my hair.

I slip my hand under the hem of her dress.

She moans into my mouth.

I groan into hers.

She opens her mouth wider.

My tongue finds hers.

And then it's a tangled mess of need. Of eagerness. Of everything I've ever fucking wanted, and it's right here, available for the taking. I'm not letting go.

I can't.

Her hand slides up to my jaw and she grips me tightly. "Unzip my dress."

"What?" I ask breathlessly.

Her eyes connect with mine, the gold in them shining in the yellow glare of the nightstand light. "Unzip my dress, Jonah."

My cock instantly grows hard. Is this real?

Is she real?

Am I fucking dreaming?

Because that's what this feels like—a dream where I'll wake up just as I grip the small zipper of her dress. I'll be rudely disrupted, she'll disappear, and that empty clawing feeling will return.

"Baby," I whisper, my forehead touching hers. "Is this...is this real?"

"Yes," she says as her lips fall to my jaw. "This is real."

"But...your date?"

"I sent him home," she whispers as her lips move over my mouth again. "I realized…" She kisses my cheek. "Very quickly…" She kisses my mouth. "That the pain I felt walking away from you…" She kisses my other cheek. "Brought me to my knees." She lifts up and looks me in the eyes. "I think I've wanted you for a long time, and it took me walking away to confirm that."

I attempt to swallow the lump in my throat, but fail miserably. "What does that mean?"

She brings her hands between us and slowly begins to unbutton my dress shirt, one button at a time. "It means that I'm yours. All yours."

"You're not…you're not leaving?" I still can't believe it.

She tugs my shirt out of my pants and slides the sleeves off my shoulders, leaving my torso bare to her. Her hands slide back up my tense arms, over my carved shoulders, and down my rumbling pecs. She wets her lips as her hips move gently over my lap.

"No. I'm staying. I want…I want you to ask me out."

Fucking hell. I feel the sting of tears at the backs of my eyes. I'm not a goddamn crier, but for the life of me, I can't stop the ugly emotions seizing me. Not sure the last time someone chose me…for me.

For all the ugly I have to offer.

For all the half-hearted seriousness I sputter out.

For all the insecurities, the demons, the baggage.

She's seen it all, in the flesh. And she's choosing me.

Wetting my lips, I stare into her eyes and say, "I want you as mine. All of you. Your beautiful mind, your insane organization, your sexy-as-fuck body, and your loving heart."

"Then"—she pauses and brings my hand to the back of her dress, to her zipper—"take it. Take me."

Two words—who knew they could undo me?

I slide the zipper down and the straps of her dress loosen so she can push them off her shoulders. She gathers the hem of the dress and lifts it over her head, leaving her in a one-piece lingerie set.

"Did you…did you wear this for him?"

Her seductive eyes flash up to mine as she shakes her head. "No. I wore it for you."

Fucking hell.

I drive my hand into her hair again and bring her mouth to mine, showing her just how much I want her, how much I've longed for this. When she grips me back, her fingers digging into my skin, I realize she wants this just as much as I do.

I'm not letting go, neither is she, and with that knowledge, I slow down my kiss. I part my lips and tangle my tongue with hers as I twist her to the mattress, laying her carefully down while I hover over her, my arm propping me up.

Together, we explore each other. Her hands sift through my hair, down my back, across my chest, over my shoulders.

I drag my fingers over the lace of her lingerie, over the sides of her breasts, down to her hip, and then back up to her delicate neck.

"I've wanted you for so long," I whisper as I bring my mouth to the column of her neck. "And not just for sex. This isn't just sex for me." I lift up so our eyes meet. "Do you hear me? This isn't just sex for me."

"I know." She brings my hand to her heart, pressing down so I can feel how hard it's hammering. "This isn't just sex for me either. Feel that? That's what you do to me, you make my heart beat faster."

"Why didn't you say anything?"

"I didn't think you felt the same way."

"Babe." I grip her jaw and tilt her mouth up. Inches away from her mouth, I say, "I think you know how I feel now."

"I do," she whispers before I press my lips to hers again. She sighs and loops her arms around my neck. I toy with the strap of her lingerie, then tug the strap down a few inches, waiting to see her response. When she doesn't protest, I pull it all the way down her arm. She shrugs out of it.

While keeping my lips on hers, our tongues colliding, tangling, I feather my fingers up her arm, across her collarbone, and then to her exposed breast. My palm connects with her hard nipple, and I groan into her mouth before rolling the hard nub with my fingers.

"Yes," she whispers when my mouth releases hers. I kiss down her neck, to her chest, and then I lift up and stare down at her.

"Fuck," I whisper, dragging my hand over my mouth. "Kelsey, you're so goddamn beautiful."

She shrugs out of the other strap and then, with her eyes connected to mine, she says, "Strip me down."

Hell...

Lifting up, I tug on the lingerie until I free her from the lace, leaving her completely naked on my bed.

"Christ," I whisper before lowering my mouth to her breasts. I squeeze one with my hand while I drag her nipple into my mouth. I lap at it with my tongue a few times, over and over, and then I suck on the nub—hard—causing her back to arch.

So responsive.

I move to her other breast and do the same thing.

Lick.

Lick.

Suck.

She moans while holding me in place.

I go back to her other breast and then trail kisses along her skin, over her belly button, and right below. Her legs part in anticipation, but instead of giving her what she wants, I move back up her stomach and to her left breast. I tease her nipple with my mouth.

"God," she groans in frustration. "I'm so ready for you. You have to know that."

"Are you?" I ask as I move my hand between us and very lightly run it along the seam of her pussy. My fingers are drenched in her arousal.

Looking her in the eye, I suck on my fingers. "Fuck," I grind out. "I've wanted your pussy ever since that first taste."

I drag my mouth back down her body, swirling my tongue around, feeling her writhing beneath me as I grow closer and closer to the spot between her legs. I drag my tongue over her hipbone and then to her inner thigh.

"Please, don't tease me...please," she cries.

"You want my mouth?"

She nods. "Please, Jonah."

Seeing the desperation in her eyes, I switch plans. I wanted to consume her with need by playing around with her inner thighs, but there's no point, so I spread her legs with my hands and move in between them. Her glistening clit is ready for me, so with one long gentle stroke, I soak her all up.

"Oh...God," she groans while her pelvis reaches for me. "More. I want so much more."

I part her with my fingers as I drag my tongue very slowly over her clit. I'm languid with my strokes, adding sufficient pressure to drive her nuts, but not enough speed to push her over the edge.

And that's how I keep her, on the edge with every press, every lick. I don't want her to come, not yet, not when I'm right where I want to be. Pleasing her. Tasting her. Consuming her.

I've dreamt of this, of this very moment, where I could own this woman. I don't want it to end; I want it to last. I want to know that I can drive her crazy with every pass of my tongue.

"JP, please," she begs.

I slowly insert two fingers inside her, giving her more, but not making her come yet.

"Yes." She shifts under my grasp. "Right there. Ohhhh, yes."

I curve my fingers up, while I pick up the strokes of my tongue, turning them more into flicks, causing a slew of curse words to fall out of my beautiful girl's mouth. And, fuck, it turns me on even more.

My dick is so hard, it's painful as it presses against my dress pants, offering no room. Between the way she fucking tastes, and her reaction to what I'm doing, I know the minute I get inside her, I'm going to come.

"JP, oh God, I'm...I'm right there."

Her confession makes me pause, and I pull my mouth from her clit to look up at her.

Her chest is heaving, her eyes are ravenous, and her mouth is drawn into a frown as she says, "What are you doing?"

"I want to look at you, see what you look like right before you come."

Her hands grip the comforter beneath us as she lies back down. "Please, JP, please don't make me wait. I want to come on your tongue."

Well, fuck.

I bring my mouth back to her clit, and instead of licking, I suck the little nub between my lips, causing her to call out my name and her legs to grip me tightly.

"Fuck," she groans. "Oh God...I'm—I'm...there."

I suck one more time before releasing her and flicking my tongue against her clit over and over again until she tenses around me and yells out something unintelligible as she falls over the edge. Her hips ride against my mouth, her arousal soaks into my beard, and I keep moving my tongue and fingers until she's begging me to stop.

I pull away slightly to see what I've done to her. To watch her unfold, to recover with her sated body stretched out along the bed.

My dick is so painful right now, and I undo my belt, unbutton my pants, and drag the zipper down. Her eyes flash up to mine and I give her a show as I slowly push down my pants and briefs, revealing my agonized cock. I take it into my hand, grip the base, and pull.

Fuck, that feels good.

"I want inside you," I say, dragging my hand over the head. "Are you on birth control?"

She nods, her body still relaxed from her orgasm.

"Good, because I want you bare."

Her teeth roll over her bottom lip.

"You want that, don't you?" I ask her.

She nods slowly.

"That's what I thought. I want it so fucking bad. I've always used con-doms, but with you, baby, I want nothing between us." I lie down so my head is on a pillow, and placing one hand behind my head, I nod for her to come over to me.

She gets up on all fours and crawls toward me, her perfect body making me grow harder with every move she makes. I've always thought her tits were amazing, but being able to touch them, suck them, mark them is better than I imagined. And it's why I'm lying down. I want to fuck her like this, so I can watch her tits bounce, her face alight in pleasure, when I'm deep inside of her.

Straddling my legs, she sits on my thighs. She smooths her hands up my hips and then in toward my cock, gripping the base.

A harsh hiss escapes my lips from her touch, warm…firm, just the way I fucking like it.

"JP?"

"Yes?" I ask, watching her small hand pump my cock very slowly.

"I really like you."

Hell. If she's trying to bury herself under my skin, she's doing a good fucking job.

"I really like you, too, babe."

She smirks and then sits up on her knees, positioning my cock at her entrance. My jaw clenches, readying myself for what I know will be the most amazing feeling of my life.

The first inch—fuck, she's warm, tight, perfect.

The second, I feel my eyes nearly rolling to the back of my head.

The third and fourth, my chest is heaving.

The fifth, sixth, seventh, eighth, ninth…I nearly swallow my tongue.

And when I bottom out, I exhale sharply. Her hands fall to my chest and her hair cascades over her shoulders and beautiful face.

"Oh my God…" she whispers. "I…I feel so…so full."

I slide my hands up her thighs as the urge to thrust up is so consuming, that it's taking everything in me to hold back.

"You okay, baby?"

Her head falls back, her hair floating with her, as she nods. "Yeah. I feel so good."

"Perfect, because I need to move. I need to fuck you."

"Then fuck me," she says right before she pulses on top of me. I move my hips with her, pumping up into her.

So warm.

So tight.

I've never felt anything like it, because I've never been bare with a woman, ever. But with Kelsey, I knew I needed to feel every inch of her. I needed to know what it felt like to be pulled into her, to feel her pussy convulse around me.

And it's heaven.

"Shit, babe, this…uhhhh, this feels so good." I open my eyes and catch her throwing her head back in passion, her perky tits bobbing with her movements, her hair swaying back and forth… It spurs on my impending orgasm.

Her hands travel up her body, to her tits, and she grips them tightly, her fingers moving over her nipples, pinching them.

"Mmmmm, yes," she says.

Such a goddamn turn-on.

I grip her hips tighter and move her faster over my cock. Every stroke is like a languid jolt of pleasure, pulsing straight to my balls, making them grow tighter and tighter, but never fully bringing me to where I need to be. Rather, I just edge myself out, riding the prolonged need to come but never getting there.

The frustration takes over and I flip her to her back. She lets out a startled gasp, and while she's still stunned, I grab her hands and pin them together over her head. I lower my head to her tits and suck her nipples into my mouth.

"Oh my God, yes," she calls out as I continue to pump into her. Now in control, I can swivel my hips just right, I can pull out slow and hammer into her hard. I can get what I need while delivering what she needs, as well.

"You feel so good, Kelsey. So fucking good."

She wraps her legs around my back, drawing me in closer. I can feel that she's close, and I'm right there with her as my legs start to feel light, tingling, and numb. My grip on her hands feels like it's growing weak as my hips pulse faster and faster.

The sound of my skin smacking against hers fills the room. I lower my free hand to her stomach, just above her pubic bone, and press down gently. Her eyes flash wide, her mouth drops open, and a silent plea falls past her lips as her cheeks redden and her legs clamp around me even more.

"Oh my God…oh my God, yes…yes. Jonah, oh my God!" Her pussy clenches around my cock and she comes, my name falling off her tongue over and over again.

That's all it takes. My balls draw in tight, my cock swells, and with one last pulse, I'm coming inside of her.

"Mother…fucker," I grind out, my molars nearly cracking from the intense orgasm that rips through me, sending me into a black hole of pure bliss.

I pulse a few more times before I collapse, right on top of her.

Holy…

Fuck.

That was…hell, that was the best sex of my entire life. And I know it's because of her, because of the feelings I possess *for* her. This wasn't mindless sex, this was meaningful. The start of something new.

"Shit, I'm sorry," I say as I try to move off her.

"No, stay," she says, wrapping her arms around me as well and slowly dragging her fingers over the short strands of hair on the back of my neck.

I press my forearms into the mattress so I can alleviate some of my weight and stare down at her. Our eyes connect, and together, we both smile, and then laugh.

"Why are you laughing?" I ask her.

"Because you're laughing."

"We laughed at the same time."

"True...I just—I don't know; it all feels right. I guess that's my response when something feels so right."

"It does, doesn't it?" I ask her, giving her a chaste kiss.

"It does."

"So, no regrets?" I ask her.

"None at all. Do you have regrets?" Her brow draws together in concern.

"Babe, I almost had a goddamn heart attack when you left this room. I'm pretty sure you could label me as the happiest man on the planet right now."

She strokes the hair that's tipping over my forehead. "Why didn't you say anything sooner? Why did you wait so long?"

"I tried telling you a few times, but we were always interrupted and then, hell, I thought that maybe if I wooed you first, you'd be more willing to give me a chance. That's what I've been doing. I planned to tell you tonight, at dinner. Until I saw you were going out with Derek."

"That must have hurt you so much. I'm sorry, JP. I never would've said yes to his date if I knew that's how you felt."

"It was an absolute gut punch, hence my pleading with you to stay."

"Well, I'm here now, and I'm yours."

"All mine?" I ask. "You realize what that means, right?"

"What?" she asks.

"That I was right, men and women can't work together—"

She claps her hand over my mouth, halting me. "I suggest you don't finish that sentence."

Chuckling, I nip at her hand until she lets go, and then I lower my lips to her neck and start kissing her all over again. She sighs into my kiss, and for the first time in as long as I can remember, I truly feel happy.

CHAPTER 19
KELSEY

MEANT TO BE PODCAST
SAWYER AND FALLON

Kelsey: Welcome, listener, to the *Meant to Be Podcast*, where we talk to madly-in-love couples about the way they met. Sawyer and Fallon, thank you so much for joining me today.

Sawyer: Thanks for having us.

Kelsey: I saw that the movie *Runaway Groomsman* is releasing this fall and that the script is based on your relationship. Is that true?

Fallon: It is. Sawyer is a fantastic screenwriter for romance movies, but his dating life was absolute crap.

Sawyer: She speaks facts.

Fallon: His luck wasn't great, either, because his girlfriend actually cheated on him with his best friend.

Kelsey: No, that's awful.

Sawyer: That's not the worst part. I was the bitter best man at their wedding, and halfway through the ceremony, I realized I didn't have to put up with having to watch them get married. So…I left.

Fallon: In the middle of the wedding, he ran out of the church right to his car, then drove to Canoodle, where we both live now.

Sawyer: In classic pitiful-life fashion, I drove to the first bar I saw and got drunk.

Fallon: It wasn't love at first sight...because we'd actually gone on a blind date a year before, but he didn't remember me.

Sawyer: Still feel like an ass about that. But, slowly—and I mean slowly—we became friends. But she was with someone else, so I remained her friend, despite falling for her.

Fallon: At the time, since I was with someone else, I couldn't reflect on how I felt about Sawyer.

Sawyer: It wasn't until after she broke it off with her boyfriend—it was a mutual decision—that I slowly showed her I could be her leading man.

Fallon: Oh my God, you're so cheesy.

Sawyer: Yeah, but you still love me.

Fallon: I do.

"Morning," JP says as he leans against the kitchen counter, holding a mug of coffee, looking so freaking fine in his navy-blue three-piece suit.

"Good morning," I say. I feel my cheeks heat up, because, oh my God, I've never in my life had as much sex as I did last night.

Six times.

Six freaking times.

It was as if he opened a dam to my libido. Anytime he even pulled away, I nuzzled back into him, wanting more.

His hands.

His mouth.

His cock.

I needed it all, and every time he was deep inside me, with nothing between us, I still didn't feel like we were close enough until we were both coming together. I've never felt anything like it, this blinding need to be attached to another human.

If I'm honest, that need has been building all week. With every time we hung out, every meal we shared, every hug before we went off to bed, I tried to tell myself we were just friends, that there was nothing more, but my heart knew better. The moment I saw the devastation on his face before the date with Derek, I nearly split in two.

I left his room with one thing on my mind—letting Derek go so I could spend the rest of the night in JP's arms. I know it wasn't fair to Derek, and I plan on messaging him later, but I couldn't leave JP. I couldn't bear the look in his eyes, the pleading for me to stay. It gutted me. And in the blink of an eye, it was as if everything fell into place.

The conversations.

The dates.

The text messages.

This was the man I was supposed to be with.

Not Derek.

Not Edwin.

Not some random guy I might meet on a dating app.

JP has been the man all along, and I've just been too blind to see it— until yesterday.

"Are you going to give me a kiss?" he asks, before taking a sip of his coffee.

Smiling shyly, I walk up to him, place my hand on his chest, and then stand on my toes and press a kiss to his lips. His hand around my waist holds me in place. Our mouths collide in a sweet connection, not carnal at all, but it's nice. It's the sweet and dreamy kiss that sends chills up your spine while your stomach flutters with excitement.

"You smell nice."

"Yeah?" He smirks. "Not sure I'll ever get used to you tossing me a compliment. You've despised me for so long."

"I didn't despise you. You were just…irritating."

"Looks like I did a good job irritating you into my arms." He wiggles his brows.

"Or you did a good job showing me who you really are, and I couldn't resist that."

"You like the real me?"

I nod. "I really do." I give him one more kiss before pulling away and taking his coffee with me. I lean against the counter opposite him and sip from his mug. "I'm sad this is our last day here, that we leave today."

He saunters over to me and presses me against the counter, placing both of his hands on my hips. "You fail to realize that I'm a billionaire and if we want to come up here every weekend, we can."

I play with the buttons on his shirt. "It won't be the same. We were in a bubble here. I mean, when we go back to LA, are you really going to come to my studio apartment and hang out?"

"If you want me to, I will. Hell, we can spend every night there, if you want."

"Do you think you'll be spending every night with me?"

His hands grip me tighter, then he lifts me up onto the counter. He settles between my legs and says, "I expect nothing from you. I'm just telling you where I'm at. If you want to spend the night with me, that's your choice. If I had it my way, you'd be coming home with me tonight."

"Aren't you nervous?" I ask.

"Nervous about what?"

"I don't know… All of this."

His thumbs rub against my hips as he calmly asks, "Are you having regrets?"

"No," I say quickly before setting down the mug and placing my hands on his shoulders. "Not at all. I don't want you to think that. We just jumped into it quickly and, yes, last night was the best night of my life. I just don't want to get lost in the physical, you know?"

The slowest smile falls over his lips as he leans in close and presses a kiss to my cheek. "I get it, babe. You want to date, yeah?"

When he pulls away, I slowly nod. "I mean, will we still go on dates?"

He chuckles. "How about this? Tomorrow night, I'll pick you up at your place and we'll go on a date? Does that work? Our first official date."

"Technically, our first one was at the blind date restaurant."

"Yes, but we both consent to go on this one."

"Very true." I move my hands to the nape of his neck. "You don't mind taking me on a date? You know, slowing down from last night?"

"Kelsey." He looks me in the eyes. "Ever since the moment you walked off the elevator at Cane Enterprises, I've been waiting for the moment to call you my girl. Slowing down won't kill me, it'll just make it better."

How on earth did I not know this man was so sweet? That he's not only understanding and kindhearted but is also swoon-worthy?

"Thank you."

"Do you feel better?"

My fingers toy with the short strands of his hair. "Much better." I lean in and give him a whisper of a kiss before asking, "You have a meeting with the mayor this morning?"

"Yeah, then I have to run across town to meet up with Edison about another building we're interested in. Unfortunately, I won't see you until the airplane."

"That's okay. Are you all packed?"

"Yup, packed this morning."

"How? I feel half-awake."

He smirks. "Babe, plugging into you last night gave me all the energy."

"Eww." I swat at his chest. "Don't say you plugged into me."

He laughs out loud and moves his arms around me, pulling me into a hug. "Nah, babe, I'm just high on excitement right now." He kisses the side of my head. "It meant more to me than you will ever know, when you came back last night, when you chose me."

"It was an easy choice," I admit, causing him to sigh into my hold.

"Fuck, I wish I didn't have two meetings today." He brings my hand up to his lips and kisses my knuckles. "I'll see you on the plane?"

"Yes," I answer. He pulls away, and as he heads toward the door, I call out, "Hey, JP?"

"Yeah?" He looks over his shoulder.

"I'm really glad you came to San Francisco. I know you really didn't want to."

"Only because I was fucking infatuated with you." He winks. "See you at the airport."

When he leaves, I practically melt on the countertop as everything he's ever said to me comes to the forefront of my mind. The glances, the light touches, the teasing, the sweet gestures—it was all there. It always has been, from when I first met him and I was so disappointed because Lottie had ruined our pitch to Cane Enterprises, to the way he showed me around the office when we were finally hired, offering me help when I needed it. The night of the gala, when he saw how upset I was, and instead of taking off, tried to make my night better. The dinners we've shared and the time we've spent together in San Francisco. His genuine care has been there, I've just been too worried to actually see it.

Worried because of his reputation.

Worried to fall for someone like him.

Worried to open my eyes and see *every* facet of JP.

But I see him now.

I hop off the counter and retrieve my phone from the dining room table. I pull up my text thread with Lottie and shoot her a text.

Kelsey: Boy, do I need to talk to you.

I walk back to my room and start packing again, and I'm almost done when Lottie texts me back.

Lottie: That text seems juicy. Tell me everything.

Kelsey: I was supposed to go out with Derek last night.

Lottie: Did he not show up?

Kelsey: No, he did. JP just intervened, told me he has been pining for me forever, wants to be with me and…well, I said a quick goodbye to Derek and wound up having sex with JP…six times.

Lottie: OH. MY. GOD! Only took you long enough! Also, six times…welcome to sex with a Cane brother. How do you feel?

Kelsey: Excited. Giddy. Slightly nervous. But mostly…I just can't wait to see him again. Is this crazy? I mean, just a few days ago, we were at each other's throats. And now he's, well, he's kind of everything I'd want in a man. And this is JP! I never thought I'd say that.

Lottie: I saw it all along. I was just waiting for it to happen. It's not crazy. I think the great thing about you two is that you're such opposites. That's why Huxley and I work so well together. We challenge each other, but we also soothe the parts of each other that need extra care. I can see the same for you and JP.

Kelsey: Yeah, I think that's pretty accurate. I don't know. I like him, I really do. I've realized that more and more over the last few days. I'm just nervous.

Lottie: About what?

Kelsey: That I won't be enough. That he'll get tired of me. That he thinks he's ready for a relationship, but he's really not, and I'll end up getting hurt.

Lottie: All valid concerns, but you won't know the answers unless you try, unless you let him try.

Kelsey: And if he hurts me?

Lottie: Then he'll not only have to answer to Huxley, but he'll have to face me, as well, and as you know, I don't let anyone hurt my sister.

Kelsey: Edwin hurt me.

Lottie: And guess who got a glitter bomb delivered to his house with a note that said to open it in front of his computer? He's probably still plucking glitter from his keyboard.

Kelsey: You didn't...

Lottie: No one fucks with you and gets away with it. And if JP hurts you, well, just imagine the damage I can do.

Kelsey: I might be a little scared.

Lottie: Good, I always want everyone to think I'm slightly unhinged. Keeps them on their toes.

Kelsey: I somehow feel bad for Huxley.

Lottie: Don't, he loves it. And, also...don't be worrying about what could go wrong with JP. Focus on what can go right. He likes you. You like him. Start there.

Kelsey: You're right. Thank you, sis.

Lottie: Now, tell me more about this night of sex. Six times!

"You didn't have to help me up to my apartment," I say as I reach my front door.

JP gives me a pointed look. "Do you really think I was going to let you carry your luggage up here alone?"

"I guess not." I unlock my door, push it open, and then scoot one of my bags in as JP follows me, dragging my larger bag behind him. "You can just set it over here."

"This is your place?" JP asks, taking in my six-hundred-square-foot apartment.

"Yeah. It's small, I know, but it does the job. I hope to get a bigger place at some point, but it's hard to find an apartment that's in a good area and doesn't cost me my whole paycheck."

Not saying anything, JP walks around the small place, running his fingers over the bistro set I call a dining table, peeking his head into my kitchen, and even opening the door to my closet and bathroom. When he turns toward me, he sticks his hands in his pockets and says, "I like it, babe. It's very you."

"It's small, nothing compared to your house."

"Why do you have to do that?" he asks. "Put down your place? It's not a competition. This is where you live; be proud of it."

That warms my heart.

"You're right. I do like my place. It's served me well. But I do hope to have a place bigger than this someday."

He walks up to me, tugs on my hand, and pulls me against his chest. "Until then, maybe we can make some memories here."

"What kind of memories are you suggesting?"

"Well, I was thinking we can cuddle on your bed, share some ice cream, and talk?"

"Jonah Peter Cane, the man who has sex on the brain twenty-four hours a day, just wants to talk?" I give him a pointed look.

"What did I tell you? You said you want to take this slow, so that's what we'll do. I want to spend some more time with you before I have to kiss you good night and leave."

I play with the hem of his shirt. "Being the romantic girl that I am, I've always dreamed of someone saying they want to spend more time with me, but I've never heard it."

"Because you weren't with the right guy. No need to look anymore. I'm right here," he says, placing a soft kiss on my lips. "And, thankfully, ice cream will be here shortly. I asked our driver, Ramon, to stop by the corner store to grab us some, banking on you saying yes."

"And what if I said no?"

"Then I would've gone home and eaten my feelings."

I chuckle and kiss his jaw. "How about this—we eat ice cream and I unpack while we talk, because I can't possibly be in my apartment with two untouched travel bags."

"I can help. I can sort your lingerie, if you want."

I roll my eyes and push him toward my bed. "You just hang out there and talk to me while I unpack. I don't need you messing with my system."

"Okay, Monica Geller," he says, flopping on my bed.

I point at his feet and say, "Uh, shoes, mister. Those need to be taken off."

He glances down at his feet and then back up at me. "Oh, this is going to be fun driving you nuts."

"Try me. I'm pretty sure I know who'll win."

"Do you do this every time you come home from a trip?" JP asks around his mouthful of chocolate chip cookie dough ice cream.

"Yes."

"What happens when you arrive home late?"

"Then I go to bed late."

"So, you're telling me, you need to steam and disinfect all of your shoes before you go to bed?"

I set down my steamer, pick up my bowl of ice cream, and take my last mouthful before setting it back down. "Yes. If I don't, I won't get any sleep. I told you, I have a system, and that system must be followed before I can tuck myself into bed."

"I see… Why do I find it strangely sexy?"

"Because you're deranged," I answer while finishing up with my last shoe. I put away my steamer and disinfectant and then zip up my suitcases—the smaller one in the bigger one—and set them by my door.

"Where do those go?"

"In storage. There's a unit in the basement of the apartment building.

It's where I keep my holiday décor as well as any extra supplies like toilet paper, paper towels, and anything I might have purchased a surplus of because of a great coupon."

"You're so fucking efficient, it makes me want to bury my head between your breasts."

I chuckle. "Are you saying you don't have a surplus room?"

"Uh, I think mine is called a pantry."

"Ah, true. Is it organized?"

He winces. "I think your nipples would curdle if you saw my pantry."

"What about your bathroom? Is that organized?"

"My toothpaste has a specific spot on my counter, if that's what you mean."

"Your fridge, is it color coordinated?"

He scratches the side of his jaw. "I don't even think there's food in there."

"Under your sink, are there drawers to hold your dishwasher pods?"

"I don't do dishes."

My eyes narrow. "Laundry?"

"I pay someone to clean my clothes."

"Your closet, are your suits organized by color and texture?"

"Babe, I'm going to settle that craziness in your voice right now and tell you there's no way in hell you will walk into my house and feel comfortable. It is unorganized." He lies back on my bed and puts his hands behind his head. "That's why I think it's great that we spend a lot of time here."

"Oh, no way. Uh-uh, not happening." I shake my head. "Tomorrow, we shall spend our date organizing your house."

He sits up on his elbows. "That's not a date."

"It is to me. I don't think anything would make me happier than seeing you organize your shoes. Ooo, and we can go to the Container Store together, grab some food to go, and then just have a frenzy."

"That doesn't sound appealing."

I walk over to him, straddle his lap, and place my hands on his chest. "I'll wear a crop top, something where you can slip your hands around my bare skin whenever you get frustrated."

His hands fall to my thighs. "I'm listening."

"And you'll be granted one solid make-out session, because frankly, I know I'll be excited from all the organizing, and I'll want some one-on-one lip time with you."

He laughs. "Are you going to be mean about it? Or will you be gentle with my disorganized soul?"

I lean down so my mouth is inches from his. "Gentle. Always gentle."

His hands smooth up my back, and then, in the blink of an eye, he flips me to my back and covers me with his strong, warm body. "You know I want to make you happy, but do you really want to spend our first date at my place organizing?"

"I do."

He sighs heavily and then says, "Fine, but our next date is my idea. Got it?"

"I think that's fair." I grab him by the collar and pull him in close. He gently pushes my hair behind my ear, then cups my cheek before kissing me.

We spend the next half hour making out, and it's everything I could ask for.

"Kelsey."

"What?" I ask, spinning around, holding two bamboo containers that I plan on using for the protein bars in his pantry.

"What the hell are you wearing?"

I glance down at my joggers and black crop top shirt. "Clothes. I told you I'd wear a crop top for you." I came to his place with a sweatshirt on, but all the organizing has made me hot, so I ditched the sweatshirt.

"Yes, but you're not wearing a bra."

Oh…yes, that's correct.

I smile and say, "Oh, huh, must have forgotten it."

His eyes narrow, and it's quite comical.

"That's not what we agreed upon."

"Are you complaining about me not wearing a bra? Really?"

"Yes…you're making me hard."

"Control yourself. We have more organizing to do."

"It's been two hours. Can't we take a break?"

"And where do you suppose we take a break?"

"Outside. You haven't even seen my pool or backyard. We can stare at the stars, take a breath for a second."

I glance back at the pantry. "Well, I guess we could take a break. We've really accomplished a lot. Maybe a break is in order."

The relief on his face is cute. He guides me past the storage bins I purchased for the pantry, and leads me through the living room to the large sliding glass doors. After a slight pause, he pushes past the curtains to a panel on the wall, enters a code, and then presses a few buttons. Like magic, the pool lights up in a deep blue color, bulb string lights dance above us, and the larger-than-life palm trees, which line the perimeter of his backyard, glow with soft uplighting.

"Wow," I say. "This is…this is dreamy."

"I thought you'd like it." He leads me to a large white lounger in front of the pool, perfectly placed under the crisscrossing bulb lights. "Will you sit with me?"

"Of course," I answer.

He takes a seat first and then guides me down between his legs, my back to his chest. I lean against his body and use him for support. He wraps his arms around my exposed stomach.

"This okay?" he asks quietly, which surprises me, because he's always been a man who takes what he wants, so the fact that he's checking in just makes me respect him that much more.

"It's perfect, JP." And then, in the distance, very unexpectedly, I hear the telltale sounds of instrumental music. But not just any instrumental music. "Why do I know this song?" I ask him.

His voice is low, like a whisper of a rumble. "It was the first song we danced to at the gala. An instrumental version of 'Wildest Dreams.'"

"You remembered that?"

"Kelsey," he says softly, "I remember everything that involves you. Everything. From what you wore the very first day I met you—a blue turtleneck dress—to the way you smelled when we shared an elevator for the first time—like vanilla and brown sugar—to the way you tasted the first time I had a chance to be intimate with you—like a fucking sunset on a rainy day. This song...it was engrained in my brain, and I just hoped that I'd get a chance to play it for you again one day."

I almost can't hear him from the pounding of my own heart. "I had...I had no idea."

"I know you didn't. And that's okay. I soaked you up from a distance and waited until you could see me as the man I really am."

"Why didn't you say anything?"

"I tried, but also, fear got in the way. Pride took over a lot of times. You're not an easy shell to crack. You were very professional when we first met, so breaking through that wall was hard."

"Because of Lottie," I say. "Because of what she was doing with Huxley. I know she had to do what she did, both of them did. Slightly unorthodox, but not only did I understand, I approved. But that meant I had to show you guys that we weren't sisters looking for handouts, you know? I wanted to keep things as professional as possible. I wanted to show you we were legit businesswomen."

"There was no doubt that you were, but I understand what you're saying."

"And frankly, when I first saw you, I knew you were trouble. I thought...*God, he's so handsome.*"

"Did you?" he asks, shock in his voice.

I nod against his chest. "I did. I really thought you were almost too handsome to look at. My romantic mind was reeling with possibilities, but I put that to bed really quickly because I'd worked so hard to establish my business, and working with Cane Enterprises was a huge deal. I didn't want to mess that up with a crush."

"A crush, no fucking way. I don't believe that."

"I did." I lean back and tilt my head so I can look up at him. "At first, it was a crush, but I worked hard to interpret everything you said or did as annoying. That annoyance grew and I was able to block out those original feelings and focus on the business. But with every kind thing you did, I could feel my original assessment of you becoming more prominent."

"And what about Derek?"

"What about him?"

"Why did you go out with him?"

"Because I was truly looking for my soulmate."

"Never thought I'd be that person?"

"Never thought it was an option," I answer honestly. "Not just because of business, but because I know we're different in so many ways. You're more experienced, you're more outgoing, you're more... I felt you were out of my league."

"That's bullshit," he says, his voice not angry, more disbelieving. His hand slides over my stomach and his thumb casually rubs against my heated skin. "Kelsey, I'm nowhere near *your* stratosphere. Hell, I'm lucky you even looked my way."

"Stop, you know that's not the truth."

He tilts my head back and lifts my chin so my lips are at his disposal. "Babe, it's the truth." He leans down and presses a sweet kiss to my lips. It's not long, but it's delicious and causes me to groan as he leans away. "Fuck, when you make that sound..." His hand slides across my stomach again, and this time, his thumb caresses the underside of my breast briefly. "Ask me something so I don't strip you down and pull you into the pool with me."

The thought of *that* is incredibly appealing. Very appealing. So appealing that I squirm under his touch, wanting him to "accidentally" touch my breast again.

But we're taking it slow.

We're trying to not be all about lust.

So, I close my eyes and block out the desire I have for this man while attempting to think of a question.

"Umm...what, uh...what's your favorite...um..."

Position?

Way to be sucked off?

Sex toy?

God, what's wrong with me?

"What's my favorite *what*?" he asks, his hand once again smoothing over my stomach, his thumb dragging so close to my breast, my bare breast—thank you, crop top—that a low throb starts pulsing between my legs.

Body part?

Piece of lingerie?

Way to make me come...?

"God, I don't know what I was going to ask," I say breathlessly.

"Hmm, maybe I can ask you something?"

"It's going to be naughty, isn't it?"

He chuckles. "Why would you assume that?" Goose bumps erupt as his fingers dance across my stomach again. I gasp when his thumb connects with my breast.

I press back against his chest. "Because you're attempting to turn me on, and it's working."

"Babe, I'm not attempting to do anything." His thumb skims just below my nipple.

"Jonah," I whisper. The spot between my thighs is now aching.

"Yes, baby?" he asks, pressing a kiss on my neck.

"You know exactly what you're doing."

"I don't." He swipes his thumb over my nipple again, and because there's fabric between his thumb and my breast, I don't get the intense sensation that I want from his touch. "I just want to make you comfortable. Are you comfortable?"

"Not anymore." I wiggle against him and rest my head to the side, exposing more of my neck.

"Shame. How can I make you more comfortable?" His lips kiss up the column of my neck, gentle, light pecks, leaving a trail of chills along my arms.

"You know what you can do."

"Unfortunately, I'm at a loss." His lips ride close to my ear as he seductively says, "You're going to have to tell me…or show me."

God, he's tempting me. He's giving me the option to explore.

And I desperately want to explore.

Just a little teasing.

Just a little relief.

I move my hand to the nape of his neck and anchor myself to him as my other hand grips the one that's resting on my exposed stomach. On a deep breath, I bring it under my shirt and rest it just below my breast.

I feel him harden against my back and that's more of a turn-on than where his actual hand is. Knowing I can do that to him, that I can turn him on as much as he does me. This man who's unruly, who's sexy, who's someone I never thought would look my way…I can make him lose control. It makes me not only feel powerful, but also incredibly desirable, and I can't recall the last time I actually felt that, if ever.

"Tell me what you want," he whispers.

"I want to know what you'd do to me if I were naked, in your pool."

He groans into my ear, and his erection becomes even more prominent against my backside. I encourage his thumb to drag over my bare nipple, and he does just that, causing me to clench my teeth. That feels...so good.

The pulsing between my legs becomes heavy, needy, and my legs widen, even though he's nowhere near them.

"If you were naked in my pool, first, I'd make you dunk yourself completely so I could watch the water droplets roll off your amazing tits." He squeezes my breast and I moan against his hold. "The fucking sexiest tits I've ever seen. And I fucking mean that. Just big enough for my hands, perky, with these hard nipples that drive me nuts. And you're so responsive when I touch them." He rolls my nipple between his fingers and I groan before lifting my shirt completely, exposing both breasts for him. "Fuck, baby. You make me so goddamn hard. Do you feel that?"

"I do," I answer. "I love that you get hard just touching me."

"You have no fucking clue." While one of his hands plays with my nipple, the other drags over my stomach again, to where the waistband of my pants meets my skin. "But if you were naked, in the pool, I wouldn't just be touching you like this. I'd be exploring your slick, wet skin. I'd lay you across the edge of the endless pool, where the water falls over."

His fingers stroke the elastic of my sweatpants.

His other hand moves from one breast to the other, and he casually caresses my skin.

Featherlike touches that drive me crazy, but don't quite push me over the edge.

"I'd start at your tits. I'd suck on your nipples, envisioning what it would be like to slip my dick between your breasts and fuck them."

I want him to do that. The thought of it makes me even hotter. So hot that these sweatpants feel stifling now.

"And then I'd move to your stomach, to just above your pussy." He presses his fingers against the spot he's talking about, above the fabric of my pants. "And I'd tease you, over and over again with my tongue until you tug on my hair so hard that it's painful."

My fingers inch toward his hair as he releases my breast and moves his hand to my hip, where he slips his fingers under the elastic of my pants.

"You're not wearing underwear?" he asks me.

I shake my head. "Didn't think I needed to."

"You fucking tease," he whispers, spreading his hands wide so his thumbs rest just above my pubic bone.

Fuck.

Me.

I squirm against his touch, but he stills me as he says, "When I knew you couldn't take it anymore, I'd part you with two fingers and eat your pussy. Fuck, I can taste it right now, sweet and salty, fucking delicious on my tongue." His thumbs drag inward and then pull back as my pelvis rises. I grip his neck tighter.

"You're making me so wet."

"Good," he says, pushing my pants down until they just barely cover me.

Needing more contact, I lift the hem of my shirt up and over my head, leaving me topless and resting on his chest.

"You want so much more, don't you, baby?"

"Yes," I whisper, bringing one of my hands to my breasts. My touch is nowhere near like his, and all it does is frustrate me. "Please, do something."

"But I'm not done telling my story," he says before dragging his tongue over my neck. Unsure of what to do with my hands, I reach behind me and hold on to him one more time, wishing I could stroke his stiff cock pressed against me, and then listen to him moan while I pleasure him. "I'd fuck you with my tongue, over and over again until you're begging me to stop, and then, and only then, would I lower you against the edge, prop your ass up, and eat you out all over again. I'd claim your cunt, make sure you never forget who makes you come the way I do."

My legs shiver.

My body shakes.

And I shift, causing my pants to fall off the curve of my ass and past my pussy, exposing me. I spread my legs and wiggle the pants down until they're at my knees. Then I shimmy out of them and leave myself completely naked on the lounger with him.

"Here I thought we were taking things slow," he says as he drags the backs of his fingers up my stomach—*not* the direction I want him to go.

"You can't turn me on like this and expect me to just sit here, unfazed."

"I didn't. I was hoping this is where it would end up, with you writhing for more. Now, the question is, will I let you come?"

I pause and turn so I can look at him. "Don't you dare."

He just smiles.

"You realize I can make myself come, right?"

I go to reach between my legs, but he takes my arms, shifts them behind my back, and then locks me against his chest so quickly that I don't have a moment to breathe. I try to close my legs, but he loops his ankles over and under mine, spreading me even wider.

I'm trapped.

Pinned down.

And I've never been more aroused in my life.

I know if I told him to stop, he would.

I know if I told him I didn't want this, he'd put my clothes back on me and return to our conversation.

But I don't want that.

I want this.

I want him owning me.

Controlling me.

Teasing me.

"Now what are you going to do?" he asks.

I let out a deep sigh as I lean into his hold, not fighting him. "I guess listen to you."

"Good girl," he whispers and then he draws lazy circles on my inner thigh. "Now, as I was saying, once I fucked you with my tongue again, I'd let you catch your breath before I brought you over to the steps. Then I'd sit down on the top step so my cock that's begging for you is above water."

I wet my lips.

"And I'd demand that you return the favor." His lips dance over my cheek. "Would you?"

"No question, I would. I want my mouth on your cock now."

He groans and drags his fingers over the spot just above where I want him. He toys with me there, dipping lower and lower until he's playing with my slit. I try to move, try to get him where I want him, but he holds me still, his strong body taking control.

"Tell me how you'd suck me in the pool."

My lungs feel heavy as they work harder for air. "I would… I'd have you hold my hair. I'd expect you to grip it hard, guiding me as I lower my mouth to the tip. I'd swirl my tongue, around and around." His pelvis moves against my back, the movement so small that it can't possibly do more than drive him nuts. "And then I'd ask you to spread your legs so I could play with your balls while I take your length all the way to the back of my throat."

"Baby…" he whispers. "Would you gag?"

"I would. But I'd do it all over again."

"Fuck," he breathes as his fingers slide over one side of my pussy, but never dip inside.

"I'd play with your taint. I'd drag my fingers over the seam of your scrotum. I'd lick the length of your cock, and then repeat that until you tug on my hair, showing me you can't take it anymore."

"Your devil tongue would make me want to come sooner than I prefer." He dips his finger to my arousal, barely touches my clit, and then removes his hand completely, bringing it back to my stomach.

"Nooo," I groan. "JP, don't move your hand."

"Are you trying to tell me what to do?" he asks as he lightly moves his fingers over my breasts, circling my areolas, but never giving me what I want.

"Yes, you're making me so hot, so wet."

"Good." His hand moves back between my legs and rests there, his palm cupping me, his fingers present, but not doing anything. "Would you let me come in your mouth?"

"Yes."

He presses down on one finger, then the other, switching between the two and driving me so fucking crazy that I feel sweat drip down my back.

"Would you swallow?"

"Yes," I answer, my voice pleading in desperation.

"Good girl," he says, then he spreads me and presses two fingers to my clit.

"Yes," I cry out, my chest arching as I'm granted some relief. He moves his fingers, up and down, up and down, the motion so full of what I need to relieve this growing, gnawing pressure between my legs that I relax against his chest, against his pressing erection, and just let him take over. "Right there," I pant. "Please don't stop."

"I wouldn't come in your mouth," he says, bringing me back to the fantasy. "I wouldn't want to. I'd bring myself right to the edge until I pulled on your hair, tugging you off my cock."

He rubs faster, and everything around me fades to black as I feel my body climb closer and closer. This unbridled pulse throbs up my legs, down my arms, and collects between my legs. It's there. I'm right there.

"Yes. Oh God, I'm going to—"

He removes his hand and rests it on my stomach, unmoving.

"What are you doing?" I cry out in absolute shock and pain.

"Listen closely, baby…are you listening?"

Barely. My body is internally roaring so loudly that I can barely hear the light whip of wind rustling through the palm leaves above us.

"Y-yes," I stammer out.

"Good. This is where the fun begins."

"What fun?" I ask, my orgasm starting to fade away, leaving me with this hollow feeling in the pit of my stomach…something more maddening than anything I've ever experienced.

"This is where I teach you about listening to me."

"Listening to what?"

He drags his finger over my body again, up to my breasts, where he draws tight circles, and then back to my stomach. "This body, when it's naked, belongs to me. Do you agree?"

I bite my lower lip and nod. He owns me. That's undeniable, especially in this moment.

"And when you're naked, not only do I own your body, but I tell it when it can come, and you're not allowed to come yet."

"Why not?"

He rolls my nipple between his fingers. "I suggest you don't question me, unless you want to lie here all night, being teased with no relief."

My lips seal shut because I believe he would do that.

I believe he would let the only pleasure I receive be from the wind gently lapping against my arousal.

"Sorry," I say.

His lips land on my cheek, just in front of my ear. "It's okay, baby. You're learning. Tell me, how are you feeling?"

"Frustrated."

"Perfect." He drags his hand back down my stomach and once again slips two fingers against my clit. I sigh into his touch and relax against his chest as he holds me in place. "Now, back to the pool. I tug you off my cock, because I'm not ready to come, not until I own your pussy. How would you want me to take you?"

His fingers cause me to climb again, and it happens faster than before. My mind is fixated on what he's doing with his fingers as his other hand moves up to my breasts. He circles my nipples, teasing me, taunting me, driving my desire for him higher and higher.

"Yes," I moan. "Right there."

He snaps his hand away and grips my chin, forcing me to look at him as he leans over my shoulder. "I asked you a question, Kelsey."

My mind reels.

My heart hammers.

My legs go completely numb.

"I'm…I'm sorry. I wasn't listening."

He smirks and rests a gentle kiss on my lips. "At least you're honest." And then he slips his fingers into my mouth. I taste myself, and I have no idea what comes over me, but I suck on his index finger, and the most satisfied look crosses his face.

"Fuck, baby." He starts fingering me again, and this time, his pace is faster. "Now, answer me, how would you want me to fuck you in the pool?"

His fingers fly over my clit, massaging, applying the perfect pressure, driving me wild with need. Breathlessly, I answer, "From behind."

"Behind?" He removes his hand, and I squeeze my eyes shut so tightly that I almost feel tears spring forth. "You like it from behind?" I nod. He tweaks my nipple and my chest flies against his hand as my head whips to the side on a groan.

"I do," I answer. "I love it from behind."

"What else do you like? Do you like how I'm edging you? Bringing you so close to your orgasm and then taking it away?"

I shake my head. "No. I want relief."

"But, baby, we're taking it slow. This is slow."

"This is blissful torture."

He rolls my nipple a few more times before releasing my breast. Once again, he removes his touch and lets me lie there, trapped in his embrace. Like a feather, he slowly and lightly runs his coarse beard over my neck, across my cheek, and back down again, his breath tickling me right before he presses the faintest of kisses to my shoulder.

"How do you want to come?"

"I don't care," I say. "Just let me."

Fingers stroke down my inner thigh and then up to my entrance. I tilt my pelvis up as best as I can, and he slips two fingers inside of me.

"I wish that was your cock," I say.

"Me too, but I'm honoring what you want. I'm just having fun touching you." He moves his fingers in and out, but it isn't enough, it's not even close to enough, and he knows it as I writhe under his touch.

"Please tell me you'll let me come. Please, JP."

"One thing you need to know, Kelsey"—he kisses my cheek—"is that I'll always let you come. If you trust me with your body, you'll always come." Then he presses his thumb to my clit.

"Yes," I cry out. "Please, please don't pull away."

The buildup.

The pressure.

The numbness in my body since he started this is fluctuating in waves. Consuming me, then fading, consuming me more, then fading less, and now consuming me so much that I'm so close, so freaking close…

"I'm…I'm going…"

"Not yet." He moves his hand and I cry out in frustration.

"Jonah…please." Tears spring to my eyes and he twists my chin to find my lips. He parts them and open-mouth kisses me as he once again presses two fingers to my clit and rubs it over and over again. I'm so high on the feeling of him, so over-the-top turned on that I feel my body float into a euphoric state.

"I fucking love it when you say my name," he murmurs against my lips. Removing his mouth, he grips my jaw and whispers into my ear, "You may come."

His fingers fly over my clit, his permission feeling like a wall has been broken. I relax into his touch, into the overwhelming rapture that's throbbing through my veins.

Pulse after pulse, I'm driven higher and higher until I feel my orgasm crest. Just a few more strokes.

"Please don't pull away. I'm…oh God, I'm so close."

"I won't." He kisses my neck. "Come, baby."

His fingers move wildly over my clit, my stomach bottoms out, my legs feel like they're floating, and with one last pass of his fingers, I'm coming, crying out his name over and over again as wave after wave of pleasure rips through me.

"Fuck…yes, Jonah. Oh my God. Oh fuck…oh fuck." My pelvis flies up, and when I think my orgasm is going to fade, it doesn't. It keeps pulling me in, drawing me into a ball of nothing until tears fall down my cheeks and I fall into a lifeless version of myself, completely and utterly sated.

On a deep breath, he removes his hand, arms, and legs, and then lifts me into a cradled position, holding me close as I rest my face on his chest.

Lovingly, he strokes my hair, pressing gentle kisses to my forehead. Out of nowhere, he pulls a blanket over the two of us and holds me tight.

"Are you okay?" he asks in a soft voice, the demanding, controlling man nowhere to be seen.

"I'm…perfect," I answer.

I'm aware that I'm naked, in his arms.

I'm also aware that his cock is rigid beneath me.

But when I try to move out of his arms, he doesn't let me, so instead, I let him cradle me.

"You're easily the sexiest, most outstandingly gorgeous woman I've ever fucking held in my arms. And I'm still in awe you chose me."

I want to ask how he could be so blind. I want to tell him it was him all along, but I can't, because I know it took me a second to realize how I feel about him. But now that I know, I can't possibly ever see myself with anyone else.

"I'm so connected to you, JP. And I don't want to scare you, but…I really like you, and I know deep down to my very core, that you have the potential to absolutely destroy me. There would be no recovering."

"I'll never hurt you." He kisses my head. "Never, baby."

———————

The sliding glass door shuts and Lottie spins to me. With desperate eyes, she whispers, "Tell me everything."

Last night, after JP finally let me come, we spent the rest of the evening holding hands, talking, and casually organizing his kitchen. He kissed me every chance he got, and I swooned with every glance, every whispered word he said to me.

I left his place feeling one hundred percent smitten.

When I woke up this morning, he was at my door with coffee. He made me come before taking a shower, and then when I tried to make him come, he wouldn't let me and reminded me he's taking things slow. Which I think means he's showing me this isn't about his lustful needs. He wants my heart, my mind. The rest will come later.

And when we were in the office, going over the solar power plans for the Angelica, he'd smooth his hand over my thigh, steal glances, and occasionally link our fingers together. He's attentive, loving, caring, and demanding. Everything I've ever wanted, and it still feels too good to be true. We were in the middle of talking about solar panel placement when Huxley came in and asked us to dinner at his house. I wasn't sure if JP had told his brothers or not, but it seemed like Huxley was very much in the know, and it didn't seem like he minded.

Now that I'm here, at their place, I know for a fact he doesn't care. He still wears a calculating gaze, but it's directed at JP, not me.

Leaning in close to my sister, I say, "Lottie, I'm so infatuated with the man."

"Oh my God, I can tell. I don't think I've ever seen you this happy. The smile on your face, oh my God, Kelsey...it makes me so freaking full of joy."

"He makes me happy. He's so... God, I don't know how to say it. There used to be such constant bickering and irritation, but the moment the dam broke, he became this overprotective alpha that won't let anything hurt me. He possesses me in all the right ways, but he's also all about me being independent and building my business."

Lottie nods. "It's the Cane way. Don't you remember how Huxley and I were at each other's throats? And then, we just...slipped into each other and it's been hard to breathe without him since."

"Yes." I glance toward the house, where the boys are putting together dinner, most likely talking about us. "It's been a few days, and I can feel myself...God, I can feel myself falling for him, hard."

Lottie quietly claps the tips of her fingers. "Ohhhh, this makes me so happy. I just knew it. I knew you two would be perfect for each other."

"I'm just terrified that something is going to go wrong. Someway, somehow, this is all too good to be true."

"It's not. Don't think that way. He really likes you. I can tell from the way he looks at you, the way he sits near you, and how he rests his hand on your thigh. He's infatuated; he has been for a while. This is it, Kelse, this is what you've been waiting for."

I roll my teeth over my bottom lip and say, "I think it is, too. Even before we got together, when we were just hanging out as what I thought was friends, he understood me. He supported me. He knew what I needed. I'm just..." I press my hands to my cheeks. "I like him so much."

The sliding glass door opens and the boys walk out holding large wooden charcuterie boards stacked full of crackers, cheeses, meats, jams, spreads, and fruit. They set the trays down on the coffee table in front of us, and then JP takes a seat next to me, slipping his arm behind me before leaning in and tilting my face toward him to place a gentle kiss on my lips.

When he pulls away, he whispers, "Talk about me?"

I can't hide my smile. "Yes."

"Good things?"

"Great things."

"Huxley, look at them," Lottie coos. "God, I'm so happy right now."

I catch Huxley's glare toward JP as he says, "I'm happy, too."

But he doesn't look happy. Not even a little.

Later that night, when JP is walking me to my apartment door, I ask him, "Is everything okay with Huxley?"

"What do you mean?" JP asks. When we reach my door, he takes my keys from me and unlocks it for me. He holds the door open and I walk in, with him following closely behind.

"He didn't look happy. I know he said he was happy for us, but I can't help but think he might be upset. Is he mad at me?"

JP shuts the door, then leans against it. He pulls me in close. Holding my hands, he says, "He's happy for us, but he's basically shooting off warning signs to me. He doesn't want me to hurt you. I assured him that wasn't going to happen, but he's more protective of you than me."

"Oh. So, he's not mad at me?"

"Not even a little. I'm sure if you ask Lottie tomorrow, she'll confirm that. As he explained to me in the kitchen, Lottie is his everything, and what's important to her is important to him. Apparently, you trump me now, and honestly"—he rubs the side of his jaw—"I'm okay with that. He gave me the speech not to hurt you or he'll hurt me."

I smile at that. "Well, look at me having a big brother."

"That's exactly what he is, and I hate to admit it, but I might love him even more for looking out for you."

"So, does he approve?"

JP nods. "With caution. He likes the idea of us, but he wants to make sure I'm in this. I told him I was, that I was one hundred percent invested in making you happy, and that wasn't ever going to change."

My heart flutters and I close the minimal space between us. I run my hands up his chest, to his jaw, then pull him closer to my mouth. "You make me happy—you know that?"

"Same, babe." He wraps his hand around the back of my head and very slowly kisses me, the delicious feeling of his lips spreading through my veins, all the way to the tips of my toes.

Yup, I'm falling so hard for this man. Harder than I've ever fallen before.

CHAPTER 20
JP

"THIS IS ABSOLUTELY BREATHTAKING," KELSEY says as she takes in the 360-degree view of the San Francisco skyline. "I can't believe you flew us back up here for a date."

"Felt only fitting."

With the meetings piling up on my calendar, I knew waiting until the weekend would be best, and I knew I wanted it here. I wanted to spoil her. I sent her a green off-the-shoulder dress that I personally picked out because I knew it would accentuate everything I like about her—her curves, the color of her eyes, and her slender shoulders. I had someone do her hair and makeup at her apartment. When I picked her up, I blindfolded her and brought her to the airport, slipping off her blindfold as we boarded the plane. I kept my eyes on her the entirety of the short flight up, happy to see her beaming with excitement. I didn't tell her a thing until the driver pulled up to Parkside and opened the door for her.

Nothing feels more fitting than being at Parkside with her when I can finally call her mine.

"I've had the chef create a special menu for us. I hope that's okay."

She smiles—fuck, I love that smile so much. "That sounds amazing." Then she leans in and says, "Not to put too much pressure on you, but any chance we can get some honey cake before we leave San Francisco?"

"One step ahead of you, babe."

She tilts her head, such joy in her eyes. "You really do know how to woo a girl, don't you?"

"Only you," I answer just as our first course comes out.

A bowl is placed in front of each of us as well as a traditional melamine Asian soupspoon. Then, with a cloth draped over his arm, our waiter says, "Mr. Cane, Miss Gardner, I'd like to present your first course. An Asian curried soup with sweet potatoes, chickpeas, and coconut milk, artfully seasoned with Malaysian flavors. Enjoy."

He leaves us in the private room reserved for me and my brothers.

Whispering, Kelsey says, "I think this is the fanciest restaurant experience of my life."

"It's not too much, is it? Because we can go somewhere else."

"No, not at all. I mean, I like the laid-back experience, but I also love this. I'm such a sucker for a romantic evening and this, JP, it's...it's really just beautiful."

"You're worth it," I say before picking up my spoon and dipping it into my soup.

"You spoil me."

"As you should be."

She smirks and dips her spoon into her soup, as well. Her eyes widen and they meet mine. "Oh my God, this is amazing."

"This is only the beginning."

"Tell me more about your mom and Jeff. Did he help raise you?"

Kelsey shakes her head. "Not really. My dad left us when we were really young. He was a truck driver and wanted to be on the road. Mom raised us on her own. Our dad sent money, but that was about it. There was no involvement in our life. And then when I was around fourteen, my mom met Jeff. To our knowledge, he was the only boyfriend she had while we were growing up, and we didn't even know they were dating until after six months. How she did it, I don't know, but she was very protective of us. When we finally met Jeff, it was this big relief because we saw how happy our mom was. We immediately accepted him into our family, and he's been a rock for us ever since."

"That's such a good story," I say. "I've had a few conversations with him, and just from those chats, I can tell how much he treats you as his."

"He's the dad we never had," Kelsey says as the waiter removes our salad plates. "There was this one night where I came home from a date in high school and I was heartbroken because the boy I went out with said I was a bad kisser. I knew that wasn't right because I'd practiced on my hand several times." She winks and I laugh out loud. Of course she did. "Jeff was very quiet, and when my mom took me to my room to console me, Jeff left the house."

"Oh shit, what did he do?"

"Never told me. All I know is that the next day, Skylar—the guy I went out with—gave me an apology card and told me it was him who was the bad kisser, not me."

"That's my kind of man. I hope he scared the absolute shit out of Skylar."

"I'm pretty sure he did."

I lean closer to her and say, "And for the record, you're easily the best kisser I've ever had."

"Same." She winks.

———

Kelsey presses her hand to her stomach and says, "Okay...hands down the best dim sum ever."

"Told you." I dab my mouth with my napkin. "Nothing tops it."

"And those Szechwan noodles changed my life."

"Hopefully in a good way."

"The best way." She lifts the tea she ordered and takes a sip. "I've been meaning to ask you something."

"What's that?"

"Have you talked to Huxley about your job, what you feel, and the ideas you have to feel more fulfilled?"

I shake my head. "Not yet."

"Are you nervous?"

"No, I'm more focused on you at the moment."

"You don't need to focus on me, you have me."

"Yeah? Is that a promise?"

She leans over and takes my hand in hers. "That's a promise. So, now you can focus on your job. Do you need help putting together a presentation? I'm good at organizing thoughts."

"Of course you are." I kiss her knuckles. "But I think I should do this on my own."

"Mmm, I like that. I like when you're in charge."

"I know because you scream my name when I'm in charge."

Her cheeks redden as she glances around.

"It's a private room, Kelsey."

"Yes, but our waiter pops in and out."

"And he signed an NDA, so there's nothing you need to worry about. Plus, given the tip he'll get tonight, his loyalty is with me."

"Still, I don't need people knowing I'm a screamer."

I chuckle. "Nothing wrong with that. I like that you scream. I actually wish it was my ringtone."

"Oh my God, are you trying to ruin the night?"

"It can't all be roses and candles, babe. There has to be some reality to the night, and that is, even though we're together, I'll still drive you crazy."

"Oddly," she says on a sigh, "I think it's what I like the most about you."

"Liar, you like how I make you come."

She shakes her head. "Nope, I like you...you, the person. I like Jonah the sweetheart. JP the instigator. The sex, that's just a bonus."

Fuck, she knows how to make me feel whole.

Loved.

Cherished.

Wanted.

I knew this woman had the potential to change my life, but I didn't know how quickly.

When Huxley asked me how serious I was about Kelsey, if this was just fun or if this was real, I wasn't kidding when I told him she was it for me. No one else. I told him that I fell for her weeks ago, and being with her, being able to hold her, kiss her, just solidifies that feeling.

She's my person.

———————

"How are you feeling?" I ask Kelsey as I sit across from her on our private jet.

"Good. Happy. Lucky."

After our dinner, we went to the rooftop of the building and I played our song again—what I refer to as our song—and I danced with my girl under the stars while candles lit the space around us. It was romantic as fuck, and Kelsey cried when I first took her out on the rooftop. Then, we sat on a couch, shared a piece of honey cake, and talked some more. About everything and anything. Our conversations flow so easily, and it's like we've been talking for years. Once we were ready to leave, I asked her if she wanted to fly back or stay the night, and unfortunately, she has a dress fitting with Lottie tomorrow, so we had to fly back home tonight.

The captain informs us that we're free to get out of our seats, so I unbuckle my seatbelt and rise from my chair. I hold my hand out to her and say, "Come with me."

I lead her back to the bedroom where there's a bed freshly made. I shut and lock the door behind me and then turn toward her. "I want you naked."

Her eyes widen with excitement. "What do you plan on doing?"

"Something that takes us the whole flight to accomplish."

"That's over an hour."

"Exactly." I undo my shirt buttons and tug the shirt out of my dress pants. "Seems like the perfect amount of time to explore your body with my tongue."

She places her hand on my chest and slowly runs her nails over my pecs, across my nipples, and down my abs. "You know I love how you make me come, right?"

"Why do I feel like there's a *but* after that statement?"

"Because there is."

"Fuck, are you on your period?"

She shakes her head. "No, but I am preventing you from making me come tonight."

"Why?" I feel my brow draw together.

Her hand slips to my pants and she undoes them, then dips her hand past the elastic of my briefs and right to my cock.

A hiss escapes me as I lean against the door of the compact bedroom.

"I want to make you come this time," she tells me.

"But we're taking it slow."

"You making me orgasm every time we're together isn't taking it slow."

I pause and grip her hand. "Fuck, you're right. I'm...hell, I'm sorry." I remove her hand. "You're right, I shouldn't end the date like this. We can—"

Her hand covers my mouth as she presses her breasts to my chest. "Don't finish that sentence."

"Kelsey, you're right, I'm not honoring what you asked."

"What I asked was dumb. We can connect on both levels. We have. I really want to make you feel good."

"Babe, you make me feel good without having to stick your hand down my pants."

"This is different. I want to connect with you on this level, too."

"Are you sure?"

She nods. "I'm very sure." She reaches to her side and undoes her zipper, letting her dress fall to the floor, leaving her in a light pink two-piece lingerie set.

"Remind me to get you a gift card for your favorite lingerie store, because this is never going to get old." I smooth my hand on her back, grip the clasp of her bra, and undo it with one quick pinch. It snaps off and falls to the ground with her dress.

"I thought I was the one pleasuring you?" she asks as she pushes down my pants and briefs at the same time until I step out of them, removing my shoes and socks first.

"Seeing you naked pleasures me." I push her thong down so we're both naked.

I reach for the spot between her legs, but before I can, she drops to her knees, moves her hair to the side, and grips my cock at the base.

"Hell," I whisper, leaning against the door.

Her tongue peeks out past her soft lips and she runs circles over my head, swirling and swirling, while she casually pumps my length.

It's subtle.

And it drives me crazy because it's not nearly enough. I know what she's doing—she's attempting to torture me as I torture her. Little does she know, I could do this all fucking night.

That is…until her hand slides under my balls to the spot just behind them. She pushes up, and my eyes widen in pleasure.

"Fuck." I clench my teeth together as I feel my cock grow in her mouth.

"Like that?" she asks before dipping her tongue to the base of my dick and dragging it all the way up, making short flicks against the underside of the head. Her thumbs work my balls, dragging over the seam, fondling them, one at a time. It's an onslaught of pleasure, but once again, not what I need, not what's going to drive me to fucking her mouth.

"You trying to torture me?"

She smirks and brings her entire mouth over my cock, sucking me in. Fuck, yes, that's what I'm talking about. I'm prepared to settle into her mouth when she pulls off in one slick motion and brings her tongue down to my balls.

The fucking temptress.

I reach down and grip her hair in my fist, turning it over once so I have a tight hold. She doesn't even flinch. She loves it just as much as I do. She reaches for my balls, brings them close to her mouth, and sucks them in, her tongue running all over them.

"Babe, that feels good. But I want in your mouth."

"Sometimes you don't always get what you want."

My eyes narrow at that smart mouth of hers and I give her hair the lightest of yanks. She smiles before taking my cock into her mouth again, this time straight to the back of her throat.

"Fuck…me," I say when she swallows. "Yes, baby. Just like that." She allows me to thrust into her once, twice, and when I go for a third, she pulls away and releases me. "Jesus."

Sweat trickles down my back as her hands start working my length, up and down, tugging, pulling, massaging. Her hands work over the head, over sensitive veins to my perineum, where she lightly plays, tapping, rubbing, driving me more and more nuts.

"Babe, I'm about to fuck you in two seconds."

She chuckles and stands. She keeps one hand on my cock, lightly tugging on it as she kisses my chest, my neck, my jaw, and then matches her lips to mine. I open-mouth kiss her, driving my tongue against hers, aggressively taking what I want. One hand on her lower back, keeping her tight against me, I reach between her legs and find her completely drenched.

"Shit, babe, you're so turned on."

"I love sucking your cock," she says, her confession nearly making me come right then and there.

"If you like sucking it so much, then lie down on the bed, your head hanging over the edge."

Confused, she leans away, so I help her lie down. Then I guide her body so her head tips back over the edge of the bed and her throat is completely exposed.

"Have you ever sucked a cock like this before?"

She shakes her head as she wets her lips.

"I'll go slow, then. Open for me, baby."

She opens her mouth, and I position my cock at her lips and slowly press into her mouth, giving her the feel of the position first.

"Are you okay?"

She nods so I press farther. She unhinges and allows me to go even deeper.

"That's it, take me in slow." I lean forward and place my hands on the mattress at either side of her waist. "Open your legs for me." She obliges brilliantly, and I lean over and tongue her clit, swiping at it a few times.

She groans against my cock and the vibration nearly makes me shoot off in seconds.

"Christ," I groan, trying to keep my composure. "Hold my cock, baby, guide me in and out."

She grips the base of my erection and moves me in and out of her throat, sometimes going shallow, other times taking me in so deep that I nearly black out. The entire time, I try to focus on bringing her pleasure. I lap at her clit with fast flicks, something I know drives her crazy.

She pulls me into her throat, swallows, plays with my balls, presses and strokes me in all the right places, and my orgasm climbs faster than I want it to.

"So good, baby. Fuck, you feel so good. Are you close?"

"Yes," she whispers while pulling off me for a second to take a deep breath. "Can I come?"

And fuck...me, those three words have my cock surging for release.

"Good girl for asking. You can," I say, then I lower my mouth again and press it against her clit. She takes me into her throat. Her body tenses beneath me, and after three more flicks, she's moaning against my cock, tugging on my goddamn balls, and making me come so fucking fast, I didn't even have time to prepare her. Instead, I shoot off down her throat and pulse into her mouth until I'm completely spent.

I slide to the side and pull her up into my hold, cradling her close to my chest and pressing a kiss to her forehead.

She rests her heated cheek against my skin and sighs.

"Are you okay?" I ask her. She nods. "Was that too intense for you?"

"No." She kisses my chest. "It was perfect." She then looks me in the eyes and says, "You make me feel so desirable, JP. The way you speak to me is so demanding, but also like you're protecting me. You have so much faith in me even though I don't have that much experience. I don't think I've ever felt sexier in my life."

"Because you are." I nudge her chin up and capture her lips.

"This may be too deep—no pun intended, given what we just did— but I've always been insecure about my looks. Being Lottie's younger sister, it's hard not to compare myself to her. And with one failed attempt after another at dating, I have a hard time not feeling insecure about who I am and what I look like. But then you came along, and you've somehow washed away those insecurities. You've made me feel beautiful."

"Because you are." I have no clue why Kelsey doesn't see her own beauty. Sure, her sister is pretty, but Kelsey is in another league of beautiful. "I think you're the most exquisite beauty, Kelse. Lottie has nothing on you."

Her smile weakens me, and when she curls against me again, she asks, "Can we lie down and just talk?"

"Yeah, baby, we can. Let me grab you a water first."

I help her under the covers of the bed. Then I quickly wash up, grab some waters, and offer her a wet washcloth. Once we're settled, lying down and facing each other, her beautiful smile peeks past her lips.

"Didn't think I'd ever be a girl who deep-throated a guy on an airplane, but look at me now…not sure if I should be proud or not."

I laugh. "You should be. There's more to life than bamboo organization systems."

"Apparently." She dances her fingers over my chest. "So, are you excited about Hux and Lottie getting married soon? It's right around the corner."

"I am excited. Not so much about the wedding, but for Huxley to be married and start a family. He's always been a sort of father figure to me and Breaker, especially once our dad passed, so I know being a father is in his blood. It'll be good to see him take a step back for a second, breathe, and enjoy life. I know Lottie helps him do that."

"She does. I didn't think their little scheme would ever go this far, but I'm happy for them, and I'm ready to be an aunt."

"What about a mom? Is that something you want?" I ask, curious about her thoughts on starting a family.

"It is." Her eyes flash to mine. "What about you?"

"Yes. I want to be a father. I want to have a family. I have that huge fucking house, and I need to fill it up with something."

"You could always fill it up with a bunch of cats. Given your ornery disposition at times, a cat seems like the perfect pet for you."

"I do like a good pussy."

She rolls her eyes, causing me to chuckle.

"I'm sure I'll get a pet someday, and it'll hate me but love everyone else in my family."

"Sounds about right. How many kids do you want?"

"One…possibly two. But not for a bit. I don't want to be banging out kids as soon as I get married. I want to enjoy my wife first, take her around the world, grow experiences before we're deep in the trenches of diapers and temper tantrums."

"I'm the same way. I still have some things I want to accomplish, experience. I know I want a family, but I don't need it right away."

I momentarily study her and then say, "I think you'd be a great mom."

Her eyes soften. "You think so?"

I nod. "I really do. You have a loving, calm heart. You're also a beautiful leader, and when conflict arises, you don't immediately grow angry like I do. You take a step back and give it some thought before tackling what needs to be said, what needs to be done. I think that's a good quality in a mom."

"Well, I think you'd be a good dad. You're caring, protective, and even though you're annoying at times with your constant teasing, I know you'd bring great joy to your family."

"That means a lot to me. Thank you, Kelsey." And that right there is one of the main reasons I'm falling for this girl. She sees beyond the façade, sees my heart, and likes what she sees. As much as I craved time with my dad, I also wished he gave more of himself to all of us boys. We all needed a role model and someone who loved us unconditionally. *I want to be the man he wasn't.*

"You're welcome." She scoots in closer, brings her hand to the back of my neck, and kisses me tenderly. "So, I was thinking, after my dress fitting tomorrow, do you want to come over to my place? I'll make you dinner?"

"Can I help you make dinner?"

"I'd like that a lot."

"Good." I kiss her this time. "Then, yes, I'll be there."

Breaker dribbles the ball and then tosses it up to the basket, making a swish. "I'm surprised you were able to find the willpower to pull yourself away from Kelsey for one goddamn moment and play basketball with me."

"Wow, you don't sound bitter," I say as the ball rebounds and I toss it back to him.

"Seriously, dude. I'm losing Huxley. Am I going to lose you, too?"

"You're not losing us."

"I never see you guys unless we're at the office, and you don't even have lunch with me anymore." Jokes are on the tip of my tongue, but when I see how serious he is, I hold back.

"Are you really upset?" I ask.

He dribbles, sets up, shoots. "I mean, sort of, and not in a bitchy way, because I'm happy for you two, but it would be nice if you guys would carve out some time for me."

"I can do that." I pull on the back of my neck. "Things have just been… crazy. And I've been consumed. Dude, I fucking like her a lot."

"I know. I can tell. And I know Huxley is consumed by the wedding right now, which is in a week, but remember, we're all we have. Don't leave a man behind."

"I'll make a better effort," I promise. He tosses me the ball and I take a shot. It bounces off the rim, right back at me. "You know, you could possibly find someone to settle down with. The option is there."

"Oh, is it? What love connection are you seeing for me that I don't see?"

"What about Ophelia?" I ask.

"Lia?" he asks, confused.

"Yeah. Huxley and I have been taking bets as to when you two will hook up."

"Dude, she's my friend, not to mention my neighbor, *and* she has a boyfriend. That's it. There's no romance."

"You two also call each other all the time—call, not text. That's weird."

"We text, too," he mutters. "But that's beside the point. We're friends, that's it, nothing more. We established those ground rules back in college."

"So, you're telling me you never thought about getting together with her?"

"Never."

I laugh. "You're such a fucking liar." I shake my head as I steal the ball from him and shoot, missing the basket completely. Jesus, maybe I should meet up with Breaker more. I can't seem to score anything today. "So, you're not bringing her to the wedding?"

"No. She did knit Huxley and Lottie pot holders, though, that I have to take with me."

"I can't believe you didn't invite her to the wedding."

"I'm bringing some girl named Charise."

"Some girl? Do you even know her?"

"Yeah. She's Lia's friend."

"Wait." I pause. "You're not taking Lia, but you're taking her friend?"

He shrugs. "I told her I needed a date, and she hooked me up. See, that's what friends are for. I was her wingman when she met Brian. Unlike you, I can actually be friends with a woman."

"Seems like everything worked out for me." I smile at him as he takes a shot from the three-point line and sinks it.

"Do you love her?" he asks, rebounding his own ball before tossing it to me.

I dribble it a few times and nod. "Yeah, I think I do. Hell, she's all I think about. I'm constantly counting down the minutes until I can hold her and be with her. And she makes me really fucking happy, dude. I think once all this wedding stuff is done, I'm going to take her back to San Francisco and tell her. Feels fitting to do it there."

"When did you become a man who makes grand gestures?"

"Ever since I started listening to Kelsey's podcast. Have you heard it?" I ask. He lifts a brow at me, which causes me to laugh. "Well, she's all about these stories of how people met. She loves the grand gesture, and she soaks in their romance. You can feel how much she's in her element when you listen. Figured if I want to keep her around, I have to step up my game."

"Never thought I'd see the day when you matured into a thoughtful man, but here you are. I'm impressed."

"Thank you." I awkwardly bow before shooting the ball. I fade back while the ball hits...nothing.

Breaker lets out a long, drawn-out "AIIIIIRRRRR BALLLLLLLLL," like the immature little brother that he is.

Yeah, I need to get out here more often.

"Thanks for meeting with me," I say to my brothers as I sit across from them at the conference table.

Fuck, my palms are sweaty.

I've put a lot of time into this presentation, knowing that Huxley would want specific points. Although I'd planned to speak to Breaker first and toss around the numbers, I didn't want Huxley to feel we'd gone behind his back. I might want to drive this, but we need to be unified on this direction, and the only way to achieve that is if we all use our individual strengths once the idea is on the table. I spent last night running through my idea over and over, explaining it out loud to Kelsey as she sat on her bed with me. She listened to me speak until I was blue in the face. I felt ready. Right now, however, with my brothers watching me, I feel like I've lost all sense of why I'm doing this.

Kelsey and I drove to Cane Enterprises this morning. She walked me to my office, she held my hand as I went over the presentation one more time, and she gave me the most encouraging kiss and told me to call her after.

I can't fucking fold, knowing she's waiting to hear from me.

Taking a deep breath, I look my brothers in the eye and say, "I'm unhappy."

The confused looks that cross their faces would almost seem comical if I wasn't so fucking on edge right now.

Huxley shifts in his chair. "What do you mean, you're unhappy? In life? I thought everything was good with Kelsey."

"Everything is great with Kelsey," I say. "This has nothing to do with my personal life and everything to do with my work life."

"You're unhappy with work?" Breaker asks, both of them truly concerned. They're obviously surprised too.

"I am." On another deep breath, I say, "When we started this company, I joined in not because it was something I truly wanted to do—invest in real estate—but because I wanted to be close to you two. Losing Dad, it was—" My throat grows tight. "Well, you know how devastated I was. And I was feeling lost, tortured at times with memories, and the only way I knew how to preserve those memories was to stay as close to you two as I could. The jobs were simple. Breaker, you'd do the numbers because that was what you're good at. Huxley, you'd be the idea man, because you're a natural-born leader, and that left me with the leftovers, handling all media and odd jobs. At first, I didn't mind it, but as time went on, I grew more and more bored. More bitter. Angry that I didn't feel like I had a purpose."

"How long have you felt this way?" Huxley asks.

"Probably about a year now. But in the last few months, those feelings have grown to the point of bitterness. And that's not what I want. I don't want to feel bitter toward the one thing that keeps me close to Dad's memory. Close to you both. So, I sat down and thought about what would truly make me happy, what would make me feel fulfilled." I open my folder and slide the two printouts across the table, one for each of them. "I want to start a foundation within Cane Enterprises that focuses on offering affordable housing in our buildings to those who need it. Single parents, low-income families, those struggling to get their feet on the ground. I want to build a community within the housing, offer practical classes like basic DIY home maintenance and managing your finances, have childcare, health management. We're bringing in so much fucking money every goddamn day that I think it's time we give back, do more than just writing a check to a foundation."

Huxley and Breaker both look over the printout, their eyes scanning the details. I'm literally hiding my shaking hands as I wait for their response.

They have to see the value in it.

"And you'd head this program?" Huxley asks. "Starting with the Angelica?"

I nod. "Yes. I've laid out the plans for how we can make the Angelica our first affordable housing apartment building. I even spoke with the mayor before I left San Francisco, pitched him the idea, and he said not only would he be willing to work with us on securing more buildings, but he'd put money toward our initiative when it comes to education, opportunity, childcare, as well as transportation."

"Have you run the numbers on this?" Breaker asks.

"Yes." I pull another paper from my folder, knowing he was going to ask. "With the products the mayor can provide at cost, and the tax breaks, we could break even on the project, while helping others. But honestly, even if we didn't, it wouldn't matter. Profit from even one of our other properties can sustain that."

"What about your current responsibilities?" Huxley asks.

"Sustainably Organized runs on its own, and I think you know that at this point, Lottie and Kelsey don't need us watching over them. I'd be able to keep up on some of my smaller management projects, and then all the PR—well, I can schedule important meetings, but the smaller fires, those can be put out by someone we hire. It's menial work and a waste of my time." I tap the desk. "This, though, this is the big picture. We can start a wave of affordable living across the country in major cities, expand from California to New York, touch down in Denver and Atlanta, as well."

Huxley leans back in his chair and stares me down. "Honestly, I think it would be a substantial hit on our profit, because I can't see how we could make affordable housing profitable." My stomach fucking falls. "But…it's a fucking brilliant idea and I'm mad I didn't think of it myself."

He places his hand on the conference table. "One of the best things I learned from Dad about business is sometimes you have to take a hit in order to invest in yourself later. This is a hit, but it will keep investing in our company over and over again, maybe not financially, but morally. We have to run the numbers to ensure we stay viable, ensure we balance the not-for-profits with the revenue-generating properties, which I can see is possible. I'm guessing we'd need a not-for-profit license too. Spend time with Breaker and run numbers. You have my approval. Let's meet on this again in three weeks."

My chest swells as I turn toward Breaker, who's still looking over the numbers. "I agree with Huxley and we do need to go over these numbers." He lifts his eyes and smirks at me. "But I fucking love the idea." Growing serious, he asks, "This will make you happy, though?"

I nod. "It will."

He tilts his head to the side and asks, "Does this have anything to do with Kazoo the pigeon?"

I let out a loud laugh as Huxley asks, "Who the hell is Kazoo?"

"Some pigeon JP has been saving during his spare time."

"I think this was inspired by Kazoo," I say.

"Well, would you look at that, pigeons really do deserve to be saved."

After a few handshakes, some bro hugs, and some reassurance on my end that I'm truly excited about this, I part ways with my brothers and pull my phone from my pocket.

JP: Where are you?

Kelsey texts back right away.

Kelsey: Your office.

I nearly sprint to my office and shut the door behind me. She's on the couch, a cup of coffee in hand. When our eyes meet, she slowly sets the coffee on the table in front of her and stands. "What did they say?"

I smile. "They fucking loved it."

She jumps in glee and then runs to my arms, offering me the world's best fucking hug. I grip her tightly, one hand on her back, the other at the nape of her neck as she clings to me, her legs wrapping around my waist.

"Oh my God, I'm so excited for you."

"Thank you," I say, burying my head in her hair.

I press a kiss to the side of her face and hold her so tightly. It's as if the world around me is starting to make sense. For so long, I've felt lost, like I wasn't supposed to be where I was, but over the last few months, the clouds have parted and I can finally fucking see what I'm supposed to be doing.

Giving back.

Creating something bigger than an income for me and my brothers.

Falling for this woman and showing her the kind of man I can be for her.

It's all clicking into place, and I don't think I've ever been happier.

Ever.

CHAPTER 21
KELSEY

Kelsey: Welcome, listener, to the *Meant to Be Podcast*, where we talk to madly-in-love couples about the way they met. Jason and Dottie, thank you so much for joining me today.

Jason: It's an absolute honor.

Kelsey: And this potato salad you had sent over, did you make this, Jason?

Jason: I did. We're in the early stages of production, but hopefully soon we'll have my potato salad in grocery stores around the country, not that I'm trying to promote it here or anything, but you know…Best Butt in Baseball Salad, coming to a store near you.

Dottie: It's all he talks about. Like…all he talks about.

Jason: Can be used for backyard barbecues, family dinners, intimate evenings… I even licked it off Dottie a few times.

Dottie: Can you not say those kinds of things?

Jason: She's always been camera shy.

Kelsey: You know, I'm always looking for sponsorship. A potato salad for lovers could be the first one.

Jason: Don't you play with my heart.

Kelsey: Well, I just love the letter you sent in, Jason, about you and Dottie, and I'd love for you to tell the listeners how you two became meant to be.

Dottie: Please note, anything he says is going to be exaggerated, so take it with a grain of—

Jason: It was a dark, morbidly chilly evening in Chicago, where everyone was searching for hope and love.

Dottie: Oh, dear God, here we go.

"Are you nervous?" I ask Lottie as we stand outside on the patio of Huxley's and her house.

For the reception, they had the pool covered in a clear surface, decorated it with seven tables, and added some soft pink uplighting on the stone walls of the fence. Strings of flowers make for a faux ceiling, while two cellists are tucked off to the side, adding sophistication to the intimate night.

It's family and friends, that's it.

The original plan was for me to stay here tonight with Lottie and get ready in the morning, but Huxley wanted nothing to do with being apart from Lottie, so I'm spending the night at JP's place. I'll make the short walk here in the morning, where we'll all get ready, Ellie, the other bridesmaid, included.

Thankfully, she has no ill feelings toward me, given I ditched her brother. She said he understood completely and had wondered if someone else had been on my mind when we'd gone out. I feel bad that I didn't give him all my attention, but from what Ellie has said, he's dating someone right now who lives in Hawaii, and he's enjoying the "commute."

Lottie exhales next to me and then knocks back her champagne, emptying the flute. "Am I nervous? Not really." She speaks quietly, keeping the conversation just between us. "I'm not nervous about my choice. Without a doubt, Huxley is the man for me. I can't wait to be married to him. I'm just nervous about all the fanfare, you know? I really wish we just got married back here tonight, and then we could go on our honeymoon, but I understand Huxley wanted more of a traditional wedding."

"The ceremony will be short, and then you get to party. That will be so much fun."

"True. Plus, tomorrow we're going to have fun getting ready, right? Did you get those Mad Libs I sent you a link to? The bridal ones?"

"I did. I have them in my bag of things to do tomorrow. Can't wait to insert *boob* and *penis* into every category."

"Don't forget *fuck*—that can be a verb, noun, adjective…it's universal."

"Yes, there will be tons of fucks, boobs, and penises."

"Good." She taps my hand and then looks me in the eyes. "I'm getting married tomorrow. How crazy is that? It feels like just the other day I was attempting to find ways to drive Huxley nuts to get me out of our contract."

"I know. I still remember you telling me you'd met someone and were going to discuss terms over chips and guac at Chipotle."

"I think that's what won me over—he paid extra for my guac."

I laugh just as Huxley stands in front of everyone and taps his glass. The small group quiets, and the cellists stop playing. With one hand in his pocket, the other holding a tumbler of beer, Huxley addresses the backyard.

"Thank you so much for coming tonight and for being a part of our special day tomorrow." His eyes land on Lottie. "A few months ago, I made a business mistake that I thought was going to cost me our company's reputation. I did everything I could to recover, including convincing this random girl I met on the sidewalk to pretend to be my fiancée. I thought I was so clever, getting this woman to be by my side and act like the doting fiancée I needed. Little did I fucking know that I was in way over my head. She was headstrong, breathtakingly beautiful, and the biggest challenge of my life, and I quickly fell for the girl who was supposed to be temporary. But tomorrow...tomorrow she becomes my forever. Leiselotte, you're the love of my life, and you make me happier than I could ever imagine." I grip my sister's hand tightly. "You're doing me the greatest honor of my life tomorrow, by becoming my wife. I promise you, no matter what comes our way, I'll always be the man you deserve. I love you."

Lottie swipes at the tears on her cheeks. She stands from her chair, grips Huxley by the cheeks, and kisses him deeply.

As I watch them, completely and utterly in love, a warm hand grips my shoulder before smoothing down my back. "Hey," JP says, taking a seat next to me. "I feel like I haven't seen you all night."

I turn toward him, our legs twining together as I scoot in closer. "I know, but I like that I saw you and Jeff having a good time, or at least what seemed like a good time."

JP takes my hand in his and rests it on his lap, his other hand resting over my thigh. "We were talking about Jason Orson and his new potato salad. I told him Jason sent some over to you, and Jeff said he actually read an article in the *Player's Tribune*, written by Jason's best friend and brother-in-law Cory Potter—they both play for the Chicago Rebels—about Jason and his love for his potato salad. The dude has been claiming it's the best since college. I'm stoked to listen to your episode, actually."

"How did I forget Jeff is a big baseball fan? I feel like I'm failing. I should've gotten Jason to send over a signed ball or something."

"But, babe, that would be against all that he believes in. He's a Los Angeles Rook through and through."

"True."

"I told him that I'd take him to a game soon. He's always dreamed of sitting behind the backstop, so I figured I'd treat him."

"Oh my God, he'll lose it. You'd seriously do that?"

"Yeah. I enjoy his company, but not only that, he's important to you, which makes him important to me."

The words are on the tip of my tongue—I can feel them. I love this man. I can't imagine what life would be without him now. Without his teasing, his caring heart, the way he makes me feel whole, needed...sexy. He's the total package. But saying those words, here, on the night before my sister's wedding...I don't think I want to do that. I want to keep the attention on Lottie, and I know if I tell JP I love him, I won't be able to keep it to myself.

Plus, there's always that worry in the back of my mind that isn't sure if he's the same place as I am. It might take him longer to get there, so I need to wait.

"Hey, dude, can I talk to you for a second?" Breaker asks JP.

"Is it important?" JP asks, not letting go of my hand.

Breaker smooths a hand over his jaw and gives JP a curt nod, saying, "Stuff for the wedding tomorrow."

Oh jeez, for a second I thought it was more important than that, like something was actually wrong.

"Sure," JP says before dropping a quick kiss on my lips. "Be back."

Breaker pulls him to the side, and I stand to grab myself some more champagne. When I sway, I realize that maybe I've had a few too many glasses, but...then again, it's a rehearsal dinner and the champagne is flowing. It's time to celebrate!

JP

A sharp line etched on his brow, Breaker pulls me into the house, shuts the sliding glass door, then moves us into Huxley's office.

"Do we really need this much privacy?" I ask when he shuts the door and turns to me, pinching the tension in his brow with his fingers. Worry starts to hit me. "What's going on?"

His eyes flash to mine as he asks, "Remember the night you were talking about polar bears dying and donating to help the pigeons?"

"I remember the night, not the details."

"Do you remember sending an email?"

"An email?" I shake my head. "No, why?"

"Fuck," he mutters. "Can you open your email?"

I hand him my phone, and he clicks on the mail app.

"What the hell is going on?"

He taps away, and when he doesn't find what he's looking for, he presses his fist to his mouth. "That night, we spoke on the phone. You were extremely drunk, and I told you to get some food and not do anything stupid."

"Okay…" I drag out.

"Well, I think you did something stupid, but I can't find it."

"What the fuck did I do?"

"You were upset about Kelsey and the wedding and needing a date, so you told me you were going to send a generic email to girls you knew, asking if they wanted to be your date."

My stomach sinks. "Shit, I vaguely recall that." I scour through my emails. "But I don't see anything in my *sent* box."

"I know." Breaker pushes his hand through his hair. "I'm fucking confused."

"Why? Why are you even bringing this up?"

"I was tipped off by Dave Toney. He said there's an article coming out tomorrow about you sending an email to a bunch of women, asking if they want to be your date. But…but you didn't send anything."

"What?" I say, the cool, breezy attitude I had slowly shrinking away. "How the fuck would someone have known that? Is it a fake email?"

"That's what I'm thinking. But I can't be sure. Dave sent me the name of the person who tipped him off and I sent them a text, asking for more information." His eyes meet mine. "I'm not worried about Huxley and Lottie. I'm worried about Kelsey."

"Well, it's fucking fake. I didn't send anything out. The proof is in my email."

Just then, Breaker's phone beeps with a message. He pulls his phone from his pocket and opens the text message. He turns the screen toward me and asks, "Then what the fuck is this?"

I bring the phone closer to me and read the email.

Hey ladieeees,

Sending a big old cock of an email because, you know…I have a big cock, so this email has to match.

Here's the thing. Hux is getting married to Lulu Lemon and they told me I need a plus-one. Looking for a willing candidate to escort me down the aisle.

All expenses paid. Promises of pleasure.

If interested, hit me up.

I wear condoms still.

K. Bye.

JP

"Fuck," I say. "I don't remember sending this. It's not in my email. I don't fucking understand."

Breaker points to the top of the screen. "It's not your work email…It's your personal."

At that moment, I feel all the color drain from my face as I realize he's right. I never check my personal email, ever. I shove Breaker's phone at him and open my personal email. I sift through promotional newsletters until I see several responses to my email.

McKayla.

Kenzie.

Hattie.

With every reply, it feels like a nail in my coffin as I try to figure out how to fucking deal with this.

I squeeze my hand over my forehead and say, "Fuck, this isn't good. Do you know anything about the article?"

"All I know is this email is in it, it mentions the wedding, and, uh…" He winces.

"What?" I ask, a ball of twisted, tortured anxiety forming in my stomach.

"Uh, it talks about Kelsey and her business, and alludes to the girls using any means necessary to be successful, including hooking up with the Cane brothers."

"Fuck," I yell as I pace the office. "FUCK!" Hands on my hips, I say, "We need to kill it, man. We need to kill that fucking article."

"I've already contacted Karla, and she's working on it, but I don't know, JP. I don't know if we can fix this."

"We have to fucking fix this. Do you realize how damaging that assumption would be for Kelsey? She'll be fucking humiliated. Not to mention, that email is damning." My lungs seem to stop working as I attempt to catch my breath. "I'll…I'll fucking lose her. I'll lose everything." I look at Breaker, pleading. "Please, dude, please help me. Throw whatever kind of cash we need to throw at it. It just needs to be dead."

"I'll work on it. Let me call Karla again and see what I can do."

He starts to walk by me, but I grip his arm and say, "I love her, Breaker. I fucking love her so much, and this will destroy us. I can feel it. Please help me."

"I will. Just hang here for a second. Let me see what I can do."

KELSEY

"My sister is getting married," I shout as I hold my glass of champagne above my head. "Ahhh!"

We're standing on the clear surface over the pool, Lottie's arm around my waist as we sway to the music. Breaker returned without JP, only to whisk Huxley away, claiming they had "man things" to talk about. Mom and Jeff are cuddling by the outdoor fireplace, and Dave and Ellie are dancing next to a palm tree, taking great advantage of the alone time away from their newborn.

It's a beautiful night.

The stars are bright.

The champagne is pulsing through my veins.

And all I can think about is when I get back to JP's place, I'm going to hump his brains out.

"I'm going to hump his brains!" I lift my champagne glass.

"Hump whose brains?" Lottie asks me.

"JP's. Tonight. I'm going to sit on his head and hump him."

"Oh, I love sitting on Huxley's face. Nothing is more satisfying than feeling his hands ride my inner thighs while his tongue does all the work."

"I haven't sat on JP's face yet, but I deep-throated him in a plane." I turn toward my sister and grip both of her shoulders the best I can while still holding a champagne flute. "Have you deep-throated with your head hanging off the bed? Highly recommend. I never enjoyed balls in my face as much as that night."

"Oh, when a nut-sack rests on my eyeball, it's a strangely comforting thing. Like a cold cucumber, but instead, a pouch full of semen." She taps her eyes. "Hmm, maybe I'll ask for a crotch facial tonight. Huxley hates when I call it that, so now, I always call it that."

"I wonder what JP would say if I asked him for one."

"He'd probably say yes. Every man likes to show dominance by setting his junk on a woman's face. Think of it as a form of marking their territory."

"It's appealing, but I also want to use this vibrator he has in his night-stand. It's just a regular one, but I'm pretty sure he's used it in his butt..." I laugh so hard that I start coughing.

"Huxley likes things in his butt. Sometimes I twirl my finger in there." Whispering, she says, "He doesn't like the twirl."

"I haven't stuck my finger in JP's butt yet. I don't think I'm confident enough to do that."

"No need for confidence, just poke it on up there. If he moans, congratulate yourself. If he asks what the fuck you're doing, just say, 'Oh...I'm sorry, was that not where my finger was supposed to go?'"

"I don't know. I think I should just tickle his balls with the vibrator tonight."

"That's also a winning idea. Ooo, put it at the underneath part of his head. I did that to Huxley and, I'm not kidding, he came in five seconds. It was so hot."

"I like that idea. I should text him."

"Oh, yes. Great idea. Sext him."

I grab my phone from the table in front of us and open our text thread.

Kelsey: Hey, big man.

"You call him that?" Lottie asks.

"Uh, not really, but it was the first thing that came to my mind. Should I delete it?"

She nods. "Call him lover."

Kelsey: Hey, big man. Hey, lover. I'm thinking about your big cock right now.

"Oh yeah, tell him how big," Lottie says.

Kelsey: Your enormous, thick, girthy, massive, heavy, veiny cock.

"God, I love a veiny cock. You should see Huxley's when it's hard and straining. Sometimes I just like to watch it bob up and down when it wants release."

Kelsey: When we get back to your place, I want to sit on your face, but I also want your balls in my eyes, and I want to vibrate your butt.

"Yes, and tell him how you like his tongue."

Kelsey: And I like your tongue and how it...uh, how it...licks me.

"So sexy," Lottie says over my shoulder.

"You think so?"

"Uh-huh. Hit *send*."

Satisfied, I press the blue arrow and clutch my phone to my chest. "I'm going to sleep with man-balls on my face tonight."

Lottie clutches my shoulders. "What a lucky girl."

JP

"What the actual fuck," Huxley roars as he reads through the article that's supposed to be posted tomorrow. Somehow, Karla, the magician in our lives, was able to secure a copy of it, and we've spent the last ten minutes reading it over and over again.

To say that I feel sick to my stomach is an understatement. When I say this is bad, I really fucking mean it. It's not a flattering article in any way. Not flattering for me and my drunk ass—it paints me as a philandering nitwit who sends borderline sexual harassment emails when drunk. And it paints Kelsey as a gold digger looking for handouts.

It's worse than I expected.

I've now resorted to rolling up my sleeves, pacing the length of

Huxley's office, and praying to the goddamn pigeons to please fix this. I've been a good person in my lifetime. I've donated a lot of money, volunteered my time, done some real, life-changing things to afford me some good karma. So, I'm calling on the universe to toss some solid, good-natured karma my way.

Huxley turns on me. "What the hell were you thinking?"

"I wasn't," I shout at him. "I was drunk and desperate. Heartbroken. You don't know what those two weeks were like in San Francisco. Seeing her go out with someone else when she wouldn't even look my way—fuck, man, it ate me alive."

"So, you go and send a crude email to a bunch of women asking if they want to be your date?"

"Well, you fucking told Dave Toney you had a pregnant fiancée. We don't always make smart decisions," I shout back.

"Hey," Breaker says, stepping in between us. "Karla is working with the reporter who wrote the article. It seems like the website can be paid off, so we might not even have to worry about it."

"Fuck," Huxley shouts while pulling on his hair. "This is not what I fucking need the night before my wedding."

"Do you think I need this?" I ask, pointing to my chest. "My goddamn happiness rests on what happens. No matter what, Lottie is going to marry you tomorrow, but Kelsey, she might not even look my way if this gets out."

"Would serve you right," Huxley says.

"Hey," Breaker yells, pulling our attention. With angry eyes, he stares down Huxley and says, "You fucked up big time when it came to that bullshit with Lottie. The company's reputation was at risk of being demolished, and we stood by your side and helped you. We made sure to go along with everything you needed to make sure no one was harmed. So, don't turn your back on your brother. He's right, you have no clue what he's been going through, not to mention, the fact that he actually allowed someone into his life again after Dad's passing. You should be asking him how he's feeling, not making him feel worse."

Huxley glances at me, and his shoulders deflate as he says, "Fuck, you're right. Shit, I'm sorry." He rubs his brow. "Are you okay?"

"No." I shake my head. "I'm not. I'm fucking scared. I can't lose her, man. I can't."

"How about this? It's getting late, so why don't you just explain to her what's going on, be ahead of the curve, and tell her that you're killing the article? That way, you're honest with her, and stopping the possible argument that could break things up," Breaker suggests.

Huxley nods. "That's probably smart. Being caught off guard is worse than having that conversation with her."

"You're probably right. I should take her to my place, sit her down, and have an honest conversation with her." My phone beeps with a text message. I glance at the screen and see that it's from Kelsey. "She just texted. Maybe she's ready to leave."

I open the text and read it.

Kelsey: Hey, lover. I'm thinking about your big cock right now. Your enormous, thick, girthy, massive, heavy, veiny cock. When we get back to your place, I want to sit on your face, but I also want your balls in my eyes, and I want to vibrate your butt. And I like your tongue and how it…uh, how it…licks me.

What…the…fuck?

"What is it?" Breaker asks.

"What were the girls doing before you left them?" I ask Huxley.

"Getting more champagne," he says, confused. "Why?"

"Because, from the text Kelsey just sent me, I can almost guarantee she's completely wasted."

"Fuck," Huxley says.

Yeah…*fuck* is right. I can almost guarantee whatever conversation I attempt to have with her tonight is going to be absolutely pointless.

KELSEY

"You're so handsome," I say as I wait for JP to open his front door. "Like, really handsome. The most handsome."

He looks over his shoulder at me and raises a brow. "How much did you have to drink?"

"Lots." I fling my arms up in the air. "And I have a fun fact for you, JP."

He opens his door, takes my hand, and brings me into his house.

"What's your fun fact?" he asks, relocking his front door.

"When I drink, something happens to my body." Leaning in, I whisper, "I get really horny."

His eyes widen and he starts coughing. I offer him a sturdy pat on the back and then…I unzip my dress and let it fall to the floor. Before he can say anything, I grip the cups of my strapless bra and flip them down, exposing my breasts to him.

"Kelsey—"

I don't give him time to finish before I grip the back of his head and bury his nose right between my breasts. I add a little shimmy, a little shake, and then pull him away.

His hair is mussed.

His body is rigid.

And there's no smile on his face.

Umm…did he not like that?

"Kelsey—"

"Wait…did you not enjoy that motorboat? Lottie said Huxley likes it. I figured it would run in the family. Does that mean you like the butt twirl since he doesn't like the butt twirl?"

He grips his hair. "What's the butt twirl?"

With my index finger, I make a twirling motion and shoot it up to the sky. "Right up the old toot-toot."

His face falls. "What the fuck did you two talk about?"

Breasts still hanging out, I move around him and go to his staircase. I lie across the stairs and spread my legs. "Come and get her. She's ready for you. Ripe and ready."

"Kelsey, baby, maybe we should just get ready for bed."

I lift up on my elbows and say, "Oh, trying to lure me into the bedroom. I see you, Cane. I see you. Sure, let's 'just get ready for bed.'" I use air quotes.

He offers me his hand and I take it as we walk up the stairs. I drag my hand over the black stair rail, enjoying the smooth, polished surface, and I allow him to guide me to his room. But he doesn't stop at the bed. Instead, he walks me to the sink and helps me with my toothbrush.

"Are you saying I have bad breath?" I ask him.

He shakes his head. "No, babe, this is just routine. And I know how much you like routine."

I stick my toothbrush in my hand, stare him down, and say, "God, it turns me on that you know that about me."

"Seems like everything is turning you on right now."

"Show me your toenails, and I bet I come right here, right now."

"Wow, that champagne has really done a number on you."

"I love champagne. Don't you?"

"Why don't you just focus on brushing your teeth? I'll get you a shirt to change into."

"Don't bother; I want to sleep naked."

I see his Adam's apple bob. "Are you sure? You can wear one of my shirts."

I shake my head. "Naked, or I scream."

"Well, we don't want you screaming—"

"Only when it's your name, right... *Jonah*?" I wiggle my eyebrows and he heaves a heavy sigh.

We spend the next few minutes "getting ready for bed," a.k.a. prepping our bodies for the magic that's about to happen, and when I'm done, I trot into his bedroom to find him standing in his boxer briefs, staring down at his phone.

Wearing nothing but my very own skin, I grip the doorframe and say, "Yoo-hoo, look who's ready for bed." I twiddle my fingers at him.

He sets his phone down and turns toward me. I watch as his eyes practically eat me alive. *That's right, take your fill, big boy.* I move one foot in front of the other and saunter toward him in this come-hither, sexy way that I know must be driving him absolutely crazy with need.

"Congratulations," I say when I reach him and put my hands on his chest.

"Congratulations for what?" he asks.

"For growing such a large boner." I cup his crotch, ready for his rocket, only to come up with...a snail. I glance up at him. "Why are you not hard?"

"Listen, Kelsey, I think we should just go to bed, okay? It's been a long night and we have a big day tomorrow."

I take a step back. "No, you're not—you're not hard. Do you not find me attractive?"

"Baby, you know that's not true. You know I fucking love your body. You know I think you're the sexiest woman I've ever met. You know I'm absolutely head over heels attracted to you."

"But...you're not hard." I back away again. "Is it my flirtation? Do you not like it?"

"Kelsey, let's just get under the covers and go to bed. You've had a lot to drink—"

"Oh God, I turned you off." I back up some more until I run into his dresser, where the shirt he wanted me to wear is folded. I quickly put it over my body, attempting to find some sort of shield as embarrassment consumes me.

"No, that's not it at all." He blows out a frustrated breath and grips his hair. "Can we just go to bed?"

I feel my eyes well up with tears as my heightened embarrassment pushes me toward the other end of his bed. I pause and quietly ask, "Do you want me to share your bed? I can go over to Huxley and Lottie's."

"You're not going anywhere," he growls, and then he approaches me. He takes my hand in his and places a soft kiss on my knuckles. "I want you in my bed."

"But you don't want me..." I say as a tear falls down my cheek. I quickly wipe it away. "I came on too strong. I said things that probably scared you. I'm not the girl you thought I was, that's what you're thinking, right? This is why I'm always vanilla, why I don't step out of my box to do things I don't normally do."

"Baby, stop."

I shake my head and pull my hand away from him. "I get it, JP. You didn't like what I said tonight." I slip under the covers of his bed. "I should just sleep it off, you know?"

He stands next to the bed, staring down at me, tugging on his hair. I can see he wants to say something, that there's something on the tip of his tongue, but instead of telling me what's on his mind, he turns away and goes to his side of the bed.

My heart completely falls.

I almost expected him to tell me that he did like what he heard, but that...I don't know, something is on his mind. But instead, he turns off the lights and slips under the covers with me.

But the worst thing that happens, worse than his rejection, is that when I fall asleep, he's not holding me. He's on his side of the bed, as far from me as he can be.

JP

"I'm going to fucking puke," I say as I walk into Breaker's place.

He woke me up at five with a phone call telling me he needed me at his place as soon as I could get there. I sprinted out of bed, threw some clothes on, and rushed to his place.

Kelsey was still sleeping when I left. The phone call luckily didn't wake her.

Last night was fucking torture, and I still feel sick about it now. All I wanted was to take my confident girl to bed, to do all the things she wanted to do, but I knew I couldn't, not with the threat of that defamatory article hanging over my head. It not only didn't feel right, but I've been so nauseated with worry that attempting to get it up seemed impossible. That was proven when she was walking toward me, so goddamn sexy in absolutely nothing, and I didn't even have a stir of excitement. And the hurt on her face. Fuck. I hated that in particular.

"What's going on?" I ask Breaker. "Is Huxley here?"

He shakes his head as we both walk into his office off the entryway. "I didn't think I'd bother him with this bullshit. He has a wedding, so I just told him it was handled."

"Has it been? Handled, that is?"

He shakes his head as he takes a seat at his desk. "The article is currently on hold, pending our decision."

I know exactly what that means—blackmail.

Searing anger pulses through me as I ask, "What do they want?"

"Well, the good thing is, the person who sent them your email had signed an NDA with the gossip website, meaning they can't sell the story to anyone else. So, if they don't run it, she can't take it to another website."

"Thank fuck for that. But I'm sure they paid her to sign that NDA."

Breaker nods.

"And they want that, on top of what they would've lost in website revenue for clicks, right?"

"They want two million."

"Jesus fuck," I roar as I stand. "That's fucking extortion."

"I have Taylor on it, pulling as many lawyer tricks as possible. That's why it's currently pending. They, of course, don't see it as extortion, they see it as us buying out a piece of revenue."

"Bullshit," I yell. "Show me the goddamn numbers that prove they'd make two million dollars of revenue off that story."

"I know, but, dude, this is a dip in the bank that won't make a huge difference. I looked over the numbers, and I can maneuver things around and slip the damage-control fee into the books in a way that no one would know, and we'd still get a tax break for it. We're trying to convince them to see it as a donation."

"That's lying."

"Which is why I thought I'd talk to you. They said they'd use some of their website ad space to promote something we're passionate about so it looks like a donation on their end."

"What an entirely fucked-up situation. So, what, they're asking what we want to promote on their website?"

"Yes, and offered to put our name on it."

"Fuck that," I yell. "They're not getting Cane Enterprises on anything."

"Dude, I know you're upset, but given the situation we're in—and wanting to save Kelsey the embarrassment if this got out—it would be smart to take the deal. And just throw down some charity, some random... oh, hey, fucking give them the pigeon charity to promote. It won't have our name on it, but we can write it off in the books, and I'm sure the last thing they want on their website is a sponsored ad about pigeons."

I pause, the anger easing only slightly as I think about the pigeons and how comical that would actually be. I grip my jaw, my fingers rubbing over the morning scruff. "You know, there are some real ill-looking pigeons we could get for the ad."

Breaker laughs. "Not a good look for them, but it all kind of works out in the end."

"I need front ad space, for two weeks, and final say in what the ad looks like."

"Taylor has already worked that in."

"Okay." I nod and take a seat in a chair again. "Fucking do it. Get this nightmare off my hands."

Breaker shoots off a text, and when he's done, he sets his phone down on his desk and leans back in his chair. "Fuck, dude, can you just listen to me next time? I might be younger than you, but I'm pretty damn smart. Sending an email to random girls in your contacts list doesn't scream *best idea ever.*"

"Yeah, well, hopefully those days are behind me."

"I'm guessing, given Kelsey's inebriated state, you weren't able to talk to her?"

"No, and then she tried on this cute seduction thing…fuck. I loved seeing her so open and wanting to try things, but I couldn't participate. I couldn't, in good conscience, fuck her. She was devastated, even cried." My stomach twists uncomfortably. "I don't think I slept more than two hours."

"Well, this is taken care of. Maybe stop by her favorite coffee place on the way home and make it up to her now. Because our brother is getting married, and we want to be there for him, mentally."

"I know." I stand and reach my fist out to my brother. He knocks it with his as I say, "Thanks for taking the lead on this. It means a lot to me."

"It's what family is for, dude, and I meant what I said last night. I'm really fucking happy for you. I know losing Dad was harder on you than Hux and me, and seeing you out there, opening yourself up to love…I'm really happy for you. Proud of you."

"Thank you." I smile at him. "Okay, fuck…I feel like a giant weight has been lifted off my shoulders. Time to go shower my girl with love. Still meeting at my place in an hour?" I ask, checking my phone.

"Yeah. Why Huxley wants us there so early is beyond me, but he has plans to spend time with his brothers before the I dos. I think basketball is on the schedule."

"I've been practicing." I point at Breaker as I head toward the door of his office. "Look out."

"I'm not even worried in the slightest. There's no way you could've improved to be able to beat me in the short amount of time since we last played."

"What little faith. See you in a bit." I tap his doorframe and then take off. I need to grab a coffee for my girl, and hopefully, I can give her one quick orgasm before I send her on her way.

CHAPTER 22
KELSEY

MY THROAT FEELS COMPLETELY DRY as I sit up in bed.

The cold empty bed.

I lean over to the nightstand and switch on the light, illuminating the dark room perfectly. I glance around but see no trace of JP. His phone isn't on his nightstand.

Did he even sleep here?

I wish I was that person who could drink a lot of champagne, black out, and not remember one thing from the night before.

Unfortunately, that's not me.

I'm the girl who usually has the hangover attached to all the regret.

And that's what I'm feeling right now. An immense amount of regret.

Regret for how I acted. What I said. For thrusting myself upon JP when clearly...well, when clearly, I was anything but attractive to him last night. And the way he shut down as if I actually repulsed him. He wouldn't even hold me last night. No wonder he's not here this morning.

I took things too far.

I flip the covers off my body and walk over to the bathroom. I look for a note, maybe a cup of coffee he left behind for me like he's done in the past.

Nothing.

Worry consumes me as I make my way down the stairs and to the kitchen.

Nothing.

Maybe he texted me.

I walk back up the stairs—grateful I don't have a headache, only a serious case of dry mouth—and when I reach the bedroom again, I check my phone for a message.

Nothing.

Once again, that ill-fated embarrassment consumes me as the worst-case scenario plays in my head.

I turned him off last night. I'm thinking that as much as he said he likes relaxed Kelsey, drunk- Kelsey doesn't appeal. *And fair enough.*

But I absolutely hate how the feeling, this...emptiness is so similar to when Edwin left that night with Genesis. And she was stunning, intelligent, and lovely. Not neurotic and uptight like I am. Let's be honest, JP chose her first, as well. Even though I felt only a tenth of what I feel for JP for Edwin, it still stung when he walked away. So, what will I feel if JP does the same?

Devastated.

But why on Huxley and Lottie's wedding day? He said that he'd been waiting for me for a long time, so it's an awful feeling knowing I've hit the expiry date of the playboy. *Is this him letting me down easy?* Shit. This just seems wrong. Or maybe...right?

What am I doing with these circular arguments?

Either way, he's not here now.

I'm not sure when he'll return, but I know one thing for certain—I can't be here.

I go to the dresser where I keep some of my things and pull out a pair of joggers. I don't bother changing my shirt. I quickly brush my teeth, toss my hair up into a ponytail, and slip on sandals.

Phone in hand, I walk down the stairs to the entryway, and just as I'm opening the door, I hear JP ask, "Where are you going?"

Frozen in place, I turn toward where his voice came from—the kitchen—and I offer him the best smile I can muster. "Uh, over to Lottie's. Bridal things." I wave at him because I'm awkward. "So, yeah, happy wedding day to everyone."

His brow pulls together. "You're just going to leave like that? No kiss goodbye?" He walks up to me with a to-go cup of coffee in his hand.

"Oh, yeah, kiss, right." I meet him halfway, stand on my toes, and then peck him on the chin. "Okay, well, see you at the altar." My eyes widen. "Not our altar, the wedding altar, the wedding that's not happening between us, but between Lottie and Huxley." I back up toward the door. "So, yeah, see you later."

"Kelsey, wait a second."

"I really have to go," I say to him. "Lottie needs help. She has, uh…a, uh, zit." I nod. "Yup, a zit. And she needs help soothing the zit before the wedding, and if anyone is the zit whisperer, I am. But it takes time to soothe a zit and we're on borrowed time."

His brows draw even closer together than before, and as I cross toward the front door, he continues to follow me. "Well, at least let me walk you across the street."

"Oh, that's okay. I don't want to trouble you."

"You're not troubling me, babe." He catches up to me, takes my hand in his, and links our fingers, the feel of his palm connected with mine nearly making the thin grasp I have on my emotions slip. He tugs me close to him and kisses the top of my head. "How did you sleep?" he asks as we make our way to Lottie and Huxley's.

"Uh…fine," I answer, feeling so awkward, so uncomfortable. There's a giant *elephant in the room* and it's sitting on our clasped hands, tugging me down.

"Just fine?"

"Yeah, fine." We cross the street, and to keep the conversation flowing so he doesn't ask me what's wrong with me, because I can feel it coming, I ask, "Excited about your plans today? I think you have basketball and some special shave session with facials at a barbershop, and I believe some sort of barbecue tasting. Seemed fancy, when Lottie was explaining it to me."

"There's a lot going on. He wanted to plan some things with us before we walk down the aisle." He holds up the coffee to me just as we make it to their front door. "I got this for you. Your favorite skinny vanilla latte."

"Oh." I take the cup. "Thank you. That was nice of you. You went out to get me coffee?"

"Nah, I was out and figured I'd stop."

Why was he out so early in the morning? *Don't even go there, Kelsey. You're not in the right frame of mind. It'll only do you more harm than good.*

"Well, thank you." Luckily, just as I go to knock on the door, Huxley appears.

"Hey," he says, looking between us, but when he meets JP's eyes, they exchange some sort of conversation, and when JP nods, Huxley clears his throat and steps aside. "Lottie is upstairs."

"Yup. Zit control," I say as I release JP's hand and attempt to squeeze by Huxley.

"Kelsey," JP says before I can get too far.

"Hmm?" I say, looking over my shoulder.

"Are you going to say bye?"

"Oh, yeah, sorry. I've got zits on the brain." I once again give him a kiss on his chin, but as I step away, he loops his arm around my waist and brings me in close to his chest. He tilts my chin up and presses his mouth to mine.

Warm.

Addictive.

An electrifying kiss that rocks me to my very core. His affection rips through me like a gentle, but comforting, hug and it causes my emotions to ramp up once again.

When he releases me, I hold it together as I back away.

But once I'm inside the house, door shut behind me, I feel the tears stream down my face.

What on earth is going on with me?

Why am I so emotional?

Because you're embarrassed. Because you finally have something that you've always wanted, and last night made you unsure of everything you knew.

Insecurities creep in and take hold of my heart.

He didn't want you.

He didn't want your body.

He didn't hold you.

He wanted nothing to do with you.

And even though he kissed me this morning, something feels off. Something doesn't feel right. The idea of losing him is making me so emotional.

Because for the first time in my life, I can honestly say I'm in love. I'm so hopelessly, and desperately, in love with a man, and I'm afraid that he very well might not love me back.

But now is not the time for that, for those worries. Lottie is getting married, which means I need to be there for her. This is her day. I need to push aside my feelings, slap on a happy face, and focus on her. And who knows—maybe she does need help with a zit.

I wipe at my cheeks, take a few deep breaths, and then walk up the stairs to her bedroom. It's time to get the bride ready for the day.

———

"Do you think people will be able to see it?" Lottie asks, looking into the mirror.

"With our concealer, no one will be the wiser," Meredith, our makeup artist, says, reassuring Lottie.

It wasn't a zit that she needed to worry about, but rather a hickey. Apparently, Huxley wanted to claim what was his one more time without a ring. And he did in spectacular fashion, right on the middle of her neck.

Unfortunately for me and my fragile state of affairs, seeing my sister with a hickey and about to get married only made me consider my current situation, which of course led to me having a mental breakdown in my sister's bathroom. When I came out with puffy eyes and Lottie asked me what was the matter, I told her I'd gotten a charley horse while on the toilet and that it nearly made me fall to the ground in writhing pain. She told me Huxley got a charley horse the other night while pumping into her and that it was so bad, it made his penis shrivel right up. I'm not sure I'll be able to look at Huxley the same after hearing that.

But I've been able to hold it together ever since, enough to feed myself, wash my body, and even engage in conversation about how excited I am for Lottie to be getting married. It's been great.

"So, you never told me how last night went. Did you cash in on your text?" Lottie asks.

Well…it *was* great.

"Uh, not really," I say, knowing I can't lie to my sister, that she'll see right through me. "Too drunk."

Keep it at that, simple.

"You weren't that drunk. Did you chicken out on me? You didn't have to do the twirl. Was it the twirl that got you?"

There was no way in hell I was even mentioning the twirl last night.

"No, it just…it wasn't happening," I say, crossing my legs.

She frowns. "What do you mean it wasn't happening?"

"I mean…he wasn't…in the mood," I draw out, hoping Meredith signed that NDA Huxley makes everyone who walks into his house sign.

"He wasn't in the mood?" Lottie asks as Meredith blots concealer on the hickey. "What do you mean?"

"I mean, he wasn't in the mood. Can we drop it? Because I feel emotional about it and I don't want to be emotional on your wedding day. It's supposed to be happy and fun, not depressing."

"Yes, but I don't want you to have to force a smile. We need to talk this out."

"Hello?" Ellie calls from the entryway. Just great..."Where are you guys?"

"Upstairs bedroom," Lottie calls out.

"Can we not talk about this with her?" I ask. "I'm really...I'm embarrassed. Last night was such a disaster, and the more I think about it, the more I just want to curl up and cry. Trust me, I'm highly emotional, and you don't want that while we're getting ready." My eyes well up.

Lottie reaches her hand out to me, and I take it. "But you're hurting, and I can't have you hurting right now. How could you have any fun today if you bottle it all up?"

Ellie comes through the door at that moment, a box of baked goods in one hand and her dress bag in the other. "Sorry I'm late, the baby was being fussy, and I hate to be that person, but I really wanted to make sure everything was okay before I left." She studies me, then Lottie, then me again, and she winces. "Oh, he told you. How are you doing?"

Told me...

Told me what?

I sit taller and so does Lottie, her protective-big-sister instincts kicking in. "Told her what?" Lottie asks.

Ellie's face drains of all color as she once again looks between us. "Uh...what was that?" She blinks a few times.

Lottie turns to Meredith and asks, "I'm so sorry, but could you give us a moment?"

"Not a problem, gives me a chance to check in with the kids."

Meredith takes off, shutting the door behind her, and Lottie spins in her seat and asks, "What are you talking about, Ellie?"

Now Ellie's wringing her hands together, chewing on the side of her lip, looking like she might possibly flee or throw up. "You know, it's not a big deal. I just—you looked upset, so I assumed something I shouldn't have assumed. Why don't we just ignore what I said and have some cronuts? I got the raspberry-filled ones."

Speaking as evenly as I can, I say, "Ellie, I'm a borderline emotional nutcase right now. I need to know what you're talking about or I might combust. Please, just tell me."

She sighs and mutters, "Me and my big mouth." She grabs her phone and starts scrolling through it while she says, "The only reason I know is because Dave told me about it and I was preparing myself for what might happen this morning. But apparently, and I don't know when, JP sent out an email to a bunch of women asking them to be his date for the wedding."

"What?" I ask.

Ellie hands me her phone. A screenshot from an email JP sent comes into view.

"What does it say?" Lottie asks.

"'Hey ladieeees. Sending a big old cock of an email because, you know...I have a big cock'..." I trail off, unable to read it anymore, so Lottie takes the phone and finishes for me.

"'So this email has to match. Here's the thing. Hux is getting married to Lulu Lemon.'" She looks up. "Hey, why is he calling me Lulu Lemon?"

"That's what you're worried about?" I ask as a tear escapes down my cheek. Ellie is quick to hand me a tissue.

"You're right. Email is more important." Lottie clears her throat. "'And they told me I need a plus-one. Looking for a willing candidate to escort me down the aisle. All expenses paid. Promises of pleasure. If interested, hit me up. I wear condoms still. K. Bye. JP.' That motherfucker!"

"Wait, he said he still wears condoms? Why would he say that?" I ask.

"Because he's looking for sex," Lottie says, handing the phone back to Ellie. "When is this email from?"

Ellie shrugs. "I don't know. I just heard it from Dave last night, and then the baby needed me."

"Does it say on the screenshot?" I ask, my throat so tight, the words strain to fall off my tongue.

Ellie looks at the phone and then shakes her head. "That was all blacked out."

I worry my lips as I draw my knees up close to my chest.

"Hello? Where are my babies?" Mom calls from downstairs.

I give a panicked look to Lottie, who then glances at Ellie. "Want me to distract her?" Ellie asks.

We both nod and, thankfully, she takes off and shuts the door behind her. When it clicks shut, I bury my head in my hands. Lottie sits next to me.

"I'm so sorry."

"Why are you sorry?" Lottie asks.

"Because this is your day and I'm ruining it."

"No, JP is ruining it. Now tell me exactly what happened last night."

I swipe at my eyes and say, "When we got back to his place, I was all about having sex and doing all the dirty things. He was really reserved and almost standoffish. I said I was going to bed naked and he suggested I wear clothes. It was—it was weird."

"That is weird."

"And then, when I threw myself at him again, he said *not tonight*, and... ugh, it was humiliating. I ended up going to bed, and when I thought he'd cuddle up against me, he didn't. I woke up this morning to an empty bed. I was humiliated and...and I don't think he thinks I'm attractive or that he wants me anymore. Right when I was about to come over here, he showed up and walked me over. He was more loving, still a little stiff. He said he was already out this morning, so he picked me up coffee, but where was he? Was he doing something with Huxley?"

"Huxley was with me all morning."

Tears cascade down my cheeks. "God, then I have no idea. But he did give me this really good kiss before I walked up here, but he hasn't texted since and…I don't know. I've never felt more desired than I am when I'm with him, but last night…last night, I felt foolish, and now this email." Panic tightens my throat. "What if he sent that while we were together?"

Lottie takes a deep breath and says, "Let's be rational about this, okay?"

I nod, even though the worst-case scenario keeps flashing through my head.

"Last night, when we were drinking, the boys were in the house talking."

"Yes, 'man things,' they said."

"Which is code for either penis problems, or something to make us think it's penis problems so we don't go sniffing around for information."

"Do you think JP was having penis problems last night? Is that why he wouldn't have sex with me? I mean, I was naked in front of him and he wasn't even hard."

Lottie shakes her head. "No, I don't think he was having penis problems, because even Huxley was irritated last night and I doubt his brother's penis problem would make him irritated. This was the kind of irritation that I always associate with work."

"So, they had a work problem last night?"

"No, I bet you they were dealing with this email. If Dave Toney knew about it last night, he would've told the boys. My guess is, someone got their hands on the email that shouldn't have and the boys were trying to take care of it."

"But when was it sent?"

"Probably before you guys were together. There's no way he sent it after. He really likes you, Kelse."

"I like to think that he does, but…there's this feeling I have, this feeling I think I've always had when getting involved with him. I'm not good enough, not up to his level. I'm not going to fulfill what he needs in life. We're so different."

"But you are exactly what each other needs, too." She grips my cheeks, forcing me to look at her. "Your insecurities are misshaping your view of JP. He's a good guy. And the more I think about it, the more I'm convinced this is the boys trying to shield us from the truth."

"The truth being...JP didn't want to take me to the wedding."

"Stop it. You don't know that."

"Then why didn't he want me last night?" I cry. "And where was he this morning? Do you think he was with someone else?"

Lottie shakes her head. "No. He'd never do that. You should know him well enough at this point to know he wouldn't do that, either."

"But...he didn't get hard. He didn't hold me. He's been so possessive of me ever since we got together, and then, all of a sudden, that just ends? Something is off."

"Maybe he was worried you'd find out."

"Because he's hiding something?"

"Or maybe because he's afraid of losing you."

I lean back on the settee and shield my eyes.

"Just text him."

"Text him what?"

"Text him anything, see what he says. Here, give me your phone."

I hand it over to her and she types away.

"What are you doing?"

"Showing you that everything is okay. I really think this is all a misunderstanding. JP is crazy about you." She types away and hits *send* before flashing me the screen.

Kelsey: Hey, how's it going over there? You guys having fun?

"See? Casual, easy. We'll see what he says."

"That's if he texts back."

My phone beeps and Lottie gives me a know-it-all look before she leans in and we read his response together.

JP: Good, just got done with breakfast. We're off to basketball with full stomachs. If I suck, I'm blaming it on the bacon. How are you, baby? Did I tell you how gorgeous you are today? If not, you are. So fucking gorgeous.

"See?" Lottie says, tossing her hand in the air. "I told you. Having been around Huxley during work crises, I'd say this is exactly what happened—someone brought up this email that JP sent who knows how long ago, they did damage control, and JP was worried about it last night. Look at that text. You're telling me he doesn't like you? You're telling me he'd rather be with someone else?"

I stare down at the text, reading it over a few times.

A part of me believes her. It all makes sense when you line it up like that, but…what about this morning? What about his rejection last night, not holding me? Even if he was worried, he'd at least hold me, right?

But I need to store that away for now. I can't worry about it. I've already ruined this morning, and I refuse to ruin the rest of the day.

Pulling out the best smile that I can, I say, "Yeah, I think you're right."

"I know I am." Lottie gives me a hug. "Do you feel better?"

"Yes." I smile even bigger, but I don't feel it inside of me. I don't feel the joy. I just feel…sad. "Want me to grab the girls?"

She shakes her head. "No, I want to grab some more drinks. I'll be right back. Need anything?"

"I'm good."

She pats my shoulder. "Text your boy back, see just how much he likes you."

When she leaves, I stare at my phone. I'm tempted to not say anything, to just ignore his response, but I don't want to be that girl. I don't want to ignore him. I don't feel great inside, but I do know I should continue talking to him.

So, I do. Even though I'm hurting, I know that it's not right to push him away.

> **Kelsey:** Thank you. I'm doing okay. Slightly dehydrated. The makeup artist is currently attempting to cover up a deep purple hickey on Lottie's neck. We're hoping the magic of makeup wins today.

I hear laughter downstairs. *Forget your troubles. Forget your feelings.* This day is for Lottie, and I need to make the best of it.

My phone beeps.

> **JP:** Hux told us. Lottie didn't seem fazed. How's that zit…?

I bite my bottom lip. God, does he know I was lying? Hopefully he doesn't. Would Hux tell them about a zit? Who knows?

> **Kelsey:** Mellowed. Shouldn't be a problem.
>
> **JP:** Looks like you're a zit whisperer, after all. Good job, babe. Oh, hey, the boys are yelling at me to get off my phone. I'll check back in. Thinking of you, babe. Can't wait to see you in your dress.
>
> **Kelsey:** Have fun.

I set down my phone, take a deep breath, and as I release the air, the door to the bedroom opens. It's time to put on my happy face.

"I do," Lottie says, her voice tight with emotion.

I don't think I've ever seen a man prouder than Huxley at this moment. His chest fills with air, his eyes sparkle with tears, and you can see the relief in his shoulders, knowing the woman standing in front of him will now carry his last name. Absolutely beautiful.

The entire ceremony has been beautiful. They timed it to begin right before sunset, so as they proceeded, the sun set against the water behind them. The location has its own beach, so there isn't a tourist or local around. The sky is beautifully dotted with puffy clouds that reflect the sun in shades of pink and purple, creating the most stunning glow.

Lottie, in a simple mermaid-style dress, steals the show, but the men in their deep blue suits are showstoppers, too. I've attempted to avoid JP's eye contact as much as I can, but it feels impossible. My eyes are like a magnet to his. When I started walking down the aisle, I looked his way and caught him catch his breath right before he wet his lips. When the ceremony began, I glanced in his direction and saw him smiling at me, his expression so intense that I wanted to walk over to him and bury my head in his chest. And now, as the minister announces to Huxley and Lottie that they're man and wife, I watch JP rock on his heels and stare me down, open promises in his eyes.

"I'd like to introduce to you for the first time to Mr. and Mrs. Huxley Cane."

Like a robot, I cheer and hand Lottie her bouquet before she and Huxley walk back up the aisle. And because Lottie wanted me to walk with JP, he's next in line. He meets me at the altar, arm extended.

Here we go.

I step up next to him, loop my arm through his, and expect to walk up the aisle, but then he leans in close to my ear, sending chills up my spine, and whispers, "You look so goddamn beautiful, Kelsey. You take my breath away."

My battered heart beats wildly as my knees go a little weak.

I love this man. I love him so much, and hearing his voice, feeling his strong body connected to mine, it almost seems like too much.

"Thank you," I whisper back as we make our way to the reception room, where Huxley is kissing Lottie, his hand possessively on her lower back, holding her tightly.

JP turns toward me and lifts my chin. Before I can say anything, his lips are on mine and his hand gently runs through the curls of my hair. "Fuck," he whispers when he pulls away. "I missed you today." He kisses my nose, my forehead, and then my lips one more time just as Breaker steps up next to us with Ellie.

"Hell, everyone is kissing. Should we?"

Ellie chuckles and says, "Only if you want Dave to cut off your balls and serve them as a delicacy for dessert."

Breaker taps his chin. "Hmm, decisions, decisions."

The wedding planner comes up to us and says, "The guests are coming, but remember, no conversations, just a quick wave, because we need the bride and groom out by the sunset to take final pictures."

The crowd walks in, everyone happy, chatting, and heading straight toward the open bar.

"You okay?" JP asks, tugging on my hand.

I smile up at him. "Yeah, just happy for Huxley and Lottie."

Not sure he buys it, because he continues to study me, but thankfully, Lottie and Huxley head back outside and we follow behind. There are only a few stragglers left on the rooftop taking some pictures.

"Just the bride and the groom right now, if everyone else would step to the side," the planner says. "And guests should head into the reception space."

Two girls taking pictures of themselves in front of the sunset offer their apologies, and as they work their way up the aisle, one of them, the one in a skintight lavender dress, makes eye contact with JP and smiles broadly. JP shifts next to me as she presses her hand to his chest and in passing, says, "Compared to this morning, you look amazing. Congrats on the new sister-in-law." She offers him a wink and then heads into the reception area.

The world around me fades to nothing.

Compared to this morning?

He was with her this morning?

My lip trembles.

My heart thunders in my chest.

And I feel like I'm going to puke.

"Kelsey," JP whispers, "it's not what you think."

Not here.

Not now.

Pictures have to be taken.

I'll deal with this later.

Push it to the side. Blacken your soul.

Don't show your emotion.

You can do this, Kelsey.

You have *to do this.*

CHAPTER 23
JP

FUCK.

That has been the word of choice for the past twenty-four hours. I've just been living in a constant state of *fuck*. If it's not one thing, it's another.

Things are strained. Kelsey might be putting on a happy face, but I now know when she's not her normal self. And right now, her smile isn't even close to reaching her eyes. Her text messages dwindled as the day went on and when I expected her to smile at me while walking down the aisle, she tore her eyes away, over and over again.

And I don't blame her. Through Huxley, I found out that the girls know about the email. When I started to call Kelsey to explain, Huxley told me that Lottie had backed me up. She'd assured him that everything was okay and that Kelsey didn't want to talk about it. So, I held back even though I didn't want to.

But now we're here, together, and I know she's putting on a show. I can fucking feel it. I feel her slipping away, and if it were under any other circumstances, I'd pull her to the side to explain everything to her, but unfortunately, now is not the time.

And just to make things worse, fucking Jill had to go and say, *"Compared to this morning, you look amazing."* Considering I wasn't at my house when Kelsey woke up this morning, this looks bad. Really bad.

It looks like I fucking slept with the girl, after I wouldn't sleep with my own girlfriend the night before. And from the stiff set in Kelsey's shoulders, I'm thinking that's exactly what's going through her mind.

I know her from our lawyer's office. She's Taylor's secretary, so she was privy to the whole extortion fiasco. I saw Jill at the coffee shop this morning. And she was right, I'm looking better than this morning because I thought the nightmare was over.

Now…not so much.

Gripping Kelsey's arm, I lean close to her ear and ask, "Can I speak with you?"

"Not now," she says through clenched teeth.

"I need to explain."

Her eyes flash to mine. "Not. Now."

And then she pulls away as the wedding planner calls her to take a picture with Lottie, Huxley, her mom, and Jeff. My gut churns as I watch her put on a happy face and smile with her family. I see the tight grip she has on her bouquet, as if it's the only part of her that can show any sort of emotion, and when they're done with the picture, she doesn't come stand next to me. She stays near Lottie, helping with her dress and assisting the photographer and wedding planner. Some might think she's being the dutiful maid of honor, but I know she's avoiding me.

After an hour of torturous pictures, we're lined up at the entrance to the adjoining rooftop where everyone is waiting, and we wait to be announced.

Kelsey's shoulder bumps into mine as we wait and I attempt to take her hand in mine, but she doesn't allow it. It's not until we're walking out onto the rooftop that she briefly holds my hand up to the sky before dropping it at her side. Then she goes straight to our assigned seats and sits. I take my seat next to her and drape my arm over the back of her chair while Lottie and Huxley dance to an acoustic version of Fleetwood Mac's "Dreams."

"Baby, I need you to listen to me," I say quietly so only she can hear me. "Jill is the name of the girl who came up to me, she works for Taylor. She saw me this morning at the coffee shop. She was grabbing bagels and coffee for her team. I know it looks bad, but I need you to know, what you're thinking about what she said isn't even close to the truth."

She keeps her eyes trained on the happy couple. She doesn't acknowledge me, doesn't even flinch. I know she heard me because the smallest tear rolls down her cheek before she swipes it away.

"Kelsey, please tell me you believe me."

She sniffs and brings her handkerchief to her eyes before saying, "Yes."

"Do you really?"

Still watching Huxley and Lottie, she replies, "I have to, right?"

"No," I answer, concerned by the cold tone in her voice. "You don't. You can talk about it; you can tell me how you're feeling."

"The happy couple would like to invite everyone to join them on the dance floor as they finish dancing to their first song," the DJ says.

Kelsey stands and I follow her closely, but when she doesn't stop at the dance floor and keeps moving through the crowd, I catch up to her quickly. She weaves past a few tables, down the stairs, and into the private rooms below, straight into the bride's suite.

I shut the door behind me, and when I turn around, I see her shaking her hands and pacing the room as she takes deep breaths. "Don't break down. Don't break down," she says over and over again.

"Kelsey, talk to me, baby."

She pauses, and with deflated shoulders, she says, "I—" Her voice catches. "I don't…I don't know what's happening." When she looks up, tears fall down her cheeks, cascading in a steady flow. "I was so happy last night. I was…I was going to tell you I love you, for fuck's sake."

She what? Fuck…why did she say that in the past tense?

"But then, it was as if I was too happy and something was bound to happen. That's what I kept saying. It was too good to be true, all of it. And I was right."

"No, you weren't," I say. "It wasn't too good to be true."

She shakes her head. "No, it was. Because here I thought that we—that we were in a good place, but we weren't. Do you realize how much courage it took me to ask you to do those naughty things? That's not me, JP. That's not the person I am, and then to be standing in front of you, completely naked, only for you to turn me down…" She chokes up. "It broke a piece of me."

"Baby, it's not that I didn't want you. I always want you."

"Not last night. And when I thought that maybe it was just because I was drunk, that maybe I turned you off, you didn't even hold me to reassure me. You were cold. Distant. Do you know the kind of damage that does to a woman? You can't do that, JP. You can't fucking do that."

Fuck.

I step toward her, but she holds up her hand. "Don't. Please don't touch me, because I know if you do, I won't be able to say what I want to say. I'll just want to curl into you and wish that none of this happened. But it did happen. And then…then I hear about this email you sent to a bunch of women."

"Before we were together," I say quickly. "I was hurting so fucking bad for you. I wrote it that night I got wasted. I didn't even know I did it, which I know sounds terrible, but it was after you went out with Derek and I…I didn't know how to handle it. It meant nothing."

"That's what Lottie believed to have happened and I believe you, I truly do, but it only added to the pain I was feeling, the sadness. It took everything in me to ignore the fact that you didn't want me, that you didn't wake up with me, that you were reaching out to other women, but that Jill girl…"

"I told you—"

"Where were you this morning?"

"With Breaker," I say. "He called me at five." I tug on my hair. "Fuck, I wanted to tell you this last night, but you were drunk and I didn't think it would go over well. An online gossip website had the email submitted to them, they were going to publish it, and the article wasn't fucking good. So, we spent last night and this morning making sure it went away. And we did, but I had to rush over to Breaker's this morning for some negotiations. After that, I grabbed your favorite coffee, and that's when I saw Jill. I was hoping you'd still be asleep by the time I got home, but because I've had shit luck the past twenty-four hours, you were awake. I swear, Kelsey, this has just been a complete shitshow that I wanted to tell you about. You have to know I wouldn't cheat on you, that I...fuck, that I love—"

"Don't." She holds up her hand again. "Please don't say that. Those words aren't meant to save a relationship, they're meant to fortify it. Don't say it to make me feel better."

"But it's how I feel. You have to know that."

She wipes at her eyes and turns away from me.

"Kelsey, please."

Blotting at her eyes, she says, "I believe you, JP. I really do."

Why do I feel like there's a *but* behind that statement?

When she lowers her handkerchief, she looks me in the eyes and says, "I just need a second. Okay? My emotions are super heightened right now, and I don't want to say something I'm going to regret. Can we just go back out there and celebrate our siblings getting married?"

"If that's what you want," I say.

She sucks in a sharp breath and says, "That's what I want."

"Okay." I walk up to her and take her hand, but she gently tugs it away.

"No," she says. "Let's celebrate...separately."

Panic clogs my throat as I choke out, "Wh-what do you mean? Are you breaking up with me?"

"I don't know what I'm doing, JP. I just need some space right now."

"Please don't do this, Kelsey." Everything I've wanted is crumbling in front of me. "Don't distance yourself from me. I need you, baby. Don't you see that? I'd never do anything to hurt you. Last night was…fuck, I was trying to protect you. I was trying—"

She presses her hand to my chest. "Please, JP, just give me some time. There's a full-on insecurity battle raging in my head right now, and I need to tackle that first before I do anything else."

"You have nothing to be insecure about."

"That's where you're wrong. For as long as I can remember, I've been looking for the right person to complete me. But no one would look my way, and if they did, it never lasted. I've been unlucky at love, and that's damaging. It makes me think, *What's wrong with me? Why doesn't anyone want to be with me?* I've wondered that for so long."

"Baby, I'm telling you, I see you. I want to be with you."

"Yes, but last night, you didn't. That's where I'm struggling, because in my mind, no matter what you're going through in life, your partner in life should be there, by your side, through thick and thin. You…you left me out in the cold last night, naked and shamed. I understand that wasn't your intention, but given my past insecurities, I'm trying to mentally deal with the rejection. So, please, just give me that time."

Fuck.

I want to tell her I love her.

That I've never been happier than when she's in my arms.

That I don't want to go another day without making her mine.

But from the distant look in her eyes, I know my words will mean nothing right now.

Absolutely nothing.

So, I do the one thing I don't want to fucking do, I take a step back and pull on the back of my neck as I say, "Okay, take your time. But just know, whenever you're ready, I'll be here, waiting for you. I'm not going anywhere, Kelsey. You can push me away as much as you want, but I'll keep coming back."

And with that, she slips out of the room and back to the reception.

Needing a goddamn moment, I take a seat on one of the couches in the room and rest my elbows on my knees before driving my hands through my hair.

Fuck…

"How did it go?" Breaker asks as he joins me at the bar. I have a water in my hand, not bothering with drowning my sorrows, but staying close to the alcohol in case I change my mind.

"How did what go?" I snap at him, keeping my voice low. "Oh, you mean my conversation with Kelsey? Fucking great, can't you tell? We're happily in love as we speak."

"I'm sensing a heavy dose of sarcasm."

"No shit, how could you even tell?"

"Well, for one thing, you're sporting one of the most intense scowls I've ever seen. The wedding planner actually asked me if I had the magic to fix your face. Secondly, Kelsey, from what I've seen, has avoided you all night. Which, you know, seems suspicious since you two were all over one another at the rehearsal party last night, before the whole email thing went down. So, from that evidence, I'm pretty sure it's safe to conclude that you're being sarcastic."

I bring my glass to my lips and stare at the dance floor, where Kelsey is dancing with Lottie and their mom to "Fireball" by Pitbull. "I hate you, you know that?"

"Why do you hate me? I'm pretty sure I helped save your ass this morning."

"Yeah, what great that did. She still won't fucking talk to me."

"Seems like a 'you' issue."

Slowly, I turn my head to face him. He awkwardly smiles and shrugs. "Not the right thing to say?"

"Not even a little."

"Maybe I should work on my people skills."

"Maybe you should just leave me the fuck alone."

"Why is the wedding planner sending me over here to tell you to fix your face?" Huxley asks in a whisper as he walks up to us.

"Jesus, tell the wedding planner to fix her own face and leave me the fuck alone."

"Need I remind you it's my wedding day?" Huxley asks in a tone so low, that I barely hear him.

"Is it?" I ask. "Huh, is that why we're in these suits? Well, fuck, got to tell you, man, the shrimp was fucking terrible. Should've taste tested."

I can feel the wrath of Huxley ready to explode, but before it can, Breaker pushes against my chest, moving me away, and calls over his shoulder, "I'll take care of it."

"Aren't you a sweetheart?" I say as he ushers me to a table at the far back. We both take a seat. "What are you going to say to me? Offer some lecture? Guess what? I don't need to hear it from my little brother, who clearly has no idea what it's like to fall in love."

"I'm not going to lecture you. I just want to ask you how you are."

"Not good, man, isn't that obvious?"

"It is. What can I do to help? Want me to talk to her? I can tell her everything that happened, back you up."

I shake my head as I slouch in my chair. "No, she fucking believes it all."

"Then what's the problem?" he asks.

"The problem is, in my sheer panic last night, I fucked up. She was vulnerable, and I was too caught up in my own head, worried I was going to lose her. I didn't give her the comfort *she* needed."

"What are you talking about?"

I smooth my hands over my pant legs and say, "Kelsey has insecurities about being lovable. I keep telling her it's because she hasn't found the right guy, but I don't think that translates in her head. She believes it has to do with her. Last night, she was looking for that reassurance, but like a fucking moron, I didn't give her what she needed. I didn't see it then, but now that I played it over in my head, I realize that I'm the biggest fucking idiot. I inadvertently played into those insecurities. And it makes me fucking sick."

"Shit…" Breaker rests one of his arms on the table as he looks out at the dance floor with me. "What are you going to do?"

"She asked for time, so I'm going to give it to her."

"Are you broken up?"

"Not sure. Feels like it, though, and I only have myself to blame."

"Don't text her, she wants some space. Texting her will only irritate her," I say to myself as I pace the length of my kitchen island the day after the wedding. "Do not text her. DO NOT."

I stare down at my phone on my marble countertop.

DON'T!

My hand itches to grab the phone, my heart making the decision.

And before I can stop myself, I grab my phone and press *send* on the text I've already composed.

> **JP:** Good morning, baby. I hope you got home all right last night. I know you want space and I'm going to give you what you want, but I need you to know that I'm still thinking about you, every goddamn second. I sent over a morning-after basket with a few things to help you recover from last night. I'm here for you.

I curl my lips over my teeth, staring at the text, reading it over and over again. When it's marked as read with no response, I inwardly cringe, hating myself.

Should've listened to your goddamn brain.

JP: Still giving you space, but just wanted to tell you that I miss
you. I miss your warm hugs, your soft lips, the way you make
me feel when you're around. I miss everything about you, baby.

JP: Also, I just found out Kazoo the pigeon was adopted and I
didn't know how to tell you. I feel like maybe I played a small
part in him finding a good home. I hope they treat him well.

JP: I asked for his new home address and the shelter told me
that information was private. Understandable, but I really just
wanted to send him a few things, you know? I'm going to miss
looking at his picture on the website.

JP: Anyway, just had to tell you that. Miss you, babe.

JP: I haven't seen any new podcast episodes. I was hoping to
listen to your voice this morning on my run, so I just replayed
an old one. Have I ever told you what a great host you are?
You're really funny, you ask great questions, and I can truly
feel how passionate you are about romance. It's one of the
reasons why I really like you—your love for love.

JP: I shouldn't be texting you, I know, but I had to tell you that.
Okay, bye, baby.

JP: That pool float you ordered for my pool, the giant pigeon, it
came in. I laughed for a solid ten minutes, blew it up, and it's
where I am now, floating naked on the pigeon. I'd send you
a picture, but I shouldn't even be contacting you. Made me

laugh, and made me miss you more. I wish you were floating on it with me.

JP: I'm here, waiting for when you're ready to talk.

———————

JP: Fuck…I just miss you, Kelsey.

JP: I miss you so fucking much.

JP: Call me when you're ready.

———————

The front door to my house opens and shuts, the sound echoing through the emptiness of my dark house.

"Dude, I know you're in here," Breaker says. "Are you going to make me follow the scent of your unwashed body, or are you going to help a guy out and at least groan so I know where you are?"

"In here," I say somberly from where I'm spread across the couch in my living room.

I'm not prepared for the blast of ungodly light that fills the dark room when he flips on the switch to the overhead lights.

I cover my eyes with my forearm and mutter, "Fuck…you."

"Jesus Christ," Breaker says from the entrance of the living room. "Have you fucking moved from the couch in the last week?"

"Yes." I roll over on the couch so my stomach is pressed against the cushions. I bury my head into a throw pillow and mutter against the fabric, "I've gotten up to pee."

"Shocking. I thought you'd have peed in one of the many bottles of… what is this?" From the corner of my eye, I see him pick up an empty bottle. "Is this root beer?"

"All natural, made with cane sugar."

"Is it good?"

"No." I shake my head. "But I purchased six cases of it so I've been drinking them."

"Why the hell would you buy that much?"

"Wanted the feel of clutching a bottle, but without the alcohol. There's something so...poetic about clutching a bottle when dealing with heartache."

Breaker stands over me, bottle dangling from his fingers. "You know, bro, I think you've hit rock bottom."

I turn again, now looking up toward the ceiling. I pinch my brow and say, "That would be an accurate description."

"Have you made any donations lately? I know that's your MO when you're sad."

I slowly swallow and say, "The pigeon shelter I've been supporting is now renaming its building the JP Cane Pigeon Rescue. The JPCPR. Has a fucking great ring to it. There's some press going out next week about it. They asked if I'd show up for the dedication of the new name, and do you know how pathetic I am?"

"Tell me." Breaker takes a seat on the coffee table in front of me.

"I told them I'd be honored, but only on one condition." I sit up. "I asked that Kazoo be invited so I could meet him."

"Dude—"

"That's not the worst of it." I look my brother dead in the eyes and say, "I commissioned some lady on Etsy to make a matching shirt and bow tie set, one that would fit me and one that would fit a pigeon...out of Kazoo fabric."

"Oh fuck...JP."

"I know." I slowly nod my head. "I fucking know. Rock bottom. But the only thing that's getting me to keep moving forward is the idea that I could take a picture with Kazoo in our matching shirts. I actually giggled at one point thinking about it."

"Giggled?" Breaker's eyes widen. "Come on, man. We need to get you up, showered, back to the office, back to a routine."

"I paid extra for a rush fee. I also looked into classes on how to communicate with the pigeons. You can train them to deliver messages. I was thinking about writing a love letter to Kelsey and having a pigeon deliver it to her. Isn't that romantic?"

Breaker stares blankly at me. "No, man. No, it's not. It's fucking creepy. You realize pigeons are better known as the rats of the sky?"

I pop off the couch so fast, Breaker falls back on the coffee table. "You know, that's exactly what an uneducated nitwit would say. Did you know that pigeons are actually intelligent and complex? They're one of the only animals on the planet to pass the mirror test. Meaning, you stick a mirror in front of them and they fucking know they're looking at their reflection. Are rats passing that test? No, they're just sitting there, in creepy holes, gnawing at their nuts until they can find something better to chew on."

"Okay, sorry I mentioned it."

"Also, there's very little scientific evidence that pigeons carry diseases. And contrary to what's blasted all over the media, pigeons are quite clean animals."

"I'm not sure pigeons are being blasted on the media."

"And you know what?" Hands on my hips, irritation roaring through me, I say, "Pigeons mate for life. They meet their one and only, and they're set." My voice grows scratchy as I think about Kelsey. "They don't need to second-guess their decision. They just...know."

"JP, are you okay?"

I sniff. "They understand that the feathered beauty in front of them is for them and them alone." I wipe at my nose. "They mate, they have two chicks, and they spend the rest of their years, feather in feather, like hand in hand, flying off into the sunset."

"I think we need to get you out of here."

I swipe at my eyes. "That's what I need to do. I need to ask Kelsey to be my pigeon." Frantically, I look around for my phone. "I need to text her."

Breaker grips my arm. "That's not a good idea. She won't understand."

"Then I'll explain it to her," I say, feeling my expression go slightly crazy. "I'll send her a video, telling her all about pigeon mating rituals."

"Dude, really bad idea, especially with the way you look right now."

"I'll show her a video. I found this really great one about how pigeons communicate. It made me think of her, especially since one of the pigeons it focused on had some gold feathers on its neck. It reminded me of Kelsey's eyes. In my head, I named it Kelsey and—"

Thwap.

I'm knocked back on the couch, pain ricocheting through my face as I stare up at Breaker, who's shaking out his hand. I slowly process the warm spot on my cheek where I was struck.

"You hit me," I say, stating the obvious.

"I'm not even sorry. It had to be done." He lets out a deep breath. "Look around you. You're drowning yourself in sugar cane root beer that I can only assume tastes like a foot, you're attempting to twin with a goddamn pigeon you've never met, and you're naming fictional pigeons Kelsey. This isn't just rock bottom, this is crossing a line, and to hell if I'm going to sit back and watch. Now get the fuck up, go take a goddamn shower, and get your shit together, because there's no way in hell Kelsey is going to want to talk to a guy who's attempting to crack the code on pigeon communication so he can tell her how much he loves her. Newsflash—that's not romantic."

I blink a few times, and even though I've settled into the comfort of my own—if you will—nest, I realize that he's right. Who knows if Kelsey will come back, or when…but if she does, she can't find me like this. No fucking way.

I scrub my hand over my face and say, "Fuck, I'm embarrassed."

"You should be. Fuck. Now go get clean. I'm ordering dinner, and you're going to work tomorrow."

"You're right." I stand again and head toward the stairs. "You're right, I really need to get back to work, get back into the swing of things. Who knows, maybe this was the wake-up call I needed."

I.

Want.

To.

Die.

This was a horrible idea. Really fucking horrible.

I miss the comfort of my couch.

I miss the dank taste of the sugar cane root beer.

And I miss the sweet sound of pigeons cooing.

Nothing seems more appealing to me at this moment, but instead, I'm sitting at a conference table, across from Kelsey—who got a fucking haircut and looks sexier than ever with her shoulder-length curled hair—listening to her give me an update on the Angelica project.

When I found out I had a meeting with her, I rushed out of my office, ran over to Breaker's, and sank down to the ground, wrapping my hands and arms around his leg, telling him I wasn't leaving him alone until he agreed to attend the meeting with me.

He was on a video call.

With our team in New York.

He was less than pleased.

But it was a quick *yes* from him so he could shake me off his leg.

But even with him at my side, I still feel the air slowly seeping from my lungs, making it increasingly harder to breathe with every second that goes by.

And Kelsey, she looks so calm, collected, not an ounce of awkwardness from her—and that's concerning.

Very fucking concerning.

Because that can only mean one thing: she doesn't care anymore. She doesn't care about us. She's given up. If she cared, she'd be stumbling over her sentences, dropping her papers, maybe even missaying some words. You know, like…uh…*banana* instead of *bamboo*. That makes zero sense, but in this frantic state, I can't think of anything that would portray what I'm trying to say. But you get it, right?

As the Righteous Brothers would say…she's lost that lovin' feelin'.

Fuck, I should've sent the pigeon message.

"I think that's all I have for you guys. Do you have any questions?" Kelsey asks as she tucks a curl behind her ear.

Yes. I have a few questions.

Why haven't you texted me?

Have you thought about me at all?

Do you miss me like I miss you?

Have you really lost that lovin' feelin'?

"Uh, I think we're good," Breaker says. "Unless, JP, you have anything?" Kelsey's eyes land on mine as she patiently waits.

Do you love me?

Do you want to move in with me?

Do you want to marry me?

Do you want to be my pigeon?

Breaker kicks me under the table, startling me to answer. "Uh, no, nothing. Great, uh, great work on all the projects and stuff. Really liked the, uh, the storage."

Breaker groans next to me and then says, "Keep us updated on the cost of the engineered hardwood flooring."

"I will." She smiles. "Thanks." She gathers her things, stands, and walks out of the conference room. When the door shuts, I collapse on the table.

"She doesn't fucking miss me. Cold as stone. She didn't even flinch when she heard my voice."

Breaker is silent for a moment before saying, "Yeah, I actually expected her to be a little more nervous. Or at least show some feelings."

"Right?" I bury my head in my hands. "Fuck. It's over, isn't it? I lost her."

"I don't think you lost her. I just think…I think she's shielding herself. And frankly, you're a goddamn mess right now. Maybe she's nervous to approach you."

"I'm nervous to approach a mirror in fear of what I might see; of course she's not going to want to come near me."

"Then fix it, man. She liked you because you're charismatic, charming, and a good time. Right now, you're just a ball of anxiety who's one loaf of bread away from becoming a pigeon man. Show her the man she fell for. Show her the man she's meant to be with."

Meant to be…

I lift my head as an idea forms. "What did you just say?"

Looking confused, he says, "Show her the man she's meant to be with."

I grip Breaker's face, bring him into mine, and kiss him right on the lips. He swats me away and wipes at his mouth as I say, "You're so fucking smart. Why didn't I think of that?" I bolt out of my chair and lift my fist to the sky. "I'm getting her back… Watch this."

CHAPTER 24
KELSEY

I CHEW ON MY NAIL as I listen to the phone ring three times and then hear, "Hey, sis."

"I'm so sorry I'm calling you on your honeymoon, but I really need to talk to you."

"Don't apologize, I told you to call whenever you want. Granted, I didn't think that was going to be every day, but you know I'm here for you."

"I know, I'm sorry, but...I got my hair cut as you said."

"Yes, I know, you showed me a picture. You like it?"

"I do." I pace my office, knowing JP is just around the corner. "And I feel really sexy with the short look, and I put on that new lingerie you made me buy, and the green dress."

"With the sleeves?"

"Yes."

"So, you're feeling better? More confident?"

"I was...and I swore I wasn't going to call you, but then JP showed up at work yesterday, and he looked... God, Lottie, I feel like everything I've been working on this past week vanished the moment I saw him, and I was taken right back to that night. And then I had a meeting with him. Thankfully, Breaker joined us. I held it together, and I'm actually really proud of myself for acting professionally during the entire meeting. But now that it's over, my palms are sweating, and I feel this urgent need to cry, but no tears are falling."

"Seeing him didn't make you miss him more?"

"Of course it did. I've missed him every minute of every day. And his text messages have made it even worse. I just felt so embarrassed when I looked him in the eyes."

"I can understand that. You're still carrying around the burden of what happened that night."

"I am, but I can't help but wonder if I'm being ridiculous."

"Your feelings are completely valid. No one can dictate if you're being ridiculous or not, because they're not in your head. They can't understand your emotions like you can. With that being said, do you think you're being ridiculous?"

"Objectively, as an outsider looking in, all I can think about is how there's this man, this wonderfully loving man, who wants nothing more than to be with me. Being in the middle of it, I guess, I just feel a debilitating embarrassment, and I don't know how to cross that line with him again, you know?"

"Does that mean you want him back?"

"I…"

Knock. Knock.

I glance up at the door, and there, standing in the doorway, hands tucked into his pockets, looking more handsome than ever, is JP.

"Uh, Lottie, I have to go."

"Oh God, is he there?"

"Yup. Talk to you later."

I hang up before she can respond. Nervously, I set my phone down and push my hair behind my ear. He doesn't step into my office, but rather leans against the doorjamb, looking like a model from *GQ*, with his hair curling over his forehead and his dark scruff lining his jaw.

"Hello," I say, unsure of what else to say. "Is there, uh, something you need?"

"Hey, can I get your opinion?"

"Uh…sure," I say. We haven't talked in over a week, but he wants my opinion on something, that's not weird at all.

"This suit, do you think I can pull it off?"

Utterly confused, I take in the simple black suit with a matching black button-up and can't see how it's different from anything else he's worn. But given that he wants my opinion, I take some extra time to observe the way his pants cling tightly to his thighs, showing off his strong legs. I've been between those legs. I've seen them flex while I have his penis in my mouth.

Immediately, my cheeks flush from the thought, so I divert my eyes to his chest, to the lapel, and I consider the many times I've pushed his suit jacket off his shoulders, and how that one time, I wore nothing but his suit jacket.

More of a flush.

Okay, I think that's enough.

When my eyes meet his again, a satisfied smile plays on his lips.

"Uh, the suit looks good." I swallow. "You can pull it off. Do you, uh, do you have some sort of meeting or"—gulp—"a date?"

"Nah." He pushes off the doorjamb. "Just wanted to see your eyes eat me up again." He winks and then takes off without another word.

Wait…what?

That was it?

That's all he wanted?

That…that's something the old JP would've done, the one who used to tell me men and women who work together can't be friends.

Why would he do that?

Consider me now more confused than ever.

———

"Miss Gardner, please stay back so I can talk to you," JP says, sitting at the head of the conference table, hands steepled together.

The rest of the construction team makes their way out of the conference room, and when the door shuts, he leans forward and asks, "Care to explain?" He lifts a knowing brow at me.

"Uh…" I look around. "Care to explain what?"

"You really don't know?"

"I have no idea what you're talking about," I answer, clutching my notepad to my chest.

"It was thirty-three times."

What?

I'm not sure I can handle this right now. When I came in this morning, I wasn't prepared for another meeting with JP. In hindsight, what I really wasn't prepared for was to be so distracted by the smell of his cologne. I even forgot what we were talking about a few times. I swear, it was as if he sprayed my chair, and my chair alone, because it consumed me.

"What was thirty-three times?" I ask him.

"The number of times I caught you checking me out." He rises from his chair and buttons his suit jacket. "Now, I'm letting you off the hook this time, but next time you want to spend an hour-long meeting checking me out, please schedule something on your own time."

Is he kidding me right now? I did not look at him that many times.

"I did not look at you that much."

He's at my side now, that cockiness front and center. "As a matter of fact, you did."

I did not. Growing irritated, I say, "Well…if I did, that means you were looking at me thirty-three times."

"Ah, that's where you're wrong, Miss Gardner. I didn't look at you thirty-three times, I looked at you far more times, fifty-four to be exact, almost every minute." He wets his lips.

"Okay, well…then, why don't you, uh, make an appointment to stare next time?" I say in a shaky, not very confident voice.

"Maybe I will. Have a good day."

He retreats back to his office, his head buried in his phone. By the time I reach my office, there's a calendar request in my inbox. When I open it up, it's from JP.

INVITE: Staring meeting with JP CANE. 10:00 a.m.–11:00 a.m.

Bring nothing.
Wear nothing.

My cheeks heat up once again as the smallest of smiles pulls at the corner of my lips. I reply to the request with one click on the *decline* button.

TO: Kelsey Gardner
FROM: JP Cane
SUBJECT: Declined Invite Request

Dear Miss Gardner,

I see that you've declined my invite to stare at each other for an hour for the fourth time. I can't possibly see how your schedule is so tight that you can't accept my request. May I ask why you continue to reject this invitation that was born through your very own staring? Please respond in a timely manner.

Thank you,
JP Cane

Smiling like an absolute fool, I consider deleting the email, but then…I wonder how fun it might be to actually respond back. The last few days have been unexpected. Somehow, JP has created this feeling of what it used to be like between us, and I've had one stark and very large realization—I've missed this. *Us*. And even though I feel awkward…weird, I don't think I can ignore him. So, I write him back.

TO: JP Cane
FROM: Kelsey Gardner
SUBJECT: RE: Declined Invite Request

Dear Mr. Cane,

Your request has been denied four times because I fail to see how staring at each other can offer any productivity or progress to Cane Enterprises. If you can provide me with a detailed list as to how it might benefit the company, I'd be apt to reconsider.

Thank you,
Kelsey

TO: Kelsey Gardner
FROM: JP Cane
SUBJECT: RE: Declined Invite Request

Dear Miss Gardner,

I appreciate your loyalty to the company and wanting to further the success of our multibillion-dollar enterprise. As to the benefit a one-hour staring contest could provide the company,

I'd like to bring to your attention the following chart below. Please email if you have any questions.

Staring -> forced proximity -> makes boss happy.

Thank you,
JP

TO: JP Cane
FROM: Kelsey Gardner
SUBJECT: RE: Declined Invite Request

Dear Mr. Cane,

I'm flattered by your response, but I must remind you, your request is purely personal, and as I once was told, men and women can't be friends in the workplace because of the obvious attraction. I'm afraid your request borders on inappropriate behavior, something I don't partake in. Unfortunately, your request has been once again denied.

Thank you,
Kelsey

TO: Kelsey Gardner
FROM: JP Cane
SUBJECT: RE: Declined Invite Request

Dear Miss Gardner,

Your dedication to maintaining your position as a superior role model should be applauded. Perhaps we should offer you a raise…or possibly, you can give me a raise…

Wiggles eyebrows

Yours,
Jonah

I squeeze my eyes shut and inwardly squeal from seeing his name at the bottom of his email. His name that he seems to only use with me. I'm reminded of the time I found out what his real name was, after one of our outings in San Francisco. He was walking away from my room, a smirk on his handsome face as he told me. I remember the exact feeling that washed over me at that moment, too, a connection much deeper than surface level, a connection that made me feel as if I was a special part of his life.

That feeling has been resurrected. Every email response is spreading warmth through my veins, and my feelings of embarrassment are slowly slipping away into nothing.

TO: JP Cane
FROM: Kelsey Gardner
SUBJECT: RE: Declined Invite Request

Dear Mr. Cane,

You couldn't possibly be alluding to an erection, could you? I can't fathom you are, being how inappropriate that would be. I suggest you consider very carefully your next response.

Yours,
Kelsey

My stomach somersaults as I press *send*. It's the first time since the wedding that I've shown any inkling that I still have feelings for him, that I'm hoping he's still waiting for me.

It's been a difficult two weeks, attempting to sort through my feelings, missing JP, and trying to remember who the hell I am. Trying to see my worth. Attempting to convince myself that I'm beautiful, I'm wanted, I'm needed. And JP, in his small way, has helped that progress.

Knock. Knock.

I glance up to see JP once again standing in my doorway, sans his suit coat. My eyes fall to his button-up shirt and how it stretches across his firm chest. His sleeves are rolled up to his elbows and he's wearing that classic smirk of his, the smirk that has been stuck in my dreams for the last few nights.

Sitting tall, I ask, "Can I help you, Mr. Cane?"

He rubs his hands together. "You can. I was hoping to discuss some business with you."

"Would you like to take a seat?"

He shakes his head. "No, this would be better discussed over dinner."

My brow raises. "Is this a business dinner?"

"Yes."

I don't believe him, but I go with it anyway. "Okay, shall I pencil you in for next week?"

"Tonight. My place. Seven o'clock."

"I'm afraid I'm not comfortable with attending a business meeting at your place of residence."

"I understand your concern, but I can assure you, no one will be there, so there's no need to be uncomfortable, Miss Gardner. You can just be yourself." He stands tall. "See you tonight."

Without waiting for a response, he walks away.

Unsure of what to do, I pick up my phone and text Lottie.

Kelsey: Oh God, he asked me to dinner, at his place. He's expecting me there. What do I do?

Thankfully, she answers. Huxley is going to murder me when he gets home, I can feel it.

Lottie: What do you mean, what do you do? You go!

Kelsey: What if…what if he wants to get back together, or worse, what if he doesn't?

Lottie: If there are two things I know for certain in my life, it's that Huxley Cane was meant to be the man of my life…and JP Cane is meant to be yours. He loves you, desperately. Take the leap, the leap you've always wanted to take. You've told me over and over again that love is a roller coaster. You're on the roller coaster, so enjoy it.

Kelsey: I think I might be ready, but I'm scared.

Lottie: Good, if you weren't then I'd be concerned. You know, there's something I never told you, something I feel like you should know. That night, when the boys were covering up that email, it wasn't the way JP was portrayed in the article that made him put up the money to extract the article; it was what they said about you.

Kelsey: What did they say about me?

Lottie: Huxley told me the article not only painted JP in a horrible light with the borderline harassment email, but they said you were using JP to get ahead with your company. Huxley said JP lost it, and he said JP did everything in his power to make sure your company wasn't dragged through the mud because he understands how hard you worked to get to where you are.

Kelsey: He did that?

Lottie: Yes, and one of the main reasons he was so off that night was because he was frantic about what was going to happen. He thought he was going to lose you. He loves you, sis. Don't let one bad moment eclipse the magic you two share. Okay? Go to dinner. Let yourself love. I promise you won't regret it.

I stand at his front door, nervously waiting for him to open it. I wasn't sure what to wear to dinner tonight. I considered a dress but felt that was too formal. Then a pantsuit, and knew that was way too…business-y, so I settled on a black pair of leather leggings and a simple off-the-shoulder red shirt and high heels. Simple, but I also have the confidence to walk through his door and not feel self-conscious.

After what feels like forever, the door opens and JP appears on the other side, wearing a pair of jeans, no socks, and a white T-shirt. His hair is wet and he looks like he's fresh from the shower.

He scans me up and down, a hungry look in his eyes when they land on my face again. "Miss Gardner," he says, a slight crack in his voice. "Glad you could make it."

Nervously smiling, I say, "I had to move some things around. Glad I could make it work."

He steps aside, and I walk into his entryway, immediately feeling as though I'm returning home. I've had so many beautiful memories within these dark walls. He shuts the door and gestures toward his backyard. The sliding glass doors are parted and the yard is lit up in shades of purple. I feel my breath catch as I approach, the entire scene familiar, as if it was plucked straight from a movie.

"Mr. Cane," I say as I cross over into the backyard, taking it all in. The pool lights are a shade of lavender, the lights overhead are a mellow shade of gold, and the lights along the base of the palm trees are a darker purple. On the table is a pitcher of what looks to be lemonade and two glasses, which makes me smile. Next to it is…oh God, I'd know that cake anywhere. Honey cake. "This, uh, this doesn't feel very business-y to me."

He comes up to me, pressing his hand to my lower back, and he leans in and whispers, "Good."

Then he takes my hand, leads me over to my chair, and sits me down. He takes a seat across from me. He sets his phone between us, and then reaches for a file folder next to the cake and slides it in front of him.

"I appreciate you rearranging your schedule and coming tonight. What I need to go over with you is highly classified, so I'd appreciate your discretion."

Beyond confused, I nod, even though I have no idea what he has planned. "Of course."

He flips open the file folder and says, "I'm going to hand you a script, and I'm going to need you to read it word for word while I record."

What on earth is he doing?

"Um…okay."

He motions to the lemonade. "Do you need a drink to clear your throat first?"

"No, I'm good."

He takes a paper out of the folder and says, "Okay, it's important that you don't read ahead. Can you handle that?"

"I can."

"Good. Let me get us set up here." He unlocks his phone, goes to the recording app, and then hits the record button before handing me a piece of paper.

My eyes fall to the first sentence and I quickly look back up at him. This consuming, fantasy-filled feeling flips my heart in circles.

"JP…"

"Miss Gardner, remember what I said, read the script, and no looking ahead." He then winks at me, and I nearly cry right there.

Because…oh God…

Clearing my throat, I read what's written. *"'Meant to Be Podcast. Jonah and Kelsey. Welcome, listener, to the* Meant to Be Podcast, *where we talk to madly-in-love couples about the way they met. Jonah, thank you so much for joining me today.'"*

"'Thank you so much for having me. Huge fan. My favorite episode had to be Jason and Dottie.'"

I'm smiling so hugely, I can barely speak. "'Yeah, that potato salad was what miracles are made of.'" I laugh, a wet snort popping out.

"'I can't wait to get my own tub.'"

"'Coming to stores near you soon. But that's not why we're here. We're here to talk about the love of your life, Kelsey.'" A tear falls past my cheek, and before I can wipe it, JP whips a box of tissues out of nowhere and sets it in front of me. I take one and dab at my eye. "'How did you two meet?'"

"'You see, my brother Huxley, he got our company into a bit of trouble. It's a long story, but because he made a promise to this girl he struck a deal with, we had to sit down with her and her sister and listen to them pitch us a business proposition. I was kind of annoyed, you know, because Huxley was making decisions without us, so when we lined up for the pitch, I didn't expect this smoke show of a woman to walk off the elevator. Immediately, I felt something change in me, something so deep, so profound, that I could've sworn a puzzle piece that's been missing my whole life finally found its home.'"

My lip quivers. "'Are you referring to Kelsey?'"

"'I am. Unfortunately, her sister ruined the entire meeting but, that whole time, while she was making a show of it, I watched Kelsey. I watched her face turn red with embarrassment, but I also watched how she kept herself composed even though her hopes of bringing her business to the next level were vanishing right in front of her. There was something so raw about that moment that I've never forgotten. And I knew I had to see her again.'"

I wipe at my eyes. "'So, it seems like you did.'"

"'Yeah, they were able to pitch again, and her idea was absolutely brilliant. We'd have been idiots if we said no. Lucky for me, the new business fell under my management, and that's when I got to spend more time with her. It started off as playful, but the more I hung out with her, got to know her, the more I knew this girl was meant for me. The only problem, though—I had to prove to her that I was meant for her too.'"

"'How...how did you do that?'"

"'Tried to be her friend, even though I told her that was impossible. And when the moment was right, I planned this entire night where I'd tell her how much I wanted to be with her. But, to my horror, she was going out with someone else that night.'"

My heart sinks just thinking about it. My eyes fixate on the paper in front of me. "'Wow, what a harlot...'" I glance up at him and he chuckles.

"'Nah, I didn't give her sufficient hints that I was interested in taking things further. I don't blame her, but I did beg and plead for her to not leave with him.'"

"'Did she?'" I tilt my head, watching him as the largest smile spreads across his face.

"'She didn't. She stayed with me, and at that moment, when she kissed me for the first time, I felt whole again. I felt like all the stars aligned and I was exactly where I needed to be, with the girl of my dreams. It wasn't easy, and it took some convincing on my end, but we started as coworkers, then enemies, then friends...and now, I'm hoping we can continue as more than friends, if she'll have me.'"

He sets his paper down and I set mine down too right before he takes my hand in his. "What I'm about to say to you isn't a moment in time to simply rectify our relationship. It's me, speaking from the heart, letting you know how I feel, because I can't go another day without you knowing." He wets his lips and says, "I love you, Kelsey. I'm pretty sure I've loved you from the moment I watched your face fall during that first pitch. And I know, for the rest of my life, I won't stop loving you, ever, because you were meant to be with me. I know, deep in my soul, to the very marrow of my bones, that you're my girl, and I'll spend the rest of my life proving that to you."

My hands are shaking. My lips won't stop trembling as I lean forward and, with my free hand, press my palm to his cheek, look him in the eyes, and say, "I love you, Jonah. I'm so sorry that it took me this long to say it to you." I rub my thumb over his cheek. "But I do, I love you so much, and I want nothing more than to spend the rest of my life showing you just how much."

The corners of his mouth lift as he gives me the sexiest smile I've ever seen. "Christ." He blinks a few times as he moves even closer. "Come here." He pulls me onto his lap, and his arm goes around my waist as I settle my hands on his shoulders. "You love me?"

I nod. "I really do. I've known for a while. I've just been scared. This feeling I have for you, it's so powerful, it's so real, I was afraid that maybe you didn't return the feeling."

He chuckles. "You don't need to worry about that. Pretty sure I loved you before you even considered looking my way." He rests his forehead against mine. "Is it too soon to beg you to move in with me?"

I laugh as tears fall from my eyes. "How about we go on a date first?"

"Okay, date first, then you move in with me."

"Date first, the bedroom next, and then we talk about possibly moving in."

He smirks. "Sounds like a plan, baby."

He closes the space between us and kisses me. A searing kiss that tears through me from the tips of my toes to the top of my head. His kiss claims me, showing me that no matter what happens, no matter what journey we take, I'm his. He's mine. And together, we're so meant to be.

EPILOGUE
JP

"I'M SO NERVOUS. WHAT IF I say the wrong thing?" I ask Kelsey as my leg bounces up and down in the back of the car while we wait to be called upon.

"I don't think you can say the wrong thing in this moment." She brushes my hair to the side. "I think you should just speak with your heart."

I rub my sweaty palms on my leg. "That's what I'm afraid of. If I speak with my heart, I might sound crazy."

Kelsey gives me a gentle once-over and lightly smiles. "JP, honey, I think you've already reached the limit of crazy."

I glance down at my custom-made pigeon shirt and then back at my girl. "I asked you if I looked nice, and you said yes."

"You do, you look very nice. Stop being nervous and go out there and meet the bird that started it all."

I take a deep breath. "You're right. You're totally right. I need to just be myself."

"He'll love you."

"You think so?" I ask, hope springing in my chest.

"It's hard not to love you." She leans forward and kisses me on the lips, soft and sweet, helping me relax before the door is opened on my side.

"Mr. Cane," our driver says. "They're ready for you."

"Fuck. Okay. God, don't puke, JP, don't puke," I say to myself before stepping out of the car. I turn around and offer Kelsey my hand, helping her out as well.

Ever since our night in my backyard, we've been inseparable. That night, we danced under the stars, holding each other the entire time. Even when we ate cake, she sat on my lap, never wanting to be too far away. And then, when we turned off the lights, I took her up to my room where we made love. It was the best sex I've ever had, filled with emotion, and with the knowledge that this was the start of a new chapter for us.

I took her on that date she asked for. We went to one of her favorite pizza places in LA, and it was not great. She said she used to go there all the time when she was young. I told her we weren't going anywhere she went to when she was young...again. When I drove her back to her place, I stayed the night and asked her to move in.

It took about twenty more dates until she finally said yes to my question, a question I asked every night. And every time, she said *maybe*, never giving me a straight answer until a few weeks ago. She moved in last weekend, and I can honestly say, it's the best feeling in the world. Now I just have to plan when I'm going to propose, because it's going to happen. I'm not letting her go.

With my hand in Kelsey's, we walk around to a tented-off area, where Tammy, the woman in charge of the pigeon rescue, greets us.

"Mr. and Mrs. Cane, I'm so glad you could make it."

I don't bother correcting her, because I really like the sound of it. "Thank you for having me and the wifey." I squeeze Kelsey's hand and can practically feel her eye roll. "Is, uh...is Kazoo here?"

"He is. He got the bow tie you sent, and I just have to say, he looks so adorable. If you're ready to meet him, he's just in this tent, and then we can do the ribbon-cutting ceremony."

"That works for me," I say, already feeling how sweaty my hand is getting against Kelsey's palm.

"Right this way," Tammy says, parting the tent door.

We walk in, and it takes my eyes a second to adjust, but once they do, they spot a little fella on a perch, wearing a bow tie that matches the fabric of my shirt.

"Oh fuck," I whisper to Kelsey. "I might cry."

She chuckles and whispers back, "I'm not sure I could love you more than in this moment."

I give her a quick peck on her cheek and then walk up to Kazoo, making sure to walk slowly to not scare him. His little head flits back and forth, looking as confused as ever. But his bulgy eyes and his bow tie, they just about break me.

"Hi, Kazoo."

He looks to the right, he looks to the left, and then he lifts one foot.

I grip my chest and say, "Oh hell, I think I just met the second love of my life." When I look back at Kelsey, she's recording the whole thing, a huge smile on her face.

I said it once and I'll say it again—this is where I'm supposed to be. With Kelsey, celebrating the small yet weird things like a pigeon who captured my attention months ago.

What once was Huxley's mistake, has now turned into a win for me, because if Huxley never met the love of his life, then I never would've met mine.

The girl who wanted nothing to do with me at first.

Then slowly wanted to be my friend.

And then, in the best way possible, chose me for who I am.

She chose Jonah.

Read on for a sneak peek at the
next in the Cane Brothers series by
Meghan Quinn

PROLOGUE
LIA

"EXCUSE ME," I SAY, BUMPING into a lanky guy in a jam-packed dorm hallway. "Sorry, didn't see you there. I'm all kinds of lost."

"Not a problem," says a deep voice that pulls my gaze up to the tall figure with shaggy-brown hair, dark-rimmed glasses, and a mustache so thick that it almost looks fake. Who knows, maybe it is. "What are you looking for?" he asks while he brings a sixty-four-ounce Slurpee cup to his lips.

"Uh." I glance around, then whisper, "Room 209. But I keep getting turned around because it doesn't seem like there's a room 209."

A smile tugs at his lips. "Scrabble nerd?"

"What?" I ask.

He leans forward and whispers, "It's okay. I'm part of the SSS. Room 209 is hidden for a reason."

SSS = Secret Scrabble Society.

But the first rule about SSS is that you don't talk about it. At least, that's what it said in the invite I received last night. It was a letter delivered to my dorm room. A thick envelope sealed with wax with an SSS melted into the red liquid. When I saw the symbol, I quickly locked my door, turned off my lights, and switched on my desk lamp. With bated breath, I delicately opened the envelope and unfolded the sides, revealing the writing on the inside.

I had been handpicked by the SSS to join them tonight. During the grueling, three-week tryout process, I played ruthless battles against different members online. After a few losses, a few wins, and two ties, the tryouts were over, and all I had to do was wait. Well, that time has come. I have the invite in hand, and all it says is to show up to room 209 in the Pine Dormitory at 10:23 p.m. sharp, ask no questions, and say nothing. And then I'm to knock with a specific pattern and provide the secret password to get in.

But now that I'm here, lost and confused, I feel like I'm breaking the rules already.

Unfortunately, time is ticking, and I have no idea how to proceed. I don't want to show up late, especially on the first night. But I can't find the room, and...this guy with the stache and the Slurpee seems like he knows what he's talking about.

Ugh...but what if this is a test? What if he was planted by the SSS, and I already failed because I mentioned room 209 and Scrabble and... *God*, I'm a failure.

Unsure of how to proceed, I rock on my feet, my hands twisting in front of me as I glance around the hordes of people. What is going on in here anyway? It's a dorm hallway, not a cafeteria. Where are all these people going? I think I need to ditch Slurpee Boy. He knows too much already. And I will not put my position with the SSS in jeopardy. I worked way too hard for an invitation.

"You know, it was nice talking to you, but I think I'll just go look for the room myself. Thanks."

I turn away and head for a dark corridor, only for him to call out, "Not going to find room 209 down there."

I glance over my shoulder to see him sipping on his Slurpee with a smile, his playful eyes intent on my annoyed expression.

"I wasn't actually going that way," I respond with indignance.

"Seemed like you were."

"I was faking you out."

"Were you now?" he asks, that smile growing wider. "Why would you be faking me out?"

I straighten to face him and raise my chin as I say, "Because between your ungodly thick mustache and your shaggy hair, you look like a predator. How can I be sure that you're not attempting to snatch me up?"

His brows raise as he runs his fingers over his mustache. "You know, you're the third person who said I can't rock this mustache. I thought I was looking pretty legit."

The man needs to get a better mirror.

"Your mustache is offensive. I'm pretty sure it would make even the most randy of women go dry." The words fly out of my mouth before I can stop them. Lack of filter—it's my downfall.

I wince as his eyes nearly pop out of their sockets. *Yeah, I was surprised too, buddy.*

"Uh, I don't know—"

Before I can finish telling him I'm not quite sure where in the depths of my being that insult came out of, he grips his stomach, bends forward, and lets out a long-drawn-out laugh, his Slurpee shaking in his hand.

Well, at least he wasn't offended. I've got that going for me.

Either way, I don't have time for this.

Moving past him, I head down the right of the hallway, where I find an unmarked door. Initially, when I was first looking around, I thought this was a utility closet. But paying a little more attention to the door, I think there could be a faint marking of a number on the wall. Maybe... just maybe...it's what I'm looking for.

On a hopeful breath, I knock on the door three times and then kick the footer like I was told just as a tall figure closes in behind me.

"You know, I've never had a girl tell me that I possess the uncanny ability to dehydrate the nether regions of the female race with just my facial hair."

I hold back my smile. "Be glad I'm honest."

The door cracks open, and a single eyeball comes into view. "Password."

"Walla-walla-bing-bang," I answer just as the guy behind me leans forward over my shoulder.

"You missed the ching-chang part," he says.

"What? No, I didn't."

"He's right," the eyeball says. "Sorry, no entrance."

"Wait, no," I say as I prevent the eyeball from shutting the door. I pull the invite out from my pocket and say, "I have the invitation…errr, I mean…" *Ugh, stupid, Lia. You're not supposed to show the invitation.* Backpedal. "Actually…" I slip the invite back into my pocket and fold my hands together. "There is no invite, and I have no idea what this door leads to. I just know that I'm supposed to be here at ten twenty-three, and I am, so therefore, I believe I should gain entrance."

"But you forgot the ching-chang," Slurpee Boy says while sucking on his straw.

"There was no ching-chang," I reply with aggravation. "It clearly said, knock three times, kick the footer, and then say walla-walla-bing-bang. I know this because I read the, uh…thing, twenty-seven times precisely. So either this is not the right door, which perhaps it's not, or you two have not read the instructions yourself, and in which case, I demand to speak to an authoritative human."

"An authoritative human?" Slurpee Boy asks. "Is that a professional term?"

"Dumbing it down for you," I say with snark. "You know, since you have that look."

"What look?" he asks.

"One that's lacking intelligence." Call it my nerves or my irritation, or just the fact that I can't hold anything back, but I just let my insult fly.

Thankfully, that smile of his once again tugs on the corners of his lips right before he says to eyeball, "She's good, man. Let her in."

"What?" I ask, so utterly confused that I wonder if being part of the SSS is even worth it.

But then the door opens, revealing a very large room, larger than all the other dorm rooms, and it's a haven to all the things I love. Off to the right is a raised bed with a desk underneath which holds three computer screens, speakers, a massive keyboard as well as a giant mouse and mouse pad that expands the length of the desk...*Lord of the Rings* themed. Hanging on the beige walls are posters, flags, and framed art ranging from *Star Wars* to board games to a large yellow-and-blue model airplane suspended from the ceiling. To the left is a futon sofa with a coffee table and crates with cushions all along the edges. In the middle, a Scrabble board on a turntable—the fancy kind.

I could totally spend an hour nerding out in this room.

The whole collection of Harry Potter books rests on the bookshelf—and they look like the originals. My mouth salivates.

A framed poster of Adam West as Batman hangs over the sofa, Adam standing tall with a "Kerpow" in comic detail directly behind him.

And under the small television on a flimsy-looking TV stand is what looks to be an original Atari game console. If the owner of this residence owns Pitfall, we will be best friends for life.

"Wow, cool room," I say. The fantastic décor speaks to my geeky heart. And the precise organization, from the labeled folders on the bookshelf next to the desk to the stacked shoes on the shoe rack, is next level.

"Thanks," Slurpee Boy says. "It's mine. I'm also the authoritative person, as you like to call it." He holds his hand out. "Breaker Cane. It's nice to meet you. Maybe as you hang out with us more, you can lower yourself to my lack of intelligence on a more personal level."

My mouth goes dry.

The tips of my ears go hot.

And I feel a wave of sweat crest my upper lip.

Good job, Lia. Really good job.

"Uh, yeah...I didn't really mean—"

"No, no. Don't take it back." He holds up his hand. "I like your brutal and brash honesty. Made me feel alive." He winks.

"Oh, okay. In that case." I clear my throat. "Although your room seems like a dream to explore, you could have tucked the corners of your bed better, not quite 'nurse's corner' tight, your framed picture of Rory Gilmore is crooked, and you have to get rid of the mustache. It's atrocious."

He chuckles and nods while moving his fingers over the bush beneath his nose. "Still trying to perfect the nurse's corner. If you have expertise in this endeavor, then, by all means, present a tutorial. The room I share a wall with plays music loud enough that they force Rory to dance, making her crooked. I've given up. And the mustache, well, I thought it looked good. Seems to me everyone's been lying to me."

"They have been."

"But you don't seem to have that ability...to lie to someone to forsake their feelings."

"Depends on the moment and the person." I look him up and down. "You seemed sturdy enough to handle the truth, and also, stressful situations—i.e. not knowing where the room was—snatching any social decorum I might have stored away."

"Well, that can only mean one thing."

Confused, I ask, "What's that?"

"That there is no other choice than to become the greatest friends of all time."

I smirk. "Only if you shave."

"Ehhh, that's something we might have to work out." He rocks on his feet and continues, "Given that you are the only new recruit to the Secret Scrabble Society, you must be Ophelia Fairweather-Fern."

"That would be me. But just call me Lia. My entire name is far too many syllables for anyone to carry around, let alone my first name."

He chuckles. "Your name was a check in the plus column during try-outs. But your brutal use of words we've never even heard of was the real reason you were chosen, especially since we play on a timer."

"That was an added challenge I appreciated. Although the timer startled me at first and took a second for me to get used to. That and not being able to see your new letters or the gameboard until your turn started. I had a lot of fun. I'm glad I was chosen."

"It was an easy choice." He sets his Slurpee cup down. "Everyone, this is Lia. Lia, that's Harley, Jarome, Christine, and Imani." From where they're seated at the coffee table, they all raise their hands for a brief hello and then return to the gameboard. "Yeah, they're not really social."

"Well, good thing I didn't come here to socialize." I rub my hands together. "I came to play."

Breaker chuckles and then reaches for his Slurpee again. "Then what are we waiting for? Game on."

I stare Breaker down and then glance at the last two tiles on my shelf.

He has one tile left.

The room has cleared out.

The rest of the SSS has left, claiming early morning classes.

"Your move," he says while purposely running his finger over his mustache. I'd dominated this entire game until about three moves ago when he somehow pulled out an eighty-point word, completely shattering my lead.

"I know it's my move."

"Really, because you've been sitting there catatonic for at least five minutes."

"I'm making sure I have the right move."

"Or any move at all." He leans back on the sofa, a smug look painted across his face.

"I *have* a move."

"One that won't win you the game, though, right?" he presses. He knows he has this game. It's evident in his cocky disposition.

"You know, it's not polite to gloat."

"This coming from the girl who was dancing only a few minutes ago because she had a tremendous lead on me."

I slowly look up at him and, in a deadpan voice, say, "It will behoove you to know that I can dish it, but I can't take it."

He lets out a low chuckle as I reluctantly place an E after a W for a measly five points.

"Nice move." He stares down at his single tile and then lifts it dramatically, only to place an S after Huzzah, giving him thirty-one points. "But not good enough." He leans back again and crosses his leg over his knee. "I win."

I groan and flop backward onto the floor. Staring up at his model airplane, I say, "I had you."

"Never celebrate too early. You never know what can happen at the end of a Scrabble game."

"That's such a cheap move by the way, holding on to an S to the very end."

"How did you know I was holding on to it?"

"Because I watched you pick up the tile a while ago and set it to the side."

"Don't tell me you're one of those players. The one who counts the tiles and knows what everyone could possibly have."

"Not to that extent, but I watched you baby that tile and not touch it until now. You saved it on purpose."

"When you're trailing by eighty points, you have to be strategic, and I was. No shame in playing the game."

"I hate to admit it since you won, but it was a good game. I enjoyed the challenge."

"It was a good game. You're going to fit in nicely here." He starts picking up the board, and I lift to help him. "Your application said you're majoring in research and statistics. What's the plan after college?"

"Getting my master's and then becoming a survey research specialist."

He pauses. "That's really specific," Breaker says. "And not a job you hear on a list of what you want to be when you grow up."

"Not so much, but I've always been into surveys. Growing up, I loved filling them out. I spent a great deal of time filling out every survey my parents came across. I loved the idea of someone being able to listen to me and gather information to make a change. And of course, I would make surveys on my own, handwritten ones on construction paper, and pass them around at family gatherings to see how everyone enjoyed themselves. Then I would draw up a report and send out an end-of-the-year letter, showing everyone where we excelled and where we could improve."

Breaker smirks. "And did you find out anything constructive from these family surveys?"

"Yes." I nod as I hand him the last few tiles that need to be picked up. "Whenever my uncle Steve decided to take his pants off after dinner, it always led to him doing the invisible hula hoop on top of the cleared-off dining table—*which no one relished*. I made sure to convey this to the family and Uncle Steve, but unfortunately, I have no control over their behavior. I can only survey what needs to change. Changes are made from within."

"Uncle Steve sounds like a good time."

"He had a mustache...and he's known as the pervert in the family. So yeah, maybe you two would get along."

"Not a pervert," Breaker says while packing up the rest of the game.

"That has yet to be determined."

ABOUT THE AUTHOR

#1 Amazon and *USA Today* bestselling author, wife, adoptive mother, and peanut butter lover. Author of romantic comedies and contemporary romance, Meghan Quinn brings readers the perfect combination of heart, humor, and heat in every book.

Website: authormeghanquinn.com
Facebook: meghanquinnauthor
Instagram: @meghanquinnbooks